Roan Rose

Juliet Waldron

ISBN-13: 978-1492241584
ISBN-10: 149224158X
ASIN: B00FKKAN98
Electronic version of *Roan Rose* published by:
Books We Love Publishing, Ltd.
Chestermere, Alberta T1X 1C2
Canada
www.bookswelove.com

Dedication: To the Legend I met in my tenth year, sitting behind that Barbadian bar, nose in a book.

God send to every gentleman,
Such hawks, such hounds
And such a Leman…

—The Three Ravens, archaic

A Game of Chess

The King of England and I played chess, passing his sleepless hours. After years of struggling with the game, I can say, without exaggeration, that I'd become a formidable competitor, nearly his equal. I will stand firm upon this claim, even though I was a lowly servant—and female, at that.

Nightly, our forces swayed back and forth across the board, until the birds began a summons to Dawn, calling her, as the harpers say, *"from that silken couch whereon she dreams."*

We sat in a steady circle of candlelight in a small, high room at the palace of Nottingham. From our vantage point, the narrow river, spangled by summer stars, flowed below a single, open window. The distance, I might add, was sufficient to prevent the smell from blighting the view.

Of late, I had won a few these matches. This I credited in part to the King's growing distraction and exhaustion. By June of 1485, he'd realized that his rule was unraveling around him, and, that he, in no small part, had been the architect of oncoming disaster.

What other choices, however, could my Lord have made? If he had let his nephew come to the throne, his own head would, sooner or later, have become his vengeful sister-in-law's trophy. Either that or he would have been arrested and mewed up by his enemies, murdered in secret like so many members of his family. Richard Plantagenet knew history and he was not a passive man. All he'd done in deposing the boy was to strike his enemies before they could strike him.

Men now say otherwise.

There is mystery in the dark hours between two and four. The black and white squares of the board swam before my eyes. I, too, was tired to my very bones. The King's wakefulness had become his servant's. I was ready to make a move when his foot, under a long red robe, touched mine beneath the table. The contact seemed accidental, but was it?

He knows how greatly I love him, how I hunger for any touch. . . .

Concentration broken, I glanced up and met his brilliant hazel eyes, burning deep in hollows of chronic sleeplessness. For an instant, a slight smile curved those thin, mobile lips, but his gaze returned naturally to the board. Our relationship had always been singular. Only recently had it turned—let us say—customary. During the winter, his queen, the mistress I'd served and loved for nigh onto twenty years, had died. That is why his touch distracted me, made my concentration falter.

"Was the move I'd planned such a good one?"

My hand wavered over the few remaining strong pieces. Traps lay on every side. Several, I saw clearly, for I'd been playing chess with Richard since our shared childhood. Whatever *coup de grace* he'd planned, I feared I'd never see until it was too late.

"That wasn't fair." In our secret kingdom of night, titles, and much else customary between master and servant, had been abandoned.

"Check."

I'd revised, chosen to move my last knight to pin down his king. Of course, I knew quite well that second guesses are nearly always fatal this deep in a match.

"Nothing in this world is fair."

As his hand went for it, I saw my doom—a lurking bishop.

"Checkmate," Richard lifted a dark brow in triumph. Extending those jeweled, elegant fingers, his Bishop cast down my helpless king.

"You touched my foot on purpose."

"What of it?"

It was worth losing any number of chess matches to see him smile. Always glorious—and always rare—it had, lately, become a thing of legend.

"Old Dick" doesn't smile. This was well known all over his Kingdom. Like a great many other things that are "well known," there was not a grain of truth in it.

"I don't mind. It's only that you used to win by your wits, and now it seems you must rely upon the lowest tricks to best your humble servant."

He laughed shortly, but it was not an entirely happy sound. Playing with my king now, turning it between ringed thumb and forefinger, he said, "Better for all of us had I learned the game of low tricks at a far earlier age."

How to reply? Crouching at the back of this night's wakefulness lay the same old horror. *Where were his nephews?*

Pawns are always the first to go. In my Lord's case, crime had brought, as it so rarely does in this wicked world, a punishment not only swift, but apt. In the space of sixteen months, the King had lost his adored son and his dearly beloved wife, my noble mistress.

On this night, Richard Plantagenet had traveled almost to the end of his earthly course, to the haunted land where human tribulation ends. Gazing at the ruin of our board, I believe we both knew it.

Chapter 1

Little Witch!" A slap always followed the malediction. "Dost thou stare?"

This was my father. He did not like children whose opinions showed in their eyes. Large dark eyes I had—my mother's eyes—and when I displeased him, he was not slow to punish the unbroken will he saw.

I was born at the village of Aysgarth in the house of a stark yeoman farmer, Master Whitby. He was not pleased when my mother gave him a daughter, and then another and another, as if by the force of her own contrary will.

Master Whitby acknowledged me, however, as he acknowledged my sisters. I was written down in the book at the Church of Our Lady as "Rosalba Whitby, legitimate, born to Master Raymond Whitby and his espoused wife, Roseanne."

When I was old enough to hear the tale, my mother very kindly let me know matters stood otherwise. To learn I had been conceived in liberty and was not the get of that humorless, ham-fisted tyrant fills me, to this day, with satisfaction.

Aysgarth lies on Wenslydale, north and west of the great Keep of Middleham. Here our peasant houses grew from the ground like mushrooms. The poorest were of turf, but the best homes, like the one in which I was born, rose upon a costly timber frame.

Those hard packed earthen floors! In the East Wind time, rain slanted through the central smoke hole and pelted the fire of our hearth. I remember huddling close, thinking how the flames were like serpents, lowering their fiery heads and hissing whenever the drops landed. During the worst weather, the entire family, including Master Whitby's curly-pelted white cattle, sheltered with us.

Our village was linked by a single, rutted path. Beyond the stone fences lay fields, wild water and wind. The river went down rapids and over the falls, on and on until it reached the stormy eastern sea through the Great Wash.

My mother kept a garden behind the house. Well-manured with the leavings of our animals, tended by my hands and those of my older half-brothers, it flourished. Here mother grew turnips, mangels, carrots, parsnips and greens, food for us and for our animals. In a raised patch, she also grew herbs, for she was Aysgarth's midwife.

She knew how to cultivate and how to distill what was useful. She delivered children, here in Aysgarth and on the dales round about. So skillful and well-reputed was she that she lived to the age of nineteen free of the marital yoke.

Our priest, however, did not approve. My maternal grandmother had been hanged as a witch and people hereabout have long memories. Although my mother had mostly been raised by a pious woman, Mother Margery, the blood line of a witch was said to run strong.

After my foster mother died, the priest and the other men of the village decided it was best that my mother, so inclined to independence, be placed under the thumb of a strong man. Farmer Whitby, recently again a widower again, was elected to the task. My mother was his fourth and final wife.

Edward Duke of York took the throne, apparently once and for all, from the House of Lancaster during my sixth year. With the help of our mighty Earl of Warwick, Edward imprisoned the mad old King, Henry VI, and drove out his wife, Queen Marguerite, a damned French princess. Edward then declared the Queen's son by the old king to be a bastard.

Master Whitby had no love for Queens, especially French ones. He rallied at once to the idea that Queen Marguerite's son had been gotten in adultery.

"It is said that our poor monkish King cried out she must have made that little shit with the Holy Ghost! I'll tell you, no good has ever come from a single one of these French queens. They bring us only bad government and war. Their courts are filled with their lovers and prancing catamites whose only care is to plunder decent folk. Look at Great King Hal's French bitch! Popping out pups to a dirty

Welsh stable-boy as soon as the Lord Chamberlain's back was turned."

Rosalba—White Rose—was a name given to me by my mother, who favored flower names. I think Master Whitby acquiesced in it because at the time he thought it politic to have a foot in the Yorkist camp. One of my elder half-brothers still glowered about the house under the name of Clifford, in honor of that other great northern family. Supporters of the House of Lancaster, they had once been a great power among us. One of Master Whitby's favorite adages was: "Coats must go on as the wind blows."

When I was ten, the Duchess of Warwick, wife to the Mighty Earl named "Kingmaker," arrived in Aysgarth. This lady was on her way to the Keep of Middleham, and had fallen ill. This was how she came to rest, with all her train, in our small stone church.

We all went to gawk. Lords and their ladies did not pass our way often.

I say the whole village, but this is not quite correct. My mother would never dare leave the house without my father's permission. Master Whitby's rule in this, as in all things, was enforced with blows. Mother picked her battles.

I can still call the old man to mind, him with his long salt and pepper beard, lank grizzled hair, and his wide, work-thickened hand, a member with which all his dependents had close acquaintance. His gaze alone could scald you, for he was a man of choleric humor. Even his flesh bore testimony, for every exposed inch of him turned scarlet at haying time. Master Whitby was certain that while he and other men labored in the fields or among the cattle, their women were likely to waste either their time or a husband's hard-won goods. He was a firm believer that women were vain, foolish and lazy.

I shall recall no more of him, for to carp is a poor pastime. There were others in our village who suffered more. For all I know, my mother would have ended like her mother had she had remained without the protection of marriage. Master Whitby took at least as good care of his children as he did his cattle. He allowed my mother to exercise her gifts, for any reward she received only made him that much richer.

Ordinarily, during a visit by high gentry, Mother would have remained in the kitchen. Going to gape at the progress of the mighty was not worth the price she'd later have to pay. Nevertheless, this time she eventually did go, for she was summoned by a power far higher, by Lady Anne Beauchamp, Countess of Warwick.

The retainers of the earl had gathered around our church, making a better spectacle than any feast day. Mother and I walked through a forest of armed men, of horses and carts and bright banners.

I wondered at the beauty of the ladies. Their mounts were hinnies with delicate legs and long ears, decked with brasses and draped in scarlet. The Ragged Staff banner of the Countesses' husband stood before our church, snapping in a raw April breeze. The great lady's journey had been interrupted by woman's trouble. Her ladies, perhaps desiring a scapegoat, had called for the local midwife. I accompanied my mother, scurrying behind her and carrying a small wooden box of hastily assembled vials.

The dark, echoing interior of the church was familiar, but I had never seen or imagined it like this, filled with torches and retainers, their coats of mail and polished armor bright against the stone. We were led in straightaway by a sharp-nosed lady in the most beautiful dress I'd ever seen. I remember it to this day, a dashing scarlet, a kind of cloth for which I then had no name. The material fell in luxurious folds. The white scarves adorning her headdress were fine as fairy wings.

She took us to a narrow room behind the high altar, usually only visited by choir or the priests. I could feel sweat beneath my shirt, although the day was cold. Mother was nervous too, although she held her head high. Before answering the summons, she had taken time to wash her face and put on a clean apron and cap, as if it were a Sunday. Now, I understood why.

❧

I smelled blood at once. All the colors—all the clean and sheen of her numerous attendants, as fair as angels in the church windows, all—vanished with that smell. It was strong, the smell of birthing. It was not the sharp, clear smell of a pumping wound or of an animal bleeding its last under the butcher's knife, but heavy and musky—sure sign of a she-creature in trouble.

"Stay close."

I stood beside my mother, clutching the box.

"You are midwife of Aysgarth?"

My knees knocked as I looked up at the great lady, seated on a make-shift bed, a plank covered with blankets and set between stools. My father was a king in his house and we feared him, but we knew that he feared his lord who lived in Kendall Castle, Sir William. In turn, Sir William feared his lord, the great Earl of Warwick, whose knee bent only to the King in London! This proud lady, now suffering like a commoner in our poor church, represented great power.

"Yes, Milady. Mistress Whitby, at your service." Mother curtseyed low and bowed her head. Her emphatic downward motion sent me to my knees on the cold slate beside her, still clutching the box.

"Come to me quick, woman! I miscarry."

I raised my eyes and this time managed to focus upon the most high and noble lady. Her brows were narrow and perfectly arched against her forehead, the whitest I'd ever seen. The eyes beneath those brows were like a gray autumn sky. Her pallor was deep, as if she had been struck in a vital part by a sword. I followed my mother, the box held against my flat, freckled chest.

The ladies who attended, with their fair skin, their soft hands, and round plump cheeks, parted before us. They looked like queasy angels, uncertain for the first time in their divine lives. This was not a trouble which could be managed by smooth address.

Mother went straight to work. I was used to this commanding demeanor when she assumed the midwife's mantle. The Countess lay back and submitted to her handling. Great Lady she might be, but now she must abandon modesty. Like a cow in a difficult calving, she must accept our helping hands.

The small, bloody lump my mother soon delivered from between her white knees was a boy. A noble child, but he looked to me the same as any other miscarry I'd seen. The Countess of Warwick's pain and her tears were also familiar.

I knelt by mother, first handing her vials, some of precious glass and others of equally precious metal, exactly as she called for them. The ladies served, bringing basins of hot water to us and a goblet of hot red wine to their mistress.

Cures were mixed with the wine; the Countess sipped. After passing away the cup, much to my surprise, the great lady took my hand and squeezed it. I did what Mother had taught, and offered her both hands. I gazed in awe at the whiteness that my fingers—so freckled and rough—enclosed. Veins crossed the back of her hand, and I wondered if it were true, the thing men said about the aristocracy having "blue blood," different from ours.

Our priest said it was true, that he'd seen the heads cut from Lords, and that the first blood was dark as the winter sea. Master Whitby scoffed. If that were so then pigs or bulls must also be noblemen, for didn't their blood—when "struck proper"—flow just as dark?

As I held the Countess' hand between mine, her breathing eased. I could see her muscles relax. Mother helped her patient with a clout of clean cloths, and fed her the wine in which she'd let fall four carefully measured drops of distilled knotweed and nettle.

> *Knotweed to tie up bleeding.*
> *Nettle for a heated illness…*

The noble child was lost, but the Countess did not blame. She grieved that she had failed her lord and that she had lost a child of her body. My mother assured her the miscarriage was clean, that nothing remained behind to poison the blood.

"God willing, there will be others, Milady Countess." Mother ventured the common comfort.

The Countess responded with a weary smile that turned down on one side.

"Yes. God willing."

My mother asked if the lady felt much pain.

"Yes, good woman, though I know it well. This is a trial I have stood before."

I was impressed by the way she bore her misfortune, with pride and grace, even in this most wretched physical moment.

If it cannot be helped, it is best just to get on...

Mother finished by giving a draught containing poppy from one of the vials, then she brought from her pocket a smooth round stone from the river. It was gray, apparently like a thousand others, but my Mother was never without it.

"With your permission, Milady Countess; may I speak a charm to stop pain?"

"Yes." The Countess lay back and closed her eyes.

There was a silent moment while mother began to pass the stone over the lady's body.

> *"Hair and hide*
> *Flesh and bone,*
> *Feel no more pain*
> *Than this stone."*

The charm was told thirteen times. Still holding the Countess' hand, I ventured to gaze at her. Everyone knew that her husband, the great earl whose power made and broke kings, had sired only two daughters. No sons to fight at their warlike father's side! Wondering if the earl upbraided her for dereliction, I felt a wave of pity.

Mr. Whitby, my authority upon everything male, declared that blood royal had "grown weak as water" since the time of Edward III. It was, he said, the cause of England's long years of war.

"Why, a man cannot be left to farm his land in peace for ten weeks before he is marched over by armies. Every village is robbed of young men for arrays, chaste women are befouled, cattle, grain and sheep are stolen. No law anywhere, only this lord and that, stirring up factions among us. How can an honest man increase his worth in such turmoil? This is surely God's judgment, just like the plague of my grandfather's time."

In Whitby's opinion, the Earl of Warwick was an improvement over the Percies, the old Lords of the North. Recently, he'd cut away the red rose that had grown over the door and planted a white one. Upon his Sunday hat he now sported a handsomely embroidered badge of The Ragged Staff.

When the Countess drowsed, we crept away. The chief among the ladies-in-waiting gave mother a coin as we left.

"You may be called again."

"May The Blessed Mother protect our good Countess." Mother bowed deeply.

The lady's haughty demeanor softened at my mother's stolid concern. We did not quite dare to bow ourselves away, because she continued to stare at us if she had something else to say.

"Excuse me, Lady," Mother finally said, "but we must go. My husband will be angry if he finds me not in his house when he returns from the fields."

"Although you have attended your Countess?"

"Milady." Mother kept her eyes down, but I stole a glance, and saw the plucked places where the woman's brows had once been arch.

"Have no fear. Your husband may not grudge service to the wife of The Earl of Warwick, he who is master of this land and all in it."

"As you say, Milady."

Mother bowed again, and the proud noblewoman, to my surprise, returned a faint echo of her reverence.

"I observed your apprentice." The Countess looked better today, and, as her lady-in- waiting had suggested, she had called for mother early the next day. She did not, however, speak of herself, but seemed inclined to other matters.

"She is my daughter, your ladyship."

"She is young."

"It is never too early to study the craft, Milady."

The countess nodded. Her great gray eyes turned thoughtfully upon me.

"You wish her to follow you."

"I do hope and pray that she will, Milady of Warwick; God willing."

"Her touch hath healing. How does she in your garden?"

"Well, Milady. She is my eldest, obedient and clever."

"Come here, child."

I did as I was told. Sunlight fell precipitously through a window, a sudden break in the eternal galloping clouds of spring. I was walking, although I did not know it, into another world.

The Countess stretched out a long-fingered white hand. I had never seen so many glistening jewels. The danced before my eyes like blue and red stars.

"Give the Countess your hand, child!" From behind, the lady-in-waiting delivered a jab between my shoulder blades. My small freckled fingers met the elegant hand of the lady.

"Such beautiful eyes!" Hers met mine, and I knew that her spirit was exactly as hard and as brilliant as those jewels upon her fingers.

"What is your name, child?"

"Rosalba."

"Rosalba—White Rose." The name made her smile and once more I was astonished. Unlike most breeding women of our village, she had all her teeth.

"Do you have brothers and sisters, Rosalba?"

"Two little sisters, Milady."

"Speak up!" From behind, the lady-in-waiting delivered another poke.

"Do you take care of them when your mother is busy?"

"Yes, Milady, when I am not helping my mother in the garden, or in the kitchen."

"Do you like caring for your little sisters?"

"Oh, yes, Milady. When Lily was sick with croup last winter, I nursed her at night so Mother could sleep." The

Countess seemed so approving that, despite the harsh presence at my back, I gained sufficient confidence to add, "This spring our Lily is bonny and fat."

"You give your mother good service."

What happened next is hard to describe, but I could feel a wave of distress coming from my mother. Although she didn't make a sound and I couldn't see her, it was as if she had cried aloud. It was a torture doubled because I did not dare turn back to see.

"I have two daughters. Do you know that?"

I nodded vigorously.

"My youngest daughter is Anne. She is not hale and hearty like you, Rosalba."

She studied me. Then, suddenly, her focus swept beyond, with such fierce determination that I was impelled to turn my head. When I did, I saw that my mother's eyes, those big dark eyes we shared, were full of tears.

"Mistress Whitby, give me this little roan rose."

I saw my mother—*my brave mother*—swallow hard.

"We are yours to command, your ladyship." Mother folded her hands beneath her bosom. Unlike bullying episodes with my father, she did not lower her eyes.

"I wish her to nurse my youngest."

Mother's eyes were unnaturally bright, but instead of voicing sorrow, she replied steadily.

"An' it be your will, Milady Countess. You greatly honor us, who are ever at your service."

Chapter 11

1 don't want to go away!"

"You must."

We were on the way home. Mother would not look at me.

"But you need me!"

"I do, but your father does not. Already he plans to marry you away."

If she had knocked me to the ground with her fist, I could not have been more surprised. Most girls in our village were married between twelve and fifteen. I was ten, but, having little dowry, had counted upon at least three years more of living as a maid in the good care and teaching of my mother.

"You are to go to the home of Martin Thornton, by Oxnop Ghyll. His wife has begun to ramble in her wits and old Martin himself is poorly. You and Jane Cobb are to meet with his sons, Mark and Matthew, at the church door, on the Nativity of John the Baptist. You are for Mark and Jane is for Matthew. They badly need women in that house."

Cold news, more terrible than a bad harvest.

"The Thorntons will take you without dower, for they know you are a good girl and are a hard worker. To get rid of a daughter was all it took to persuade Master Whitby of the wisdom of his course."

Why had she not told me?

The Thorntons were wild as Scots. They lived on the high dales, lonely herders in a stone and turf croft, a family rough, simple, and almost as speechless, as their sheep.

"I have entreated the Blessed Mother to save you every night since Master Whitby shook hands with Old Martin at the Cross Quarter market."

Mother's fingers closed tightly on my arm. Her gaze burned.

"Oh, my darling! I feared Our Lady had abandoned us, but see! My prayer is answered! You are saved! Whitby will not dare refuse the Countess of Warwick."

Tearing my arm away, I fled, running down the street, clogs clopping and slipping. Past the smith's shed with its reek, noise and steam, across the gray stepping stones of the rattling beck, water gurgling on every side. I knew Mother would not follow. She had supper to make and news to break to the wrathful man who ruled us.

I ran until I was out of breath, then I walked, up a grassy hill that overlooked Aysgarth. A narrow, winding sheep path led to the top and I followed it. Near the crest, I turned to look back at the huddled houses trailing smoke. There were numbers of fires tonight, with the train of Countess in residence. Church bells rang for Compline, the sound clear and hollow. Wind was dying along with the sunlight. I shivered and tightened my shawl, knowing I had nearly a mile to go.

At last, toward sunset, I reached the place I sought, a bald hilltop jumble of weathered rocks which stood sentry over our valley's thin soil. Carved by rain and wind, these stones were filled with fissures, some large enough to sit inside. Shepherds caught by the gale hid here, waiting it out with their sheep.

Close to the center of this desert place, springing from a crack, one deep enough to hold a man, grew an oak tree. Blasted by storms, twisted, stunted, starved, and yet it grew. The villagers were always wood hungry, but somehow, over the centuries, no one had been desperate enough to cut it. It was very old, leaning and spare, the shape sculpted by the prevailing wind.

Mother brought offerings here in secret, as her mother had. In dry summers she carried water. In autumn moonlight, she brought dishes of blood from butchering. She poured these tributes into the fractures where the gnarled roots sank. Others brought similar gifts here as well. I knew because sometimes the rocks were stained when we arrived, but I never knew who else tended the ancient tree, and I never asked.

Somehow, this had always seemed a natural place to take my distress. Certainly, no one would be here tonight. The tree stood alone, clinging to the mouth of a crevice. Following the twisted trunk downward, I lowered my body into the hole.

The stone my palms pressed was sharp and grainy.

Crouching in the dimness, I wept upon the roots and waited for the calm of the place to overtake me. Sweat cooled upon my back. A shiver shook me and passed, born of the deep chill that always lingered here.

Looking up, I peered through the branches, lifted against that broken spring sky. In summer the leaves seemed to be whispering secrets, but this was too early. Only a few wart-like buds dotted the twisted limbs. As I sat, listening to my blood pump, staring up through the branches, I heard a fierce, sweet cry, one which spoke of beauty, of power and pain.

Out of the clouds, riding down a ray of light, sped a hawk. He seemed a lord, far removed from the humble, grubbing world of men. He shot by, faster than an arrow. He did not call again, but the perfect moment reverberated like a rung bell.

That was when I understood. As frightened as I was of leaving everything and everyone I'd ever known, of going away with strangers to a place where a peasant was less than nothing, it was better than the slavery to which Master Whitby would doom me.

Mother was right. The Blessed Mother had saved me. I bowed my head and began a *Hail Mary*.

Straining upwards, scraping my hands on the stone, scuffing my knees, I scrambled forth from the crevice, determined as a new-made butterfly. On the way home I had to keep my eyes fixed upon the twilight path in order not to slip on the greasy new grass and tumble head over heels down the hillside. The sun was disappearing, a blur in a hazy wrack. As it sank, the clouds darkened to the color of dried blood.

Chapter III

I will pass quickly over the ache and fear, the tumult of my homecoming that night. I shed tears for my mother, for my best friend Jane, for my little sisters, Marigold and Lily, for the only home I'd ever known.

It is enough to say that after he received the news, Master Whitby roared, cursed and hurled about the house shouting. Finally, he struck my mother. It seemed that he'd made an even better deal than she knew in his agreement with Thornton. Two kindled blue-faced ewes were to have been traded for me. The loss of those fine creatures piqued him beyond measure.

The next day, the proud lady who had tended the Countess, appeared at our door, took my hand from my mother's and led me away. I was too exhausted from the alarms of the night to be frightened when a great burly man-at-arms all suited in mail and with the face of a battle-scarred bear picked me up. He lifted me into one of the high-sided lumbering carts that carried the baggage.

There I sat, beside bolts of fine cloth, furs, fine trunks of tooled leather and a hooded hawk in a cage. We were baubles picked up along the way, gifts from suppliants and subjects. Miserably, I found a place to sit, upon a hay bale thrust between two stacks of rugs. At least, I reasoned, if these fell, they would not crush me.

Behind I could see knights in armor mounted on horses taller and broader than the most enormous oxen I'd ever seen. The horses, too, were armed, their heads and necks protected with jointed plate. Like scales on a fish, these accommodated their bravely curved necks. The armor between their eyes was decorated with twisting silver horns. The men rode without their helms, and, unlike other soldiers I'd seen, they wore their hair long. Pinioned lances sat easily in a single hand, the butt thrust securely against a stirrup.

Exhausted by the terrible night, I lay down in the swaying, jolting wagon, but there was no way I could sleep. Hollow-eyed, I sat up again and watched as a gray jennet carrying two riders came pelting beside the marching line. One of the knights turned his head, and after a shout to his mate, they both laughed.

The jennet wasn't pleased to be hurried. Her long ears were laid back, but she obeyed the feet thumping her ribs. As she paced beside the wagon, I saw a slender young man, a servant in soft boots and red livery, his fair hair very long. Behind him, clutching his waist and smiling even more widely than the joking knights, sat a barefoot woman. She was astride, so the wind blew her skirt up to her plump thighs.

"here've you been, Pretty Lucy?" One of the knights greeted her.

"A poor riddle!"

The couple on the jennet ignored them. Much to my surprise, as they closed alongside the wagon, the girl turned to grasp the upturned bars that held the side slats, and swung free of her mount. The jennet, reined sharply away from the wagon, gave a honk of protest and then was left behind.

"Rosalba?" She was beside me now, as uncaring and limber as a boy. I admired her strength.

"Yes, Mistress."

"I'm no mistress, as you must certainly see, goose. Just Lucy, a servant like you."

I stared at her dumbly.

"You are to be the Lady Anne's new poppet?"

I nodded, although I felt sure my duties would be more important than that.

"Good! I'd rather scrub pots than take care of babies. I was afraid the Countess would make me serve her."

"Lady Anne isn't a baby, is she?" I had a flare of real fear. Babies were messy and difficult to care for. Noble babies died as easily as ordinary ones, often a dangerous happenstance for the luckless caretaker.

Lucy was amused. She flopped onto her belly and waved bare legs carelessly in the air.

"Thank your lucky stars! Lady Anne's five-years-old, and hasn't shit herself in ages, if that's what you're worried about." Just as I began to feel some relief, she added, "She's a weakly little thing, fair as an angel—which, mark my words—she will soon be. Don't you worry, though. She's easy enough to care for, except when she's got the croup. Then she cries all night."

I wanted to say that I had had the croup myself, and that I thought anyone might cry from it, but Lucy was already rushing on.

"Did you see that fine fellow who rode me here?"

I nodded. How I could have missed her arrival?

"Well, he's one of the earl's ushers, and we were just married! Isn't he handsome? Aren't I lucky?"

It was clearly expected, so I nodded agreement. It was easy to take her measure. She was one of those who *must* talk. Let them run on, my mother always said, for with this kind there's nothing else to be done. Soon, you will know all—and more—than you ever wished to.

"And you are almost as lucky as I am. Yes, indeed! Aren't you from that shabby little village?"

"It is not shabby." Shabby was a place like Oxnop Ghyll, where the people and their sheep dwelt together in turf huts. Aysgarth was a big village. We had stone houses and wooden houses and the privilege of a fish weir. We had gentry close by at Nappa Manor and people of all ranks filled our stone church of a Sunday. Besides, the cattle only entered *our* houses during the worst part of the winter.

"I myself was born at Middleham. If you work hard and always do as the Countess and the Lady Agnes say, you shall never have to go back to that wretched sty! If you are clever, you will have fine clothes like me and eat meat. Not the same food the Lady Anne eats, of course, but plenty of beef and bread from the best kitchen in the North. Have you ever been to Middleham?" Her thoughts seemed blown here and there by some inner wind.

"No." I'd lived in Aysgarth, walked around the falls and watched the men fish the rapids and the weir. I'd gone for lonely rambles across the dales, looking for lost sheep or making secret pilgrimages to the oak. I'd been to Nappa Manor, and several times to Bolton Castle, but, of course, never nearer than to help unload a cart at the kitchen door.

"I have seen Bolton." I spoke proudly. To me, that was a large and fair abode.

"Bolton? Bolton? Why, Bolton is nothing! Hardly worth the name castle, that poor little heap of stones!" The words did not quite fit in her mouth. I wondered whose she echoed. "Ah, just you wait! The Great Keep at Middleham will start the eyes from your head! It is the biggest castle in the north. A whole village, far bigger than yours, sits at its feet. All of it, and all that do dwell there, do naught but serve the great Earl of Warwick, his noble lady and his daughters."

As Lucy foretold, the castle took my breath away. It was enormous, appearing before my simplicity like a many-headed beast reclining upon the grassy rising dale. It was massive, gray, and very old, having been built, as I would learn, in the time of William Rufus, son of the Conqueror. The actual size was not apparent until we came close enough for me to recognize the houses against the outer walls. They appeared as small knots of rubble clustered at the sides of a giant. There was a guard tower spiking the sky, a drawbridge, and a green, slimy moat.

Plumes of smoke rose from many fires. Some were black. Some were pale, trailing in the wind. I would learn that these fires belonged to smiths, to the armories, to the kitchens, as well as to the cottages of retainers. At first sight, however, watching the smoke circling the stone towers and swirling about the battlements, it seemed I was about to enter the yawning mouth of the underworld.

The first few hours at Middleham were indeed a kind of hell. After we'd crossed the muddy bailey, I was lifted down from the cart by a great man-at-arms and delivered like a sack of meal through the kitchen door. No sooner had my feet hit the slates, than a hard-faced woman grasped me by the hand and marched me across the room.

In one shadowy corner, as unceremoniously as if I were an aged, moldy ham delivered from the smokehouse, I was stripped naked, and ordered into a tub of very hot water, where I was scrubbed by a strong-armed, red-faced woman who, after a curt "This is her, then?" spoke not a word.

Scalding water and embarrassment turned me scarlet, but staying seated in the tub seemed the best way to keep what little I had hidden. Not that anybody seemed to have a moment to look. They were all far too busy, rushing to and fro, in the throes of preparing a welcoming meal for the Countess. Vegetables were chopped; mallets pounded meat; fires were raked; bread was kneaded.

I was too terrified to utter a word, even after the woman poured a pitcher of water over my head and scrubbed my scalp mercilessly with her stumpy fingers, each as tough as a tree root. I had seen my family naked for the bath and on hot summer nights, but I'd never been the only one stripped, or in front of so many strangers. I can't explain why—shock, perhaps—but, for the first time in my life, I was quite unable to protest.

"Them freckles don't wash off, do they?" My tormentor laughed as she sloshed more hot water over me. The end came when a startlingly cold rinse of stale beer was poured over my head. Then, I was jerked from the tub and roughly toweled. Stunned, I simply stood, shuddering all over, dazed as a calf dropped from his mother's warm belly into the icy mud of February.

"Here!"

A linen shift was thrust at me. Fast as ever I could, I yanked it over my head.

"Put these on."

I was pushed to a stool and handed a thick pair of knit stockings and a pair of clogs.

"My shoes . . ." These were the first words I'd dared since entering the nightmare of the kitchen. They were the most valuable things I owned.

"Off to be cleaned. Your foot will be traced for new ones. You can't wear those nasty things in the upper chambers."

Feet sliding in large new shoes, I was led out into the bright, cold bailey and ordered to sit on a step. At first, after the shadowy, smoky world of the kitchen, I could barely see. I shivered hugely as the woman who had bathed me continued with her task, searching my hair for lice.

Beyond I saw gardeners lugging manure in leaking wheelbarrows to a garden where others dug it in. By the door, pale as a corpse, a scalded pig hung by the back feet, guts trailing into a tub, while bloody-handed women worked at butchering. Across the bailey, boys in red and white jacks were fiercely pounding each other with wooden swords. A line of archers, similarly attired, practiced at the butts, arrows singing as they flew. Wagons from our journey still stood in the yard, but the horses were unhitched and gone.

Bright pennons cracked on the battlements. There were glass windows in the upper stories, fine as those of our church, blazing back at the sun. The lower levels of the castle were punctuated by gaping mouths that spewed smoke, noise, and more people than I'd ever seen in my entire life. I sat still, enduring the woman's tugging and tweaking while she braided my hair. My brain buzzed and my ears rang, just like the last time Master Whitby had struck me on the back of the head.

※

"Anne, dear, here is your new servant. Her name is Rosalba."

In a stone chamber, treading upon sweet smelling herbs and rushes, the Countess pushed me toward a small girl child, who looked up with what I decided were eyes of fairy blue. Her skin was white, so fair I could see the veins. The braid that fell down her back was a pale copper, like metal buffed to sheen. It was neither blonde nor red, but some color perfectly in between.

Her dress was of a brilliant blue, not cut down from the

old clothes of grownups, but made in miniature, just for her. I'd never seen a child so richly attired. A steady, slightly perplexed stare cast back and forth between her elders and me.

"Marta will come no more?"

"She has other tasks now."

"Good." The fairy child declared with crisp decision. Her mother smiled.

"How old are you, Rosalba?" Anne's next question came straight to me.

"I am ten, Mistress Anne," I said. It seemed odd to be addressing someone so small so politely. I had not, however, been sufficiently respectful.

"My Lady Anne!" A harpy I would learn to know as Lady Agnes corrected me. "Always address her as *My Lady Anne!*"

"She will learn." The Countess patted my shoulder, which made me at once feel better.

"She has spots," Anne said, anxiously glancing at her mother. "Is she well?"

I was momentarily at a loss. Freckles were not unusual in Aysgarth.

The Countess laughed. "Those are freckles, Anne. Like Tib's."

"Tib's spots are gold." Anne knitted her fair brows and studied me.

"Rosalba's are brown, but what isn't freckled is as fair as fresh milk. She's like Roan William."

"Oh!" Anne's eyes brightened with understanding. The explanation had reassured her, and she took a step closer. I would later learn I'd been compared to the Earl of Warwick's favorite *destrier*—a war horse.

"Curtsy!" Lady Agnes prompted, administering a poke to that particularly vulnerable spot between my shoulder blades. I obeyed awkwardly and then extended my arms so Anne could see them.

"Do you have any dolls?" Anne took a step closer, experimentally tracing the flesh of my arm with one finger. I saw that for all her splendor, she was, after all, simply a little girl.

"No, My-Lady-Anne. I left them at home for my sisters, Lily and Marigold."

Delicate white fingers, moving with a mixture of shyness and command, caught mine.

"Come, then," Anne invited, with a sweet smile. "You may play with mine."

The Countess nodded when I glanced anxiously up, so I followed Anne to the corner. Here was an open chest, full to the brim with dolls. Some were finer than I'd ever seen, the kind with painted wooden faces and silken clothes. Others were rag, much like those I'd left at home.

It was one of these Anne chose. "This is Lady Katherine," she said, holding the doll up for my inspection. "I have had her since I was a little, little baby."

Lady Katherine was grubby and faded. She had yellow hair of worsted yarn, a crumpled green dress and kirtle, rouged cheeks, and painted lips and eyes. Her features, skillfully rendered, separated her from the rag dolls I'd had at home, whose eyes and mouths were rough embroidered.

"Say how do you do."

"How do you do, Lady Katherine." I dropped another awkward curtsy.

"How do you do, Rosalba," Anne spoke in a squeaky voice which I understood to be Katherine's. She plumped down in all that finery onto the sweet rushes and Our Lady's bedstraw. Anxious about my own new clothes, I slowly got down beside her. The flooring in the private chambers of nobility were changed monthly, the rushes mingled with all kinds of fragrant herbs, lavender, rosemary, and that deliciously scented bedstraw. A pleasant, dusty bouquet arose as we settled in to play.

That night, I lay by myself for the first time in my life, in a narrow pallet pulled from beneath the great curtained bed which Anne and her older sister, Isabel, occupied. Beside this was another high bed in which slept Nurse Cole and her daughter, Elaine. A mighty wind full of rain sobbed about the castle walls. I joined with it, crying softly as I could.

I'd never lain by myself, and although this bed was clean and marvelously soft, it was also cold and lonely. I missed my mother, missed Lily and Marigold. All my life we'd slept together, snuggled close as puppies, warm and safe when the North Wind howled down from the moors. Tonight that same wind moaned, hunting around the stone pile of Middleham. The room was like a cavern. Fire flickered in the hearth, casting monstrous shadows. I desperately wished I had something to hug, even if it was only a doll.

"Are you crying?"

I started, peered into the darkness. From the enormous four-poster, I saw my pale charge looking through the curtains, her fair plaits dangling. I tried to answer, but all that came was another sob. She surprised me, slipping through the curtains, and climbing down into my bed. Quickly, I pulled the covers close around her narrow shoulders. Even in tears that first night, I remembered my duty.

"Do you miss your Mam?" Anne cuddled against me. Quickly, we scrunched into the warm bed together.

"Yes."

"I would miss mine and Nurse Cole, too, and I would miss Middleham. I pray never to leave, not even after I am married." She hugged me, utterly trusting, convinced of her ability to give comfort. I hugged her back. After a time, my tears stopped.

She is good, I thought. Then sleep came to claim me.

"This one will do very well."

The Countess of Warwick stood above us, candle in hand, gazing down with approval at the bed where her daughter and I lay, curled together. Beyond, a rainy dawn seeped through the amazing glass windows.

My days were more regimented than at home. Mornings were spent dressing Anne, hearing Mass, serving breakfast to her, and then sewing, a tedium I loathed. After dinner, I sat with the Countess, her daughters, and her ladies. They embroidered while the rest of us spun, all gathered into a large, chilly room with two great windows.

A huge tapestry loom was erected there and weaving was always in progress. I had never seen such an immense device and my curiosity eventually brought me work there, where I learned the craft from the clever weaver women the Countess employed.

.⁂.

"Father!" Anne ran toward him, scampering like a puppy across the dense carpet of reeds that lay beneath the banners of the hall. Still a little uncertain about being among all these great personages, I hesitated before realizing I was supposed to go after her.

The Earl of Warwick was a magnificent figure of a man, very fair and muscular, with a neatly trimmed beard and broad shoulders. In his gray eyes I saw a cheerful sparkle that echoed the delight of his child.

As she approached, the knights drew aside. Suddenly, Anne tripped on something hidden in the reeds. To my horror, she pitched headlong, fell, and began to cry. I was close by this time, but not close enough to catch her.

My precious charge!

One of the pages, a thin, sallow boy, got there an instant before I did. I'd noticed him before, because in this castle world of the well-fed and strong, he alone appeared to be thin and small for his age. Not only that, Nature had not formed him well, for he carried one shoulder high. This young fellow now knelt beside Anne, then most tenderly lifted her up and comforted her, even kissing her cheek. Feeling useless and afraid, I was torn between concern for her and apprehension of the expected chastisement.

"Do not cry, Lady Anne." The page helped her up.

"Thank-you, Dickon." Immediately, she'd begun to master her distress. Lifting her blue skirt, she solemnly examined her childish knee. "I think I broke it," she said, gazing at him with those astonishing sapphire eyes.

"No, Milady." A smile graced the boy's features. "You have not, Praise God, for it bears your weight."

A red bump was forming. *Holy Mother protect me! A bruise on that fine white skin!*

Agnes had promised me two bruises for any one upon Lady Anne....

"You must kiss it and make it better." Anne held her skirt tightly back on either side of the injury.

The Page kissed a long, elegant finger and then ceremoniously touched her knee. I was impressed both by his gentleness and by his adult discretion.

"'Tis this big bone." I dragged what appeared to be the front leg of a cow from beneath the dusty reeds. Not knowing what else to do, I had searched for what had tripped her.

"The mastiffs must have dragged it in." The boy shook his head at the size of the thing.

We gazed at each other for a moment and then made an exchange. He took the large, chewed-to-whiteness bone, while I took Lady Anne's little hand into mine.

"Um—thank-you—gracious sir." Ludicrous as it seemed to speak so to this thin, small boy, I'd quickly learned that everyone at Middleham was far more important than I. Agnes had slapped and then lectured at length on the subject of proper address after a first day full of such mistakes.

"Dickon, this is Rosalba, my new nurse," Anne said. "Isn't she pretty colors?"

Hazel eyes, in which I detected a gleam of amusement, calmly looked me over. He was, I thought, near my age.

"And, so you don't get in trouble, Rosalba, he's 'Lord Richard' whenever you speak to him. He's the Duke of Gloucester, our King Edward's little brother."

Just as I was absorbing this startling fact, a voice right on top of us boomed.

"How does my girl?"

It was the earl, that tall, shining deity. In the next instant, he'd swept Anne away, up into the air, high onto his shoulder. She let out a squeal of delight. To have garnered so much of her father's attention sent the rest into oblivion.

"See! It's nothing. Just a little bump! Nothing for my brave daughter to bawl about."

The earl sauntered away with a beaming Anne perched upon his shoulder. All of us, men-at-arms, knights, pages—and my humble self—trailed after. I caught a final glimpse of "Lord Richard, our King's little brother," headed away toward the kitchen, the offending bone in hand.

I've often thought of that day. In this brief interchange, the earl's character was plainly figured. He wished his Anne was a boy, and, as that could not be mended, he wished her strong. Now, by simply speaking the words, it was as if he could make it so.

About two weeks after my arrival, while Anne learned reading at her mother's side, instead of the usual sewing, I was taken into the kitchen and left standing by one of the outer doors.

"Wait here. Mother Ash will come for you."

These servants who bustled on every side were like the people of my village. Their clothes were worn, of lumpy wool and linen, even if their aprons were of better stuff, and recently washed. Their accents, their laughter and their cussing when things did not go well, sounded like home.

A fire in the open hearth blasted the room. The door where I waited had been opened to let out some of the excess heat. Outside, men still cultivated the kale yard, turning a dark soil stippled with straw.

A sly-faced girl with hair like a fox's brush sidled close and whispered, "You are for Mother Ash?"

"Yes." I was keenly aware of the way she had been studying me. It was strange to be cut off from my own kind simply by a bath and a new dress. Before it had happened, I never would have believed such a thing possible

"Mother Ash is mad, you know. She's a mean old witch." The malicious smile let me know that she wanted to scare me. I'd heard such things said of my mother, too, so this didn't alarm me. Before I could reply, the girl turned on her heel, and returned to the big table where mountains of vegetables were being cut.

"The fool brings you here like this?"

I startled and turned back to the door. A woman, heavy, square and white haired, stood behind me. There was nothing frail about her, nor really so many years in her face. She looked me up and down, arms akimbo. Her accent was strange to me. I would learn she had originally come from the fat region of Oxfordshire, where lay the Countess of Warwick's Beauchamp dower lands.

"Mother Ash." I curtsied. Something told me that in spite of her plain's dress, this was the proper course.

"Yes, that I am, and you are Rosalba, for yours is the only silly face hereabouts I haven't seen before." She clamped it between one of those work-hard hands. "My Lady of Warwick says your mother has taught you something of healing?"

"A little, Mother Ash." I spoke as well as I could, cheeks pinched in that grip.

"Do you know aught of the cultivation of useful herbs?"

I had to search for the meaning of "cultivation," but finally I managed.

"Gardening? Ah, yes, Mother Ash. Some."

"Some? Some?" She twisted my face this way and that, gazing into my eyes. For a moment I had the sensation of being a mousey dinner caught in an owl's foot.

"It's a wise child who knows her own father, and a wise child who knows how to make an answer which says nothing! Come along then, Roan Rose." I bristled, although by this time I should have been well used to these Middleham people mocking my freckles like that.

"Come. We shall learn this morning a little about what you don't know."

The kitchen had grown quiet as the cooks and maids

paused to watch.

A burly male cook shouted, "Be easy with her, Mother Ash! Don't pop her in the pot and cook her for your supper like the last girl."

Everyone began to laugh as the old woman caught me by the back of my neck and pushed me through the door.

"Fools," she muttered.

We went down the steps and along the slate path. On either side shabby kale and pale new turnips ruffled, the only greens in sight. I thought this castle garden was large, but, after we left the bailey and passed beneath the wide, fanged portcullis, I spied another, even larger tilled plot, facing south. Beside the gray presence of the massive outer wall, we trod a narrow path between thatched cottages.

"How does your mother make a soothing bath?" Mother Ash suddenly asked.

"With hops, lavender, and thyme."

"Easy! Now, something harder." She fixed me with her dark, cold eyes. "What is used for colic in infants?"

"Fennel seeds, chamomile flowers, and fragrant valerian." That preparation was often in demand.

"And, then?"

"And, then?" I trembled, wondered what I had missed.

"Well, how is it prepared, girl? And don't mumble!"

"It is steeped in half cup of boiling water, then strained and given in five or six doses a day."

"Always recite the preparation when you make an answer." She paused, thinking again. "How would you treat congestion of the lung?"

"With lance leaf plantain, lungwort, and speedwell. Steep with one cup boiling water and mingle with spring water. Take a cup or more a day sweetened with honey." I thanked my stars I had a good memory

"That will work, but you may also use milfoil with two parts lungwort, nettle leaves, and the plantain. It is, I think, a more effective mixture. I will show you how to prepare it, as we are not yet out of the season. And catnip is for?"

"Chronic cough."

"There are other uses, but that will do. What about celery?"

"Air in the stomach, Mother Ash."

"What about chickweed?"

"For the bringing on of spitting, and—and—to move—reluctant—stools."

"Reluctant? Is that what they are?" Mother Ash broke a smile for the first time.

Again, I stared. I was beginning to wonder if there was something very excellent in the water of Middleham, that the women hereabouts should be able to keep so many teeth.

"Very nicely put, Rosalba. Not only have you been paying attention to your Mother, but I see the makings of a lady-in-waiting into the bargain."

We reached the cottages. We entered hers, marked by a pestle hanging alongside the door.

Embers glowed on a small hearth, revealing a pair of gray cats lounging beside it. The floor had boards, which made it finer than the house from which I'd come. There was a spinning wheel, a long table by a glass window covered with herbs, scissors, knives and at least five different sizes and styles of mortar and pestle. A bed against the far wall was shielded from drafts by a hanging. Instead of a smoke hole, there was a chimney at the end of the room.

Dried plants hung from the beams, and the room had a fragrance beyond the smoky remains of the fire. I warmed to the place at once, and even dared to imagine that someday I too might have such a house

"We will talk today, and then I shall show you my garden. Return tomorrow in old clothes, please. Rootstock must be moved, seeds planted. You will get your hands dirty with me, Rose."

"I know how to plant and weed—but—I must be clean, under my nails and all, to touch Milady Anne. Lady Agnes says so."

"Lady? Ha!" The old woman snorted. "She was begot on a kitchen slut by a knight not worthy of his badge. We will put gloves on you, girl, or haven't you heard of those?"

"Yes, Mother Ash."

"And you will come to me straight, no dawdling, every morning as soon as Lady Anne goes to her Mother, and race back in bare time to wash those precious freckled hands and that precious freckled face and change your clothes. No idling for you, girl."

"I am not idle, Mother Ash." It came out a bit more tartly than I'd anticipated.

"Time will tell." Her reply was equally sharp. "Now, tell me the name of this." She began again with her quizzing, moving about the room and pointing to the dried herbs that lay here and there upon the table.

I knew most of the answers, and was beginning to feel quite proud of myself until she opened a hinged, red wooden chest. Within, sparkling, was a host of mysterious glass vials, sixteen in all.

Reaching in with a muscular hand, she withdrew one, uncorked it, and then passed it close to my nose. An acrid smell flew up, vicious as a hoard of demons with pitchforks. I sneezed violently.

"What was that?" She corked the bottle and returning it to the box with a clink.

"I do not know, Mistress." I replied when I was able to speak again. My eyes were tearing violently, so I wiped them on my sleeve.

"Always use your handkerchief!" Sternly she pointed at my bosom. Inside the laces that closed the outer dress was tucked this new—and still unfamiliar—accessory.

"Now I know where to begin your instruction."

Chapter IV

ady Anne," I said, holding out a shawl. "If you go out, you must wear this."

Eyes shone back me, bright as her mother's. When I bathed her, sponging her arms or her chest, wringing warm scented water from the basin, I marveled at the sight of all those branching veins within the translucent flesh. There it was, flowing through this little girl—genuine "blue blood." Tributaries of the heart's river opened in the fine skin of her wrists and elbows. Others—slate colored ropes—fanned across her thin little bosom. In spite of Lady Anne's apparent fragility and tender nature, will was present in formidable quantities.

"Oh, Rose!" She protested as we made our way up the narrow, spiraling stair, "I don't want to. 'Tis far too warm."

I had learned a great deal about my charge in the last weeks. Putting my hand on her forehead, I checked for excess heat. *No fever.* Moreover, she was correct. The June day *was* warm. Warm, that is, for our dales.

I was warm myself, but I never judged Anne by how I felt. She was a rarer kind of being with her thin skin, her careful, adult enunciation, and the unfortunate susceptibility of her lungs of which I'd heard so much.

"Well," I said, "while we are climbing, I shall carry your shawl. When we are there, we shall see how the breeze feels."

Wind at that height could be stiff. The earliness of summer would make it fresh. If she broke sweat while climbing, I would have to pay attention and wrap her up before that turned to chill. However, Mother Ash had told me that climbing would not harm Anne—or anyone—unless they were old and fat.

Common sense, not coddling, was what I learned from my teachers. All the fuss in the world is useless when a person is marked for the grave. And unless we are wicked, what is to be feared in death? Are we not on our way to the bosom of

God?

"You'll see, Rose. We'll be quite warm enough." Anne flashed me one of her pretty smiles and took my hand. We began our march from a south-facing, sunny room by entering a torch-lit dreary hall. A sleepy young man-at-arms with a red and white tabard over his mail came to attention as we passed. The darkness of the station made it hard to stay awake.

Anne was excited, and, to tell truth, so was I. Today was a feast day. The household had been to Mass in the chapel, and now the young knights in training would display their skills at a mock tourney. I had never seen such a thing, although I had watched the squires and pages exercise in the yard.

They drilled daily, their execution criticized and sharpened by a master. These were mock melees with wooden sword and buckler, with the pike, with mace and battle-ax. The final step in their education was the management of weapons on horseback.

Tilting at quintain was the most exciting. If the boys were too slow riding past the target, they would receive a mighty buffet in the back as the tail piece swung around and they'd be tumbled off the horse and onto the hard ground.

During this rough practice, the boys wore layered jacks stuffed with tow. In jousting, the protection went up a step, and they donned brigantines—jackets with hide and pieces of tinned metal sewn inside. Then these sons of lords began to practice in odds and ends of plate, for they must also acquire agility and speed under weight.

Today, Anne's long fair hair was in a single braid down her back. A white cap tied at the chin covered her head. This would give adequate protection against the wind, if it wasn't too chilly. It was her throat and neck that might need wrapping, so I followed, carrying the shawl draped neatly over my arm.

I was learning to be comfortable here. The Countess relied upon me, and simply believing that this great lady trusted me ensured the best I could give. Anne, with sweet docility, had attached herself to me. It further eased my task that she was naturally kind. In spite of so much privilege, she was not in the least spoiled, which, I'm sorry to report, was not the case with her older sister.

Even had I been inclined to neglect my duties, the memory of hairy Mark Thornton, smelling of sheep dung, should have been sufficient to keep me on the straight and narrow. Master Whitby, too, was an angry presence I did not miss.

At first, a night did not pass in which I did not pine for my mother or for my poor friend Jane, but even that ache was quickly fading. Ease, good food I did not have to labor to produce, warmth and cleanliness, were seductive. The fact is I had taken to living at Middleham like a duck to water. Always one who watched and listened before opening my mouth, I doubtless seemed wiser than I was—at least, about the ways of the castle.

Mistress Cole, the woman who had supervised the child nurses was no longer spry. She was heartily glad to no longer be called upon to trot for hours after active little girls—or, as in the case of my predecessor, wayward nurses. Nursey Cole didn't look a gift horse in the mouth. She answered my questions and instructed me patiently.

Besides, Mother had instructed me to seek the guidance of "the little Lady's old nurse. Be humble, courteous and respectful, for she possesses all you must immediately learn." I had followed Mother's advice, and so pleased Nurse Cole. She and I got along well, and she always gave good advice, brief and to the point. Now that I cared for Anne (her own daughter, Elaine, attended Isabel) she was free to sit and chat with friends by the fire. As she had served the Countess faithfully since childhood, she had earned every moment of ease.

"I believe we shall make a lady of you, Rosalba." Standing before the Countess, scrubbed, braided, coifed, in a new linen dress and a white cap, I'd dropped a deep curtsy, feeling well on my way. My heart swelled with gratitude every time I saw the Neville crest—white bear and ragged staff—and for this world of marvels to which these mighty folk had transported me.

Anne and I continued to climb. Bright, narrow bands of light intruded from bow slots in the wall. When we reached the top, Anne's cheeks would be pink and her breath hard. So would mine, but there was a difference. It always took her time to recover from any exertion.

At last, we emerged into breeze and sun. There were seats set in the out-of-doors gallery, and all the folk of the house occupied them: the Countess and her ladies, the bailiff and his wife, the chamberlain and the chief usher, all chatting. Veils and shawls billowed in the breeze.

Anne, excited, pranced toward her mother, pink dress fluttering. In my old world cloth was dyed in colors which came easily from plant and earth. The blacks, purples, and the host of pastels of the rich still amazed me.

"Oh, have they already begun?" Anne cried. "Everyone's here!" Before anyone could answer, Thomas, a favorite among the burly men-at-arms, held out his arms.

"Thomas! Thomas! Lift me down."

Not waiting for anyone to scold this unladylike behavior, Anne sprang into his big hands with all the trust of a puppy. Grinning, Thomas swung her over the stone lip, effortlessly lowering her into an empty space beside Isabel. Gaily, Anne turned and waved.

"Do you also wish my help, Mistress Rose?" Thomas winked at me.

"I can walk." I headed for the stairs. I knew I must be on my dignity. Thomas and his friends chuckled. Teasing a new servant girl was always good sport.

Squeezing past others in the narrow aisle, I thanked my lucky stars that the Countess was talking with the bailiff's wife. Either Mistress Bailiff was more interesting than usual, or the Countess had chosen to ignore Anne's prank.

Lady Isabel, however, did not. She said loudly, "What a baby trick!"

As I inched past a pair of fat male knees covered in a noisy diamond pattern of red and white, I noted Isabel's disdainful heart shaped face. The Neville girls were sisters, no doubt about it, right down to the gilt hair and sapphire eyes, but

Isabel was haughty and sharp. Daily, I breathed a sigh of relief that gentle Anne was my charge, not the older girl, who was much taken with her own beauty and high station.

She was jealous, too. Everyone flirted with the handsome bear, Thomas, and though he was only a man-at-arms, it seemed to pique Isabel that he had not paid so much attention to her. Anne, of course, was still young enough to be the pet. Isabel Neville and I were of an age, young women. Entering this new estate, we had lost some privileges and gained others. How like Isabel, I thought, to covet the best of both worlds.

Looking down at the ground below where the games were, I had a moment of vertigo. The gallery inclined precipitously. In the courtyard knights and squires rode brightly caparisoned horses. When they trained or served in the house, the boys, all sons of high nobility, wore the badge and color of the Nevilles. Today, because of the tourney, they wore their own badges, signs of proud lineage. Below I saw the crests of each family—the quarterings and crossings. Instructed by Anne, who had been schooled in heraldry since she could lisp, I had begun to learn them all.

There was the Bear and the Ragged Staff of Warwick, the Dun Bull of another branch of the Neville family, and the Fish Hook of Falconbridge. There were white and red lions, shackle-bolts by the score, collared dogs, stag's heads, griffins with teeth bared, ravens and falcons with spreading wings. Covering the wide rumps of the sweating horses was cloth dyed indigo and white, red and yellow, purple and black. Murray and blue, colors of the House of York, appeared as well.

"Pick one for your champion." The bailiff's wife encouraged while the young men paraded in the yard. Wagers were offered and taken—little things—scarves or ribbons among the ladies, and daggers, rings, or badges by the men.

First came jousting, with a rush and shout. Next was the melee. The boys began on horseback, and then fought on foot. The clang of metal and the thud and crack of wood rang in my ears. Showers of dirt flew. Loosing the last of their weapons, one after another, the fighters would be forced to yield and withdraw.

With the notable exception of Anne, who sometimes covered her eyes, most of my companions, even True Thomas, laughed and joked when a young contender fell and did not rise. Trained to see in another way, I could not look again until servants ran upon the field to help away the injured ones. Even as young as I was, I knew there would be scars and broken bones, or perhaps even the killing fog of a head-wounded sleep for some of these fallen. Despite that, soon excitement seized me like the claws of those heraldic beasts. The thunder of hooves and harsh clash of arms, the dangling red foam on the bit, blinding flashes of sun upon plate, the alarms of trumpets, thrilled me to the core.

Through it all, Anne and I hugged each other. Sometimes we joined the others, pointing and cheering. Sometimes we covered our faces. The full armor of the knights rang like a bell whenever a helm or chest plate was struck. Around us, men and women leapt up, red-cheeked, cheering and clapping, or groaning and booing and turning thumbs down, as the fortune of their wagers changed.

After the men, the violent game was taken up by squires with blunted weapons and odds and ends of plate. Finally, as the earl and the others of importance were settling wagers and reliving the show, the youngest boys put on a display, such as their fledging talents could provide.

"See!" Anne yanked at my arm and pointed. "There's Dickon!"

Sure enough, there was the diminutive duke. He swung a wooden sword and hefted a wooden shield, both of which were too big for him. His clothespin legs—one blue and the other murray—stuck out beneath a bulging tow jacket. The ground had been churned to mud by the earlier passage of horses, and the little boys stumbled about, whacking each other like mad men, whipped to frenzy, I guess, by the manly display they'd just witnessed.

The earl cast a casual eye upon this field, and then began to laugh. Indeed, there was much to amuse, for none of the armament fit, except in the case of the very largest of these most junior contenders. Battered helmets, much dented, slipped over the boys' eyes. One lifted a heavy sword for a huge downward swing, tottered and then fell over backwards. A lunge launched by one boy to knock down his opponent ended in an ignominious collision with the wall.

A few old timers stood around the melee, refereeing and intervening to call "Quit." The boys were supposed to beat their opponent to his knees or strike "a killing blow." Then the loser was expected to surrender and abandon the field.

The boys hammered each other with those wooden swords. If they lost a sword, they fought on, battering with the shield, while attempting to snatch their opponent's weapon away. The field thinned. I saw the duke matched with a much bigger boy, who simply charged, using his body like a warhorse. Richard fell, but managed to keep hold of his sword. Aiming upward, he shoved his opponent away by jamming the point beneath the tow of the jack at an angle.

"A good blow! A killing blow!" True Thomas, who had joined us in watching, cheered. "The duke has gut-stuck 'im beneath the fauld!"

The larger boy, Rafe Vaughn, staggered backwards and gasped. An old soldier came forward to declare the duel over, but Rafe came hurtling back at Richard, sword swinging. Richard, exhausted, and believing that the contest was over, had dropped his guard.

Rafe's blow, on a downswing, struck Richard's high shoulder. The duke staggered backwards. His sword fell into the mud. Somehow, he managed to stand against the following push, clinging to his shield. His right shoulder and arm drooped uselessly. I knew he'd been hurt—badly.

"Yield!"

Richard didn't shout, but we knew his answer was defiant. An instant later, they were both on the ground. Fortunately, a huge man-at-arms yanked the older boy off and carried him away by the back of his jack, still cursing and flailing. Richard lay like a dead fish.

Before I knew what had happened, Anne was over the back of the stone seat, skirts flying, skinny legs pumping. I raced after her. A rail had been affixed to the wall to help older folks up the stairs and now Anne used it to go down, holding on with two hands and pushing off to take several at a time. I followed.

We raced through the great room with hanging banners and reedy floor, today dim and abandoned. Then, we descended another level, where we left behind a chorus of "Ladies! Be careful!"

We flew into the kitchen and straight across to the door that gave onto the courtyard. It had been opened for the folk below-stairs to see the contest, and there, as my Lady seemed to have known, was a mob. Some were boys, some were the old soldiers. Kneeling in the midst was Master Gray, who supervised the boys' training at arms.

Contestants leaned against the walls, nursing bloody noses, cut lips, bandaged hands and blacked eyes. On the stone floor, lay the skinny form of the Duke of Gloucester, his ruddy dark hair tumbled, his head bolstered on someone's cloak. Beneath the streaks of dirt and blood, his face was gray.

An argument was going on among the boys. Richard's opponent, Rafe, was out of doors, puking—whether from Richard's gut blow or one delivered by someone else, I never learned.

"It was a killing thrust!"

"It would have been caught by the fauld."

"Are you blind? Rafe was gut-stuck! He was done!"

"War is no game. No one is ever out 'til they're stone dead."

"Exactly! Rafe would have seen his guts spill!"

"Watch your tongue, Lovell, if you don't want the same."

A scuffle began. Francis Lovell, not a very large boy himself, had punched one of Richard's detractors.

"Take it outside, young sirs!" Master Gray pointed at the open door.

The man-at-arms and a pair of the half-grown squires added their voices and authority. The quarrel spilled outward, into the sunshine of the bailey.

Anne had wormed her way through the mob and now

knelt beside Richard. I joined her, and we silently watched while Master Gray slit the arm of the jack upward to the shoulder.

"Saint Anthony." He shook his head and looked grim. The tow within was red. I saw a gleam of white, where bone had pierced flesh. Richard groaned, moved his head. Fresh blood bubbled from his nose.

"Be easy, young sir. Don't move."

A hand rested on my shoulder; it was gnarled, spotted and wrinkled.

"Take Lady Anne upstairs. There is naught for either of you lasses to do here." It was Mother Ash who spoke.

"But my dearest Cousin Richard may die! You—good Mother Ash—good Master Gray—you must make him well!" Anne began to sob piteously.

"We will do our best, My Little Lady," said Gray.

That evening, the boys received a lecture from the earl himself regarding the rules of the tourney, about how the judges must be obeyed. A sorry lot the younger ones were— black eyes and bruises everywhere. The dispute that had gone outside had ended in a fist fight, but there would be no punishment. Boys fought. Men fought. That was what noblemen did.

On the battlefield, just as Rafe's defenders said, it was yield or die, and Duke Richard had chosen the latter. To die in battle, after all, was the noblest end any soldier could make.

Our duke had suffered a broken shoulder and arm. The setting, we heard, was difficult. Mother Ash said too that because Richard's spine had lately begun to grow with a curve—the cause of his high shoulder—he wasn't as strong as other boys. In Aysgarth, I'd seen a boy die from a green stick break, not from the injury, of course, but from the gangrene which came next. This was a fact I was not about to share with Anne, who fretted constantly about her cousin.

When Richard started a fever, both Master Gray and

Mother Ash stayed with him for over a week, treating him with humble willow bark, with expensive myrrh and mysterious clots of spider web, with leeches and frequent lancing, until the pus and swelling subsided. Finally, slowly, the little duke began to mend.

For a long time his fever returned every afternoon. His meager body was beset with pains from head to toe for the shock of so much injury to a frail body was hard to bear. However, Richard was the King's brother, not some peasant lad, left alone at home to heal if he could. Master Gray and Mother Ash hovered over him. Special broths and soups came from the kitchens. His wounds were twice daily washed and dressed.

When he began to get better, Anne and I were sent to visit. The first time we found him sitting up in bed in a loosely belted robe. I could see through the gap that his torso was tightly wrapped in a kind of harness of muslin and canvas, with straps to hold it in place. Mother Ash later explained to me that even before his injury, Gray insisted that the Duke of Gloucester wear this device at night in the hope it would prevent his spine from curving more.

"Do you know how to play chess?"

The question, of course, was directed to Anne, who blushed and shook her fair head. She was quite in awe of her solemn older cousin, perfectly aware—and at ease with the notion—that they would eventually wed.

This is how Richard became our instructor in the rules of this ancient game. He remained patient with Anne, who was, to her dying day his "Sweetest Cousin." After a time, however, he grew merciless to me, just as he was to Francis Lovell— who, sporting his own black eye and bruised knuckles from the tourney, was occasionally set free of duty in order to visit his friend.

We played many other games, too, in those days: backgammon, games with dice and *jeu cart*. Mere girls, we were not expected to ever win.

Nevertheless, Richard had been born to a strong mother, and he seemed to have sucked in with her milk the notion that while women might be weaker in body, this flaw did not necessarily extend to their minds. Never voiced, it appeared in his attitude. Having let me into the game, he then gave no quarter.

In the beginning, Anne was distracted by the personalities she saw figured upon the board. She loved the horses especially, crying when they were taken. Richard teased, telling her the game was not about horses, but about kings, and that she would do well to remember it.

He was kind, though, because she was younger. Soon all the games he played with my lady left the precious horses "alive" upon the board. She and I often played him together, consulting, but in those days we never could defeat him.

"The King falls, but the horses shall ride away." Anne smiled happily, the first time he engineered such an end for her. Richard sighed softly, reached across the board and tugged one of those long golden pigtails. Over her shoulder, he winked at me. His eyes were hazel, but close as we were I could see that they were strongly flecked with green.

"Dickon!" Anne cried, sweeping her braid free and slapping. "Ow! Stop!"

He let her hit him, next caught her small hand with his. The duke's fingers were long and graceful, though in those days the nails were thoroughly gnawed.

"'Tis unfair to strike me, Lady Anne." He spoke with boyish formality. "As a knight and a gentleman, I may not defend myself."

"Well, then, don't laugh at me, Sir Knight." She pouted prettily. "I saw you wink at Rosalba."

"Pardon me, dear Annie." In a flash he was all cousin, all courtier. He drew her hand to his lips and gave the fingers a kiss, in a perfect imitation of his elders, lowering those beautiful dark lashes as he did so. The sight gave me a never-to-be-forgotten chill.

How old was I? How old was he? I have never forgotten the gesture, for in that instant Richard of Gloucester became my *beau ideal* of gallantry.

"Perhaps I <u>may</u> excuse you," Anne fell into her part,

acting it out with a toss of her shining head. He had unsettled her, although she was too young to know exactly why.

So early starts the dance!

Nevertheless, Anne had excellent instincts. She knew her cousin was managing her in some unfair, masculine way. Seizing her knights, she pushed backward, dropping in a flurry of skirts from the bed. "Come on, Rosalba! Cousin Dickon shan't have my horses, no matter what!"

Like magic, the door opened for her. Children placed so high are never alone, and we always played beneath the watchful eyes of a servant. Though the man had been sitting on a stool, apparently daydreaming in his red and white livery, as soon as Anne ran in his direction, he hopped up, ready to do her bidding.

With a backward glance at the small duke, who was now smiling at this willful feminine behavior, I, too, regretfully slipped from the high bed. Richard of Gloucester was the nicest boy I'd ever known, certainly the nicest to girls.

One afternoon, so late the shadows had grown long, after the duke had begun to heal, Master Gray called upon Ash for a soothing draught. We compounded it in the castle kitchen, and then I was sent upstairs with it. After I'd tapped and been called in, I discovered the physician at work, manipulating Richard's thin, scarred arm. I'd never forgotten his white face or his tears, so fiercely dashed away at the sight of me, nor the glow hanging like a willow-the-wisp about the old healer.

"I am cosseted." Naked to the waist, his twisted spine in plain sight for the first time, Richard turned to face me. Nonetheless, he took the draught from my hand. I looked down, seeing his discomfort and thought instead of Mistress Ash's instruction:

> *Some for sleep.*
> *Some for pain.*
> *Some so the palate well receives.*

"Tis healing, my Lord Duke, not cosseting."

As Gray spared me a look of silent approval, I'd tried not to look at the duke's poor arm, the scant flesh reddened from the massage.

"You are the king's brother, Lord Duke." Gray's voice had cut sharply between his patient's shame and my wondering. "Never fear! Mistress Ash and I shall make you strong again to ably serve His Grace."

When Richard was back on his feet again, we were allowed to visit the stables. True Thomas escorted us. He often was detailed to what his mates called "nursemaid" duty.

Thomas' eyes were the shattering gray of a Yorkshire winter sky. His hair was white, perhaps prematurely. How old he was, I do not know. Perhaps, he was one of those lucky men who remain agile, hale and hearty 'til they die.

I'd heard it whispered he was a Neville bastard. He had the family look, and always stood about a half a step higher than the rank and file of ordinary servants. True Thomas had a fine hand with children. He gave many a frightened new page comfort and advice while they learned the ways of the castle. If Anne wanted to go somewhere ordinarily forbidden—like the stables—she could appeal to him. Even the Countess did not fret so long as he was our escort.

Anne had wanted to take me to the stables so I could see her pony. I'd been kept very busy through most of the first summer by Mother Ash, for it was gardening season and there was much to do. Now, in late summer, there was a pause, after haying and before the final gathering in, however, we'd followed the chain of command in order for me to receive permission. First, we'd appealed to Lady Agnes. After Anne coaxed a little, Agnes relented and summoned Thomas.

"And, please, Anne, do look where you step!" Agnes cautioned. She always had to have the last word. Behind her, Isabel and Elaine Cole sat in the window embrasure, demurely sewing sections of the most beautiful outer robe I'd ever seen. It was almost finished, embroidered on the turned back cuffs and around the collar with the standing bears of Warwick. In their claws they held the ragged staff, and beside them were suns and white roses, indicating the family's alliance with the House of York. The older girls paused, and then shared, with a glance, their superiority. What a little girl thing, their eyes proclaimed, to be interested in horses!

Richard appeared outside the door, breathless, still straightening the tabard he'd thrown over his white inner tunic. He must have been summoned from some other duty, one that did not require him to be in livery. The forelocks of his ruddy brown hair were held back with a bit of eel skin.

"Your hand, Lady Anne." Richard bowed and offered his arm. He could walk beside her, not a half a step behind, as a boy of lower rank must. He was a prince, ranking every man in the place—including the earl. Thomas and I followed the diminutive blue bloods down the gray twisting stair. Their formality was still new enough to amuse me. Such airs in mere children!

I glanced at Thomas, to see what he thought, but he wore a good-natured expression just this side of a smile. The most even-tempered man I've ever known, Thomas took the whole world, and all of us dwelling in it, in stride.

Passing through the kitchen, I was handed a basket with green apples. Outside, on the other side of the yard, the boys hammered each other with wooden swords and shields. For a moment, Richard's attention, so carefully trained upon Anne, wavered. He sent a longing look at the knightly exercise and released an audible sigh.

"You will heal soon, dear Cousin." Anne's small white fingers pressed his. He appeared surprised that he'd been caught out wishing to be elsewhere.

"Yes, Milord Duke." Thomas brought us to a halt, and then rolled up a sleeve. "You don't want to have another break at the same place. See here what happened to this arm of mine after two bad breaks?" He extended a forearm. Lumpy, scarred and knotted beneath blond thatch, it was no pretty sight. "It is almost half a finger shorter than the other and all winter it sends me pain which could set a saint to cursing."

"But you can still fight, can you not?" Richard asked.

"Indeed. I can and I do, noble Milord," Thomas said, "but not near as well as might have been. Still, praise Saint Wilfred, it serves me well enough to uphold my good Lord the Earl!"

In the stable we walked carefully, as instructed. It was clean, as such places go, the stable boys scrambling to pick up manure as soon as it dropped. Tall war horses gazed over their boxes. Some were friendly and curious, others looked down with rolling eyes and then drew their lips back, as if they contemplated taking a bite of us. Great dappled rumps shone in colors of sorrel, strawberry roan, chestnut, and gray. Manes and tails were braided and filled with ribbons.

I gaped in awe. These animals, bred for carrying men and armor, were the biggest I'd ever seen, even taller than Master Whitby's finest white ox. No one in our village had horses, except for old broken down ones soon slaughtered and stripped of meat and hide. Even the royal children stared. I was visited by an irreverent thought, wondering when Richard, Duke of Gloucester, would ever be tall enough to mount such a creature.

Anne adored real horses as well as chess pieces. She examined these with as much pleasure as if she'd never seen them before. Her cheeks flushed pink. Solemnly, to please her, Richard named them. I could tell he loved and longed for them too. To me they were beyond astonishing, another sign of the wealth of this place to which I'd been so magically transported.

"This is gray Dominus, and that is Questor, who has a nasty temper." Richard turned to say, "So keep clear." We obeyed, moving away quickly when the big chestnut stamped and then suddenly thrust his head over the wall to show us his teeth.

Over our heads, in the dark rafters, swallows twittered and flashed. The business of raising young was in full swing, and the trails of their leavings streaked the walls.

"And there is Boadicea!" Anne pointed. A beautiful sorrel mare stood easily in her white socks, munching hay. After the stallions, she appeared quite placid and ordinary. I wondered why she should be of such interest, and then I saw that curled on her broad back was an orange cat, such an exact match to her hearty color that at first I hadn't noticed her.

"Her good friend puss is well seated." Thomas smiled.

"Oh!" I cried, forgetting myself. "Are the great horse and the little cat truly friends?"

"Oh, yes," Anne said "They are always together when Boadicea is in the barn. She even teaches her foals to love her cat."

As they said, I thought, a cat may look at a king....

I was enjoying my visit more than I'd imagined. To me, the place smelled comforting—of animals, of hay. I had a flash of homesickness, for the frigid times when the cattle shared the door end of the house.

Further along, we came to low stalls where smaller animals, rugged dales horses of black and brown, were kept. Most stalls were empty, as they were in the yard for tilting practice. At the far end, where the walls were low and made of slats instead of heavy boards, a snow white pony thrust out her head.

"There is my Precious," Anne announced proudly. "Isn't she wonderful?"

"Oh, my goodness, yes!"

She held out her hand and I placed one of the green apples in it. My Lady was that day a fairy maid in a blue dress, braid dangling from beneath a flaxen veil. Precious might have been her unicorn, with a face which was chiseled and strongly dished. Her eyes were dark, yet the lashes were white and long. Her mane was brushed and left hanging, not hogged off or braided like the others.

As Anne displayed the apple, the pony's lips wrinkled, revealing creamy teeth, a pink mouth and a pinker tongue. With a relishing crunch, the apple disappeared.

"Oh!" I sighed, full of wonder. "She is the most beautiful horse I've ever seen!"

49

"Yes, she is." Anne smiled. "Now you see why I am in such a hurry to go riding when you go to Mistress Ash."

I noticed that sharing the box with Precious, back in the shadows, was another pony. She was smaller, shyer, too, for she didn't approach, even when the apples appeared.

"What pony is that, My Lord Duke?"

"That is Strawberry," Richard replied. "She keeps Precious company."

After a time, the other pony moved closer. She proved to be an ordinary dales pony, stocky and strong, though she was colorfully marked. Strawberry looked as if someone had sprayed red wine all over her milk-white coat.

"We will feed Precious and keep her busy. See if Strawberry will come to you, Rosalba," Richard said.

I did as I was told, supplying them with the basket and then moving away a little. Next, I put my arms between the slats with the apple I'd selected flat on the palm. The roan pony approached slowly, snuffling. There was a moment of hesitation, and she glanced at her stable mate, now being indulged straight from the basket by the duke and my mistress. I had a perfect view of my own freckled flesh beside her freckled muzzle, as she took my offering. As she crunched, studying me gravely with dark liquid eyes, I decided that being called "roan" was not entirely a bad thing.

Richard rode beside us, guiding a stocky, feather-footed chestnut gelding. Anne was mounted on her Precious. I perched upon Strawberry's fat back. A mounted austringer, a hooded goshawk upon his fist, brought up the rear. Richard may have been lord of this and master of that—but at Middleham, he was also a boy sometimes.

Today we were for an outing on the moor. Except for the austringer, we were quite unattended. The earl and his countess were gone away to another castle, taking Isabel, Elaine, and much of the household with them.

When they marry, I mused, as Strawberry and I trotted

along behind, it shall not be hard for them to sleep together. Had they not spent time in bed already? Actually, the three of us—seated cross-legged or belly-flopped upon a heraldic coverlet, the chess board between us, along with a three-colored money cat—a famous mouser who'd become as privileged a commoner as myself—curled warmly against Anne's back.

I knew of the other things done in bed, as much as any common child would learn by living in a crowded house. More important to me seemed the chess, the talking, the things done together in daylight. As for the other, well, it appeared as blind and instinctive as what I saw in the fields of autumn, an act that neither party could resist, a momentary reflexive madness. The male became quieter after the deed was done, briefly close to tractable. The female continued about her business with as much dignity as she could muster. The hen soothed her feathers. The sheep or mare might run off after attempting to land a kick upon her mate's muzzle. The Queen Cat jumped up, shrieked, hissed, and dealt the puzzled Tom a head-rattling box.

Perhaps things were more mannered in the private bedrooms of the great folk at the castle, but I often wondered. At least this couple would have teased, played, squabbled, and kissed each other, cousinly, on the lips, before they were expected to breed. For my part, I thought Richard would make a good husband. He was tender of Anne's feelings. He was even thoughtful when it came to me, as if I mattered, as if even a servant girl was worthy of a measure of respect.

I remember the strong wind that day. Blue and mare's tails arched overhead. At our feet was the grey moor, the patches of rocks and glowing heather. Larks sang. Released, the goshawk circled, floating on sunlight, like a taloned magician.

Our Dickon was cross, I knew, although both Anne and I were elated to be allowed onto the moor with him. Even now, Francis Lovell and the other boys were at knightly exercises in the yard. Master Gray still refused to let him return to tilting at quintain yet, insisting that he was not well enough healed. The King's brother lived a life that was far different from the other boys.

Of course, it was also well understood that the earl liked to often put Anne and Richard together. Despite the breeze, it was warm that day, one of those days when we might be sent outside anyway, to bring color to Anne's pale cheeks.

This is but a scrap of memory, I know, but they are all so precious to me.

Chapter V

Have you ever kissed anyone, Rosalba?"
An odd opener! However, considering our age this year, it was time for such conversation.

"Only my mother, my sisters and My Lady Anne."

For once, aimless, we were leaning against a low stone wall, eating strawberries pirated from the garden. Warm summer sun, something sufficiently rare on the dales to be made the most of, bathed us.

Richard had been sent away from his great passion—the aviary. Even a duke had to obey the Head Falconer while the young hawks (called "branchers") were walked into submission. The mews would be in darkness, the faloners all in attendance, passing the new caught birds hand to hand in an endless circle in order to break their will.

Richard spent all his free time in the mews. Falconry that did not simply comprise flying a trained bird from the wrist was a craft with a long, humbling apprenticeship and he willingly pursued the knowledge. His reserve and his observant nature particularly recommended him to the falconers, who shared those characteristics.

Today, idly talking of kisses, the duke sighed pensively. I knew his age mates often teased him. Because he was slight for his age and took the bigger boys' jokes so seriously, he was an easy target. Even this simple rite of passage loomed before him like a mountain.

"Celia is very pretty. Bob says he has done it with her."

"Kissed her?" I hesitated, wondering how much it would be proper for me to admit to know. "Or—or…?"

"Well—*or*—I should rather think." Richard flicked away the green cap from his berry.

"Bob's eyes are bigger than his stomach." I had a servant's angle on these stories. The young squires liked to attempt seduction upon servant girls. For their part, the girls liked to flirt, to play one fellow off against another, to ask for and receive rings and trinkets—even silver coins—in exchange for this or that. Naturally, in the telling, the boys liked to enlarge the size of the territory they'd conquered, while the girls magnified the value of what they'd received.

It was a way for a girl to collect a mite toward her marriage, especially if she was wise enough to avoid the consequences attendant upon actual surrender. It has always been this way between rich boys and poor girls.

"So, you don't think it's true." His look became inward, considering. "It is said that Celia kisses—and the rest—most willingly."

"So," I said, starting a giggle. "Will you offer Celia a coin and discover what she gives for it?" It irritated me that he was, as usual, planning, in this case, to take the next step toward adulthood.

His lean cheeks were still bright from the morning's exertion, splintering lances in the yard, so I couldn't tell if I'd provoked his flush. This year our young duke was far stronger, sometimes a winner at these daily games of war. As he'd done to all earlier opponents today, he parried my thrust.

"I'd rather be kissed for free. T'would mean a deal more." His long fingers reached into the bowl for another berry.

"So would all you gentlemen." I echoed what I'd heard older girls say. "But you fellows must not be allowed to run Scot free; you must pay the toll. After all, you may kiss and whisper sweet words 'til the cows come home, but you can never marry us."

As I made my speech, his eyes steadily brightened. I thought he would laugh and then do some boy's nonsense, like flipping the corner of my apron and sending the bowl and its contents flying.

"A servant may be commanded by her betters."

"If I must be commanded to yield a kiss—" I thought quickly, and, I hoped, cleverly. "—then my betters are hardly better than Scots, who steal what they are too lazy to earn."

"You compare the Duke of Gloucester to a Scot?" He sounded about half way to pulling rank.

A little anxious now, I met his grin. We were behind the wall, backs to the bright wind, hair blowing, mine escaping in wisps from the braid. In the strong light, his locks, which indoors appeared black as a raven's wing, had a touch of bronze.

"If you must be paid for a kiss, doesn't it follow you may be paid for more than a kiss?" He was rallying, playing the lawyer. "And, if you are paid many times, by many different men, doesn't that make you a harlot?"

"We may be poor and humble, but we are free born." All very well for him to be pious about Celia and the others who did these things! They were only making use of the one object of value they possessed. I was, however, not tempted to follow their lead. Not from any high moral standard—a girl who sleeps through Mass can never claim that—but simply because I couldn't imagine putting my lips against those of any greasy, hairy male who offered a trinket for the privilege.

"We common folk do what we choose—but, more often—we do what we must. We confess later, and hope for God's mercy. You, My Lord, should consider that before you judge."

"Well spoke, Rosie."

Rough, sunburned summer lips met mine, taking me completely by surprise. When I trembled, yet did not recoil, he caught my face between his long hands and kissed me harder. Trust Richard to have well studied the matter before he assayed. Nature, thus invited, asserted herself. We were warm friends. We were wildly curious. Drawn by my response, he tasted. It was shocking—wet and surprisingly sweet—full of strawberry.

After, we embraced with all our might, faces buried against the other's shoulder, embarrassed by so many startling new sensations. My flat girl's chest pressed against his padded jousting jacket. Even through thirty layers of wool and linen, I swear, I could feel his heart beating. I could smell him, too, the sweat and horses of the tilting yard, his dark, sun warm hair. The berries spilled into the grass. In that instant, with a strong boy's arms locked around me, my heart was lost forever.

And why should this have been so? I have plowed and planted beside a prudent, hardworking husband. I have borne and raised children of whom I am justly proud. I have healed the sick of every kind, and soothed the passage from this world of those I could not save.

I have taught the lore of herbs. I have brewed ale, and raised pigs, all to the benefit of my family. Why should a kiss, the whim of a royal boy, be so perfectly remembered?

Rain, and we stayed inside, Mistress Ash and I, and worked at what could be done. These were the days I liked the least, for she would make me study reading and writing, as well as cleaning and other tasks which did not get done in good weather.

I don't know who taught her to read and write. As a child, you don't really ask such questions. It is sufficient that someone is drumming it into you. I remember sitting at a table with a slate, trying to copy sentences from an open book. Over and over again I wrote:

To make an Infusion, soak in boiled water.
Decoctions are made from root and bark and are boiled not steeped.
Ointments are made with lard or beeswax.

She also taught things I liked better, word charms and how to cast stones for fortune telling. The last was an art she told me was a dark secret, knowledge for which women were sometimes hanged. There was the charm for stopping blood:

Three ladies came from Northern lands
With bloody knives in their hands,
Stand blood, stand!

Bloody wound, in Holy Mary's name, close up!

There were charms for burns, fever, and inflammation:

Three ladies from the East had crossed
One brought fire, two brought frost
Out fire, in frost
Out fire, in frost
The fire is out;
The frost is in!

To remove burns, you moved your hand from the trunk of the patient's body outward. As your hand moved out, you were to blow upon the burn, letting your breath follow the same path as the hand.

For Headache we said:

Tame thou flesh and blood,
As Our Lady closes the lion's mouth!

I learned to use my hand to catch, cup, and throw away the headache, saying as you did so, "I throw this pain away."

You could rub stones upon warts and then throw those into water or bury them to make the warts go away. For healing of any sort of malaise we said:

Holy Mary Mother of God
The Body is Whole
The Body is Strong!

Ash also told me what she called "true and very old stories," which came from the time before the priests kept the holy things all for themselves. We went together, early on Lammas morning and dropped a coin into the well and thanked "the lady who lived there" for the water of the past year. Further we'd ask she would continue to supply "plentiful water and good health" to us in the next.

This was allowed, Ash said, because we called her "Saint Alkelda," who, the priest said had been strangled by the Danes for her Christian faith. In fact, Middleham's village church was named in honor of this long ago martyr.

Mother Ash, privately scornful of such stories, said it more likely that "Saint" Alkelda had been a healer who had been charged with protecting and praying for the continued health of the well and the people to whom it gave water. She believed that Alkelda had been slain *by* the Christians for keeping the old ways. She said that in the ancient Saxon tongue, *Hal Keld* merely meant "holy well."

Ash also taught me the signs in the heavens, and when by the moon it was best to plant or cut herbs, when it was the right time to wean calves. She also taught me weather signs. All of this was learning I had to brush up in later years, and it stood me in good stead when Fortune's Wheel turned and carried me down, down again, back to my humble beginnings.

Chapter VI

Time flew and our quiet years at Middleham abruptly came to an end. The Earl of Warwick and King Edward fell out over the King's imprudent marriage to Lady Gray of Groby, "a nobody," a widow with two grown sons. She had been a lady-in-waiting, but "only of the second order," to the deposed and exiled Lancastrian Queen Marguerite. King Edward was known for taking what he wanted from women without a great deal ceremony, but Lady Elizabeth had proudly told him that "she was too common to be his wife, but far too good to be his mistress."

Prodded by this sally--and by who knows what agonies of lust--Edward IV had married the reputedly fair lady, in a secret ceremony with only members of her own family present. Even the timing of the marriage seemed suspect: May Day morn, which led to whispers that black magical arts had been used to seduce our king.

This story came, of course, from our betters in the castle, but soon it was on every lip that our handsome King had married the fair Lady Elizabeth only "after spells cast upon him by her mother, who is a foreigner and a witch." To compound bad judgment, the King did not tell the Earl of Warwick, but allowed him to go on negotiating a royal marriage with the King of France's sister, so that our Lord was left looking a fool. As you might imagine, the earl was furious.

The new Queen was formally crowned. As everyone expected, she brought her numerous family to London, and the King began to hand over estates and honors to them by the wagon-load, insulting the old nobility. Next, Richard was called to court to wait upon his brother. The King doubtless thought it best to have his little brother under his wing than to remain by himself under the influence of the offended, brooding earl.

Which came first in this battle of wills between the King

and the most powerful man in the Kingdom, it is now hard to say, like the riddle of chicken and egg. In those days, like all other dependents of Warwick, I was certain my Lord had been badly used.

Anne and I only knew we would miss our "Dickon." As soon as things were so ordered, Richard withdrew from us, so the ache of loss began even before he was gone. No longer familiar, he became, almost overnight, a high and distant princeling. He continued to perform his duties in the house, but then would stay as long as possible with the schoolmaster or with the other boys at the practice of arms. When he was free, he'd ride on the moors or go hawking or hunting with Lord Francis and his other friends. Afterward, he'd remain in the stables wiping down his horse and walking the animal cool.

"He won't marry you now." Isabel taunted her sister when Anne as we sat together in the solar plying the needle.

Anne continued her embroidery and kept silent, but I saw how she paled. My humble self was there, mending, as usual. Embroidery was not for the likes of me, and, frankly, I was just as glad. All a lady's maid must really know is how to mend, darn and press. Daily, to my sorrow, I did plenty of both.

I would have been as bored by it as I was with other tasks involving the needle, except that Mistress Oakes insisted that it was good practice for the stitching of wounds. As with many other things I did not like, I eventually learned to do it well.

"The King, our cousin, is ungrateful to Father. Because he has married that climbing Lady Grey instead of the French King's sister, Edward must now arrange foreign marriages for his brothers. What other way will there be for the King to make alliances?"

Anne said nothing, simply stuck her needle fiercely into the fabric of the tabard she was embroidering. It was useless to quarrel with Isabel, who was older, and knew everything. In fact, there were whispers in the air of a marriage for Isabel, and this enforced her superiority.

❦

I woke Anne before first light. Then, brushing sleep from our eyes, we slipped into the anteroom and threw on the clothes I'd concealed there. We knew Richard would be leaving early. In order to see him away, we'd have to avoid servants and slip unnoticed down the stairs.

We managed this more easily than either of us had imagined possible. Sure enough, there in the great hall, amid a group of gentlemen who would escort him, we found our quarry. Although he was small—and looked smaller, sitting between those tall men at arms—he was not hard to pick out. Arrayed for a journey to London, Richard was dressed in princely scarlet. A heavy golden collar, the Suns of York, lay about his shoulders, glittering beneath the smoky, predawn rush lights.

One of the earl's body servants hove into view, carrying a salver of hot water, coming straight for us. We shrank into the shadows. If any of the upper chamber servants caught sight of us, we would be sent away at once.

"Quick!" I grabbed Anne's hand. We hiked our skirts and tore up the twisting stair that led to the musician's gallery. My heart thundered as I climbed. I would certainly be whipped by Lady Agnes for my part in this escapade—a notion which was only now beginning to alarm me.

Once in the gallery, we peered down. Now we were closer, right over the heads of the early breakfasters.

"We have to get his attention." Anne peeped over the edge.

The shadowy gallery proved to be in high disorder. We had to be careful not to stumble over the clutter and be discovered. In one of the chairs lay a set of pipes, which would have let out a great groan if we'd happened to sit on them. There were empty bottles, mugs, and other things not necessary for music. A loaf had been abandoned upon a plate, and our arrival interrupted the feasting of a veritable pack of mice, so many they might have filled a bucket.

"Shoo!" I hissed at them. I'd had an idea. The mice, however, remained so bold I had to smack them repeatedly with the hem of my skirt to run them off.

Breaking the bread apart, I tossed the hard parts to the wall. The mice, who had bravely held their ground close by, now rushed after what I'd tossed like hounds after a bone. In the center, I hoped, the loaf would still be elastic. Finding some that was pliant, I began to make balls, rolling them on the surface of the bench. Anne understood what I was about and instantly seized the first two. A moment later, she was leaning over the gallery edge and taking aim.

She'd been growing and it was odd to witness the change. Anne, who had been so dainty—our fairy princess—had lately shot up. She was now taller than Richard. (What a misery it is for boys, the long wait some endure, before they reach manhood's full pride!)

I gathered all the pellets I'd made and joined my lady in leaning over the balcony. Below a voice complained, "Someone plays the fool!"

Her first shots had gone awry. The first bounced across the table, while the second fell with a splash into the mug of Richard's tutor, who was seated beside him. This mischance had wet the tutor's sleeve.

"Look here! Two! Two, I say, and a fine mess they've made."

Anne made a face. I stopped my mouth.

Below a wave of laughter and denial ran along the board.

"If we are caught, there will be trouble!" The image of a birch rod striking my poor legs arose again unpleasantly.

"That cow, Agnes, shall not touch you." Anne reassured me. "Now, hush, and give me the rest. I've got the range."

I delivered all the pellets and sent up prayers. Anne was a good shot with her bow, quick of hand and eye. She took aim again, flexing her wrist a couple of times to feel it. As the next pellet left her long fingers, she and I breathlessly watched the arc.

Her aim this time was perfect, if a tad high. This ball struck Richard right on the top of his chaperon, hopped off and bounced across the table. Across from him sat True Thomas, who looked up—up, while everyone else was watching the bread ball tumble across the board.

As one, we ducked.

"Did he see us?"

"I think he did, My Lady." I now heartily wished I'd never let her talk me into this.

I was the one who concealed clothes in the anteroom. I was a servant, the one who would be punished....

"I believe there are fair ladies in the gallery who crave an audience with the Noble Duke of Gloucester," said Thomas.

Laughter followed, while the tutor grumbled. There was the grating sound of a bench pushed back. Anne and I covered our faces and peeped at each other through parted fingers. We'd gotten Richard's attention—and that of the entire room, as well.

"Saint Winifred!" Anne gasped.

Not only Richard, but from the number of footfalls on the stairs, half his entourage too, was on their way up. After a moment's consideration, she shot to her feet, grabbed my hand and tugged me upright. I watched as she composed herself, folding her hands together beneath her budding bosom. She lifted her chin and straightened her back, as she'd been taught. At this age, she was sapling slender. The pleasant abundance of her later years was not yet in evidence.

When Richard entered the gallery, we both curtsied. Then, beside me, Anne resumed her proud stance. True Thomas, Sir James Walker, Sir Robert Alcott and their servants, as well as several men at arms, entered behind. Richard would, for the rest of his life, be attended.

Although near fourteen now, "our Dickon" looked a deal younger. Despite his jewels and golden collar, his youth was even more pronounced, framed by those grim-faced soldiers in the dim gallery. In lavish court clothes, the high shoulder was concealed.

"You wished to speak with me, Lady Anne?"

Royal children playing at decorum, but none of the onlookers so much as cracked a smile. From now on this lord and lady would be surrounded by ritual—and by dissembling.

"Yes, My Lord of Gloucester. To wish you a pleasant journey and to let you know you will ever be remembered in my prayers."

I was so proud of her! She carried off that grownup speech, in spite of the girlish way she'd delivered her summons.

"I very much hoped to see you too, Lady Anne."

Stepping forward, he removed a ring of braided gold. Carefully, he took Anne's fingers in his. With utter daring, he slipped it on. The tutor cleared his throat loudly. Richard ignored him.

"By this small token, I pray you shall remember me, Lady Anne."

"By this, I shall, My Lord of Gloucester."

It was matter-of-fact, a pledge between boy and girl. So simple! They belonged to each other.

Richard leaned forward and kissed her cheek, and then he put his long fingers beneath her chin, tilted, and brushed his lips chastely against hers. If it had been me, I would have thrown my arms around him, pressed him close. There would have been no way I could have restrained myself, but they were royal. The steel was already in—fired, tempered, set—so their last moment, formal, gilded—was like leave-takings I'd seen pictured in books.

Richard stepped back, and the cousins made another courtesy. When he turned, his men parted before him. Without a word, they followed their small lord down the stairs. The tutor alone dared a measuring backward glance.

Of course, there was hell to pay. Before we'd got half way back up the stairs, Lady Agnes met us, switch in hand.

"This is your doing, you blighted imp!" She pointed the slender birch at me.

"Don't you dare!" There was a moment in which Agnes simply stared at Anne. Then, abruptly, she slashed at me. I pushed past her, springing up the stairs like a goat, but the first blow cut my ankle bitterly.

"Stop at once, you wretched old cow!" Anne shouted it.

A chase began, and Agnes didn't catch me again. I was much faster; her knees were aged. Anne, these days tall and strong, with plenty of breath to spare, followed along in her wake, threatening every step of the way.

"I will tell my mother you did not obey me!"

"The Countess switches harder than I do, little Lady!" Agnes puffed, still in hot pursuit.

So it went, until we reached the solar on the upper floor.

"Anne Neville!"

Everything stopped. In the light of the upper windows stood the Countess, an unbelted scarlet robe thrown over a long white shift. A heavy length of sand and silver hair fell below her waist. We sank to the floor, as did Agnes. The tone the Countess had employed was unmistakable.

"Come." The Countess extended a thin white hand, rings flashing. Two ladies-in-waiting flanked her. One held a brush, the other dangled a pearl-beaded satin ribbon. The Countess had been alerted in the midst of her toilet.

"I beg your pardon, Lady Mother, but Rosalba must stay with me. Agnes will whip her, and nothing is her fault."

The Countess looked me coldly up and down, then amended. "Rosalba, attend!" With not so much as a backward glance, she marched away across the solar. I didn't know whether to be relieved or even more terrified. Leaving behind the simmering puffing bulk of Agnes, I followed Anne into her mother's chamber.

"You are of an age to be married, Anne. That was childish."

"I only wanted to see Cousin Richard again, Lady Mother."

"The Duke of Gloucester, Anne," The Countess corrected. She was seated in an arm chair now, heavy ashen locks flowing about her shoulders. The two of us—*foul miscreants*—knelt on the carpet at her feet.

Red, blue, black, white, a maze swirled before my eyes. It was easier to stare at the queer patterns on the carpet from the Holy Land than at the Countess, whose eyes blazed.

"Please, Mother. I—I may never see—the Duke of Gloucester—again."

"King Edward has injured your father greatly, first by his ingratitude and then by his marriage, that astonishing folly. The queen and her upstart kin are preferred over us, showered with lands, with high offices and rich marriages. This, despite the fact we are Edward's blood, despite the fact we share the ancient lineage. Richard of Gloucester knows his duty. He has always behaved in this house with perfect propriety, and now he goes to court to serve his brother. You, Anne, likewise have duties, and are subject to your father's command. We Nevilles have parted ways with Edward of York and his brothers. So must you."

Anne said nothing. I wondered if the Countess would learn about the ring, and whether Anne would be allowed to keep it. She and I traded a furtive glance as we trembled on our knees. I knew her mind was working furiously.

The Countess had chosen to make our punishment all the worse by making it public. Her ladies and upstairs servants had crowded into the open door of the chamber, and I wondered what tales they might bear. Still, with the exception of Thomas, the men who had come to the gallery with Richard would soon be gone, on the road to London.

I could see Anne moving her hand inside the folds of her dress. I knew what she was doing—slipping the ring into an underlying pocket.

"Speak to me, daughter," the Countess said. "Say what you understand."

"I am deeply sorry, Lady Mother, for my careless and improper behavior. I understand your displeasure and now understand my duty better. The Duke of Gloucester is—is—no longer our friend." I guessed what it cost to say, but she bravely lifted her head as she spoke. Her eyes glittered with tears.

Lies! All lies! The first she'd ever spoken to her mother, I'll warrant, but hardly the last dissembling I'd witness or take part in on that day.

After dismissing Anne, the Countess dealt with me. She did not call for the switch as I'd feared, but lectured me on where my loyalty lay.

"Come here!" She spoke in such an angry voice that I did not dare get up. Instead, I crept to her on all fours like a dog. When I arrived at her knee, she leaned down, seized my loose braid and hauled me upon her knee.

"Now listen, girl! You owe more to Warwick than you can ever imagine," she shouted. "And you owe this duty to me, even more than to my daughter, the Lady Anne. Do you remember who it was raised a poor thing such as you so high?"

"You, my Lady Countess! You!" Tears spilled down my cheeks. "I owe all I have—all I am—all I have been taught—to you." She slapped me twice, hard across the face and twisted my braid so that I thought my eyes would pop out. It hurt terribly, both my head and my pride, for not since leaving home had I'd ever been punished so ferociously.

"Lady Anne is of marriageable age. Any favor my daughter shows to any lord, no matter how high that lord's rank and no matter how familiar, you shall report to me, forthwith!"

She kept a tight hold on my hair, and asked what they had said to each other. It was now my turn to perjure myself.

"Only that the duke and my Lady Anne promised to remember each other as loving cousins, my good Lady Countess." Easy enough, after that, to be pitiful and grovel weeping at her feet. "They—they—exchanged a threefold cousin's kiss, as they always have done."

At once, I feared this was more than I should have said, but the part about the kiss seemed to make the Countess think she had heard the truth entire.

"Remember well what I have said to you, Rosalba! Do you swear upon your soul to remember your duty and tell me everything? Otherwise, I will send you home, back to that nasty sheepfold from which you came."

"Oh, please, no! Not away from My Lady! Yes, an' ever I shall do your will, my good and great Lady Countess."

She gave me her hand to kiss, and it seemed my troubles with her were—for the moment—over. I was dismissed and sent back to Anne.

I found her, not repenting, but sitting in a high window seat. In the distance, dust rose along the southern road.

"Did you see Duke Richard go?"

"I did," Anne said, with a faraway look in her eyes. "He looked so brave riding at the head of his company."

Anne was kept close by her mother. I was dispatched to Mistress Ash and set to scrubbing her empty medicine bottles and grubbing in the dirt of the garden and a host of other disagreeable and menial tasks, no doubt so ordered by the Countess.

It was a week before we were permitted to ride. As usual, True Thomas came to accompany us. He lifted Anne onto her Precious, and made certain the saddle was tight by surreptitiously punching the pony in the stomach. Precious coughed, stamped a back foot and glared, but she had a naughty trick of bloating her gut, and this would make the saddle slip.

I climbed from the mounting block onto the little strawberry pony, mine to ride with my lady. Every time I did this, I wanted to pinch myself. Horseback was an exhilarating experience a commoner rarely enjoyed. Horses were for gentlefolk. Ox carts or "shanks' mare" sufficed for the likes of us.

Anne, in a hurry to escape the confines of the castle, had already started away.

As I quickly gathered the reins and found my seat, Thomas walked over.

"Gotten yourself up, have you?"

I began to say that I had been getting myself up for the last year, then realized it was a ruse. Thomas had something in hand, something he wanted me to take.

"For you, Rosalba," he whispered, "from a young Lord who says he will miss you, too."

I gazed in astonishment at an enameled white rose, a pendant strung on a fine strand of braided horse hair.

"Thomas—"

"My Lord of Gloucester prays you will take special care of Lady Anne," Thomas said. Then, with a wink and a knowing look, he added, "Further, the duke also says you are to understand that this is a gift—and—no wage."

Leaving me gaping, he walked away and swung up onto

his mount. From the messenger's point of view, the deed had been done. Besides, he must catch up with Anne, who, in her hurry to escape the castle's confines, was even now approaching the portcullis unattended. Blushing fiercely, I slipped the necklace through the slit in my dress into a pocket.

My Lady and I kept our secrets. She, with absolute daring, hid hers in plain sight, wearing the ring Richard had given her on a chain, between a medal of Saint Anne and one of The Blessed Mother under her shift, so it touched her fair skin. I, too, kept my white rose close. It was all we would have of our Dickon for a very long time.

Chapter VII

My daily work in the garden increased, so I spent less time with Anne. Another girl, one of gentle birth, Grace Poleyn, was introduced into the house as one more suitable to wait daily upon my Lady. I think it had been planned to put me aside entirely, but Anne, not known hitherto for ill temper, cried and stormed, demanding to keep me.

"I cannot sleep without her! She keeps me warm and company, she knows how to loosen the knot in my chest, and chases away the nightmare. She has ever been with me—and so she ever shall!"

"You will soon sleep with a husband, Lady Anne," Agnes countered. "You will have no need of Rosalba to keep you warm."

To this remark, Anne replied only with a cruel snort of derision, copied from Isabel.

"And what would you know of that, you old maid?" In her parent's absence, my Lady was overruled, however, and I was banished to Mother Ash's cottage. This was no absolute hardship, for I had always loved it there, so clean and snug. The only problem was that my teacher snored so loudly that the rafters shook. It took me quite a while to learn to sleep despite it.

I did miss Anne, and had my own hard times away from her bed. I missed the scent and touch of her, the sweet warmth of her body in my arms at night, quite as much as of her company. It was a kind of love, such as young girls often feel for each other, especially if they are kept from the company of men. Some call it unnatural, but it seems to be quite ordinary in nature. Observe the way heifers will leap upon each other, before they are strong enough to carry the bull on their backs. We were chaste, with just the need to hold and press a sweet kiss or two upon the cheek or neck, sufficient to send shivery pleasure into innocent flesh.

If Anne rode out, I would see her, run to her, and she would stop her pony, and extend one of those pretty long hands for me to kiss. Just to lean my forehead against her leg, to touch and be close, even if only for a moment, gave us both solace.

When the Countess and her husband returned from a long circuit of visiting their castles, Anne demanded to have me back again. After this, I was allowed to come to her bed whenever she didn't feel well. I was always summoned when she had trouble breathing. However, our old way of living like tender sisters had passed and gone, as do all things in this life.

A second lady-in-waiting was introduced at this same time, Lady Margaret Neville, a plump blonde with watchful gray eyes. She was actually Anne's half-sister, one of the earl's bastards. She had been raised mostly at Warwick castle, because her mother's family lived nearby.

Perhaps because she was the second interloper, I was always less jealous of Margaret. Perhaps it was simply because Margaret was so quiet and so wary. Her blood was bluer than Grace's, but from her demeanor you would never have guessed. A bastard, I suppose, stands always on a quaking bog.

It must have been her mother's intent to wean Anne and me from each other completely, for I spent longer hours in the garden every day. Mistress Ash and I tended not only the castle folk, but the people of the village, too, and we were busy that year. Ash and Master Gray taught me about surgery: to cut boils and cysts, how to open and clean wounds that have pus, how to set bones, when to apply leaches and when to let blood, and demonstrated the horrible business of cauterizing flesh. More happily, I went with Mistress Ash to assist women in childbirth. To see the fat squalling baby come, to see the tears and shrieks of the mother turn to joy as she put the child to her breast, this was a miracle!

With my teacher overlooking, I assumed near all the work in her herb garden, pruning the rangy hyssops, the yarrow and mint, and those that invaded more than their space, harvesting, drying, and preparing all the standard cures. Washes of burdock for pimples, garlic for wounds and infections, hip syrup for winter tonics, borage for nursing mothers, sage, rosemary and thyme for seasoning and for purifying the blood, nettle and raspberry for woman's troubles, comfrey and myrrh for bad gums, the list went on and on. This summer my teacher rested beneath a tree and watched me work in her beautiful, scented garden. On rainy days, we sorted and dated all our stores. We threw out what was old, replacing it with the newly dried. My mistress quizzed me, as she always had, as we went along.

She set me to reciting the spells which went with certain cures, and refreshed me upon the saints' names to exchange with some charms my mother had taught me. This, in case "priests come sniffing with their long snouts, thinking 'twill advance them to hang a wise woman."

The moon sent the blood curse to me when I was with Mistress Ash that summer. She presented me a dagger upon the occasion, small and bright, the hilt bound in leather, and in such a fine sheath of soft leather that it almost made recompense for this new trouble.

"It is what your mother would have given, and what every woman must carry, as we live so close to the Scots. I will show you how to wear it beneath your skirt and True Thomas has said he will show you some ways of using it that may save your honor, or, even more important," she added with a stern look, "your life."

"Is not death preferable?" I repeated what I had heard on the lips of Lady Agnes.

"It is better to live if you can, for how else will you get revenge?"

I considered this, and it sounded like something my mother would have said. That was still the way I tested the merit of things I was told.

"But," I went on after a pause to consider, "are not sins of the flesh—even insults--a result of woman's temptation?"

"Men, of course, say this." Ash spoke with the grave

contempt usual when such a topic came up. "Sins of the flesh are commonly instigated by men, although you will never get one of those sodomite priests to admit it."

There was not much I hadn't seen, between village and castle. I did not stay, but ran from whatever coupling I'd stumbled upon, be it the soldier and kitchen maid grunting against a pantry wall, or robes like ghastly wings enfolding some hapless, weeping boy, or young squires on a hunt, who have caught a village girl in the glade instead of a hind. A woman, no matter what her age or station, was wise to keep a sharp look out.

"And while we are on the subject," my teacher continued, "you will hear that the man's seed alone makes generation. What do you think?"

"I think," I said, for this was another idea I'd begun to ponder, "that I look like my mother and not at all like my father."

"Well," Mistress Ash smiled slightly, "that is not a bad way to say that something is contributed by one's mother. Men, however, will laugh at you for that answer and say your father was a cuckold."

"An' so he was," I replied stoutly. "I am proud to be my mother's daughter and would be proud to be hers alone, an' it was possible."

Ash cackled and slapped her knee. "By the Black Lady! Her hand was in the business when you became my last pupil." The business about being the "last pupil" bothered me, for, old as the hills though she seemed, I didn't like to think of her dying. Mistress Ash waggled a bumpy, crooked finger at me and pronounced, "Only between wise women, Mouse, such talk."

True Thomas did indeed show me how to use my knife, how to keep it where it could be drawn quickly through my skirt pocket. He also showed me where to strike openings in mail or through a stout brigantine, how to strike fast and avoid losing the knife to my attacker.

"Strike and run. Strike hard and deep enough and perhaps you can escape. Any man that wills has the strength to rape you, will—even wounded. He will break your jaw, break your back and have his way. Never be caught off guard; keep your eyes open. Use your teeth, bite off his ear, try for an eye. It may be all the revenge you will ever have."

His stories—terrible things he'd seen at war—frightened me, and for months I could hardly go anywhere without wishing for eyes in the back of my head.

"Oh, Holy Mother!" It was Anne, sobbing.

I had been summoned into the castle because "Lady Anne is sick at her stomach and calling for you." I found her crouching white-faced over the chamber pot, too embarrassed to move.

"Rosalba! Come quick!"

It had come to me but a short two months ago, and was, in fact, upon me now, for it was new moon, the time I ever had my courses. It didn't come every month, yet, thank the Blessed Mother, by now I knew the signals of onset: backache, nausea, cramps—the curse of our disobedient Mother Eve, which brought discomfort, inconvenience, shame—and, danger, in the form of a terrible vulnerability.

"Patience, My Lady. I'll bring what you need."

"Oh, Rosalba! It's so horrible!"

After gathering a handful of clean rags from the cupboard in the anteroom that held a store of such things, I returned.

"Where is Grace?"

"I sent her off on an errand to the kitchen."

"Do you need me to help?" I crouched down beside her.

"No. It's too awful. But stand outside and don't let anyone in. I know what to do. Then, please, get me something for the pain. Oh, dear Blessed Mother! Why so soon? Why? Dear Saints and Angels in Heaven! I am lost!"

"It comes to all of us." Hunkering down beside her, I was having a pang of indecision. "I should tell the Countess."

"Don't! Oh, Rosalba! Please don't! That's why I called for you!"

"It can't be hidden, at least, not for long." I looked down at her, clothes wadded miserably around. A bloody smell rose from the pot. "Look." I pointed apologetically to her kirtle, peeking out from beneath her skirt. "There's some." Sure enough, a gout had stained it.

In the end, I stayed with her, helped her get comfortably cleaned and padded. I tried to offer what solace I could, but in the end we simply retired to bed together, hugged and sniffled. I cried for her, and for myself, as well.

Pain and blood! It was the end of our childish freedom, the beginning of the servitude to the body which is woman's peculiar office.

"Now my Lord Father will find me a husband," Anne whispered. "I will be married to someone I don't even know—and—and—then—all the rest—whether I will or no."

I knew she was thinking of her lost, sweet Dickon, and of the terrible breach between the King and her father, the great Kingmaker. I hugged and tried to cheer her, but I had fears of my own.

If she married, would I be allowed to stay with her? Would I want to? Or would the family keep me here to make medicine and tend the gardens at Middleham? Mother Ash had taken a bad turn during the past winter. Her mind and will were strong as ever, but her body had weakened, and she moved slowly as a snail. Of course, the worst end, as I then saw matters, was banishment to Aysgarth, where I would doubtless sleep for the rest of my life with a sheep for a bolster.

Anne finally crawled deep under the covers and I went to concoct the pain medicine she needed. As I slipped off the bed, I knew that as soon as I was gone she would break down and bawl like a baby.

On my way out, chamber pot in hand—for I aimed to give my dear lady as much help as possible—I encountered Lady Agnes, sneaking into the anteroom. She pretended to be busy with linen in the cupboard, so I ignored her and continued on my way.

I knew she'd been spying. News of Lady Anne's submission to the moon was all over Middleham before dark.

❦

During the time Anne and I had been kept separate, she had found a new solace. Climbing into the musician's gallery one afternoon, hoping to relive her last encounter with Dickon of Gloucester, she made a new friend, Anthony, the lute player.

Nothing in the way of adventure here, for kind Anthony was weak-chinned, slumped, and thin as a broken reed, with eyes so bad he couldn't see the butts at Sunday archery practice. He could, however, coax beauty from every string instrument ever devised. Richard, in fact, had favored Anthony, for the duke was one of those whose heart was touched by music. Anne had a sweet, white voice, and Anthony often accompanied her. That Anne was able to sing without shortness of breath was a sign of her new strength. Her parents were as much delighted by this, I could tell, as by the innocent charm of her performances.

Anthony cheered his sorrowful little mistress with songs. One thing led to another, and now he came every day to give her lessons. Isabel, naturally, must have lessons too, though she was more interested in being the center of attention than learning anything. The sisters did master a few showpieces in beautiful close harmony, which they performed for their father like a pair of shining, golden angels. It was, however, Anne who stuck with practice, Anne's long fingers that mastered the art.

The songs my Lady worked hardest at were those her Dickon had loved most. Mild, chinless Anthony was a great help, remembering which ones had "found favor with the young Duke of Gloucester." He taught Anne all the verses, too. At first, her stumbling hours of practice drove the servants near to madness, but we all respected her diligence. After a while, her graceful fingers proved to have the perfect touch. Her sweet, clear voice was pure as a boy's.

The sad songs she sang brought tears to my eyes—and, to the eyes of pale Anthony, who now fancied himself a *Trouvere*, romantically attached to an unattainable, chaste and lovely mistress. He was forever tapping on the door, bringing "my Lady Anne" another new song.

"And you shall be the Queen, Milady," prompted Elaine.

"I shall be married to George of Clarence, and then our father shall depose Cousin Edward, and George shall be King."

"So shall I be!" Isabel struck a pose before the window. "Then our father Warwick shall call the tune for England."

I mending in the corner, gawped at treason so lightly spoken. Anne, however, managed a retort.

"You will need a dispensation. Cousin George is within forbidden degrees."

"Cousin George has gold enough to get whatever he wants from the Pope," Isabel said airily.

"You wish to *marry* with my Lord of Clarence?" It was not my place, but the words came tumbling out.

Isabel leveled her blue gaze. "Why shouldn't I, you silly fool? Did you not see The Duke of Clarence at my father's great feast? He is the king's equal in every part."

I stood and dropped a low curtsy, prudence taking belated hold. After all, these days it wasn't often that I was allowed to sit with them. It was left to my Lady Anne to pursue the thought.

"For myself," Anne said coolly, "I only noted what a deal our Cousin George drank."

"Trust you to be jealous!" Isabel habitually attributed her own worst faults to those around her. "The Duke of Clarence is tall, handsome, and witty. Not a thing like drab, crooked Richard."

"He may be crooked, but he rides and fights as well as..."

Isabel interrupted. "Our father says the Woodvilles daily spit upon Richard, but he is such a weakling, so in love with his brother, that he will not listen to any proposition our Father makes. Richard of Gloucester will not even change his course," Isabel added, smiling cruelly, "though Father secretly offers him your hand."

I watched Anne swallow hard. Down in the kitchens, or in my village, these sisters would have next flown at each other, shrieking and slapping. Without a word, Anne got up. Marching across the room, she grabbed me by the wrist, and cried, "Attend me!" Leaving Isabel, Elaine, Grace and Margaret behind, we marched away. As a servant snatched the door open, I could feel eyes following us.

We ended in the chapel, kneeling side by side. Among the candles and lingering incense of the place, with the cold, carved faces of saints inspecting us, My Lady prayed earnestly, whispering Latin, telling her beads.

For what did she pray? That Richard should, somehow, continue to love her? That her father and King Edward would be reconciled? Or, simply, for the strength to endure whatever fate awaited?

My thoughts were a jumble. Besides, to me the chapel was like death itself, the darkness, the silence, the unending chill, those ghostly statues. For me, religion happened in other places. I felt a thrill of holiness by Alkelda's green and mysterious well, or when I saw a hunting peregrine fall like a bolt from the sky. My heart stirred at golden sunrises and blood red sunsets, or at the sight of the great-bellied, rising moon. I loved and believed in Our Lady, the great preserver of my life. I prayed to her silently, several times a day, in the Latin my mistress had taught. At Mass, I knew when to cross and bless myself, but escaped the oppression of long, mostly unintelligible devotions with a series of catnaps. I had even, over the years, learned to doze while kneeling.

Here, beside my mistress, I wondered how the Duke of Gloucester could break with the brother to whom he had sworn allegiance, even for the sake of the great Earl of Warwick, even for the sake of his love? After all, *Loyaulte me lie*—Loyalty Binds Me—was Richard's chosen motto.

Choices! At each fork in the road, hearts are broken, and eternal partings made. I did not know what anyone, divine or human, could do to soothe my mistress. The fight between her Lord Father and the King had already brought us unhappiness. How much more was to come—to the principals, to the hundreds of soldiers and the innocent commons who fell in their way—I'm glad I could not know. Foresight is no blessing!

The earl refused to attend the King's Councils. He said he would never attend as long as his enemies, the Woodvilles, were present. King Edward shrugged. Then he destroyed the last of the goodwill Warwick had created with King Louis of France by giving his own sister, Princess Margaret, in marriage to Charles, Duke of Burgundy, a ruler who was a perennial thorn in the French side.

It was, certainly, a better marriage for the wool trade. This opinion I heard on a visit home, from the men of my village. King Edward remained popular enough with common folk. Burgundy was our natural market, our major trading partner. Better to make an alliance with there—to send them a princess—than to those "treacherous catamites," the French. So, even here, in his own country, my Master the Earl found himself second-guessed.

To visit Aysgarth was queer. I had been back but one other time, and I'd become a stranger. Everyone regarded me with the same wary indifference they would any other traveler. I was the girl who had gone away to the castle, who returned in fine new clothes with clean, smooth, hands. I was unmarried, too, at the great age of seventeen. I might as well have arrived sporting two heads.

Since my last visit, Master Whitby had grown old. Falling sickness had begun in him. Barely able to walk and not always coherent, he sat in the sun in the square with other old men, all of them trailing beards and maundering on about some imaginary "good old days". Mother ministered to his needs, but, more often, my unlucky sister Lily was the one left caring for the old brute.

Mother was free now. No longer a prisoner of our house, she trudged back and forth with her wares between dale villages, frequently disappearing for days. She did cures here and there, for which she was blessed and thanked, paid whatever folks could give. She hunted the rarest wild herbs, and, at certain seasons, mushrooms, which she found in the southern groves. These had good value at the kitchen doors of the gentry. She also made cheese and sewed for a womanless shepherd who had moved nearby, a local character and ex-soldier named Alban.

Whitby's remaining local son, Clifford, and his hatchet-faced wife, Aldgyth, ran the house and did the farming. They were busily raising another blonde brood. They treated my mother with respect, for she had never come between them and the old man. Besides, Mother was no burden to them.

They did not want my sister Lily to marry, for she had such a way with her cantankerous father. The old man, of course, was of like mind.

"I won't be among you long," Whitby declared with a self-pitying sigh, "but I must have my Lily to cheer me while yet I live."

Mother and I sat in the sun by a pool, nodding greetings to the local women dipping their buckets. We absently tossed crumbs to the ducks who swam by. When I said that "Poor Lily will never get free," Mother had simply patted my hand and smiled.

Her smile was not what it had been, for her front teeth were missing—the result of Whitby's violence, the last before his abrupt decline into senility. Explaining this, Mother had nudged me companionably and whispered, "When the signs are right, I have a nice draught for him."

I knew what she meant, for Mother Ash was even now teaching me something of this most dangerous and forbidden of all physician's arts. Still, it was something of a shock to hear it so coolly said.

"By the Black Madonna! Be careful!"

Mother winked, long bronze lashes flashing over one hazel eye. "Aldgyth would kiss my ass if I'd do it. But where on this green earth did you learn such an oath?"

"It is the oath of my teacher, Mother Ash. She has such a Madonna, from her grandfather who made a pilgrimage to Montserrat in Spain. The Lady is all black, carved of ebony. She is strong to defend."

"Indeed! I think our plain English Lady has done well enough by us. Has she not, White Rose?" Mother's wrinkled, freckled hand touched my cheek. Though it was rough and hard, her caresses and smiles were so precious.

While I was visiting Aysgarth, Anne and her family were away on the continent. The earl, pretending to mend fences with the king, had taken them to witness the royal progress of Princess Margaret, now on her way to marry the Duke of Burgundy. Anne had not wanted to leave me behind, but her mother had insisted.

The Countess had taken to continually disparaging my appearance. What would the Burgundians say if no fairer girl than this "freckled heifer" could be found in all of England to tend her daughter? I was dispatched to Aysgarth with one final kick, this from Agnes, who remarked that I should take "close note" of the village where I certainly would end my days.

Anne and I cried together, saddened at parting. She kissed me, hugged me, and promised that hereafter I should always be close. The family were to travel to Burgundy and then to our English port of Calais before returning home. Margaret Neville and Grace Poelyn would be the ones to tend her. For their journey, Mother Ash and I distilled drops, gathered dried mixtures and tonics by the score to be packed into a traveling chest for our noble family's benefit.

"Naught but piss and pestilence across the water." Mother Ash muttered as we worked. "The French are the dirtiest people in the world. And, although it pleases our master not, King Edward has done the right thing, trading his princess sister to the Duke of Burgundy. In that land, she may continue to enjoy a decent measure of good health."

There were strange doings that summer. A gentleman calling himself "Robin of Redesdale" was marching about the countryside with three hundred archers, all well clad and carrying long knives, calling men to arms against the "injustices" of King Edward, complaining of "misrule." Unlike most local rebellions, this one was said to be well-disciplined. It was well funded, too, for there was no plundering of villages which lay in Robin's path, and his soldiers paid for what they took.

Men who had plied the trade of war in the old days were

back in brigantine again, sharpening their weapons and marching in bands. Some went with the army of this "Robin," others were for the banner of John Neville, the earl's younger brother, who lay in York, loyal to the King.

When Robin of Redesdale reached the gates of York, he had 15,000 men at his back. Still, John Neville was ready for him, and he sallied out, captured the leaders and 'headed the lot. The common soldiers, as was the rule in King Edward's time, were pardoned and told to go home.

Many, however, did not. Only a few months later there was another "Robin" and another army, said to be twice as big as the first, this one on its way to present grievances to the King in London. I was happy to be safe at Middleham again, for armed men were everywhere, and small villages like Aysgarth stood in danger.

True Thomas said, "Looks to me like the bad old days have come 'round again."

Chapter VIII

Word came that Anne was at Warwick Castle to the south, ailing, and I was to be brought to her at once. The Countess had remained in France with Isabel, who had been married in Calais to King Edward's brother George, Duke of Clarence. As the King himself had forbidden this marriage—well, the King was not pleased—but by this time, he had other, more immediate troubles. All over the countryside, men were taking up arms. It seemed the Earl of Warwick and his friends were on the move.

When I arrived at Warwick Castle, I found my dear Anne quite ill. It was not her lungs, but guts and bowels, puking and purging from something she'd caught over there. It took a long time to get her well, for she'd lost a deal of flesh. As a result, I spent that summer in lush Warwickshire, at her father's most beautiful and luxurious castle, caring for her.

We cried with joy at our reunion. Anne, as she recovered, had a thousand stories to tell, of all the places and people she'd seen and of her sister's wedding to the Duke of Clarence. We were well tended, but left pretty much to ourselves by the other servants, which was all right with us. Busybodies like Agnes were far away, attending Lady Isabel and her mother.

I had seen both King Edward and The Duke of Clarence on several occasions, and their size, strength and good looks had dazzled. Such was the golden spell cast by these two stalwart sons of York.

"George can be funny and charming—when he is not crawling on the reeds, babbling drunk—which, unfortunately, is the latter part of every day."

"Your father married Lady Isabel to a drunkard?" I was shocked. The earl did not share this vice. To his wards and young knights in training he constantly extolled the virtues of hunting and hard training as far better ways to exercise youthful high spirits.

"You know it doesn't matter what George does while he is the king's heir. My father will unseat King Edward and put George in his place. That is what all these rebellions are, my father's friends a-stirring. Isabel shall be queen and bear royal children and The Earl My Father shall pull the drunkard's strings."

She now spoke this treason as if all was a matter of course. Even then, to my young and simple mind, none of it seemed likely. I wondered where Dickon was in all this. I couldn't believe Anne had so quickly forgotten him. I certainly hadn't.

"How is Isabel?" I asked to avoid a doubtful subject. "Does marriage please her?"

"She seems happy," Anne said. She shook her head, puzzled. Clearly, she did not see how Isabel could be happy, but she was, so there must be a reason. Anne began to suggest some, hoping to convince herself along with me.

"In spite of how scandalously he drinks, George is handsome and he makes a big fuss over her. He is always kissing and hugging, and telling her she is the most beautiful woman in the world. He gives her jewels—oh, heavens, Rosalba! You should have seen the ruby ring! It was big as an egg!"

She blushed, put a hand over her mouth to hide a smile and then leaned forward, blue eyes sparkling, long braids shining. She shared, in whispers, things Isabel had confided about what went on inside the ducal bed curtains.

"But—a drunken man—cannot—" I blushed at what I knew.

Anne's shoulders shook with laughter. "When he can't—he does it—with—his tongue!"

We both screamed and fell over in bed, shrieking with disgust, giggling wildly and kicking our legs. The image of George Plantagenet's blonde head bobbing between Isabel's white thighs was supremely undignified. Far more so for the duke than for his wife, who was, after all, the one pleasured.

When I finally stopped laughing, I said, "That won't get her a baby."

"No." Anne turned onto her belly, waving pale, bare legs

in the air. "She says he tries to make a baby in the morning, when he's sober, if his head doesn't ache too much."

Illness had turned my mistress into the courtly ideal of beauty. She was starvation thin, fair skin tautly stretched over breast bone and ribs, with a waist you could span with your hands.

No peasant in his right mind would have bartered for such a bride. In my village, they would have said Anne Neville needed a great deal of "feeding up." They would have joked about bruising themselves on her prominent hip bones or say disdainfully that they "don't jump boys."

On the other hand, each and every nobleman who saw Anne that summer wanted to ravish her. Her pallor, her forehead, the hair line plucked high in French fashion, her chest with a pair of lemon halves, her sharp angles, were the pinnacle of fashionable desirability.

There is no accounting for taste.

Warwickshire was green and lush, warmer and brighter than Middleham. This splendid castle was a fine place for Anne to recover and a safe haven for us during that disturbed summer. Things were falling apart all over England. Old blood feuds were rekindled and neighboring lords began to attack each other, to ravage one another's property. The king himself was under siege and there was no one now to put a stop to the ever-growing turmoil.

Months passed. Uprisings took place in those ancient seats of disaffection, Devon, Wales, and Kent. Some rioters favored the restoration of Henry VI, the deposed Lancastrian king who was imprisoned in the Tower, some were simply looking to settle ancient feuds, which burst through the civic flesh like cysts draining.

At one point, the earl actually captured King Edward and sent him north under guard to Warwick Castle. Here, Anne and I, from a distance, again saw him, tall and fair, the best looking man—I swear by the Holy Well—I'd ever in all my life clapped eyes upon. From Warwick, he was sent north to safekeeping in the heart of the earl's domain, Middleham.

Anne could not ask, but I could, so I found out what had befallen the Duke of Gloucester. It seemed he had been with his brother, traveling to Our Lady of Walsingham's shrine with only a few hundred archers when her father had captured the royal entourage.

Warwick had freed Richard and a bosom companion of the king's, one Lord William Hastings. Richard and Hastings had ridden off, no one knew exactly where. Anne and I wept and prayed for our Dickon. Nothing but a horse and few archers between him and who knew what mischance!

The earl, now in control, began to clean house. To start, he ordered the beheading of his court enemies. The hated, upstart Woodville Queen's father and one of her many brothers were among the first to be topped.

The devils my master had set loose could not be kept leashed. As always happened when things fell apart in England, the Scots came over the border to burn and plunder. I prayed for my Aysgarth home place. I prayed for my mother and sister, for only too well I remembered True Thomas' bloody stories.

This forced the Earl of Warwick to allow King Edward a certain freedom in order to raise troops to deal with the foreign invader. The King first went to seven-towered Pontefract Castle, ancient seat of the House of York, and who should next appear at the gate of Pontefract, but Richard of Gloucester, Lord Hastings and other loyal lords of the Court, with a heavily armed force of their own? The Scots were successfully beaten back, and several disaffected Northern lords, taken in battle, were beheaded.

King Edward had simply walked out of the earl's cage. Suddenly, the shoe was on the other foot, and Warwick and his allies were on the run. Anne and I found ourselves collected— along with baggage and treasure—and sent to take ship for Calais. I was terrified. I'd never even seen ocean before, much less traveled upon it.

It seemed the earl was a power at sea as well as upon land. He'd found gold here in earlier times, preying upon the ships of other nations in the channel. With his fleet, we embarked for Calais, where a welcome was supposed to be waiting. However, Lord Wenlock, captain of the place, whose allegiance the earl thought he had in his pocket, changed sides and said he was, once again, King Edward's "loyal servant." Instead of welcome, Wenlock gave our ships cannon fire, and we had to lie offshore in those heaving channel waters.

We were all desperately sick, of course, standing in rows clutching the rails, showering puke over the side. Another ill star sent Lady Isabel, now great with the Duke of Clarence's first child, into labor. As there were only supplies laid in for two days, not enough for a long time at sea, wine ran out. At first, Wenlock would not even send a bottle to ease poor Isabel's suffering. We had loaded in such disarray our apothecary chest had been placed in another vessel. Though row boat messages were sent between the earl's ships, no one could locate it.

I had never felt so helpless in my life! The countess, Anne and I, and a new woman servant, a pretty dark woman called Ankarette, did what we could, ministering to Isabel in that cramped low cabin. Opium we could not give for fear of slowing the labor down and killing both mother and child. We had simples: nettle, wise hemp and raspberry; we had the bitter beer of the sailors. None came near the pain Isabel suffered, trying to force a child through her too narrow passage.

Ankarette was an experienced midwife, and I was glad the terrible responsibility was hers. She and the countess conferred, gave what aid and comfort they could and instructed the rest of us. We took turns with the duchess, holding her and listening to her scream, crammed into that narrow, dark cabin, trying not to upset the lamps and set ourselves afire, trying to see what we were doing, to give that Isabel comfort and prevent her bleeding to death. Ankarette and I let mutual suspicion slip and were soon sharing what we knew as well as charms to stop blood, charms to free the child. We tried everything, but to no avail.

Isabel labored for nearly two days and was close to dying when the baby came. Toward the end of this dreadful labor, her mother had called in the priest. The child paid the price, a full term son born still. We wept again for the duchess, but there was not a blessed thing more we could do.

And, ah! The Duke of Clarence, her adoring husband! He of sweet lust, of compliments and rubies! Upon entering the cabin drenched with blood and birth, faced by that poor half-dead girl, now passing in and out of consciousness, Clarence said sternly, "You have sorely failed me, My Lady. I hope you do not prove as poor a breeder as your mother."

He turned on his heel, slamming the door behind him. I heard the Countess of Warwick roundly curse him to eternal flames, while Ankarette wept and bathed Isabel's forehead with cold, new fallen rain water.

Anne and I, and a few sailors watched from the tossing deck while that same priest who had given Isabel unction blessed the dead, blue-faced child and then dropped his corpse over the side. Though weighted with a ballast stone it barely made a splash, and was swallowed at once by the angry waves.

Finally, we came ashore at Honfleur, arriving as exiles, not moving an inch out of doors except in the company of soldiers. Around us a port town careened; a strange language hummed and buzzed in our ears. I hated the dirty closeness and I feared the French.

I think Anne was not as frightened as I, partly because she knew the language. Still, I was the one who had to go to the kitchen of the inn we occupied, the one who endured smirks hidden behind grubby French hands and laughter at dirty jokes even the deaf could understand.

From Honfleur, the earl and his soldiers raided the channel, taking prizes from every country, a new and terrible fleet of pirates. After a few months of that, Louis, King of France—truly called "The Spider King," spun a new web, woven on purpose to get peace for his kingdom, by tearing our dear England apart.

"Edward of Lancaster!" Anne choked.

I'd had moments of jealousy when we'd been small, but not for an instant since her father's intrigues had begun. Fortunately, I was on my knees when the Earl of Warwick made his design known to us, or I would have fallen down in shock. Never, ever, could I have imagined such a plan. To put King Henry back on the throne, that old prisoner in the Tower! To bring back his Queen, Marguerite, the "bloody-minded French whore," of my childhood, the "She-Wolf" whose army had blazed a trail of murder and rape across England! And, worst of all, to wed my dear mistress to this evil woman's son!

Noble ladies had a soft life, yes, but there was a piper to pay. And, here he stood, pitiless hand outstretched! As Anne twisted a sapphire ring helplessly, lip quivering, I thought I'd never felt so completely sorry for her. The Earl of Warwick arched a blonde brow at her dismay. Her mother remained expressionless.

We do as we are done by, I thought. Her mother had been given no choice, either. The Countess, once Anne Beauchamp, had long ago been delivered to the Earl of Warwick, whose primary interest had been, of course, her vast inheritance.

The earl cleared his throat. A look of daggers went toward his wife, as much as to say, "Woman, in how many ways you have failed me!"

The Countess took her cue.

"This is not the proper response, Anne, when your father proposes to make you Queen of England."

"What—what—of our Cousin of York, King Edward?"

"Edward of York is a thrice-damned fool! I shall show him what it means to be a king—to be—by Christ!—a leader of men!"

"My dear Lord Father, I—I thought Queen Marguerite was our enemy and that George of Clarence and our dear sister Isabel—"

"My plans have changed." Her father cut her off. The plain fact was, he'd been seduced by King Louis, who had whispered this idea in his ear. Louis had thought of a way to get all these armed English out of France and back home destroying each other as soon as possible.

"I—I—don't want to be Queen." Anne stood proudly as she'd been taught, head up. She was a shining angel at fourteen, the fairest fair of every illumination, all blonde hair and pink flesh, the blood royal shining.

"Anne!" The Countess said, all of her considerable force of will aimed at that bright, lovely daughter. "Your duty!"

Anne drew a deep breath, but, instead of collapsing in tears, she threw back her lovely shoulders. Then, slowly, gracefully, eyes open, tears tracing her rosy cheeks, she subsided in a profound, straight-backed curtsy. The sight of her regal submission came near to breaking my heart.

"I am your humble, grateful child, dear Lord Father." Her voice came cold as January. "Your wish is my command."

"Good girl." He fetched up a smile—a poor reward.

All at once, I despised him, saw my golden benefactor as mean and false, a foolish, petty tyrant. To know this so suddenly was terrifying, as if once solid ground had shaken beneath my feet.

"I only ask one boon, good My Lord Father." Anne spoke again.

"Eh?" The earl's blonde brows drew together in a frown.

"Please, Father, I must have Rosalba always with me. I will do all I am asked, by you and mother and by Queen—Marguerite—but—but—she is the one who knows best how to keep me in health."

Chapter IX

Queen Marguerite, whom I had been raised to fear as the Devil, proved a refined beauty. What had once been a confection of gold and sugar, time had spoiled. The fine lines on her lovely, sculpted face all drew down. Her eyes were polished agate, gray and hard. Wearing a purple gown and a crown over a gold-embroidered caul, Marguerite was the most terrifyingly regal female I'd ever beheld. At Amboise, in their cathedral, filled with candles, incense and blazing windows thronged with bright saints and angels, the Earl of Warwick begged the queen's pardon upon his knees.

Pardon him for calling her beloved son a bastard. Pardon him for stealing the throne from her dear husband, King Henry. Pardon him for making war upon her and driving her and her royal child from England.

The queen kept the earl on his knees for twenty minutes, looking for the world as if she had changed her mind and was ready to go back on the reconciliation she'd promised King Louis. Her sixteen-year-old son, Prince Edward, was beside her, French elegance in scarlet. His chestnut head was topped by a turban with a trailing liripipe. His tunic had a pinched waist and was short and fur-trimmed, showing handsome scarlet legs to advantage. The heir of House Lancaster stood during the interview, as befitted a prince, only a step lower than the King of France. While the earl begged forgiveness of his mother, he made a show of arranging the drooping petals of his scarlet sleeves.

Anne wore a blue dress. Her steeple head piece carried a floating butterfly veil. Her thin, white shoulders were bare. A pearl choker embraced her long neck. She kept her lovely hands folded, her eyes downcast, looking like the Virgin waiting for an angelic visitation.

Prince Edward showed his mettle by munching hazel nuts. As time passed and sweat began to drop from the brow of the kneeling earl, the prince began a great show of studying Anne. He nudged the gentleman next to him, who responded with a wink.

When Queen Margeurite finally allowed Warwick to kiss her hand, some conversation passed between them and King Louis. As it was French, I could not follow. The great French King, Louis XI, was an ugly, squat man with the calculating narrow eyes of a rat. His clothes were none too clean—that I could see, even at a distance—and around his scrawny neck hung a heap of chains and holy medals.

Finally, Warwick and Prince Edward were introduced. The prince barely managed a nod. He went at once, talking boisterously in his own tongue, straight to Anne. First, he walked around her, like a buyer at a horse fair. Instead of prodding her with his hands, he used words to test her mettle.

Anne responded in French. She did not deign to turn as he circled her, but kept straight and steady. When Prince Edward chucked her under the chin and said something that must have been impudent, she slapped his hand away and snapped something in return which drew surprised titters from the courtiers.

"Very good." Prince Edward spoke for the first time in a heavily accented English. "I shall marry her."

The queen laughed, followed by the French King. They were immediately echoed by the assembly, a singularly hollow sound in that cold, echoing space. Marguerite and her son joined hands and stood there, facing Warwick and his daughter, four pieces on a royal board.

The earl smiled now, but he looked uneasy. Anne held that formal pose, head up, eyes down, one foot forward, studying the hands which she had clasped just below her meager bosom.

.⚜

"When I return and bring our dear father, the true king, from the Tower, there will be a reckoning. I shall head those lords of York, hang their gentlemen and put their chief towns to the sword." The lords who surrounded the Prince of Lancaster smiled indulgently, as if listening to a poem. Around us torches flared in that dark cavern of a room. Over his head, a fabulous rose window shone blue and scarlet.

"Edward the Usurper shall die, as will all his kin and every man who resists us. The House of York shall drown in its own blood." Here stood a youth, who by his own prideful account, had ordered, and, cheerfully witnessed, his first beheadings at the age of eight.

"She's pretty enough, for a thrice-dyed traitor's child." Today, apparently for our benefit, Edward spoke English. With utter presumption, he tilted Anne's chin and gazed into her eyes.

I saw her flush with rage, but she was determined to be her mother's well-schooled daughter. She did not object; she made no reply.

He turned her face from side to side, examining her. I had a feeling that if he'd dared, he would have looked at her teeth.

"Nice eyes." He was playing to his entourage. "But what I really want to see is your pretty red muff."

Anne pushed his hand away and regally stepped back. Her eyes blazed, the veil swirled about her shoulders.

"What I want to see is whether you know as much about war as you pretend to know about women."

I stepped between them, clasping Anne and carrying her away from him. I was ready to take the blow—*or knife in the ribs*—for now it was the Prince's turn to redden. He did so, mightily.

"A snapping bitch from an English kennel!" Edward shouted. "You had better prove a better breeder than your sister!" He lunged at us.

We both sank to floor and lifted our hands to ward off the momentarily expected blows. I thought we were lost, having provoked that young lunatic's rage, but, fortunately, the queen picked that moment to enter the room. Behind her came a graying, lean Welsh lord, Jasper Tudor.

"Ah, there you are, dear son," said the queen. She did not speak loudly, but everyone in the room jerked to attention.

As the prince turned, I wondered if he would tattle about Anne's slight, but he did not. At least he was enough of a man for that.

"Only playing, Mother." Edward bowed to his formidable dam while attempting to laugh the whole thing off. "I am teaching my bride-to-be to understand me."

The queen arched a brow. "She shall learn soon enough, of that I am certain, Your Highness."

She gazed down at us, huddled upon the floor. I'd never seen such ferocious malice in the eyes of any woman. Later, of course, I would meet eyes of an equal ferocity, those of yet another pitiless she-wolf—Margaret Beaufort—but none before or after were ever so beautiful—or so terrible—as the eyes of Marguerite de Anjou.

"My Lord of Oxford has news which concerns Your Highness." Her cruel expression only softened when her eyes fixed upon Edward, that pretty monster she'd doubtless made with some good-looking blue blood about her monkish husband's court.

"Excuse me, Lady," Edward promptly said, turning to offer Anne a mocking bow, "but we shall certainly continue this conversation at some future time." The threat was unmistakable.

While they withdrew, I watched, from my place on the slates, the nicely made scarlet legs of the prince as he marched up the stairs. With pikes of immodest length upon his shoes, each attached to its respective knee with a fine gold chain, he was a picture-perfect French gallant. The room speedily cleared without so much as a single backward glance toward us.

"Holy Mother of God!" I could not believe what a pit of vipers the earl had sent his family into. First, Isabel, given to duplicitous, drunken George, and now, Anne, soon to wed to this vicious boy....

All that play-acting at love! Carrying those little girls upon his shoulders, giving them ponies, hawks, toys and servants! To what did these indulgences and professions of love come? To the cruelty of putting his cherished innocents to bed with men in whose hands any Christian man would tremble to abandon the wiliest whore!

I was afraid my lady would be in tears, but daily she showed me how strong her heart was. A little water lapped within the blue, but it did not spill. Rage had carried her into new, brave terrain.

"I pray my Cousin of York kills him," she said, and not softly, either. I glanced around, but the room had emptied, servants and gentlemen alike following power.

"We may hope, Milady." I replied, getting to my feet and helping her, encumbered with the hennin and all the rest of her voluminous court clothes, up as well.

We both overlooked what logically followed. If she were rid of Edward of Lancaster, she might also be rid of her father, not to mention her great inheritance.

One misfortune at a time!

Still, I could see no other way back to England and Middleham, the place we both longed to be. Imagine being exiled forever in some foreign place, like this, where every hand was, both by nature and by nurture, against us!

Anne prayed. She wept buckets of tears in the days before her wedding. I honestly thought her poor heart would break, as she kissed Dickon's ring over and over. I was not much help, either. I wept right along with her, for England, for our happy times at Middleham, now lost and gone forever.

The night before the ceremony, the Countess, who came to lock us in at night—such was the danger, even for noblewomen, in France—gave her daughter a ferocious lecture on duty and *sangfroid*.

"Enough is enough!" Grabbing Anne by the elbow, the Countess yanked her to her feet, away from the statue of the Virgin where she knelt. "You should be ashamed! Ashamed of this sniveling! You, daughter of Despensers, Beauchamps, Nevilles, Plantagenets, the noblest of the realm! You, begot of bluest blood, must not behave in this ridiculous fashion. Everyone is laughing, saying the Nevilles can no more control their children than they can control England!"

A ringing slap followed, and Anne collapsed, clutching her jaw. Naturally, this treatment did not stop her tears.

"And you!" The Countess turned to me. "Useless spotted cow I picked from a dung heap! Are you helping my daughter see her duty? Are you calming her, soothing her with medicine? No! No! By Our Lady, no! You are encouraging, blubbering right alongside her."

I crouched to avoid the blow, and got, instead, a hearty kick in the side that left me gasping. Swirling in a fury, the Countess picked up a cane and came back with it.

Anne threw herself upon her mother crying, "No! No! Please! Mama! Rosalba is good! She only loves me! Nothing is her fault."

In the meantime, the cane rose and fell upon my back. On all fours, I scuttled as fast as I could under the bed. Fortunately, it was high and set close against the wall. Once I was well under, the Countess, red and puffing with rage, could no longer reach me.

❧

The wedding was without joy. It was, after all, only a move in the greater game, a gambit. Anne was the piece to be sacrificed.

She got through the ceremony in the cathedral without tears. She sat through supper, chin high, eyes downcast, like a statue. Still, everyone who looked into those lovely eyes could see how desperately she had been crying.

The prince said very little to her, or anyone else, even his mother. For once, he seemed preoccupied. When he kissed Anne in the service, he let her know he was as cold in the matter as she. He barely spoke to her at table, and all they exchanged was the expected ceremonial language.

We servants watched on our knees, and were fed, if at all, as was French custom, from the plates of our masters, like dogs. Anne fed me, but ate little. It was exhausting, especially when all I could think of my dear mistress at that arrogant little monster's mercy.

At last came the withdrawing, taking Anne to the bridal bed. Not accustomed to kneeling for such a stretch of hours as the French servants were, at first I could hardly stand.

Anne wobbled as if about to faint. Surrounded by the French attendants Marguerite had sent, by Grace and Margaret, she was undressed, and her glorious hair let down. Finally, she was put into the high bed naked and quaking, a lamb to the slaughter. I wanted to weep, seeing her shaking so. I wanted to comfort, dreading for her, but I dared not come too close, for fear her mother would have me whipped away.

The bedroom door opened. Queen Marguerite and the Prince, accompanied by a group of courtiers and English exiles, paraded in. Now, with the same ceremony, Prince Edward was also undressed, hidden behind robes of red and black emblazoned with ostrich feathers, supported by gentlemen. Randy jokes were passed in French, while the tone made the subject obvious.

When Edward stepped out, he revealed a cleanly made young body, well-muscled for his age. He climbed in beside Anne. While she huddled deeper beneath the covers, visibly shaking, he sat, waving and smiling at all the ladies blowing kisses. The bed curtains were pulled. I covered my mouth, fighting not to cry out loud.

My Anne! Would he hurt her, humiliate her?

I was so terrified I could hardly breathe. No one moved. I began to imagine some hitherto unsuspected, barbaric French custom.

Surely, we weren't to remain?

Then Queen Marguerite gestured, and the curtains were opened. Edward, now deep under the covers with Anne, quickly turned over. He appeared startled. The queen gestured and barked an order. Her son flushed scarlet, all the way up his back, but he obeyed, sliding quickly out of the bed. The emblazoned robes again received him. Those who had been on the side to see went about the next day laughing and telling everyone that the Prince of Lancaster had displayed "ample and ardent nature."

The Countess and the Earl of Warwick were puzzled,

speechless, but the queen did not long keep us in suspense.

"Fulfill your promises, My Lord of Warwick. Every one. Rescue my dear lord from the Tower! Carry my son and me safe into London and place my husband, King Henry VI, of the rightful and royal House of Lancaster, upon his throne in Westminster. Then—and only then—shall there be consummation."

There was a whispering pandemonium, people hissing to each other in English and French. Almost everyone appeared surprised. The earl and the countess, stone-faced, followed the prince, now wrapped only in those glorious robes, out of the room.

Pushing my way to the bed, I fairly leapt in. A moment later, I clasped my trembling, naked friend. She grabbed me, laid her head against my shoulder, clenched her knees together and began a kind of hiccupping noise. Ladies of the French court kept calling something. They were amused, but, also, for the first time, they sounded sympathetic.

The door closed and suddenly we were alone again, forgotten. Then, those hiccups, which I feared would lead to coughing or crying, surprised me by turning into giggles.

"Oh, Blessed Mary! Dear Rosie!" Anne gasped for breath. "Do you know what the ladies say?"

"No," I said, thumping her back and giving my nurse's lecture. "Dear Milady, please don't start a cough."

"They—they—were saying: *Poor little bride! Do not be sad! The queen will relent, for her dear son the handsome prince truly desires you!*"

Just when I began to imagine she had got through this awful trial without much harm, the laughter turned to tears.

"Oh, Rose! He put his hand—his fingers—straight down there. And—and—I had to let him!"

Queen Marguerite had given Anne reprieve from the final rite of marriage, but there was a strange and unforeseen effect. Prince Edward suddenly was very much in evidence. Every day there he was, either in person, attempting to make conversation, or boyishly peeping at us from behind the arras.

He began to pay Anne compliments, even deigning to use English. He tried his hand at chess with her. I am proud to report that the very first time he did, he was soundly beaten. After throwing the piece that had failed him across the room, he gave a shout of laughter, seized and kissed her hand, and told her she was "*tres intelligent!*" This was followed by a boyish, rueful grin.

The Countess of Warwick and her ladies watched, heartened by the groom's change of heart. My Lady Countess appeared exhausted; her fair long face was suddenly as lined as Queen Marguerite's.

What a thing to be a woman, and have to silently watch your husband hazard everything—including your life and the lives of your children—upon a single cast! The earl was mad, and we, all of us women, knew it. Like his soldiers, however, it was our bounden duty to obey, to fall upon our swords if necessary.

We were kept well enough. We even had an English cook who prepared food after our own custom. By this, the Countess hoped to keep Anne well, and not repeat what her daughter had suffered on that last visit to France. This meant meat or fish was boiled or roasted, and presented with plain mustard or horseradish for seasoning. The French sneered at our plain fare. Theirs was God knows what smothered in odd-tasting gravies. Just the smell of some of these dishes was sufficient to send me rushing for a breath of fresh air.

The prince now handed Anne to table at every meal, always behaving with a kind of charm I could hardly believe from this spoiled mother's darling. Anne actually began to relax around him, to talk easily and not wait to be drawn out. I didn't know which I feared more, the old Prince Edward or the new one.

"And, pray, for what lucky man is that pretty song?"

Emerging from behind the arras, he caught Anne playing and singing one of our sweet English love songs. Edward, in that red tunic with the scalloped, hanging sleeves! As beautiful as it was, it had become clear that he did not have many changes of clothing. A long exile makes for a lean purse.

Anne had been singing:

Ah, Westron Wind
When wilt thou blow
That the small rain
Down can rain?
Ah, that my love were
In my arms,
And I in my bed again.

It was one of Dickon's favorites. I even imagined I knew the room of which she sang, the tower room at Middleham, the one with the sweetest view over the dales, where four little girls and Nursey Cole had once–upon–a–time slept so safe.

Anne focused upon him as he spoke, and I knew she, too, had been remembering. Marriage to a prince of Lancaster, exile in a land where only French was spoken, had never been any part of her dream.

She looked down, into the full belly of the golden lute, and moved her long, sapphire-covered fingers absently over the strings.

"It is just an old song, Your Grace."

"Come, come," Edward said, sitting beside her, "you have sung it many times."

There was more, but he fell into French. Anne sat still, as if considering. She readjusted herself upon the bench, as if she were making room for the neck of the lute, while in fact she was acquiring more distance from him.

"Would you like to hear another?" She flashed a brave smile. In the backdrop of that chilly, ancient room, she wore high French fashion, a parti-colored *houppelande* over-skirt layered atop a gown of white satin. On her head was a padded linen turban ornamented with pearls and thick white satin braid. Not a bit of her glorious hair was in evidence.

"I would, but, I pray you, will you not tell me who it is you sing for?"

"It is only a song, My Lord."

Abruptly, Edward turned his charm upon me. "My wife had a sweetheart in England, did she not, Rosalba?" I think it was the first time he'd ever addressed me by name.

"Come, come, I command you. You must tell me the truth. She has left a lover behind, has she not?"

"Lady Anne is an innocent maiden, Your Grace," I replied. "I pray you will remember My Lord, that England is not France."

"Ah! A Rose with thorns!" Edward grinned, flashing his white teeth. He shook a finger at me in playful admonishment. "They say the best servants always have sharp tongues."

"Let me play you another song, My Lord." Anne's voice came between us.

"The Duke of Clarence says it is his little brother, Richard, whom you love. The one you were to marry before your father—returned—to his proper allegiance." Edward's pleasant mood seemed to be bleeding away.

"We were never betrothed, my Lord, so I could not have loved him."

"The Duke of Clarence says that his brother is neither tall, nor handsome, nor even very clever. He says Richard is a drab fellow with a crooked back who ought to have been pledged to the church. Could a lovely lady pine for a cripple?" Suddenly, we were back to playing cat and mouse.

"I miss England," Anne said, flushing. Cornered by the young brute, she did well, tears and temper rising in her eyes, even as she ignored his provocation. "I miss my father's beautiful castles—Warwick, Nottingham, Sheriff Hutton, and Middleham. You are not very clever, my Lord, if you cannot understand that I am homesick."

Perfect!

The young dog backed down. "Soon, I hope," he said, relenting, "with the help of your father, and the friends of my own dear father King Henry, we shall all of us make return to

Angleterre. When my mother and I own London again—imagine, Lady Anne! The whole land and every castle in it shall be yours."

Anne managed a silent nod. She returned her gaze to the lute and simply began again to play. She chose a song of war, about a northern lord and his battles with the Scots.

The embellishments were many and elaborate, but she kept perfect time and tune, the subject calculated to give a man pleasure. Pushing her fingers over the strings fast and loud was as good a way as any to silence him.

For a moment, Edward seemed annoyed. Then his face grew forlorn. Relenting at last, for she really was a very good player, he gave her the courtesy of attention.

As she rippled through that elaborate fingering, I saw an involuntary smile come to his lips. Suddenly, Edward appeared sweetly handsome beneath his tumbling chestnut curls. It was odd, to keep catching glimpses of what was tender in this young man and then to run against the wicked folly of his schooling.

Of the country France I say simply: I did not like it.

The castles we saw were enormous, terrifying. Their crenellated heads reared above the countryside with a silent menace you could feel in your gut. The farmlands were meticulously cultivated, but the land was clearly overworked. Everything that was not King's or Lord's Forest was scalped and tilled. Good soil had washed away. The stream banks gullied, a sign of too many animals grazing upon too little ground. There were only a few trees, mostly sprouting from the stone dikes between the fields. The common people looked exhausted and were poorly clothed. Both they and their animals appeared thin and hungry.

They didn't resemble English free men, and I soon learned they were not. They were serfs, as laborers had once been in England. In our country, the custom of holding men in such bondage had hung on only in some of the southern counties.

In France, this injustice was the rule.

As I watched the villagers harvesting their grain, I felt a pang. They were commoners the same as me, yet here they were considered no more than domestic animals, kept as we at home kept sheep or cattle. Ever and ever more strongly, I longed for England.

⚜

A few weeks more and I was set to sleeping outside Anne's bedroom door on the slates. One of the archers, in a moment of pity, offered an old wool cloak for me to rest my head upon.

Many things had changed since Warwick had gone back to begin the war in England. The most immediate, as far as I was concerned, was that Queen Marguerite had allowed her son to share Anne's bed.

I did not see Prince Edward emerge on the first morning, though I could hear the laughter and teasing which followed his egress. The room they'd occupied did not open into a hallway, but into other rooms. Always buttressed by attendants and soldiers they were, these French nobles, ever in fear of assassination.

When I was allowed back to Anne that first morning, I could not help but shed tears. There she sat, tousled, pale, and weary, in the act of handing the stained linen of her show, to one of Queen Marguerite's ladies. The sight of this, of course, set me to weeping.

"Stop blubbering, Rosalba!" Anne flew into fury. "By Our Lady! You should rejoice that I am at last come into the Queen's favor."

The French maids who had brought warm water in a salver, began smirking and elbowing each other. A rush of anger, at them, at the disgusting things they doubtless thought about me, quickly choked off my tears.

I retrieved Anne's robe and wrapped her up before helping out of bed, all the time feeling like a kicked dog. Even worse, as I cast the robe about her, I could smell it, the rank

103

smell of coupling. The French maids tried jollity, but this got no better reception than my tears.

"Be silent! All of you!" Anne shouted. I had enough French now to understand that.

She was stern and matter of fact, sitting in the basin upon the floor and using the wash cloth on the inside of her long thighs. In the end, we helped her through her toilet in utter silence. She dismissed me without a glance, instructing me to "go away and help with the packing."

With French ladies to carry train and sewing basket, she departed along the dark hallway for Isabel's chambers. Her sister's recovery from that nightmare childbirth had been unsurprisingly slow.

Isabel now sat up most days, her dark, devoted Ankarette in constant attendance. The Duchess of Clarence, Anne and the Countess of Warwick, too, found surcease with handwork, laboring over tunics and robes, with coats to be worn over armor, embroidering them with heraldry: the White Swan & Ostrich Feathers of Prince Edward, the Black Bull of the Duke of Clarence, the Fleur de Lys of France quartered with the Rampant Leopards of England.

We were soon to travel to the port from which we'd sail back to England. I silently blessed Saint Alkelda of the Well, for packing was work enough for many hands to do. Still, my heart ached. I had suffered all night, praying for my lady, keeping watch as close as I could, lying upon cold stone, grieving for her. A public rebuke had been my reward.

Anne's coldness did not end. Nights, she dismissed me early. Grace, Margaret and the new French ladies put her to bed. They were the ones to wait with her, to see if the Prince would come. If he did not, they shared her bed. This hurt me terribly, but I had not needed Middleham to learn pride. That had come at my mother's knee.

I did my work, slept on the floor like a loyal dog, curled up around a bolster and covered with the old cloak. When I was free, I marched up the long, winding stairs to the battlements where I could look out over the countryside. Facing North, I wished myself a bird to fly away home.

The guards there were archers, most of them English, because we have the best. Thank the Blessed Virgin, while they grinned and teasingly greeted me, they kept to their stations. I badly needed to be left alone.

How could Anne so forget herself? Forget Dickon?

I could not stop thinking of him—of his dark hair—of his body—tough, twisted and thin as a root. I imagined him standing upon the rolling green dale, glove raised, head thrown back, one of his beloved falcons coursing. The joy in his eyes, as if, for one shining moment, he, too, could conquer the sky! Then, the image of Anne's prince would intrude. I'd envision him tupping her, making free with my own beautiful friend, now begun her life's work as a broodmare for the Red Rose.

At first, it filled my heart with rage. There was jealousy on Dickon's behalf—not to mention my own—that Edward should be the one to hold her, to kiss her. There was anguish, mixed with self-pity. At the end, however, I found that all my pity returned to Milady. Anne had made the promise before God and man and now she must lie down, as women always must. Lie down, just like a common woman, just as my mother had, and let a husband she could never love breed her.

I closed the traveling chest, trying not to weep. Anne—and the Countess her mother—were correct. Sorrow helped neither of us.

When the Countess called for me, I folded the last of the veils, those made of that most special flax, fine and pale as a web. I walked slowly to answer her summons through the dark, torch-flaring passage. The Countess of Warwick was herself within an hour of departure. She would return to England through Portsmouth, where she was to meet her husband and his army. I expected another scolding, or, perhaps, a beating. You can imagine how slowly I walked!

"Would the queen had seen fit to allow it earlier," The Countess said, after I'd curtsied low. "We might be returning to England with a royal heir."

I bowed my head, said nothing. I was exhausted and aching from my nights upon the floor. A pretty poor peasant I'd become!

"I suppose I don't need to tell you to take good care of my daughter, do I?"

"Lady Anne is my life." In spite of how things were, it was—and always would be—true.

"Watch her diet, and you can ask Lady Van der Wey about any woman's trouble you don't understand. Now, Rosalba," she continued, precise as always in her instructions, "Although I know Mother Ash has taught you well, you are still a maid, and there are things about being a wife which only experience can teach. Never be too proud to ask for help if there is a problem you do not understand, for it is your mistresses' health at stake. As the Duchess of Clarence and Ankarette will be traveling with me, you shall be all of home there is for my dear daughter. You alone bear a very great trust."

"Yes, Milady. I understand. Everything shall be exactly as you say." I bowed my head and waited.

"Buttermilk is good for the whites." I could tell her mind was this morning full of a thousand cares, but she strained, as always, to command every detail.

"Yes, Milady. Mistress Ash has taught me that brides often suffer this. Also milfoil, as a douche."

"Good. Good. Yes, the Prince is now most eager to breed her. He is a pretty young man. My daughter should have little to complain of on that account. I wonder what changed the queen's mind?" She'd again changed course. "I heard the prince has just spent another night with my daughter. Did Lady Anne receive him properly? Did she seem of good cheer this morning?"

"Yes. Yes, Milady Countess." At this precise moment, I was the wrong person to ask for such a report.

"Good. Good! That will do, then, Rosalba. I charge you, in my absence, to always remember your duty to your mistress and to the Nevilles."

"Until death, Milady." I curtsied low again and humbly

kissed the proffered hand.

She dismissed me, and I retraced my steps along the gloomy hall, wondering at how she'd rambled. Anne's fate was no longer central in her mind. That much was clear.

Certainly, the Countess feared the outcome of her husband's military adventure. All her thoughts had turned to England, to this making and breaking of yet another king, the game in which our great Earl of Warwick now hazarded all.

Anne and I returned to Honfleur with Queen Margaret and Prince Edward. Anne's mother and her sister sailed first, braced to meet Clarence and Warwick, who were already under arms in England. Their destination was Portsmouth, and theirs the last ship to set sail from France before a spell of evil weather set in.

We had heard news that King Edward had fled before the army of the earl and his new, cobbled-together alliance of Lancastrians and Neville kin. Edward IV and his brother, Richard of Gloucester, were again fugitives. They had fled with little but the clothes on their backs to the Court of Burgundy where their sister was bestowed. Old King Henry had been taken from the Tower and raised again to the throne. Nevertheless, Queen Marguerite had hesitated to leave France, and then that terrible weather set in.

For a month, the channel churned like a gray rapid. Foul weather, which would not give over, prevented Queen Marguerite's army from embarking. Every once in a while there would be a break, and we'd sail out, but each venture ended in our return. The gales and high seas that met us were simply too dangerous.

Anne and I were sick every time, in spite of the mouth-burning ginger root Lady Van der Wey gave us to chew. We did not know what had happened to the Countess of Warwick and the Duchess of Clarence. They had set out and had not returned. Either they had made England, or they were on the bottom with the fishes. The unending apprehension left my

Lady pale, off her feed and complaining of headaches and malaise.

During one of our aborted attempts to cross, the waves were so huge that water poured into our cabin. We had to sit with crossed legs like beggars, our dresses tucked around us. Watching the water surge back and forth across the floor and seep through the leaking walls, feeling the ship heave and hearing the timbers groan, I couldn't decide which was worse, the constant gut-wrenching nausea or the terror of drowning.

Anne believed our time had come. Turning to me, she suddenly cried, "Dear Rose! Forgive me for sending you away. I felt so sorry for myself, and I couldn't do what I had to if you were near."

I had been sick and scared, but when she said that, I grew angry.

Why would I not understand? I was only a common person, but had we not grown up together?

"You are in love with your husband, the prince." I spoke with all the scorn I could muster. "So what does your servant's love matter?"

"Don't be angry!" Tears spilled.

(Blessed Mother! That year, all we did was cry!)

"You don't know—what—what it's like. I—I can't talk to you anymore."

Didn't know the tenderness of hugging, kissing, holding? All I knew of that was chaste, gentle, fragrant—*Her!*

"Oh, no, Milady! Matters are far contrary. You do not wish me near you."

She looked guilty. Then she blurted, "You will speak of— Dickon." She spoke his name as if it burnt her tongue. She tossed her blonde head while fresh tears spilled. She started to unfasten her necklace, but she couldn't do it.

"Help me!" Suddenly, she was impatient, commanding.

Bracing myself and praying the next wave didn't turn the ship over, I leaned close. There she was—alabaster, blue, copper—beautiful as an angel. Despite the sailors shouting, the boom of the ship as it rose and fell, the water sloshing around us, the roar of wind and the smell of vomit, this moment of accord and our old friendship held a perfect peace.

As I clutched the chain, fearful I'd drop the precious pendants upon the floor, I saw what she must be after—Dickon's ring, that fine braided gold. When she took it from me, sure enough, she let everything else fall into her lap.

"You must keep it, Rose." She handed the ring over and began restring what remained. "I must not wear it any longer. To keep faith with my husband, whom I swore to obey before God, I must break faith with my own dear cousin."

When I tried to give it back, she curled my fingers about the little ring. "Please! You must keep it. Put it beside your White Rose. As I cannot give it back to him myself, you are the only safe place I know." Her tears fell fast as the rain, spilling more salt into what was rushing back and forth upon the floor. Tears, and more tears.

What a tedious tale! At least, we did not drown. Neither did we sorrow alone, but in a kind embrace.

Chapter X

After several weeks, in early May, the winds relented and we finally passed over. Getting to land, even as part of an invading army, was preferable to riding the back of that terrible water. I prayed The Blessed Virgin that I never again would have to cross the ocean, and she has made it so.

No sooner did we land in England than we heard the terrible news. George, Duke of Clarence, had turned coat again, going straight back to his brothers and taking his soldiers with him. Shortly thereafter, the Earl of Warwick and his brother, John Montague, were slain and their army utterly destroyed during a great battle at Barnet. Anne's father and her brave Uncle were dead, their bodies lugged off for display in London by Edward of York.

Anne wept bitterly for that arrogant, cruel father. My reaction was terror.

Without the earl, what would happen to us? The marriage—even consummated—would come into question, and then—then—we would be at the mercy of these new "friends" who had once been enemies. How long would their loyalty last? Would we end as exiles in France?

The tall earl, trailing his flags, his heralds, his brave retinue, beautiful horses, stag hounds, men-at-arms, archers, and armies—was slain. His naked battered body was lying fly-blown on London slates. It had seemed impossible.

There had been a battle in the fog. Part of his army had taken the Blazing Star of the Lancastrian Earl of Oxford for the Sun in Splendor of York and had fallen upon its own flank. Cries of "Treason" ran along the lines, and part of the army panicked and ran. That which held met the young Duke of Gloucester and his brother, the tall red-gold King, who had come to win or die.

Queen Marguerite, whose confidence was badly shaken, was encouraged by her commanders to proceed, to do battle again with the remaining half of her army. They'd come so far, and it seemed their last bolt at the bull's eye of England for these Lords of House Lancaster.

Anne and I huddled in light cloaks beneath an arch of the cloister walk. We were at Tewksbury Abbey now, and we were hiding. Hiding from Queen Marguerite, hiding from the Lords of Lancaster, hiding from soldiers of whichever side would appear. We pulled our cloaks around to keep out the chill of the gray stone priory where our party had taken refuge. No matter how hot the summer, these ancient piles ever seeped cold.

The queen did not call for Anne, although Edward continued to. My lady spent her nights in his arms, and not a whisper of what passed came to me or to any other. The prince seemed happy, less angry than I'd ever seen. This new cheer was pleasant, even though he was full of himself as ever. He did not seem a bit worried about the death of Anne's father, but listened to the reassurances of his mother's captains.

What the Countess of Warwick thought, neither of us knew, for she had landed in due course at Portsmouth, and then had to escape straightaway into sanctuary at Beaulieu. If Marguerite won this morning, consummation would maintain Anne's marriage until her ability to breed was proven.

If Edward of York won—well! Anne, once heiress of castles and lands, could find herself stripped of everything, including her freedom. The nunnery, that oubliette for inconvenient royal women, was ever at hand. During the day, we trundled along amidst the army, half-forgotten baggage, lagging in the train. Even with the prince taking such interest in his wife's body, getting supper every evening was a conjuring trick.

Anne grieved for her father and bore the rest with dignity. The prince still came to her bed, but since our shipboard conversation, she'd drawn closer to me again. Frankly, I had been surprised by the prince's continued attention. Had sex become more interesting than all those heads he had so long dreamed of chopping off?

The army of York had found us. On the night before battle, no one slept long. Prince Edward rose from where he lay with my lady and went to arm. She, too, arose, and I helped her into a beautiful black and red dress, colors of Lancaster. After this was done, I accompanied her to Edward's tent, and watched as she watched her husband dressed for war.

Queen Marguerite was already there. When we arrived, she and a man-at-arms had already fastened the gussets of mail and mail collar onto his arming doublet and hose. The sabetons, greaves, the cuisse that covered the thigh, poleyn at the knee, were also in place. At this point, he was a man half of metal, half of flesh. At the end, they would attach the breast and back plates.

Edward was solemn, but did not appear in the least frightened, although this would be his first battle. It was, so it seemed to this humble onlooker, the final move in Queen Marguerite's great game. She, pale, but apparently self-possessed, offered her son drink from a table set near, holding the cup to his lips as is the custom. She barely spoke. Outside rooks began to call, a sign that the sky had begun to lighten.

Later, we heard the sounds of battle muted by distance. Dawn hadn't cleared the mists from the meadow before there came the thud and boom of the *gonnes*. The ring of metal upon metal, as knights in full armor joined battle, struck a higher note. We went to prayer along with the other ladies of the queen's train. Speaking for myself, my private prayers were somewhat different from those of the Lancastrian ladies kneeling on either side.

Finally, as time dragged on, the queen stood, regal as always. She began to pace and at last to weep. Suddenly, she was a thousand years older, her magnificence ravaged by fear and helpless rage. What could even a queen do—but wait?

We heard the foul traitor come, Sir Thomas Stanley, that infamous turn-coat, a man who played every side in these wars of roses, a man whose betrayals were far, far from over.

"Lady Margaret! Lady Margaret!"

Red-faced and blood-covered, he rode his sweating war horse right under the arches, up the steps that led to the sanctuary. The queen went out, standing straight. We watched from the shadows as she faced him, in her black and red, the Swan badge proudly riding her shoulder. We knew what Lord Stanley's news must be.

In the distance, smoke rose above the spires of the town. It was close to seven, an April sun at last burning the fog from the water meadows. Soldiers of Lancaster, injured and exhausted, had already begun to gather here, seeking sanctuary beside the altar of the abbey.

"Your bastard's dead!" Stanley bellowed, lifting his sword. His soldiers raised gruesome pikes, cheered and hooted, called "French whore!" at the queen, while we watched from the shadows.

Anne leaned against my shoulder. She began to cry, and I could feel terror in her long, stiffening body. So much grief in the last years, tears without number, as many as the stars in the sky, for this was indeed our time of tears. At midnight she had lain in his arms. Only a few hours ago she'd seen him sip from the jeweled battle cup. Before riding out, Edward had kissed her lips, her hand, and said *au revoir,* while she had wished him *Bon Chance.*

Blessed Mother! To be young, to be suddenly wrenched away from every loyalty you have been taught! Then, to lie naked, if even for the briefest span, in the arms of a handsome prince who tells you that you are beautiful, that he loves you in spite of your father, in spite of his mother! Who is to say what may happen in a fifteen-year-old's heart?

There came the clank of armor and chink of mail, the echoing tramp of soldier's booted feet through the stone cloisters. You could smell them before you saw them, for the stench of their battle madness came before them.

So covered in dirt and blood were these armed men--and we so frightened! We could not see their badges where we huddled in the jeweled light of a side chapel. We had prayed that the holy abbey would protect us from the victors, now rampaging through the countryside, killing and looting simply because they could.

I heard a shouted inquiry for "Anne of Warwick." A slender knight in fine white armor, his dark head uncovered, with a guard of five, all blood spattered, swords drawn, burst through the arras. A terrified priest pointed him toward the altar of Saint Catherine, where Anne and I had taken refuge.

The young knight, hair matted with sweat—and God knows what else—marched quickly forward. As he did, he signaled his men to put up their awful, dripping swords. His face was lean and young, not a whit older than My Lady's dead husband. Though streaked with dirt and gore, he was familiar.

Gazing into those burning eyes, I knew him. Anne gripped my hand hard, and I understood that she did too. Richard of Gloucester did not come any closer, only bowed.

"My dear Cousin Anne, I have come to see you are unharmed." His voice was hoarse from battle. His coat badge, the White Boar, though much stained, gleamed across the chest plate.

"I thank you for your care, My Lord of Gloucester." Anne took swift refuge in formality. "I pray you, cousin, let there be no violence in this holy place." What followed, however, was the truth of the matter, an absurdly long moment in which they simply gazed into each other's eyes.

Anne's face was pale and heavily streaked with tears, her poor eyes swollen. Her hair had been braided and coiled on either side of her head, and she wore a ruby swan brooch at her bosom. She was a reed in black and red, those violent colors of Lancaster. At dawn I'd helped her don the dress even while, nearby, her young husband had been arming.

She solemnly studied the blood-spattered features of the knight before her. Our Dickon was a man now, still spare, but strong. He straightened from his obeisance with grace, even after hours of fighting in that full plate. The blood which stained him showed he had not shirked the field's dangerous places. The laurels he'd earned were as plain as the gore that coated his armor and daubed his lean cheeks. It was present in the devoted way the eyes of his guards, mastiffs at the heel of their master, fixed upon him.

"I shall order you safe, My Lady Cousin."

I noted his armor had taken some mighty blows. Both *pauldron* and belly plate were dented.

"We are grateful for your care of the vanquished, Cousin of Gloucester."

He bowed his dark head respectfully, and then said, "I am sorry for your losses, dear Cousin. The Earl your father, before he challenged my brother the King, was always kind to me. As for—your—husband—I am told he fought bravely in a manner worthy of his blood. My dear Lady, I do wish with all my heart that we were met again in another place."

"As do I, my Lord."

"I thank The Blessed Mother that I have again had sight of your face."

"We are—grateful—for what help you can lend, my Lord. We are at the King your brother's mercy."

Clearly, Richard wanted to say a hundred things, but he only replied, "We shall speak again, Lady, hereafter."

Then he was gone. His men followed. Anne and I embraced again. Next, we fell on our knees and began again to call with all our strength upon the Blessed Mother and every saint we could remember. After a time, my Lady caught me by the shoulder, and said, "For so long I have yearned for the sight of his face! And to see him now—on this most evil day! Blessed Holy Mother! My heart is broken—broken ...." New sobs threatened to tear her apart. "Oh, Rose! You know I did my duty! I was Edward's wife! I loved him! And, now, now..."

I held her, tried to give comfort, while my head spun. The immediate appearance of the Duke of Gloucester proved there was a certain way out of this hell her father had made.

Seeing Richard was, for me, sight of land after shipwreck. In spite of war, in spite of death and betrayal, our young duke had not changed. He would not let any harm come to his cousin, of that I was certain.

.⁂.

And who should come with an even greater host of men, not an hour later? Not Richard, but George, Duke of Clarence. George, in fine fettle, helmless, blonde hair blowing, knuckles on his hip, riding a great black horse and grinning ear to ear. He appeared nowhere near as battle-worn as Richard. Except for one great gout of blood across his chest, he was almost clean.

There was not apparently a thought in his head about what he had done—all his betrayals—all his lies. On this day, George was perfectly full of himself, as if he'd single-handedly won the battle at Tewkesbury. He gathered us up and took us away, but not before we heard his soldiers turned lose upon the wounded men of Lancaster who had packed into the sanctuary...

Separated from the queen, Anne and I were carried in Clarence's train all the way to London. As we rode, we had the bad fortune to view the heads of the great Lancastrian lords, sixteen of them, all set upon stakes. George, of course, had to stop to admire them, to explain to Anne how they had been induced to come from sanctuary with a false promise of safe conduct. Seized, they had been summarily tried before "my brother of Gloucester and John Mowbray, Duke of Norfolk, and adjudged guilty of treason. We knocked their heads off and then went to dinner." These men, many of whom Anne knew, were only guilty, as far as I could see, of their attachment to the losing side.

"Got off easy, they did." George ambled slowly past the fly-buzzing gallery. "The King could have had them disemboweled and then quartered."

There they were, a row of men to whom we had both

curtsied, now horribly dead. Among them, I spied the once beautiful face of Edmund Beaufort, Queen Marguerite's favorite, now twisted in death and streaked with his own blood. These grisly tokens were to be dispatched, each to the places where they had once ruled, to be displayed upon city gates. Here was King Edward's justice and a traitor's reward!

We were not conveyed along with the spoils—the armor, the horses, the jewelry, the fine possessions looted from the tents of the lordly dead, but Queen Marguerite—*the Bitch of Anjou*—was. I had never felt a drop of charity for the Queen of the Red Rose, but I could not endure to see what was now done to her. Once an anointed Queen, once beautiful, once young and full of hope, Marguerite de Anjou, her face a mask of grief, was paraded in an open wagon. The people pelted her with showers of dirt and insults, while in her bosom lay far worse, a mother's broken heart. The only creature she'd ever truly loved—her handsome, arrogant young son—was dead.

Chapter XI

The Duke of Clarence was drunk—again. I suppose, the past considered, he had reason to be. What makes a man like George Plantagenet, a man without conscience, honor or self-control? Words cannot express how perfectly I had come to loathe him.

I could see Isabel, paler than ever at the mere sight of her husband in bad humor. From her seat, close by the sharp light of a May-time window, she watched with all the wariness of an often kicked dog.

"Stitch, stitch, little Neville girls!" George snickered, indicating the ever-present embroidery. "What brave heraldry do we work this afternoon?"

Ankarette and I were sitting knee to knee, adjacent to our mistresses. The room was a townhouse of the duke's. A luxurious Turkey carpet lay beneath our feet. There was good light for handwork from a cluster of glassed windows.

As George approached Isabel, I could feel Ankarette tense. She and I were joined to our ladies far closer than they to any husband.

"Ah, a noble black bull!" said George. "For my new arming coat? Very nice, my dear. Very nice." He made a great show of kissing Isabel on the cheek. She made a great show of enjoying it.

"Such talent with the needle," he said, baiting his drunk's ugly trap. "Such beauty in my lovely duchess! Such honoring and obeying!" He bent close, breathing into Isabel's paling face. "But no sons! No goddamned sons!"

Isabel closed her eyes, sat perfectly still, waiting for the blow, but this long summer's afternoon, George had an audience. A nasty little play was an amusement he never could resist.

He stood back and smiled lopsidedly upon his captive audience.

"Would you ladies like to hear a story? A thrilling story about the great war just passed?"

He put his fists into his waist, standing legs apart before our small fire. He was tall, and could still cut a good figure in tunic and hose, but an ever-growing gut took a deal away. Young as he was, drink had already blurred his elegant features. Blue eyes glazed, blonde hair a bit too long for a man of war, he was, in my eyes, a player's likeness of his older brother, King Edward.

"Not a word? Not one word from these chattering busy ladies?" He had to steady himself against the back of Isabel's chair. "Chatter, chatter, chatter! Yes, they chatter like a cage of canaries—until George comes!"

"You would not be interested in us, Milord." Anne spoke. I knew she was trying to draw him away from her sister, but, for my part, I wished she wouldn't. Isabel was safe—at least, until George had got his hands on all of the Earl of Warwick's property he coveted.

Anne had no one to protect her now, and if something were to happen to her, George would seize the great inheritance, every bit. I now feared George more than anyone else in the world.

"And why wouldn't I be interested, dear sister Annie?" He sallied toward her, wine spilling from the jeweled goblet he habitually carried at this time of day.

"It would bore you."

"Women's talk."

"As you say." She studied him levelly.

I was terrified that he'd take it into his head to strike her, for in each response she'd omitted the honorific "sir" or "cousin." I knew he'd caught the omission, and knew, too, that she had done it intentionally.

"Get up!" He waved his goblet, shouting. The last of the wine spattered Isabel's dress and the floor. Anne half started from her chair, but the command was for me, seated beside her. I hastily did as I was told, but took up a stance just on the other side.

George dropped onto my stool, tossed the goblet in the

general direction of the door, where he assumed someone would intercept it. As it hit the floor with a clatter, he seized Anne's hand.

"My story is really only for you, pretty sister Annie." He stuck his red mug close to hers.

She focused on his hands, eyes down, prudent at last. There was a moment of silence, of no sound but George's drunken puffing and a creaking, dying fire.

"What are you gawping at? Spotted bitch!" Suddenly, his focus changed; he was roaring up at me.

"Only Milady, Your Grace, as is my bounden duty."

"Duty?" He lurched back to his feet so he could face me. "Duty? Who asked for an answer, you—spotted bitch?" He was too drunk to think of another curse. Wine spittle flew.

I took a prudent step backwards. Lady Anne caught his hand. "M'Lord Clarence," she prompted. "Do tell us your story."

"Spotted she is! Spotted as a January apple." He mumbled, evil blue eyes slewing. After a moment, his gaze wavered and then shifted back to his original target.

The duke swayed slightly. You could see him deciding that perhaps it might be safer to sit back down, which he did. I took a careful step backward. From here, I thought, I will watch, and perhaps he will not notice me. I resolved, however, to stay close enough to rush to my lady's defense.

"So, you would like to hear my story, Annie?"

"As you will, my Lord brother." She was now all meekness.

"Why don't you get rid of the spotted creature? Her face is enough to make a fellow puke."

"She has served me long and well, sir. Her face makes no matter."

"Like Ankarette's ugly black skin makes no difference to my darling Isabel?" "Ankarette is not ugly." Anne tried a soothing tone, but all that can be done with a drunk is to humor them. Even that is generally impossible, for the whole point of the drink is to find a reason to rage, to punish the world at large, to humiliate and demean. Isabel's white face floated above the embroidery frame. She knew far better than Anne the doomed course of this conversation.

"Ankarette is not ugly." George mimicked her. "Listen, Widow Lancaster, it's what the Duke of Clarence thinks that counts in this house!"

"As you say, Milord." Anne lowered her head. The hennin and veil tipped forward, shrouding her fine features.

"Learn faster than your sister, you do, Annie." George smirked. "I believe you are cleverer."

Silence followed. Everyone sat entirely still, praying, I guess, not to attract his attention.

"Wine!" George bawled to an evil-looking man-servant who slouched by the door. "Where, by God's nails, is my wine?"

There followed the scuffling of slippers on the stairs. A silver jug, and a silver goblet, the sound of pouring, and a sullen boy brought it forward upon a tray. George took aim and grabbed, as if the wine might, at the last minute, elude him. Of course it spilled, all over his gloves and onto the page.

"Clumsy brat!" He kicked. I believe he missed, for the boy jumped with alacrity, then shot away through the door. We heard him skipping downstairs. Apparently, he was accustomed to serving George. "S'blood!" George pulled his face into an exaggerated mask of disgust. "Is no man in England worse served?" There was another pause, while he swallowed whatever was left. The smell of sugary Malmsey rose from the floor.

After it was drained, the empty goblet was again launched across the room. This time his man intercepted it, waving it in the air with a cheerful flourish.

"Ha!" George was delighted as a child. "Ha! Well done, Robinson!" He turned to Isabel. "Quick as a hawk, Robinson! It was well caught, was it not, Lady?"

"Yes, Your Grace."

"Was it not well done, Little Sister Annie?"

"Yes, Your Grace."

"Now, my girls, we shall have our story." The drunk sat, extended his long legs to the fire. Another thing about drunks—they seem distractible, and, up to a point are. However, when it is their ire they follow, nothing can divert them for long.

"My story is about Tewksbury, and what befell there." He began with sinister satisfaction. "Pretty meadows—water meadows, they are called. Very green, good forage for cattle, although one must beware the leeches. Water runs all the time. Rather wet this year, they did say, making lots of pretty yellow and white flowers. You like to see tender spring flowers, don't you, ladies?"

"My Lord—" Isabel began plaintively. She knew where this was going.

"Well, do you or don't you?"

"Yes, spring flowers are most pleasant." Anne plunged her needle into the embroidery and let it sit. Her elegant hands clasped in her lap. I knew it was to control the trembling.

"Liked daisies, didn't you?" George leered at Anne. The daisy, of course, had been Queen Marguerite's emblem. No one missed the allusion.

"Not as much as roses."

"Oh ho! Not as much as roses!" George flung his body around to face his wife. "She's clever, your sister!" He turned, mouthed a grin, and wagged a jeweled finger at Anne. "Not as much as roses! Ha, ha! Very good, Little Widow Lancaster!"

"Thank you, My Lord."

"But—your father decided he liked daisies—and swans, and ostrich plumes—if I remember right? Didn't he?" George continued. "Didn't he just, though?"

"I don't believe he ever truly liked daisies or swans, not really," Anne replied.

"Aha! Again, very good! But he believed he had a found a use for daisies and for those bloody little swans, didn't he?"

Anne said nothing. Isabel had nothing to say, either, and her blue eyes blazed with anguish, a pain I could see even through the veil of the hennin. The sisters had always viewed their father as a man who walked on water. Not even the horror just passed seemed to have altered this.

"My Lord," Isabel spoke, a quiver in her voice, "Please

spare us your opinion on this matter. Anne and I mourn our most beloved and noble father."

"You mourn a damned old fool. King Louis used him and then threw him away like a rag full of snot!" Having unburdened himself of this, he called over his shoulder loudly, "Robinson! Where's the wine?"

"Whatever he was, he was our father," Anne said. "I pray you, respect the dead, Your Grace."

"Dearest little Sister!" George let out a snigger. "I have respect for no man living, much less the dead!"

The beleaguered page appeared, another goblet balanced on the tray.

"Where comes this stain upon your doublet?" George leaned forward, eyes focusing on the boy with difficulty.

"Wine, My Lord."

"Wine, My Lord." George squeaked the words. "Clumsy brat! Do you know how much Malmsey costs? Can't you carry a pitcher upstairs without spilling it all over yourself?"

"You spilled it upon me, My Lord."

"Oh, did I? How clumsy of me! Like this?" George took the goblet and abruptly emptied it over the page's head, following the assault with yet another kick.

Again, in the nick of time, the page jumped. He took the worst of the wine, but he did avoid the foot.

Training for knighthood in the house of the noble Duke of Clarence! At least, I thought, the poor boy will always beware the low blow.

"Get out of here and change, impudent ape! By Christ! The service I receive!"

There was another pause, in which his man came forward with a cloth to blot what had splashed upon George's doublet.

Isabel said, "We should withdraw."

"And leave this jolly, jolly gathering? No! You can't go yet. I still have to tell Annie my story 'bout—'bout—the great big terrible battle at Tewksbury."

"I know about Tewksbury, Your Grace," Anne replied. "I was there."

"No you weren't! You lie, Sister Annie. You and the

wicked old whore—'scuse me—queen—were hiding in the priory. You saw nothing of the slaughter in the meadows, and that is exactly what I'm trying to tell you. Saving all these damned interruptions," he muttered in a deeply put-upon tone, "I would have finished long ere now."

"Soldiers killed sanctuary men upon the altar at Tewksbury."

"Shocking, wasn't it? Still, when you get down to it, that sanctuary business is silly monkish nonsense, nothing for true soldiers to worry about. And don't think they wouldn't have done the same to us, had it been the other way around. Besides, posh! That little splatter round the altar wasn't near as much blood as I saw. Oh, no, nothing like. I was making it spurt from arms and legs and necks on every side of the battlefield, yes, indeed I was."

"Indeed." Anne's disbelief was palpable.

"You don't think I was risking my life and killing the enemies of my royal—my most royal—brother of York, do you, Little Annie?"

"I believe everything happened as you say, sir."

"No, you don't!" He waggled a finger in her face. "You think I am a coward and turncoat, don't you, Sister Annie? You think I got your precious father killed! My dear Isabel does."

"I have never said any such a thing, My Lord."

"Nor I, My Lord," said Isabel.

"But you think it, don't you? Oh, yes, both of you. I can see it in those big blue eyes."

"Nay, My Lord."

"My big brother Edward and my little brother Richard are the brave ones, the true knights! *Chevaliers!* Aren't they? No one has any respect for poor old George."

If I could have plunged a dagger into that man's heart, I would have done so, and gladly suffered the agonizing consequences. A traitor, a weakling, a liar, a hundred times forsworn, a cowardly tormentor of women and children, the Mighty Duke of Clarence!

"Ah, you shake your head, but inside—ah, yes—inside—I

know you are thinking very bad thoughts 'bout me, Sister Annie." Satisfied with having bullied her into silence, George sat back.

"So, allow me to tell you how puny crooked Dickon himself, with his own quick hand, cut down your dear handsome Prince Edward, your late—however, not particularly lamented—little boy husband. It's really quite a relief, you know, the way things have turned out, to discover that you, personally, were never too fond of daisies. Frankly, Sister Annie, I'd say you know how to change sides with the best of us."

It was like a nightmare from which you cannot awaken. We were all transfixed by his malice.

"Our men brought Prince Bastard into our camp, trussed like a Christmas capon. Remember how he used to make all those fine speeches about all the heads he was going to cut off? Well, it was really quite funny to see the Heir In-apparent, all dirty and crying and snotty. Shaking in his French booties, he was, after a sharp taste of some real fighting."

George leaned forward and caught Anne's hand, drew it forward and lipped it moistly. It was all she could do not to tear away, but somehow she endured the vile creature's slobber.

"Dickon has always been sweet on you." He leaned close, his voice a drunken caress, "Now he's a sensible grown up, and he's sweet on your father's lands and castles too. It's a romance, you see, just like me and your dearest, darling sister Isabel. Both of you are passing fair ladies, passing well left."

"The Duke of Gloucester and I were once promised." I knew it was all Anne could do to hold her voice steady.

"Could I ever forget? A pair of sickly runts holding hands! It was sufficient to turn a fellow's stomach. Come to think of it, though, it does explain what he did," George said cheerfully. "I never thought of our dull Dick as the jealous type—but, there! Seems he's as hot as the next man. You know how I know? You don't, do you? So let me tell you about the willows—nice, big willows—pretty—weren't they? They had long trailing branches and made a lovely spot to lie, there by the river. Not this year, of course, the place is a crow's banqueting hall—but, after they and the worms have finished, it will be quite pleasant there again."

His voice trailed away, as if he'd forgotten where his tale was going. Anne said nothing. What could she do now, but wait for George to end?

"Where was I? Oh, yes! Poor little baby Prince Edward, your braggart husband! Well, he tried to speak to the king my brother, to beg for mercy, wretched brat. He had his hands bound and he'd lost his sword. He was standing there, all muddy and bloody and shaking, when Richard, just as smooth as you please, strolled up behind and slit his throat. It was funny, actually, how astonished the little bastard looked, to find himself stuck. Our Dickon was handy as a butcher with an autumn pig!"

Anne blinked. Otherwise, she did not turn a hair.

"You know, Annie," George went on dreamily, "the eyes of a man so slain are full of surprise. The look is always there when you silence a man like that—or—a woman," he added with a sinister wink, as if he had done both many times. "They know, you see. It's no more than a sting, but they understand they are bleeding out from that great vein. It's over in less than a wink, but 'tis a very long wink for the one who is dying. Not an ounce of Prince Edward's blood flowed blue, for I watched most carefully. It made a lovely scarlet mess all over that fine embroidered arming coat. You know—the red and black with the swan and the ostrich plumes upon which you ladies worked so long and hard."

George paused to gauge the effect. Anne tilted her head, hiding her face beneath the veil. Her shoulders rose and fell steeply. I prayed she was not starting an attack.

"Hey, Ned of Lancaster is food for worms!" George sang in a golden slur. "His last view of God's earth, those willow trees, long arms trailing in the water.

Dickon laughs, his blade runs red!
For naught the Queen-bitch span in Somerset's bed.
Her bastard's slain, her loss, York's gain,
Down in the green, green meadow!"

The fire spit softly. No one moved. George had a good

voice and his foul song cast a malevolent spell.

"Yes, little twisted Dickon is a man now. A valiant soldier, a fierce dog who bites at Brother Edward's command! He was at the Tower, too, you know, the night King Henry died and broke the coot's head in with a mace while he knelt at prayer." George giggled, pleased with the misery he'd created.

"There's another useless Lancastrian object helped to heaven. Did the job himself, you know. Why, can you believe it? Dickon told me that his soldiers were afraid of God's damnation if they killed such a saintly old man. Murdering a helpless fool on his knees before God doesn't give my little brother a pause, as long as it serves his best-beloved Edward. Suppose he would have done for your father, too, had he been the first to catch him. I wonder if he would have had your father's head chopped off, or if he'd have rather broken his head, like Henry? Dickon says he's found there's nothing quite like doing the job himself."

Anne choked, reached for her handkerchief. Her shoulders lifted, and I knew a spasm had begun. I stepped forward, my fingers clasping the aromatic bottle I always kept in my apron.

"Get thee back, spotted cow!" George exclaimed with playful menace, pointing at me. "I'm not done yet. Certainly your mistress—dear sister Annie—would like to know a thing or two about my brother, now so eager to warm something of his in that red muff of hers."

"George!" Isabel cried. "Enough!"

"Ah, my little wife is a scold!" George said. Leaping out of the chair, alarmingly quick for one so drunk, he seized Isabel's arm, and dragged her upright. "I have always had a strong fancy for angry women."

Isabel's curtained bed was visible through the open door. Kicking over a chair to clear the way, George began to pull Isabel toward it. Ankarette rushed forward, caught George's arm and began to plead.

"My Lord of Clarence! I pray you, have a care! It is too soon."

"As I have no son," George shouted, "it cannot possibly be soon enough!"

Anne's choking was well started, but, somehow, she managed to get up. I put my arms around her waist to give support, and we fled Isabel's day chamber. I am sorry to admit cowardice, but Anne was my first care. As we fled past the evil smirk of Clarence's man-servant, I could hear Ankarette pleading.

"I pray you, sir! In heaven's name, have a care for your wife!"

"She should have a care for me!" George shouted. "Where are my sons? Why, men laugh behind my back, saying I do not know how to breed her!"

The door crashed shut. Shouting continued, now, blessedly, muffled.

Anne leaned against the wall, slowly sliding into a sitting position on the steps. I settled beside her. She was struggling, trying not to choke, not to let her throat to close. She fought for each breath, swallowing over and again. I opened the aromatic vial.

The pungency seemed to help, although from my point of view it seemed hours we huddled on the stairs. I knew I must take Anne away and back to her room as soon as possible. We'd deal later with the filth George had spewed.

I understood something about the madness that takes men in battle, something about the similar madness which takes men in politics. Nevertheless, I'd be willing to bet that Clarence had made up every shred of what he'd just said about Richard.

A good story was not to be confused with truth, that much had become clear to me, a witness to oh so many strong oaths of fidelity sworn upon sacred relics. All those solemn promises—so soon forgotten! None of these elaborate ceremonies had any force nowadays, in this world of liars and cheats. Perhaps, I realized, in a sudden epiphany, they never had.

⚜

"Do you believe what he said?" Anne was curled into a window seat, looking as forlorn as only fifteen can.

"I believe nothing George says. He is a perjured, vile, drunken, traitorous dog."

"Good, for I believe less than nothing of his maunderings. It serves his purpose to make you hate the Duke of Gloucester."

"Yes. I understand what he means to do, Rose. I am not a baby anymore."

"No, not since you were a wife." Still, I wasn't entirely certain. She had a great imagination, my Anne, and a fearful one, that I knew. Everyone had betrayed her, even her beloved parents. Why should she not now suspect that other love of her young life—her own dear Dickon?

"Do you think he killed Edward?" She spoke after a lengthy silence, confirming my intuition. George's web had snared her.

"Soldiers in the field killed your husband the prince, hoping to get some extra reward from the king. Such things often happen." I watched her face, knowing she was still watering the seed George had planted.

What to say?

That if she'd failed to birth sons, Edward of Lancaster would have put her away in a heart-beat? That as soon as the thrill of bedding her lovely self wore off, this pitiless young man would quickly discover that he also "loved" others? Privately, I was of the opinion that if Richard of Gloucester had slit Prince Edward's throat—even, exactly—as George said—it was for the best.

"Dear Sister!" Anne started up, all anxiety. "How are you?"

"Hush, Anne, and do sit down." Isabel was all cool elder superiority.

The duchess looked none the worse for wear. After some of the stories I'd heard below stairs about the mixture of violence and sex George was said to particularly enjoy, I was surprised.

"Don't get the servants talking," Isabel said sternly. "They chatter enough already."

"Indeed," Anne replied, settling. Her time with Marguerite d'Anjou had taught her a great deal about changing direction and maintaining her poise while doing so.

Isabel arranged her skirts, and waited for Ankarette to bring the embroidery basket.

"If I may not enquire about your health, may I ask how is My Lord the Duke of Clarence this morning?"

Isabel, cool as a pickle, replied, "Sleeping late."

"As might be expected."

"Anne, dear," Isabel said, heaving a great sigh of exasperation, "everything is fine. You just don't understand. George has a good heart. He never means what he says when he's deep in his cups."

Anne stole a glance at me, and I knew exactly what she was thinking—or, at least, something close enough. We'd seen it time and again, his drunken abuse, followed by tears of repentance and a tender reconciliation sealed with a thousand liar's kisses. It was George's pattern with the world.

Later, Ankarette confirmed this suspicion. Yes, she said, the duke had roared, and Isabel had wept, and then, suddenly, as was his wont, he, too, had begun to cry, and talk about how he was misunderstood and maltreated by the whole world. They had ended in bed, weeping and comforting each other. George had fallen asleep—Ankarette had heard the snores—and Isabel, still dressed and quite unmolested, had sent her out.

"He will be tender and thoughtful for a few days, and then it will begin all over again. Lady Isabel will beg him not to drink, and for a while he will refrain, at least not too much and not in her presence, and then something will pique him, and he'll be off again, head first in the Malmsey, and ready to pick a fight with the first person who crosses his path. He tells her he loves her, and she, poor lady, wants so much to believe. She loves him, that's for certain." Ankarette paused, shook her sleek dark head with distaste. "Plantagenet men are the devil between your legs. Women will do anything to get more, from their lady wives to foolish serving girls. Once they've had you,

you'll scorn the touch of any other. I've seen it before. Yes, indeed! Who can say where this will end for my poor lady?"

"Who knows how it will end for any of us?" I confess, of late, I'd been worrying about my own freckled hide far more than a perfect servant should. Little did I guess what mischief George had up his magnificent scalloped sleeves, for I came by—of all unexpected things—a suitor. After being assaulted with "spotty" every time I turned around, it was the last thing I expected.

A guard in George's house—one who had come as a soldier of fortune into the service—began to follow me about and make friendly talk. At first, I thought of him as merely lonely, a man who heard my Yorkshire tongue, in use when I was down in the kitchen and found that it made him think of home.

When others began to tease, I came face to face with his true drift. Not only was it hard to believe, but it seemed mightily ill-timed.

Hugh Fletcher was not young, being thirty at the time. He was a big, square fair man born in my own county. He had strong legs, brawny arms, broad shoulders, and a big, hard, gut. By trade, he was an archer. For fun, we watched the men practice at the butts on Sunday afternoons, as the ancient decree of England required. Here I saw with my own eyes there was not a man in the household who could come anywhere near the aim of Master Fletcher. Not only could he pull the heaviest bow, but he could hit the eye out of a squirrel at 200 paces. All the other men stood aside, watched and cheered while he shot.

Hugh had gone on the continent after his village had been burned in Queen Marguerite's time and had joined a Company of Saint George, English mercenaries. Later, he'd returned to England and waded through the latest battles of York and Lancaster. When Clarence had changed sides and left the Earl of Warwick in the lurch before Barnet, Hugh had changed his badge too. He said it had turned his gut to fight for Marguerite.

Eighteen now, I was no longer young. Whatever bloom had been on this poor plain rose was long gone in the trials and tribulations of the last few years. In secret, I availed myself of Anne's polished metal mirror and gazed into it. There I was, same as ever, only a bit plumper. There was my white skin, lips and face, the fat roan freckles splashed over all. There were two thick, short braids of burnished brunette that set off my hazel eyes. In a moment, I'd wind the braids and cover all with a white headscarf. There I'd be, plain as a nun in a gray dress, with those damned freckles standing out against white linen.

Hugh was, of course, well paid, as any archer of such exceptional skill would be, but it was further rumored that he had money put into the wool trade. That he was, in fact, a man of enough substance to give up soldiering and settle down, something of a catch. There were girls in the house who had conceived (through this news, perhaps) a fancy for him.

Extra was carried to him at the servant's table with a sauce of winks, banter, and swaying hips. The girls even cooed he was good-looking, although there was too much bulk—and not enough hair beneath his brown felt hat—for my taste.

His hair was that ashy color which is the fate of half of the English nation, with high color in his cheeks, sharp gray eyes, and bushy brows tinged with white. He could speak fair and speak coarse, one as well as the other, and he could read and write a little, too.

Where on earth a poor boy gone to the wars had picked up writing, I had no idea. It was, however, rather intriguing, like many other things about him. When the fellows all stripped their shirts at archery on a hot Sunday, I saw his broad back was covered with whipping scars, a sign of some long ago transgression.

Hugh Fletcher nevertheless stood proud as a lord while drawing his great bow. Beneath the extra, there was muscle in good quantity. As he shot, Katy, one of Isabel's housemaids, ardently clapped, blushed, and giggled.

What on earth was there besides my Yorkshire accent to attract this hardy yeoman? One afternoon, when Ankarette teased me about Hugh, I put the question to her. She, dark eyes merry beneath her shapely black brows, replied, "Don't play the fool, Rosalba Whitby! Your lady adores you, as all the world knows. She will take good care of you, and Hugh, with the nose for money he has..."

"Without her father and under attainder, my Lady Anne is not in a position to take care of herself, much less me. And, how do you know Hugh Fletcher has a nose for money?"

"How many soldiers keep their pay?"

"Not many, but, goodness, this is all supposition."

"Is it? Timothy the scrivener helped Fletcher with a letter only last week. It was a letter about his money, placed with one Master Cooke, a wool merchant right here in London."

I must have looked shocked at this bit of household espionage, because Ankarette giggled and responded with a friendly shove.

"If you paid attention to anything except your herbs and hovering over your little lady, you'd hear a deal more, you know."

Hugh and I were seated at a side table in the kitchen, watching others at work, a most relaxing occupation. The room was a cavern of brick with a deep fireplace. Over our heads, timbers, half trees, cut long ago, hung with herbs, strings of garlic, onion braids, and drying slices of apples. There was a comforting smell of smoke, grease and spice.

On the slate floor nearby lay a snoring hound. Cats rested higher, atop the indoor wood pile. Kitchen maids in kirtles with their overdresses looped up to stay well off the floor, scrubbed at the slate sink, or stirred pots while standing beneath the mantel of the yawning fireplace, which was so deep and tall that several small cooking fires could be laid within. Some of these were for pot cooking, others for roasting. The spit dog, lop-eared, short-legged and long backed, trotted with a big smile inside a squeaking wheel.

Hugh was telling me his story. This was more than my polite inquiry had hoped to draw forth, but I had naught else to do, and the man seemed pleased to do it.

"I was born in the village of Sandal Magna. Grew up

there, married there, and saw the whole damn place burnt to the ground. After the Battle at Wakefield, Clifford and Queen Marguerite's soldiers came to our village. They slew almost everyone I held dear, my wife, baby, my old father, my mother, three brothers, two sisters, neighbors, and all my friends. I lost everything but my life that day."

He paused to see what impression this made. Easy enough to offer sympathy! These were the bad old days of which Master Whitby and True Thomas had spoken, the southern march of Queen Marguerite's army after the Battle of Wakefield, a blood-soaked trail of plunder, murder, and rape. Like a passage by the Devil, the queen's soldiers had scorched the earth beneath their feet.

"A grievous loss, Master Fletcher. I have often heard of the terrible things that happened in those days. My village was fortunate. We did not fall in the way the queen's army."

"It was a time ago," Hugh said. He shook his great head, as if to clear it. "Afterwards, I went myself to soldiering. Faith! There was nothing else to do. I was in Burgundy for a time, and then came home to England again and threw in my lot with the Sons of York. I am a Neville man by birth, which was the reason why the She-Wolf plundered us. I fought in second St. Albans, where I just got away with my skin. I fought at Towton, where Edward of York paid the French Bitch some on her account. I was at Hexham with John Neville—the Earl Montague that was—and at Edgecot with Warwick Kingmaker, next at Barnet with the Duke of Clarence. Last, I was at Tewkesbury, where I settled scores, once and for all, with that murdering French whore. A fine battle for a fightin' man, was Tewkesbury."

"You fought for both the White Rose and the Nevilles?"

"I have, and make no bones about it. I'm a soldier. It's a trade to be followed like any other. As long as I'm paid and given a little respect, it's all one to me."

This last I judged professional swagger. After all, he'd just admitted to fighting in order to "settle accounts" with Queen Marguerite.

Hugh slipped a hand into his pocket, and drew forth a

thick golden ring. When he held it out to me, however, I would not touch it.

"'Tis pure gold; feel how heavy."

"No thank-you."

"Oh, don't be so stuck up!" He snapped the ring into the air and caught it, "Yes, 'tis loot, but it is better than coin."

"It came from a man's dead hand."

"So does this." Hugh proudly displayed a massive thumb ring. "These fellows didn't need 'em anymore."

"But their family might have had a need."

"Well, then, they shouldn't have been so proud as to wear 'em to battle, should they?" Hugh stuffed the first ring into his pocket and studied me from beneath those shaggy white blonde brows. "What's the matter, lass? Don't you fancy a brave soldier?"

"I like soldiers well enough, especially when they fight on the proper side."

"The House of York?"

"The proper side is that which defends My Lady. To me, she is all that matters in this world."

"How old are you, Mistress Rosalba?" He grinned and leaned back in his chair. From around the room I could see the other girls—maids, kitchen wenches, cooks—smirking behind their hands. Other servants said I was too proud, that I had forgotten where I had been born, that I talked like those whom I served and thought myself better than the rest.

"Eighteen."

Hugh shot a glance at a man-at-arms who'd been chatting up one of the handsomer maids. A wink passed between them.

"Old, it may be fairly said, to so much in love with her mistress."

Someone laughed. Angry now, I went to get up and leave, but the rogue dared to catch my arm.

"Your fair young mistress will soon have that hardy stripling, the little fightin' Cock of Gloucester, to keep her warm at night. She won't need you anymore. What then?"

Before I knew what he was up to, he had me off balance and falling, straight onto his knee. "There," he said regarding me with satisfaction, for I was forced to steady myself against his broad chest. "A goodly backside you have, little woman."

This brought a chorus of "Ooooh!" Even the greasy scullions dared.

"Fool." Declining to struggle, I sat still.

"Suit yourself," Hugh replied. "Still, be you warned, Roan Rose. I've always had a strong fancy for freckles."

He released me. He judged well, for I wasn't in the mood to make any more of a scene than we'd already played.

Getting off his knee with as much dignity as possible, I stamped out of the kitchen. A flood of laughter spilled as I closed the door. I could have killed them all.

"Do you know where I first saw you?" It was Hugh, again, sidling up as I gathered peppermint. I'd paused at my task to take a deep breath of our good English air.

"No." We no longer bothered much with preliminaries, Hugh and I, though I was still locked within my stony castle keep.

"On the battlements at Amiens, looking north."

"Really?" I'd been in such a fog of misery those days, I actually couldn't remember much, except for the feeling that everything was wrong—everything in the world.

Hugh spoke softly, looking over his shoulder to see if we were truly alone. "I wanted to say that I shall soon leave this house, for my service is up. These lords are all wolves, but, By Christ, this one is naught but a thieving dog."

I joined his survey of the garden, but all our company was a honeybee, buzzing within the bright, early flowers and a wren rattling like a mad thing among the wilting lilacs.

"The Duke of Clarence is a wicked man. I hope and pray the king will soon take my lady into his protection. I worry every moment we are here."

"As you should," Hugh said. "I wouldn't let her out of your sight."

I could see again that hopeful look in his eye—*girl*—

garden—spring!—and decided to cut the conversation short.

"You are correct, sir. And so, it follows, I should be going."

I turned and started across the grass. Undaunted, Hugh trailed after.

"I would like to go with the Duke of Gloucester," he said offhandedly. "That would take me north again. It has been a long time since I saw the dales."

This brought me up short. That notion was dear to my own heart.

"If all goes well for My Lady, I may soon see home again, too. I was born in Aysgarth."

"I would never have guessed." He smiled. "Let's see. There are two kinds in your village, the tall, fair ones that came on the long ships, and yours, with all the freckles." He wore an older, wiser look, full of amusement.

"Easy enough after I have said."

"I thought of the falls at Aysgarth the moment I saw you upon those French battlements, Mistress Rosalba. You made me long for my home place, a feeling I have not had since I lost my young wife and baby, all those years ago." When his big, warm hand moved to clasp mine, I did not pull away. That would have been cruel. Knowing I'd be kind, he'd begun to tame me, with a touch, as is done with all wild creatures.

As for Anne, she'd closed up, like an oyster pulled from the water. She would not talk about Prince Edward, not a word. Unlike Isabel, who had apparently detailed every passage of George's hand for her sister, Anne had nothing to say.

By nature she was modest. When, at first, Anne stopped sharing her inmost thoughts, I wasn't surprised. I knew she could hold her peace, but I had never suspected so much strength. Quite alone, by choice, she went through whatever Edward of Lancaster and their brief marriage had meant to her, then she packed it away, in some deep and private place.

There were days when she grieved. She prayed a great

deal, said her rosary time and again, and often wept bitterly over it. When not on her knees; however, there remained a plain, grave determination to get on and not to wallow in the "what-if" of a ruined past.

When it became clear she wanted to be alone with her thoughts, I let her. For me, it was enough to hold her again, to smell her fragrant hair and feel her long limbs sleepily moving against mine through the night. It was not that I could never give her up. Teased to death by everyone, I often reassured myself on this score.

I would be glad to leave my lady behind, when, and only when, I delivered her to the one who should rightfully have her. Putting her into Richard of Gloucester's bed was what should have been—and what might yet—come to pass. When that wedding night came, I should go to sleep, perfectly contented and alone. At least, that's what I told myself.

One beautiful June morning, my lady went riding. The Duke of Clarence, not usually much for anything except dice or the bottle, made an exception and went along with the party. At dinner time, I saw the accompanying ladies and gentlemen returning, faces pink, laughing and bright. They trooped at once into the hall for their dinner. I looked for My Lady, but did not see her, although I did see Clarence going upstairs to Isabel, passing by the room where Ankarette and I sat sewing.

I stood, wondering where Anne was. Ankarette followed me and then abruptly seized my shoulder.

"Listen!"

Through the thick walls, there came the sound of screaming, shouting! It was another battle royal between the Duke of Clarence and his duchess. Ankarette promptly started for the stairs. I followed, thinking that perhaps, somehow, Anne had passed me by. As we entered the stairwell, the duke's villain of a servant, Robinson, met us. We both recoiled at the sight of him.

"Get you to your mistress, Ankarette! And you—Rosalba—" He paused to grin, his usual tired trick of finding humor in my name, "go pack everything of your lady's. You must be gone from here before supper to Westminster."

From above our heads came a crash as something shattered.

"Good luck to you and your dear lady. I'll come see you later." After squeezing my hand, Ankarette hastened away, past Robinson and up the stairs.

"Where is my Lady Anne, Master Robinson?"

His smirk grew wider. "Why, while they were out riding, who should they meet but our King Edward among his court? The King asked your lady to accompany him to his palace, so what could my master do but relinquish her?"

"My Lady Anne has gone to Westminster?"

"She is with the king, wherever she has gone," Robinson replied waspishly. "I say again, get you to her room and pack. You shall be conveyed thither, along with your lady's belongings, before supper today."

Wondering mightily—but also mightily relieved that we were leaving—I did as I was told. Help came in the form of a housemaid and a man to move the trunk when I had finished. There was not much to pack, when all was said and done. The daughter of the great Earl of Warwick had been plundered along with the rest of Queen Marguerite's train, and this single trunk was all that remained of the splendor that had once been hers. Isabel had given Anne clothes and linen out of her own store when we'd arrived here.

From the kitchen came buttermilk, cheese, and a round of hot loaf, a kindness I had not expected. I was excited about our fortunate escape, and, truth to tell, excited about the prospect of seeing the Court of Edward IV in all its new, conquering splendor.

Chapter XII

Approaching the river, Tom, my driver, drew our cart to a halt. I did not inquire why. It would only lead to some leering remark about the call of nature and did I want to see what he had? The place was thick with willows, and beyond, I could see the Thames running strong, carrying leaves and branches downstream, a ruin caused by a recent rain.

Tom got down and walked away to duck beneath the willows. I didn't look until after the sound of branches cracking indicated he had thrust his way through. There followed a lengthy pause.

This Tom was a big fellow, a mate of the slippery Robinson. The knowledge had worked on my nerves as we traveled, for there had been a host of odd things, beyond this sudden turn of events. For one, Ankarette had never come to say good-bye, although a few others with whom I had grown familiar had waved me off in the courtyard.

A movement caught my attention and I spun around. After all, so soon after a war, who might be lurking in such a secluded place? It was only Tom, but I startled, for he had come up quietly. He seemed disconcerted when I saw him, but he quickly sprang up onto the wheel and seized my wrist.

"This is as far as you go."

I began to kick and yell, but he was strong. With the free hand, I got into my pocket for the blade, but he only used that to get me off balance, to throw me down upon the ground. The landing knocked out my wind and the knife fell from my hand. In a leap, he was on top, using his legs and weight to hold me. While I fought and tried to reach the knife, he twisted a silken cord around my throat. To do that, though, he had to let my hands free. Struggling with all my might against him, I went for his face. My nails dug into flesh, but he had me fast.

❦

I heard a terrible roaring, next, a man shouting.

"Rose! Rose!"

I coughed and choked, drawing a breath that rushed into my lungs like a burning spike. Hands had pulled me into a sitting position, while I gasped for air and coughed violently.

"Are you all right?" I could at last recognize who my rescuer was.

I couldn't answer. I was too busy sucking air. *Alive!*

Grey clouds rushed overhead. On a nearby willow, a raven croaked, bobbing his heavy black body. He seemed more than a little put out.

Lost your supper, I thought, but I'm not sorry for you. No, I'm not.

Next to me lay the unmoving hulk of Tom, the livery of the Duke of Clarence all muddied, face down in a reddening pool. The sight of him made me jump.

"Easy." A chuckle followed my alarm. "That bastard isn't going anywhere."

"He tried to kill me!"

"Yes, with Clarence's blessing. Sorry about the blood."

I collapsed into his arms and let him hold me, which he did very kindly, wiping sticky blood from my face and neck with his sleeve and patting my back while I shook, coughed and sobbed.

"Can you get up on the cart?"

"Yes." The hysteria had gone. Abruptly, I felt as if I could flap my arms and fly over the trees. Maybe the river, too!

"Good. Get up there while I put our Tommy in the water."

As Hugh grabbed Tom by the boots and began to tug, I lurched toward the cart. It was astonishingly easy to put my foot on the wheel and spring up.

Only a few minutes later, Hugh was in the seat beside me. While I watched, he wiped his knife on a rag and then settled it into the sheath at his side.

"Now you must marry me."

"What?" I stared at him as if he'd grown another head.

"I would think that a woman whose life has just been saved might be grateful."

"Grateful? Holy Mother! I am! But—but—Fletcher! I have said! I cannot marry anyone! Lady Anne needs me!"

"Damn you! I should have known that's what I'd hear! So now it's 'good Fletcher run to the Duke of Gloucester and save my precious Lady'! Well, hold tight, stupid bitch!" Seizing the reins, he slapped them upon the fat back of the pony. We went off with a jerk, me hanging on for dear life. His rage was visible all over his fair skin. I could actually feel it, roaring off him like a hot wave.

"Hugh Fletcher! What on God's earth—"

He dragged the pony to a stop, impetus slamming the cart into the traces and almost knocking the poor creature over.

"What's the matter?" He roared into my face. "The matter? Shall I knock you on the head and toss you into the river? Go back and collect the reward from the Duke of Clarence? Or will you—by Bloody, Suffering Christ—keep out of the Thames and marry me?" His gray eyes bulged. His face was purple. It was clear that a man who has just killed one person may very easily kill another.

"Um—Yes! *Certes*, I'll marry you." My face began to twitch like mad. I wanted to rub to stop it, but did not dare to let go of the seat.

"You only say that because you're frightened!" He stared at me, cheeks puffed like an angry dog's. He pounded the seat between us with his fist, striking so loudly that the pony again hopped forward. He was, if possible, even more furious. I thought it best to sit absolutely still.

"Will you?" Yanking a ring from his little finger and seizing my arm, he cried, "Then have this." He jammed it onto my wedding finger. It was some of his loot, but his grip was what occupied me. I thought my wrist would come apart.

"Don't speak!" He stared balefully. "Especially to take is not to give, or some bloody double talk, or—or—by Christ's bloody wounds, there's still time to fucking drown you." He gestured widely at the roiling river.

"I—I—thank-you from the bottom of my heart—for—saving my life, good Master Fletcher." The words came hissing from my bruised throat.

"Ha! But you don't mean it, do you?" He slapped the reins again on the poor pony's back. "Miserable, ungrateful woman! S'Wounds! If Clarence wishes, he can have me hanged for what I just did! What's a man got to do to get a woman's goodwill these days? Bleeding suffering Christ, I should have let him finish choking you!"

On the way, Hugh, though still thoroughly riled, explained how he came to be there. He said that, curious about this sudden turn of events, he'd done some spying and had overheard Robinson talking with Tom. After a little chat about putting me "to silence," Robinson had boasted to Tom that "Little Gloucester will never discover where we've stowed the lady, which our lord likes very well."

This news sent another wave of terror through me. My heart pounded, and I felt as if I could have run to Crosby Place, the duke's townhouse, twice as fast as the pony trotted.

We were fortunate to find Richard at home. More, the blood with which I was stained gave our urgency credence. As a result, Hugh and I were quickly escorted into the duke's presence. We rushed with the breeze through an arched walkway. Within the house were dark wooden floors, the white daubed walls crisscrossed by timber frame, and a high ceiling. We approached a table, where a host of gentlemen gathered. Richard of Gloucester rose from the head to meet us. So unlike his brothers, I thought, so small and dark, "More Mortimer than Plantagenet," or so I'd heard some among the old servants say.

Still, it was clear this was a man of power, in a gold-riveted mulberry brigantine, with a shining golden collar of suns and leopards. Men-at-arms stood by the doors like falcons, falcons with their hoods removed, roused to fly, erect upon the fists of their keepers.

Hugh stopped behind me and removed his hat. I took a few steps more before dropping a shaky curtsy. Richard came to meet me. He took my hand, and raised me, a high mark of favor.

"Rose! What is this?"

Yes, a man now, I thought looking into those shadowy hazel eyes. The boy who had conquered illness, injury and a twisted spine, now tempered to manhood in the fires of war.

"My Lord of Gloucester! My Lady Anne is gone!"

He did not let go of my hand, and his touch brought back something of our past. Like the rest of him, the hand within the glove was hard.

"Speak quickly!"

"Your brother the duke, told us my Lady Anne had gone to be with King Edward at Westminster, and I was put to packing..."

"Lady Anne is no longer with my brother?"

"No, My Lord. She went for a ride this morning with the Duke of Clarence, but she never returned. We have come to..."

"John!" Richard interrupted, calling over his shoulder to his servant, "My horse."

A servant hurriedly left the room. Richard's eyes returned to me.

"Quick, Rose."

A strange mantle was growing before my eyes, a blackness which obscured everything but his red and gold shape. "They said I was to Westminster after my Lady, but by the river—" Swaying cattails, high water. Tom, his face so grave, his hands, tightening—ever tightening . . .

"I slew the dog as he attempted her murder and have brought Mistress Rose straight to you."

Much to my embarrassment, I was now seated in my lord's chair, the sort with broad wooden arms. Here I rested an elbow and my swimming, aching head in my hand. I could not remember how I came to be there.

"You have broken faith with the Duke of Clarence, Fletcher."

"I have, Your Grace," Hugh replied. "I can no longer serve him."

"Where were you born, Fletcher? Yorkshire is on your tongue."

"I was born in Sandal Magna, my Lord. I have been a soldier since Queen Marguerite killed my family. Through service to the Earl of Warwick, I came to your brother Clarence. My Lord of Gloucester, pardon a plain man, but of your brother the duke I have had a belly-full."

"Stay with me then, Fletcher of Sandal Magna." Richard extended a gloved hand.

Hugh dropped to one knee before Richard and bent his fair head to kiss the ducal signet.

"I am yours, my Lord."

"You were mine from the moment you saved Mistress Rose and brought this news. Attend my Sergeant at Arms. He will give you livery and a place among my men." You never had to sketch the obvious for Richard.

I tried to leave the chair, but he insisted I stay. I cannot tell you how uncomfortable I was, sitting in his presence.

"My Lord! You are the only man in England who has a care for my dear lady."

"No. My brother of Clarence cares, of that be certain." Richard's eyes flashed. I wouldn't have wanted to be George—and within reach.

"She has been brave, sir, but what she has borne has come nigh to breaking her heart."

"Near to breaking all our hearts," There he stood, right royal, long dagger by his side, among his soldiers. Had our Dickon, as George claimed, killed Prince Edward at Tewksbury, like a dog tearing the throat from a royal hart? Had he, zealous for the right of his brother, performed the awful necessity of murdering the old king?

All I can say is there was something new hovering over Richard, a ferocity I had never observed in boyhood. It has been said that the spirit of the badge a man chooses overtakes him. I prayed that with such a powerful and wily champion as the boar, my dear lady would be speedily saved!

Richard rode to court and then to his brother Clarence and found matters exactly as we'd said. George declared that he neither knew nor cared where Anne was. Lady Isabel, eyes red, said the same. The entire household, it seemed, had gone deaf and dumb.

What had George done with her? It seemed impossible that all Richard's inquiries and searches led nowhere. Richard even confronted George before the king, and still he received no answer.

King Edward seemed perfectly willing to sidestep the matter and let his brothers fight for possession of the Warwick property. Perhaps it was simply good politics to let George and Richard quarrel. At least this way, George would stay out of the king's hair for a while.

Duke Richard was busy, but a few days later, I was summoned to his presence again.

"Are you better, Rose?"

"Yes. I thank the Blessed Mother for her continual protection—and, ah—for Master Fletcher's great bravery."

"At Tewkesbury, you were in the priory with my dear cousin. Did you see any of the fighting there?"

"We heard, sir, the soldiers enter the sanctuary. Others came to protect us, but we heard.... The—the—imagination—embroiders fearfully."

Richard nodded while I bowed my head, shuddering at the memory. He seemed to understand. I don't know what came over me, but his apparent sympathy sent me babbling.

"Sailing the channel, My Lady and I were sore afraid! Oh, yes, My Lord, such waves, such deeps! But then, at the French court, they smiled to our faces, but their knives were always ready at our backs. Lady Anne and I spent hours upon our knees, calling upon The Blessed Mother to save us."

"Our Lady has delivered you," Richard said. "Continue with your prayers, Rose. The Holy Mother of our Lord must not forget your dear mistress now."

Richard wanted half of the Warwick inheritance, certainly. What man would not? Nevertheless, if anyone could bring Anne home safe again, it would be the Duke of Gloucester.

"Tell me, how did she fare, when last you were together?"

"She has been very brave, sir." My Anne was a wildflower, bearing all weather with grace. "She never cried until they told her about her father. She carried herself like the lady she is, no matter what affliction of body, soul, or heart was visited upon her." I had slipped into nursemaid's hyperbole, but Richard listened.

His eyes searched mine as I spoke, and I saw that in one way, at least, he had not changed. Excitement agitated the green when I spoke of Anne, made it bright as springtime.

A good sign for my Lady, that green!

Anne wasn't certain of her Dickon anymore, but from that moment I was. So much had changed, so many vows broken! Men had learned from these endless wars to distrust everything, even the evidence of their senses.

Then my old playmate's face closed. Before he schooled himself, however, I caught what he didn't want me to see, like sun breaking through clouds above our beloved dales, so I dared to speak again.

"I have prayed things would be better since your brother, King Edward, is come home, but—oh, Your Grace! What can Clarence have done with my poor little lady?" Tears caught me, but this was a time for tears, after all.

"If I have to pull down London," Richard said, "I shall find her." Reflexively, those strong, long fingers gripped the handle of his dagger. I was relieved when, with a snap, he pushed the blade back into the sheath. He had, for an instant, seemed ready to find an outlet for his rage in the body of the person nearest.

Chapter XIII

Every house needs these services."
Richard had set me to work here, gathering and
preparing simples. It was a large task, finding a place for
myself in the kitchen of his house at Crosby's Place. It was
good to have something to do, something useful, when so
many of my thoughts revolved around my poor little lady.

"He says you are trained in surgery, Mistress Rose."
Richard's squire, John A'Parr eyed me uncertainly. He was a
little older than I, but one born to a higher station. There was
nothing beautiful about him, except the ancient depths of his
gray eyes. He had a long head and jaw, a bowl of short brown
hair and an upright carriage.

"The duke won't to the king's surgeon again, but he's got
a wound under the sword arm, down along the ribs, which he
got at Barnet. It doesn't look good to me."

I was astonished. Neither Richard nor his men had made
any fuss. So little, in fact, that it was the first I'd heard tell of
any such wound.

"I've talked His Grace into letting you look. I'll tell you
right now, I think it needs opening." A'Parr's tone indicated
that he'd be glad if anyone looked at it, even a young, female
herbalist. "I can do the cutting," he said. "But perhaps you
know something which will help it to heal, something I don't.
The wound is swollen again and that's dangerous."

"I am sorry to hear the duke took a wound. I didn't
know."

"He's royal tough, raised not to make much of such
things. Still, he does not mend."

"I will certainly be glad to help and hope I can. I thank
you for your confidence. Only tell me what kit is in the

house."

"I will show you what we have, Mistress Rose. If you think we need aught, we shall to the apothecary."

John A'Parr was good as his word, and by evening we were ready to make another treatment of his master's injury. On that day, his squire and I formed a bond in service that would hold until the death of our Lord, Richard Plantagenet.

The duke was above stairs, in his chamber, which was lit with clear burning candles in a candlabrum, not the smoking rush lights of my world. In the background was his bed, the curtains showing a scene of Daniel and the lions. Richard, wearing a knee-length cote-hardie, sat in a chair beside a small table.

On the table was all we'd need: the sharp steel we'd use to open the wound, silver pitcher, basin and goblet, plenty of wool. I'd arrived bearing the last contribution, a bit of sponge and a bowl of Mother Ash's favorite wound wash.

Wearing a face that clearly said *let's get this over*, Richard stood and opened the cote-hardie. He shucked the upper undergarment, made of coarse knitted worsted. John helped him unwind the bandage, and I assisted, applying warm water to the spots where pus had stuck the cloth. I was surprised to discover that he was bandaged all around the torso.

The sight his bare body moved me. All of skinny Dickon, even around his bent spine, was braided muscle. His chest showed a cross of dark hair, a ridged belly, and, By Our Lady—so many hurts! His body was a mass of bruises, but the worst was the pouting purple gash beneath the guard arm. The pain must have been continuous and sharp, but, from his carriage, I never would have guessed.

"My Lord!"

"I've done what I could, Mistress Rose," John said, "We've drained it three times, but his grace will not rest and he doesn't heal."

"The king's brother cannot rest." Richard used a tone that said he and A'Parr had had this discussion before—and that he was heartily sick of it.

"What troubles most?" It was hard to know exactly where

to begin. Of course, as John had said, the wound would have to be opened.

"Here." Richard indicated a large bruise upon his left side. Plate had protected, but his body had still suffered from the blow. Chain mail had bitten straight through the arming doublet into underlying human flesh.

We persuaded him to first swallow wine into which I had stirred a powder. A'Parr, noticing my sleight of hand, winked approval. We both wanted the duke relaxed during the cutting and it would certainly do him good afterward to sleep. I immersed the sponge in the mixture and gently squeezed. It had been a long time since I had dressed a wound.

Not so much that it runs…

Richard lifted his arm and allowed me to apply the potion to his macerated side. At my touch he drew in a sharp breath.

"Saint Paul!"

A'Parr held the bowl, a mess of vinegar, honey and juices of onion and garlic. As I dipped my sponge again, Richard wrinkled his long nose.

"It stinks like a damned French cook shop."

"It will help you to heal, My Lord."

"By the Blessed Anthony, Rose!" Richard switched saints in the stress of the moment. "They'll say I haven't bathed since Easter."

"Never mind, My Lord," A Parr said. "The ladies will have The Duke of Gloucester anyway."

"Your tongue, John! Hold what you wish to keep."

"The sting is cleansing." Pus began to run and I cleared it with bandage.

"Stinks and stings! You call this medicine, Rosie?"

There was more slights as he winced and endured my ministrations. The jokes were uncharacteristic. A'Parr and I knew it came from the combination of exhaustion, pain, wine and those strong powders.

"I think you've a cracked rib, my Lord."

"More than one, if you ask me," said John. "He can barely tolerate binding." The squire was right where I needed him to be, dried moss in hand. It took all four hands to apply the poultice. Then, while he held it in place, I wrapped it down, winding a long strip of clean bandage about the duke. As I did so, I admired the muscle he'd made, flesh gracefully grown about d his crookedness.

"How long has this been so, Your Grace?"

"Stabbed at Barnet, the ribs during the Kentish rising." John answered for his master.

"This needs to be opened." It was clear after only a cursory examination of the gash.

"Exactly as I said, Your Grace." A'Parr couldn't resist an 'I told you so'.

"Then do it." Richard sat perfectly still as we worked upon him. How it reminded me of the old days! His grim silence was the same, but the sickly, skinny boy with the crook in his back had grown into a man who was as slick as a greyhound and hard as the proverbial rock. His way of battle had not changed, either.

See you in hell!

"I am glad you have come, Rose," A'Parr said softly. We shared a look across the strong bare back of our Lord.

I worked close, carefully winding. There was not an ounce to spare on Richard. Even at rest, he was taut as a drawn bow. His hands retained their almost feminine beauty, even though they had become strong from constant contact with sword and bridle. Their natural elegance was enhanced with rings, a sapphire on the pointing finger, heavy gold upon the fourth, a flat cut ruby for the thumb.

His skin was fine and clear. He had the long, dark lashes I remembered, but there was something about his face that still tugged at my heartstrings, an uneasy mingling of youth and age. He'd worked hard to create this man's body, to overcome the mistakes Nature had made. Past and present pain, past and present duty—strain and suffering were drawn in every premature line.

My work took time. Hot water helped with probing the underarm wound, taken below the protection of the *rarebrace*. While he'd fought from horseback, a dagger had entered from below, through an opening only protected by mail. There was pus, swelling, and worst of all, odor.

"I cannot use it as I did. I cannot extend it."

"You go too fast, my Lord," A'Parr chided gently. "Let it heal a little and then work it a little, heal a little and so on, as the king's surgeon said."

"You and the surgeon are both old women. With Lord Falconbridge and the Kentishmen inside the gates of London, when was there time?"

John A'Parr sighed. He and I had earlier agreed, after a long discussion, that I would be the one to open the duke's wound. "He knows when I am about to do it," John explained, "and then he stops me."

"Christ's Blood!" Richard exclaimed. I had steeled myself, and, without prelude, slit the infection. Sweat popped out all over his torso; trickles raced each other down his hard sides.

"Looks to be on the mend," A'Parr declared. "The pus runs clear, my Lord."

"Ring bells!" Richard bared his teeth in the semblance of a grin, but he'd gone white.

"I will cleanse it and pack it with bee jelly and spider's web. Mother Ash always swore by those."

A'Parr and I were busy for a time, absorbed in the business. We wanted to clean the wound, dress it, sew it, and then let his body finish the job. Infection, no matter how slight, can poison the blood. We were almost done, when my necklace slipped out. I paid no mind and finished tying up the bandage, but Richard's saw it.

Playfully, one long finger inside the chain, he tugged. "What's this, Rose?"

The braided silk with the white rose pendant, my holy medal—and Anne's ring—tinkled forth.

"This is not your only finery, is it, Rosie?"

"Oh no, my lord. I have others my dear lady has given, but these I like best, for—for—they remind me of happier days, when—we—we were all at Middleham, Your Grace."

"Happier days for me, also." Curious and ready to tease, he caught the ring, which I think at first he took for a love gift. My heart stopped.

Oh, his look! Sharp as the blade I'd just used, and, I swear, it hurt me every bit as much.

"This is of my great-grand-dam! Why is it here?" He shouted the last words, unfettered both by his Plantagenet disposition and the drugs. His hand closed upon the cord and for a moment I feared he would choke me. By that strong silk, he drew me close. We ended nose to nose.

"My Lady Anne said…"

"Yes?" His hollow cheeks were livid. In the background, I could see John hovering, afraid, but not daring to intervene.

"She said I was to keep it safe for her! She said…."

"Yes?" This was a prince, holding me as much with his eyes as with his hand.

"She said she mus' gie her husband—th'Prince o' Lancaster—th'faithful obedience whi' she promised a'fore God." I gabbled the words, fast as I could.

There was a long pause in which the fire in his eyes went out. When he released me, I straightened and took several prudent steps back.

"Leave us, John." A wave of his ring covered hand. He seemed suddenly weary, as if the burst of rage had exhausted him.

"My Lord, may I…" John began.

"Out!"

Knowing the better part of valor, John withdrew. I'd never been afraid of Richard before, not even at Tewkesbury when he'd come to us, covered in fresh gore, but here, I was terrified. Even more so when I heard the snap of the latch and knew we were alone.

Richard cleared his throat. The eyes I met were bitter.

"The truth, Rose."

"Yes, Your Grace." I folded my hands and cast my gaze down.

"Look at me."

"Yes, Your Grace." I lifted my eyes, though I didn't want to.

"The marriage of Lady Anne and the Prince of Lancaster…" Richard got only that far. We stared at each other, and then I answered what he could not seem to ask.

I swallowed hard. "Consummated, your Grace. Just after we reached Honfleur."

When he said nothing, just continued to sear me with that stare, I dared, "My Lady only did as a wife must, Your Grace."

"I do not need a servant to explain!"

I fell to my knees, stiff with fear. In the far off back of my head, I could hear my mother whispering scornfully:

Men are mad, mad creatures, especially when their passion is thwarted. Look to the bulls fighting in the pasture, my daughter. There you see figured the proud reason of men!

"Here to me!" Richard shouted again, as if I were one of his dogs. He'd picked up his own dagger, laid with the bowl and the rest of our mess upon the table.

Swallowing hard, I began to crawl across the broad dark boards toward his feet. He stepped forward and caught the cord, and, in a flash of steel, cut. The floor received everything.

"Oblige me."

A moment later I'd retrieved the ring and handed it up. Those long fingers accepted, touching mine with unexpected gentleness. His attention turned away from me and entirely to that ancient braid of gold.

"Leave me, Rose." He gazed at the ring, as if it could speak and tell him the rest of what he longed to know.

Quickly, I scrabbled on the floor, picking up the white rose. The figure of Saint Alkelda was harder to find, but finally my hand brushed the jet pendant. Once in my grasp, I backed up swiftly. Close to the door, I stood, spun around, and seized the latch. Escape was in view.

"Rose!"

I didn't want to, but I stopped. "Your Grace?"

"We will speak again."

"Your Grace." Another curtsy and I was through the heavy, metal braced door. Here I promptly ran against John A'Parr.

"Are you all right?" He grabbed my shoulders.

"Yes."

"John! Come here!" From within, Richard called.

John shook his dark head, gave my arms a parting squeeze, and, with an "At once, Your Grace!" went to his master.

Slowly, medals gripped tightly, I walked along the upper balcony, on my way to the stairs and the servant's quarters beyond.

Would her lack of virginity matter?

I supposed it was foolish to worry. The land was still attached to the lady, after all. However, I knew that a dream Richard had been holding like a treasure had been lost. Duty had cheated these courtly lovers.

I had another worry as well, a dark secret. Anne had not bled since France, and she and I were the only ones who knew. Could she, my poor lost lady, be carrying Prince Edward's child? I wondered if Richard, if Anne, if any of us, could weather such a storm.

As for Master Hugh and I—well, I returned the ring and he accepted it from me—grumpily—but, apparently, without great rancor. We continued to speak, a relief to me, for now there was a blood bond between us. It would have been pure folly to put such a staunch friend aside.

In the kitchen, we often took our bread and ale at the same time. He did not speak of marriage again and I imagined—I prayed—he was done with it. I was glad, for though I did not wish to marry him, he was not only a good man, but an interesting one.

"Gloucester killed Prince Edward?" Hugh snorted when I asked if he knew anything of it. "Ha! That's a good one! Clarence made a fine tale of it, did he? I'll wager he did! You know why? 'Cause he's the man as done it."

My jaw dropped.

"Oh, yes," Hugh said, leaning back, pleased he knew something else I didn't. "There in the meadow, in the shadow of the abbey, the young prince came to ask his brother-in-law for help. Cold steel is what he got."

"By Our Lady!"

"I know a pikeman—as right a fellow as ever lived—who saw it. The duke said he would help and when the young prince came to him, George fell upon the lad and slit his throat with one of those slender French daggers."

"He tormented my poor lady, said Gloucester did the deed." I shuddered, thinking of all the fine detail of his gruesome story.

Surprise! Yes, I could imagine it all over Edward's elegant features as he, invincible seventeen, felt the fatal sting, saw his life's blood running down the beautiful coat of arms the Neville ladies had so thoughtfully embroidered.

❧

"Rose!"

I sat up in the room that I shared with the other females of house. There stood John A'Parr. A flaring, sputtering reed light held by a bleary-eyed maid at his side pierced our night.

"My Lord is calling for you. Do not stand upon ceremony. Come at once."

He tossed a knee-length cote-hardie at me and then backed through the door, perhaps intimidated by a room full of women, all naked beneath the covers. The maid with the light remained.

I dragged myself out of bed. Hung for the night upon pegs, I found my shift among the others. Then, I picked up the cote-hardie. It was light wool, old, worn, but made very fine, perhaps one of Richard's. I threw it on over my shift, found a girdle to belt it beneath my bosom and then followed him out.

"What is it?"

"Hush 'til we get there."

A kitchen wench stood outside, my basket of supplies over her arm, so after collecting this, the two of us went straight upstairs to the duke's chamber. I couldn't imagine what was going on. John didn't seem fearful, so whatever had happened mustn't be too serious.

Richard was seated when I came in, just like the last time, except tonight he was on the edge of his bed. The curtains were opened, and he was ready, white undergarment opened. A blood-stained cloth was wrapped about his upper arm, the same side we'd last treated.

"Not again!" It was out before I could stop myself. Over my shoulder I caught a glimpse of solemn John A'Parr.

"Not exactly, Rose." Richard was rueful.

"Let me see, My Lord."

"The Duke of Clarence..." John began, but Richard interrupted.

"John!"

Of course, this was already too much. I lifted my eyes from the bandage to Richard.

What had George dared now?

"My Lord?"

"Never mind. Only tend to it." Richard sounded weary.

I saw that it was not the old wound, but a long gash on the outside of his bicep. As I began to unwrap the hastily made dressing, fresh blood oozed. This was not bad, for bleeding cleansed.

"'Tis fresh and clean, but not too deep, thank The Blessed Mother," John said.

"How comes this, My Lord?" I tried a question, while gently lifting the gore with a clean cloth.

"Curiosity killed the cat," Richard said. "To work, Rose."

As before, John assisted. First, he brought his master a draught for the pain. While Richard downed that, I cleaned the area so I could see.

The duke winced. Once he even swore, as I stitched over the deepest part. Ever in mind of his high place, he was always loath to exhibit any weakness.

"This is so near the first," I said by way of explanation, pausing for a moment to let him rest, needle in hand. "Flesh likes not to be put another trial so soon."

"Nor do I." He joked, perhaps by way of apologizing for his earlier shortness. "Just sew it, Rose. Don't mind me. One of these days, I'll learn to keep my guard up."

My mind was full of questions, even while my hands

worked. This was a neat wound, made with a sharp, clean weapon. It was the kind of injury you'd see at a tourney, when one of the participants had lost his temper.

After the new injury was firmly closed, I took a moment to reexamine the old, to be certain it was still healing. I was relieved to find it unopened and looking far better than even a few days ago. As I wrapped and secured a new bandage there, A'Parr went out with the basin of bloody water.

In leaning over the duke, my braid, made loosely for the night, slipped over my shoulder, and began to slowly unravel. When he caught it, I went on working, thinking he meant to push it out of the way. Instead, he tugged gently, running his free hand along the length.

"Beautiful hair, Rose, as beautiful as when we were children."

These days it was always braided, modestly tucked beneath veils and caps. A passer-by might see the end of a braid, but that was all.

To my surprise, Richard did not relinquish his hold. Elegant fingers continued to sample the weight, the softness.

"'Tis the same color as those freckles of yours. Remember how the men-at-arms used to tease? Roan Rose, one of them called you. You pitched wash water on him from the tower window."

I remembered it well. That long ago flirting had made me think of myself in a grown-up way I hadn't been ready to do.

I looked up and met Richard's eyes. A dangerous green tide sparkled. His strong hand, full of my hair, slipped to catch me about the neck. His lips met mine. An instant later, he'd pulled me into his bed.

What he was about was clear. A thousand emotions, a thousand cautions, tugged and pulled. I did protest, resting my fingers against his lips as soon as they left mine.

"My Lord," I said, "I—I have never—never—"

"Hush, Rose." He kissed my fingertips and smiled. "Don't tell me you're still a virgin."

"Indeed—I am."

"If that is true, you must yield to me at once."

I stared at him, jaw dropped like a fool. There was a sudden familiar smile, the boy who'd kissed me by the strawberry patch. Slowly, a long forefinger stroked my nose and then moved outward, drawing a line along my cheekbone.

"Lie with me, Roan Rose."

He was a prince, used to submission. He was my old friend, now miles ahead in what he knew. I was a maid, but, he—he was a man.

The kiss that came was sudden, sweet. When I let him taste, he caught my hands and pressed me back and down— deep, deep into his bed. There was wine in his mouth, the lusty dregs of an evening at King Edward's court. Holy Mother! He knew how to kiss, and he knew other arts, too....

An actual, earthly door creaked—John making his return. I could have stopped Richard then, for if I had asked, he would have, but I did not. Quietly, discreetly, the door closed again.

The act is shameful if reason is engaged, and the unavoidable, awkward pause as he stripped off the rest of his clothing brought me to my senses. A stripped man is a stripped man, no matter how good looking he is and how much you may have been—but an eye-blink earlier—lusting for him.

I studied my fate—hard, lean, ready! Lost now, I shucked my kirtle. He helped me pull it off over my head and then put his arms around me. There we were, flesh on flesh. Eagerly, he laid me down, getting between my legs with not a whit more prelude. I trembled at the shock and then cried out.

"My Lord!" The virgin knot was not quick to untie.

"There, there, Rose." He spoke gently, even while seeking a better seat. His lips encouraged, distracted, as he bent above me, a taut and limber bow.

"Your knee, Rose. Here. Like this." He was gentle, panting a little from the strain of self-control. "Otherwise, it hurts my arm."

Oh, yes! The wound I'd just sewn and bound. We women are ever and always accommodating.

Innocently obeying, I had a glimpse of his hand—the rings—my freckled knee. It was not, as he well knew, a position from which to resist. There were sounds, all of which

I'd heard before, my cries and his triumph, the whisper of flesh upon flesh.

On the other hand, the creaking of the bed, the bodily effusions, shocked and embarrassed. I remembered Master Whitby and my mother and what I had once believed she endured beneath him.

I thought of Anne and her Prince, the dance more beautiful as the partners were so young and fair, yet ever and always the same. Now, here I was in the ancient and often-performed role—woman—wriggling and gasping underneath.

He stayed, savoring, kissing, whispering silk and honey, of long ago strawberries, calling me his "Roan Rose." He said other things that were not true, although, in such passages, men always say them.

Even in sin, I wished for absolution, to hold fast to my innocence. For years after this night, I would have to strive to silence my heart; to forget the words the Duke of Gloucester spoke to me.

His after-the-fact wooing led us to further repetition. This time, he left me in a deep languor, lying-loose limbed in the fine linen, his lithe body still topping me, his lips and fingers moving at will. He showed me what he knew, how the fiery animal spirit rises from the altar of humble flesh. We danced. We wrestled. At last, we drifted to dream, his arm around me.

The next morning, there at dawn, I woke when he did. My eyes met his, and I saw the change. It was over.

"Ah—Rose!" He spoke my name, but his voice was so sad. He shook his dark head in slow dismay, as if he'd been knocked cold and was only now returning to consciousness.

"This was not well done."

It had been very well done indeed, but I lay silent, feeling his hands—in spite of the words—linger. The lines etching themselves upon his melancholy face showed my dear Lord headed straight from whitest heat to coldest, ashy repentance.

May the Blessed Mother succor a woman when the man

who has hotly bedded her turns down this road! Not a minute later, he was up, hastily belting a long white under-robe over his thin self. It was like suddenly being adrift in high, rolling water.

When he turned to face me again, his face was so strange, so dark, I shrank against the bolster, afraid. Would my beloved Dickon prove to be one of those men who laid his sin at the woman's door?

"Dear Rosalba." His voice was so strained, and I understood his fierce displeasure was mostly with himself. "I swear to you that this will never be again."

I began to weep in good earnest. Men and women, always at sixes and sevens! Not only the differences of temperament between ewe and ram, but Holy Church, which says this act, done by all creatures alike, is sin—to further confuse and damn us!

Richard's cast of mind was absolutely serious. In spite of the exquisite breach he'd made, he'd probably not had so very many women. I don't think he quite understood that I had followed his lead because I trusted him, because, deep in my heart, I loved him.

"The fault is mine," he said. "But if aught comes of what we have done, I shall acknowledge." Then, stiff as a tin soldier, he faced about and left the room.

I rolled over and cried. Cried and cried, until I could cry no more. He would hate me! Hate me! Despise my woman's weakness! And, Anne! Anne! What had I done? Even if he did find her, I would now, certainly, be sent away.

It would be impossible to keep a woman he'd so fervently swived in his household. Especially one to whom, only a few hours before, he'd confessed such tenderness!

Unlike his brothers, Richard took the sin of venery seriously, but I knew the rules. Women were the ones who must say "no," who must insist upon it, for men, especially young men—most especially a young lord—could not be expected to control themselves.

At least, I thought, the sin was not the mortal one of adultery. Nevertheless, I knew that in some way deeper than

161

church law, our trespass had been huge. Richard belonged to Anne and she to him. Who knew this better than I? Yet, I had imprudently lain with what had been Anne Neville's from the first day she had drawn breath.

God's teeth! What a fool!

Someone entered the room. I knew, without even looking, who it was. Miserably, I pulled the blanket over my head. Hair flowing loose, I was nothing this morning but a naked, fallen woman, one old enough to have known better.

Stripped, heartily swived, and abandoned, as significant as the remains of last night's supper!

"Mistress Rosalba." John A'Parr was formal. "I have brought water and towels. Knock at the door if you need aught else. When you are ready, I shall accompany you back."

The head disappeared. I stared at the quivering curtains and shuddered, now afraid, into the bargain. Nothing a prince did was secret. Even if A'Parr held his peace, the maid who had led us down the passage—as well as those with whom I shared a room—knew that I had not returned from a late night summons by the Duke of Gloucester.

In one lightning stroke, the applecart that had been my life was upset, more terrible to me than the whole war. Pieces of my life rolled around me, scattered, like a shattered crock.

Anne! Anne! Suddenly, all I could think about was her. Little white points of light, tiny, captive stars, dashed about between my eyes and the gray stone wall. It is not the sex itself which is the sin, but the tangle it makes.

Dragging myself out of bed, I found the basin. My knees shivered in a strange way, an uncoordinated weakness coming from the part taught that nightlong lesson.

And, oh, what if this single night, as he had so ceremoniously suggested, bore fruit?

I had been taught that strong pleasure led to conception, most particularly of sons. The depth of my despair reached to hell's fiery pit! At last I tapped at the door to be let out, but John, instead of letting me out, entered. At first, this frightened me, as if he, too, might want a share.

"I didn't know, Mistress Rose!" He held up his hands in

gesture of harmlessness. Apparently, he, decent fellow, felt it necessary to explain his part. "I never imagined the duke so intended."

I nodded, but I could barely meet his eyes. It didn't help, either, that he could barely meet mine.

"I don't know what devil got into him. You know—you know—he isn't like the others. And, and," he went on with a kindness I shall never cease to bless, "neither are you, Mistress Rose."

"I love him very much, but I should not." I was ready to break down again.

John nodded, his long face full of pity. "We who are close to the Duke of Gloucester, we all love him deeply, our brave young lord."

I templed my fingers over my nose and drew a deep breath. Perhaps, it would calm me.

"The Duke of Clarence wounded him?"

Two body servants alone, at last we could speak. John nodded.

"In torchlight where the horses were being held at the palace, my lord tried to question his brother about the Lady Anne."

"Clarence! With a skinful, I'll wager."

"Yes, bloated as a toad. He said My Lord of Gloucester would never find Lady Anne and that all which was The Earl of Warwick's would be his alone. Our lord held his temper, but Clarence—Clarence—"

"George drew."

The first name slipped out, but John, usually so correct, only answered, "Yes."

"'Tis beyond anything! Dukes—brothers—brawling at the king's door!"

"My Lord did no more than parry until his brother cut him. After that, he put the big fool down." John's lip curled with disdain.

"Clarence was wounded?"

"No, but my Lord knocked him into the finest, deepest pool of horse piss ever seen. There's a fine French suit he shall wear no more."

Heaven help us, at this bleak moment, we shared a smile.

"Your discretion?"

"I heard nothing, Master A'Parr."

"And you may ever trust me with this of yours. Now, come. I will see you safe away."

He did so, negotiating the passages so we were not particularly noted. To this faithful servant, I was another secret to be kept, part of the strange night just passed.

For the next few days, I never strayed from kitchen or garden. I grubbed in my oldest clothes, patiently teaching the cook's children again and again which were weeds and which were not. I showed them how to wash the growing salad to keep off thrips. I picked and chopped vegetables for the cooks. I harvested and cleaned sage, thyme, parsley, lemon balm, rosemary, feverfew and hyssop, getting help from a kitchen lad in hanging them from the wooden beams.

Of course, the news flew about the house like a loose bird. Soon, the housemaids came giggling to ask what their stern "praying and fighting lord" was like "between the sheets."

A man-at-arms, a gruff fellow with one eye, caught my arm and whispered tales of girls at Edward's court with whom Richard had lain. One had died in childbed, leaving "a fine boy whom my Lord acknowledges." The other bastard, he said, was a daughter, carefully tucked away with the mother's family on the Marches.

It was useless, I knew, to deny, so I looked the man in the eye and said, "My Lord of Gloucester wishes nothing more from me."

The rogue regarded me, his single eye glittering. "Told you he was done, didn't he?" He grinned, speared an apple from the basket and began to quarter it upon the table. "Always heartily repents, does that pious gentleman."

It rang of the plain truth. I blushed, while wanting to cry.

The blush couldn't be helped; the tears I fought back. This fool would never understand. How could he? I hardly did myself.

"My Lord Duke will grow mad like old King Henry if he does penance for mere swiving." He took a slice of apple upon his knife and carefully put it into his mouth. "King Edward, now, there's a man with no monkish tattle on his mind! Changes his bedmates more often than his linen. Drinks and fucks all night, they do say, one lady after another."

He closed his eye, to savor the lewd vision he'd conjured up. I went on chopping, wondering when, if ever, this conversation would be done. Who says sins are only paid for in hell?

"Religion is all very well for an old man who can't get it up anymore and is soon to die, but not to regularly plow and plant when young? Why, 'tis most unhealthy." He gazed at me in a reflective way that let me know that if he were the Noble Duke of Gloucester, he'd summon a far lovelier girl with whom to perform this essential task.

Each and every one of these conversations were sojourns in hell's fire. I loved Richard. I loved—and I feared—for my sweet lady. The winks, the jokes, were like scalds. I prayed to The Blessed Mother, telling my Aves fifty times on my knees morning and night, but I did not make formal confession. Of all gossips on this earth, priests are the worst.

A lord would be unlikely to show his face in the kitchen, or its adjunct, the garden. He had councils to meet, judgments to make, soldiers and messages to send, accounts and deeds to examine over the shoulders of inky fingered clerks. I felt safe in my world, well hidden, and the duke did not summon me.

This was permitted for a week, but I should have known that to Richard, so meticulous, we were unfinished business. Here he came, tan boots up the row, slim and elegant. I glanced up and saw him, a padded round hat upon his head, a long dark cote-hardie making him look more like a sage councilor than a young courtier. Today, he looked more than usually unhappy.

My heart sank when I saw him approaching. At least, one fear had been put to rest. This morning I'd had to jump out of bed and tie on the rags. I was cramping and bleeding like a fountain, which did not improve my mood. I hung my head. I loved him, but the shame I knew we shared was unbearable.

"My Lord," I said, looking down at the dirt and his fine leather boots. I prayed to faint right there among the sprouting salad. "Have you—have you—found my dearest lady?"

"Not yet, Mistress Rose. Though news I have this morning makes me more hopeful than I have been in weeks."

"Ah, My Lord!" I gained courage when he followed my lead away from our terrible subject. "Please tell me."

"I have hold of a fellow who will—soon—point us at the mark, Mistress Rose. However," he paused, miserably, "there is another matter upon which you and I must speak." He stretched out a jeweled hand in that familiar gesture of affection and command. There was naught to do except to clasp—so warm and strong—and rise.

"I have done badly." He said it again. We had gone where he led, to a bench beneath a trellis of trailing hops, where we were screened. Nevertheless, I could feel eyes upon us from every window.

"On'y what ma'come to pass 'tween a Lord and his handmaid." I'd been reduced to a Yorkshire mumble.

Richard smiled slightly, perhaps at the dialect to which agonies of embarrassment had driven me. Then, his lips tightened, and he said, "But, Rose, 'twas unkind."

There was nothing I could say in return. He called what he had done "unkind," so he did not love me, not in the way I loved him. How could he? What we'd done was wrong, wrong for all three points of our childhood triangle. I stared at the dirty, freckled hands now huddled in my lap.

"Oh, Rose. You have lost what was the right of a husband."

This nearly sank me. It was beyond unsettling to see him so guilty, worse than the years in hellfire I doubtless merited. Unable to stop myself now, I began to sob. Hazel eyes fixed me, the only steady point in a whirling universe. "You—you—know," he struggled to speak, suddenly no prince at all. "I do not—love—lightly." His hand reached for mine, pressed my fingers hard. Just as quickly, as if my flesh burned red hot, he let go.

"Please, my Lord, the highest matter is that my dear Lady Anne must never know. I could not bear to cause her pain."

Something larger than gratitude sparked his eyes. At that ragged instant, I would not have traded anything in the world for what I saw there. We gazed at each other, relieved that we'd found our remedy.

"Nor I."

We would continue to do what we had always done. We would set lust aside and care for Anne, center of our world.

"For your sake, Your Grace," I whispered, one last speech in this final moment of intimacy, "I imagined myself free." Free as my mother had been upon the night she'd conceived me!

It was a bold speech, but I'd thought of almost nothing else for the past week. It was, I knew quite well, the only time we'd ever speak of this, the last time he would acknowledge what we'd done.

He nodded understanding, holding me with his eyes, green sparking the brown, his emotion a visible bright tide.

He cares for me, I thought, as much as ever a lord may care for such as me. Whatever happens next, at least this once I've seen it in his eyes.

Chapter XIV

I have been thinking, Mistress Rose."

"Yes, Milord." I curtsied, eyes low, and waited.

"I wish you to remove to St. Martin Le Grand."

If he'd struck me with his fist, I couldn't have been more surprised. I was being banished, sent from his house—and, worse, sent to a place where a woman could disappear beneath a nun's black robes—forever!

"Your Grace?"

"You will stay there until such time as you may be of service to your mistress."

I tried to swallow the lump in my throat. I tried to hide my feelings in another curtsy, but my knees failed. I remained a sorry, quivering heap upon the floor.

I suppose he waived the others out of earshot. At last, when I finally managed to look up at him, we were alone.

"Rose, this is best. You know why."

"Because—because—there is talk, my Lord."

"Yes." Contempt sounded thickly. His privacy had been breached; he violently resented it. "But when I find Lady Anne," he continued in a gentler tone, "she must be placed in the protection of the church. It would not be proper to bring her here, for that would place her under an unseemly obligation."

"Yes. It is as you say, My Lord." He was right. Yes, he was, but I knew Richard was equivocating. I must be sent away, out of reach.

A further suspicion grew, like a poisoned mushroom. I feared that Anne would never be served by a living soul who knew what had happened at Crosby Place.

"You will allow me to tend her, My Lord? As I have always done? Oh, your Grace, you know she is my heart." I was a raven trapped in a tower, wings beating upon stone!

He nodded, but he did not speak. I knew he was holding

back, something I would not be told until later.

"Up now, Rose." He offered me a gloved hand and assumed a faint smile, one intended to be encouraging. "Pack your medicines. My Lady Abbess expects to welcome you before the bells of Compline."

I left his presence shaking. No one spoke to me, just drew back as I passed, as if I bore the mark of leprosy. I was to be sent away, into a nunnery, where, for a modest price, troublesome women may be cast forever....

On my way to gather my medicines as he directed, I knew I could not enter the kitchen, now in the after-supper lull, and face all who would be there. To collect myself, I passed into the garden, intending to circle amid the green for a few minutes.

Pick a sprig of lavender, I thought. *Calm yourself.*

No sooner had I begun my perambulation, bruised herbs to my nose, then a brawny hand reached from a hedge to catch me, then slam my body against the smooth daub surface of a wall.

"I hear you played handmaid to the Duke of Gloucester, you miserable, ungrateful bitch!"

It was Hugh, not only drunk, but straight to the point. We were hidden, but not out of earshot of the usual traffic about the house.

"Let me go, Hugh Fletcher. I am not yours to command."

He obeyed, after a fashion, slamming me against the wall once more, this time so hard I saw stars.

"Slut!" The expression on his face made me wonder if he had a knife, if he intended to assuage his anger with my blood.

"As you say." I loosed a helpless shower of tears. He couldn't have caught me at a worse moment. After the interview with Richard, I was weak as a kitten.

"Christ!" His gray eyes bulged in a mad and terrifying way, his face blotchy red. "You assent?"

"Why sin again by lying?" I clutched my medals. *This accursed life,* I thought, backed against that wall, *will soon be done.*

"S'Blood!" Hugh roared it. Spittle flew into my face.

I cowered before his great, clenched fists, but he only

smashed one into the wall, cracking plaster before bolting away across the garden. Heedless, he crashed over bushes and crushed cabbages and herbs alike, a perfect madman.

Chapter XV

"istress Rosalba! You are to come at once."
A strange, disheveled man had rushed into the kitchen at St. Martin's. He wore a filthy cloak, the kind that has seen better days on the back of a gentleman.

"Gather your medicine!"

How he'd come within the sacred precinct was anybody's guess. He grabbed my wrist and held up his token: Isabel of Castile's ancient ring.

In this unlikely garb came Richard's surrogate, from his mouth, the command. Although I did not know him, I certainly knew the ring. My heart skipped a beat,

Reaching beneath the table, pulse pounding, I seized the basket I had so carefully prepared. It was heavy, containing everything for which I could imagine a use.

"Who is this?" The cook stepped up, his enormous arms bare. "What do you want, Rags, here in my kitchen?" He hefted a meat chopper from the block.

"It's right, Master Clipsham. He comes from my Lord of Gloucester."

Unconvinced, Clipsham stood like a statue. How this garish beggar could belong to a lord was a monstrous puzzle. Ignoring him, I dropped the basket on the counter and swiftly checked the contents one last time. Bandages, clean wool, burnt wine, an expensive vial of poppy, powders that would break fever, honey, camphor and ground pepper.

Clipsham the cook stuck his blade into the greasy block with a chunk. The buzzing kitchen fell silent. Without another word, I picked up my basket and headed for the door. As the beggar held it open for me, quiet reigned.

Once beyond the sacred walls, in the rutted, muddy alley, he took the basket and swung it into a waiting cart. Then, taking my hand, he helped me step from the stairs to the wheel, and onward, into the seat. The waiting driver flipped his reins and the shaggy pony moved off with a jerk. Like a bundle of tossed garbage, the "beggar" flung himself in behind.

We trotted from St. Martin Le Grand straight to a river wharf, where the well-mannered beggar helped me down. A boat waited. Stepping aboard, we were rowed at a great rate, with the current, down river. Here, in the hazy summer light, I had a chance to study my companion.

He was tall and strong, saturnine and sensual, with full lips and large eyes, like a Frenchman, or that yet rarer kind of foreign beast—an Italian. On close inspection, his disarray smacked of art. I noticed that while his clothes were smoky, filthy and ripped, he did not have the foul, rotten cheese body smell of a genuine beggar.

Viewed from a distance, the Thames glinted magically. Up close, it was dark, muddy, and odorous. All manner of offal floated by, thickening as we rowed deeper into the city. On shore, the world went on, the cries of hawkers sounding as we sailed beneath bridges upon which shops crowded. Wagons, throngs of folk, curtained litters—the city pushed, shoved, and shouted from the banks. Slops came showering from a window overhanging the water, nearly landing in our boat.

In Yorkshire, the rivers were rapid and bright. They sang, merrily begging you to trail your fingers. Here, just looking into that syrupy darkness seemed to pose a threat. Digging in my pocket, I came up with a small sachet—rosemary, cloves, and scented geranium—which I held to my nose.

"Stinks today," observed the beggar. His phrase was colored by an unfamiliar accent.

"Yes. It is horrible."

He gave me a sly smile, which set off a distant tingle of alarm. *What if he came—somehow—from George?* If so, I would soon meet fate in those dirty depths, of that I had not the smallest doubt.

"You are from the north country?"

I nodded, kept my nose against the sachet. The stench around us grew as a bloated dead dog floated past.

"Pink cheeks do not come from this air." He waved a dirty paw, a strangely elegant gesture. I did not reply, just gripped the handle of my basket. We were approaching Southwark, the opposite side—the bad side—of the river. Here were the notorious stews and houses of ill-repute.

The boatman steered toward a dilapidated dock. I was beyond grateful to disembark. Handed to the wharf, basket in hand, I was glad to leave the narrow, rocking boat, and close confine with this queer person. Once on land, however, gazing at the buildings that leaned over the stale water, I had a moment of hesitation.

The sign of the house upon whose dock we landed dangled from a lopsided, sinking post, as off kilter as the neighborhood. Of flexible daub and wattle, the buildings seemed caught in the act of sliding down the bank. The advertisement showed a naked woman mounted upon a monstrous chimera, a cock's head upon the body of a horse. Ride a cock horse! Pagan fancy was not my first notion.

Plain enough what kind of establishment we were about to enter. I would not have taken a step further, if John A'Parr hadn't suddenly appeared, loping toward me, hands extended. His long pale face held, perhaps for the first time ever, a bright flush.

"This way! Hurry! The duke awaits."

We entered by the river door, guarded by a familiar pair of men-at-arms. Inside, the place was occupied by others, all wearing *Blanc Sanglier,* the duke's badge. There was no one else. A malefactor with branded cheek and a huge girth leaned sullenly upon the bar. His face was bleeding and raw-meat red. A blousy woman stepped up, made a trembling, submissive curtsy, and then asked, "Milord's midwife?"

I could feel the blood drain from my face, but John said, "Lead on!"

Ducking beneath a low doorway, I followed as she waddled along the curving, sagging corridor. The house had drifted so far out of plumb you couldn't see one end from the other.

Windows had been cut in the inside walls. The views were rooms of such squalor and disarray they would have shamed the meanest hut on Wenslydale.

173

We paused at a door, while the woman nervously fumbled with the latch. As it opened, a small candle appeared, held in a hand I knew was Richard's. At once I scented the reek of a woman with the moon heavily upon her. Without so much as a by-your-leave, I rushed past him, gripping my basket.

There Anne sat, knees curled under her chin, upon a sheeted pallet. She and the bed were the only white things in the room. A fine cloak was wrapped around her, but she started as I appeared, and I saw she was stripped to her kirtle and her head was wrapped in a linen turban. Only her eyes, that incredible robin's egg blue, were exactly as I remembered.

"Rosalba!" Anne stretched out a piteous hand.

I dropped the basket and threw my arms around her. I could tell she was feverish, and the smell of blood strong. She began to weep against me and I could feel her narrow shoulders shaking.

The door closed. Richard was gone. Only the candle, placed in a wall sconce, remained.

I rocked Anne against me and let her cry. The duke must have stayed with her, but she had waited to cry her heart out until she found my arms.

"My Lord has you safe at last." What a blaze of feeling! Joy at finding her alive, joy at holding my sweet friend! At the same time, a spinning, shrinking figure that was my Dickon went whirling away from me forever. "You are safe now, Milady! Safe!"

Anne cried as if she would never stop. I rocked her, remembering the croup, when I'd been a green ten-year-old, mothering a sickly noble child. While she soaked my shoulder with tears and snot, I kept repeating that she was safe, that I would never leave her again. At last, she quieted a little.

"Are you injured, Milady?" I was weeping myself. "Have they—they—abused you?"

I prayed the question would not start those sobs again, but I had to know. There were medicines she must have, and quickly, if those vermin had dared to so insult my precious Lady!

She understood what I was asking. That she did not at once answer, but only began that hopeless weeping made my blood run cold.

"You are safe." I retreated to that, stroking her poor shuddering back, "Safe—safe—safe."

"I will never be safe." Anne's voice was low and desperate. "For when I sleep—oh, dearest friend! Of what shall I dream?" When she had calmed a little, I got a valerian tincture mixed with brandy into her. There was a good supply of bandage, so, as soon as she'd swallowed her medicine, we discarded the bloody rags and fixed on new. She would feel a little better simply by being cleaner.

Ready now, I opened the door. Richard was there, standing like a black statue. He came in and settled the cloak once more around Anne's thin shoulders. Like a parent dressing a child, he tied the cord beneath her chin. She stood, accepting his service, face glazed with tears, eyes lowered. I could feel her humiliation rise like a fog.

Richard did not address her. He did not even seem to be seeing her, but, like a good servant, he did what was needed, then picked her up. One bare white arm encircled his shoulder and she hid her face against his chest.

In a curtained litter, the duke conveyed my mistress to the sanctuary at St. Martin Le Grand. Although the nuns were shocked by my decision, as soon as hot water in quantity could be produced, I bathed her, sitting her in a wooden laundry tub lined with sheets. From my basket, I retrieved rose petals, geranium, powdered thyme and lavender. After steeping, as if for tea, I added this to the tub.

Once I had her comfortable, I washed the remains of her glorious hair, now short as a boy's, in Spanish soap. She told me it had been cut and sold to a wig maker the day she'd been taken to the Cock Horse.

Last, I wrapped her in dry sheeting, and, sitting where the sun came in, I cleaned her head of lice. Her fair skin was almost blue-white. Her ribs rose so you could count them. And, the pain in her eyes—I could hardly bear it! My sweet Anne looked even more ill and frail than the summer she'd caught the French flux.

A few days later, squatting on the pot, sobbing, near to fainting, she gushed blood and clots. She said she'd never bled once in the four months since her abduction. Outside, in a hidden spot in the garden, I crouched over what she'd passed, using a twig to search, looking for the tailed creature, first sign of life. As it was my duty to care for her, I must know the truth, no matter how abhorrent.

If well formed, the miscarriage I suspected would be noble—last of the doomed House of Lancaster. Or—and, even more terrible—if it was small and gilled, the get of some unspeakable vermin....

It was several days before I dared to question her. Before it was all nursing, keeping her clean of the incapacitating menses, feeding and dosing her, holding her in my arms so my strength could enter her frail body, watching as she slept.

"How was it the duke found you?"

"I don't know how he ever did," Anne finally replied, "for they kept moving me. First, I was in a kitchen at the house of a man who was a dependent of George's, where they set me to scrubbing pots. Then, they took to me to another house, and then to another. Each place was meaner. Last," she shuddered all over, "to that—that—tavern."

"How long do you think?"

"A week, maybe. I'm not certain because I was locked into that room and there was no window. They told me a man would come, that if I wanted to see the sun again, I must submit to whatever he desired." She covered her face with long hands while her shoulders rose and fell.

"Every time I heard feet coming down the hall, I was afraid, so afraid!" She buried her face in her hands and it was a time before she could continue. "Oh, Rose! If I live to be a hundred I will never forget. Never!" Her eyes, when she lifted her head, were lost in memory. As I watched, her eyelids closed, fair lashes settling against alabaster.

"Then one day, I heard coins clink just outside the door. I heard the key scrape. I could not move, just curled into the corner and prayed to be struck dead. The room was so dark at first I only saw a hand holding the candle. There were many rings and I thought, 'twas a gentleman, so, perhaps, if I asked for his help, and he would not insult me." She paused and I took it for a good sign that even after all that had happened, she still didn't seem to completely understand that gentlemen could be brutes as easily as the rest of mankind.

"He was all covered in a dark cloak, but when I saw his face, I could not believe it. I thought I had finally gone mad. He didn't say anything, just set the candle in the sconce. I could not move; I could not speak. I just sat on that awful bed, shaking and hugging my knees. He told me not to be afraid. He took off his cloak and covered me, and then went to the door to speak to someone. I heard him say to fetch you. That's when I believed he wouldn't harm me, that it was all George's doing, every bit." Suddenly, she was sobbing again. "Oh! Mary Mother of God! Protect my poor sister from that wicked man!"

Great Warwick's folly ...

"'Tis a hard fortune to be born, and hardest of all to have been born a woman." I quoted my mother. Not only poor women like those who had birthed me, but this lady, her sister and her mother, blown from England to France and back again, hunted, condemned, tormented, for no fault of their own, but as a result of the pride, the wrath, and the greed of their men folk.

I thought of Isabel, like to die upon that ship, of the dead baby we'd dropped into the waves. I thought of the Countess, trapped in sanctuary at Beaulieu, while the victorious king and his brothers quarreled over the spoil, as if the Countess of Warwick, an heiress in her own right, had died alongside her husband.

I wondered, as I held Anne, what else she and the Duke of Gloucester had said to each other. Perhaps nothing, in such a sink of shame.

Richard sent messages daily, but until many weeks passed, Anne would not see him. She had a hundred reasons. First, she was too ill. Next, she said she was mortified to her soul by the wretched state in which he, her noble cousin, had found her. Then, she said she was such a fool to have believed George when he'd claimed to be sending her to the king. She could not bear to face Richard, now that he'd seen her folly and weak-mindedness. Last of all, she told me the truth, which was she feared what he must imagine.

"I have been Edward's wife and thereby broke the promise I made to the Duke of Gloucester. But, dear Rose, please believe me, those blackguards did not befoul me. If they had—if they had—I would have asked him, my kinsman and cousin, to drive his dagger into my heart—and, then—then—if he refused to end my dishonor—I would have begged you for the same mercy."

I began to believe her. She passed no sign of life. Except for bruises and sickness, she bore no other marks of violence. She had been terrorized, oh, yes, but the kingmaker's daughter would have resisted rape tooth and nail, and in consequence would have received terrible injuries.

I think the moon saved her, coming when it did. Fear, and her lack of flesh, might have continued to deprive her of the flow, but she was so overdue—six months—that it had broken through at last. Fortunately, there is a deep repulsion in most men for a woman flooding in blood.

If she was not able to speak to Richard, I was. Anne did not forbid me, and so I related each of these excuses and what little else I was able to learn. He was all business, Master to servant, but, sometimes, when he was close, I'd catch the scent of him, and feel a stab of yearning. There would be an ache, a desperate longing, but I'd force it away.

We were done.

I had my lady to care for. She needed my help, my undivided attention, my perfect loyalty, and she would have it.

In every house, Anne had been told it was "King Edward's Pleasure," that she "entirely disappear." At the Cock Horse, they suggested she must do more to earn her keep. They had introduced her to the sights of the house, just as they would any girl they'd picked up on the streets.

Richard asked but once about what had happened to his cousin in that terrible place, and when I did not answer, saying only that I did not know—which was the truth at the time—he never spoke of it again. His face hardened; his eyes froze. I knew he would make them pay.

Hugh told me, many months later, that he and some other picked men had burnt the tavern to the ground. Further, they were ordered to "cut the throat of every rat which runs out." Even common folk who had frequented that house were tracked and put to silence. Vengeance was also visited upon certain men belonging to Clarence, those believed to be directly culpable.

No civil authority remarked upon these events. Neither did George of Clarence.

"Clarence is faithless to his own blood." Hugh asserted. "Why should he bother keeping faith with those who merely do his bidding?"

As for me, I wasted no pity on any who had bullied and terrorized my poor, innocent lady. A knife across the throat was, indeed, too easy an end for such abominable creatures.

At last, Anne did tell me a little. She spoke of her brief servant's life, of how hard the work was and how they'd mocked her with "useless" and "stupid," how they'd struck her and laughed. Then had come the finality of the Cock Horse. Here, she'd been taken to peepholes to watch loutish patrons, lunging and grunting between fat, quivering thighs. The heavy bleeding she'd started had embarrassed her, but the onset perhaps spared her an immediate introduction to a customer of the kind who would pay well to brutalize a lady.

Within the holy precincts of St. Martin, sounding only of bells, birds and chants, she became calm again, but I knew it would be a long time before I heard my little lady laugh. As she recovered, we followed the nuns on their daily round of prayers, the exception being those two sung in the dead of night. Anne was of a mind to attend these as well, but I put my foot down, saying she needed to be asleep more than she needed to pray.

Spooned against me, she did sleep, too, with an ever-lessening supply of bad dreams. Having me with her, the way it had been, skin to skin, was a better charm than any sleeping draught I could make.

As for her slain husband, Prince-Chop-Off-Their-Heads, she did not speak of him. I comforted her, but in my heart of hearts, I was heartily glad he was gone.

Meanwhile, the news from court, which came to me through A'Parr, was that George continued to wrangle with Richard over Anne, and that he continued to demand the whole of the combined Neville and Beauchamp lands as Isabel's right.

"He says my Lord of Gloucester may have his lady sister-in-law, but he and his wife agree, they shall part no *lyvelode*."

Richard argued he had served the king faithfully and that half of the great spoil should to be his. Gloucester intended to have Anne and he intended to have her inheritance, too.

Never mind that both dukes were in the wrong. The Beauchamp lands belonged to the Countess, who was still very much alive down at Beaulieu. King Edward, however, soon devised a way around that problem. His new parliament was instructed to simply declare the Countess of Warwick officially "dead."

After robbing the mother, those great tracts of land could be split more or less evenly between Isabel and Anne, and, of course, their respective husbands. King Edward, wanting only to keep George quiet, was no help at all to his loyal brother. At his Court the Woodvilles reigned supreme, even more thrust forward than before Warwick's rebellion. You would think our handsome king might have learned something on that score, however, while in sanctuary at Westminster, his queen had at last given birth to a son, the longed for male heir of the House of York. Elizabeth Woodville's star had risen high.

Once home in London, with a sturdy new son, the king returned to his old pleasures. He chased the wives of burghers, hunted and feasted, all while handing over titles, royal wards and treasure to his wife's relatives. There were plenty of them, too. The queen had four brothers, two sons by her first marriage and seven sisters, and all needing to be matched with the first peers of the land. Perhaps the King thought by this to create a power in the kingdom to use against his dangerous noble cousins, a counter power that was loyal to him alone.

⚜

"It was horrible to have him see me like that." Anne repeated it again and again. "Blubbering like a baby, naked to my shift, in that low, filthy place."

We had been in St. Martin's for almost five weeks. She sat beside a pool in the courtyard, studying her reflection as it floated above the pond fish. Pale and languid, carp lifted their round mouths and nibbled the surface of the water, hoping this visitor might have a treat. Anne obliged, scattering crumbs.

The fish took them. Above our heads, bells stirred, sending a blur of notes into the breeze. It was clear who "him" was, so I simply nodded.

"The duke would like to see you, all the same."

"It is hard." She set her jaw in a way which reminded me of her mother. "So many terrible deeds now lie between us."

"Nothing can be undone, My Lady, so it must be water under the bridge."

Truth to tell, I was weary of St. Martin Le Grand, of the nuns and their prayers, of the sameness of every day walled about, first by the confines of the church, and, beyond, by the dirty city. This could end but one way—with the two of them married and home to Middleham.

Richard wanted it. Anne—if she could just see clear—wanted it, too. I, though of no importance at all, would have sold my soul to see home again.

Oh, to be back on the dales, to smell fresh air, to feel the bracing wind, hard and strong as boar's bristle, scouring us clean of the ugly past! For my part, I was foolish enough to imagine things would return to a semblance of earlier, happier times.

With a finger, Anne skimmed the surface of the greenish water, pushing crumbs here and there. The fish followed, their great eyes and broad fins swiveling.

"Do you know when he will visit again?"

"The duke said tomorrow afternoon, Milady."

After another moment's consideration, Anne turned her big blue eyes toward me.

"Let the duke know I will speak with him."

"At once, My Lady!"

It was the end of her self-imposed exile. She'd been pushed by everyone, by her beloved parents, treated as a despised necessity and then as a bedroom toy by the fickle prince, and, finally, cast into the pit by George. Even Isabel had abandoned her, not offering Anne protection or forewarning of what Clarence had planned.

Richard and I were the only two constants. Of course—terrible to remember—we, too, had betrayed her, but this could not be undone, so it must be forgotten.

Richard, alone in her world, had not demanded, had not forced. He had rescued, placed her in sanctuary and waited politely. Even if his motives were not unmixed, patience was the honorable course. I gave him credit for respecting her fears, but, in truth, my lady had nowhere else to go—except to a nunnery! The duke, however, was sufficiently tender of my lady's feelings to present himself as a suitor.

I settled a plain cap over her short hair and covered it with a linen gorget. Over this we placed a long veil, which hid her face when she looked down. I'd tried to persuade her into a blue dress from the trunk I'd packed that fateful spring day, the day intended to be the end of us both, but Anne would not have it. She donned the Lancastrian black slashed with red, the dress she'd worn at Tewkesbury.

"He wants to see you," I said, impatiently shifting the veil. "You look like a widow about to take holy orders."

She fixed me with those blue eyes and lifted her chin.

"It is a choice I yet may make, Rosalba."

"Rubbish," I muttered under my breath, drawing the veil back over her shoulders to make hiding behind it more difficult.

"I will wear this, or I will not see the duke at all." She tugged the veil impatiently out of my hand. Confronted by her haughtiest manner, I knew I had better hold my tongue.

Let her have her way. I'd leave it to Richard. He understood women well enough!

Still, it was hard to stay out of things entirely. I picked up a small nosegay of herbs and late blossoms which I'd fashioned and offered it.

"What is this?" Anne gazed down her long nose at my pretty handiwork, her expression as disdainful as if I were presenting her with something lifted from the chamber pot.

"I thought you might like to carry something sweet alongside your prayer book. The Duke of Gloucester has done you no harm, after all."

"Only killed my husband! Rosalba, many men say this, not only the Duke of Clarence."

"Men say?" I was quite out of patience. "Men say? Whose men? In which kitchen full of The Duke of Clarence's dependents did you hear it? You, Milady, owe the Duke of Gloucester your very life—and—and—he is still exactly who he was at Middleham—our very own Dickon!"

And, by the Black Virgin, so much more...

Unable to bear the memory—his kisses, his words, his wanting—I slapped the nosegay on the table, bobbed, and left the room.

Once in the gallery I spied him, a quick stride carrying him through the yellow and brown of an autumnal garden. Grasping my rosary to steady myself, I watched him approach. The Duke of Gloucester was elegant and somber today as well, in a knee-length black tunic with slashed burgundy sleeves and a hat with a badge jewel at the brim. His dark hair was shoulder length, a handsome frame for a thin face. No servant accompanied him, at least, none close enough to see.

Early and anxious bodes well!

Swallowing hard, I dropped a far deeper curtsy than the one I had just offered Anne.

"Your Grace! Milady will receive you."

"I have been looking forward to this moment since your message."

"Come into the gallery, Your Grace." There was a breezy length to walk, a view of the garden, and benches to rest upon beneath the ornamental arches.

As I walked along the gallery, heading to My Lady's room, I began to worry about quarreling with her so near the time of his arrival. What if she now refused to see him?

As I approached, however, Anne came through the door. She wore the veil, yes, but she had not waited to be called. Turning in her long fingers was my nosegay.

They bowed and curtsied, a formal greeting full of titles. Then, my most royal loves walked to and fro within the gallery, books of hours in their hands. The sun obligingly shone, and the cloister garden glowed like a many-faceted jewel. Golden leaves drifted past. As if it were still high summer, birds caroled in the windless warmth of the afternoon.

Richard did not touch her, even kiss her hand, which was wise, I think. Following at a discreet distance, I could not hear what they said. Although there were many long pauses, and, on her side, a few tears, these did not signal an end to the interview.

Anne's expression was solemn. I knew she was asking hard questions. Even though this would not assist a quick return to Middleham, I was proud of her. When she lifted her handkerchief, I told myself that this must be for her father. I could not bear to think of the prince, for thinking of him made me jealous, even though I now had pity for his wretched end.

Anne asked; Richard made spare answers. The intervals, I noted, were not on his side. They walked the square of the gallery around and around while I trailed in their footsteps.

In the garden, nuns in black robes and three servants in simple doublet and hose, labored to trim and weed the flowerbeds, now mostly marigolds. Orisons rose and fell from a side chantry as Mass was sung for some departed (and well-to-do) soul.

Finally, Anne paused. I, too, came to a halt. A swallow's mud nest filled the hollow of a stone trefoil. The last fledglings, with their tan throats, had come out to perch and exercise their wings. The fond parents hustled back and forth bringing bugs to stuff into those comic, eternally gaping, yellow-lined gullets. It was a tender show, beautiful blue-black feathers, swift flight and sweet cries of encouragement to their young. Such faithfulness to their duty! I confess to spending lazy moments every day watching these paragons, so hard at work raising their brood.

When I glanced back, I saw Anne offer Richard my little nosegay. She'd twisted it this way and that during their long *tête-à-tête*. Solemnly, he stood at attention while she pulled a pin from her dress and secured it to his shoulder. There was a momentary pang, but I swiftly buried it with an avalanche of common sense.

This is your way home.

Time for a kiss! Richard bowed over her white hand, today the graceful, trim image of a courtier. A brush of his lips followed, and a long, silent moment in which they held hands and gazed into each other's eyes. Gently a bell began to toll, signaling it was time to pray, to recite the *Parvum Beatae Mariae Virginis* in the chapel. In they went, most formally together.

After prayers, he departed. Nothing in his movement betrayed the emotion he certainly felt. The sight of his imperfection as he walked away returned the past. A small stubborn boy beaten almost to death at that mock tourney, and later, working his broken body relentlessly through the pain, walking up and down a thousand stairs at the castle, carrying trays heavy with golden service, lugging plate for the knights he tended. Never a whimper, never an excuse!

Master Grey and Mistress Ash had helped heal Richard, true, but if he had not worked, had not willed it, he would never have made such a recovery. I'd seen him now in full armor at Tewkesbury, covered in sweat, dirt and the blood of his enemies. I'd lain in those arms, muscle braided with steel. An ugly raised scar atop the high shoulder was all that remained his near fatal childhood injury.

Lady Anne stood quite still, watching his soldierly figure disappear into the shadows beneath the farthest arch. The dark veil fell around her shoulders. Poor little widow!

I approached, sensing stillness. After all she had suffered, she was as easily startled as a deer, but somehow I knew that what I desired—what the duke desired—had begun.

Life would return to the predestined path. Richard and Anne would marry and go home to Middleham.

I dropped a deep curtsy to her, but did not speak. Water was rising in the well. It would only take time to fill.

·❧

Thoughtfully her long fingers stroked the lute strings, releasing delicate chords, rainbows of harmony. She was dreaming. I knew the way of it, pretending to gaze at the strings, but actually examining her heart. Winding wool, I listened, heard phrases of songs I knew, songs Anne had once played because her Dickon loved them. As fate would have it, these had become the self-same songs she'd played at Prince Edward's request.

At first, her husband had asked for these sweet laments because he knew quite well they were for another. He'd wanted to cause her pain, but he'd changed. Gradually, they'd become Edward's songs, as well.

Two young men—one alive, one dead—I could almost see their shadows on either side of her. Memories were in those songs, many I could not share. As so often these days, I tasted bitterness. Anne and Richard! They were still so much of my world, but all the time I was less and less of theirs.

I remembered Hugh's taunt, that I was "old to still be so much in love with a mistress." Like a thorn which drives deep, his words festered.

·❧

The next visit they arranged to confess and hear Mass together. This they did at dawn, attending the chant of Prime. In court clothes and jewels, they walked hand in hand into the dark maw of St. Martin's with its hundreds of flickering votives, heavy incense, and glowing stained glass. Pale of face and hollow-eyed, they were a pair of royal penitents.

After, they broke their fast with solemn ceremony at a table specially laid in My Lady's receiving room and served by the duke's servants. They hardly spoke. Outside it was gray and cold, an echo of the mood. They did, however, exchange a three-fold cousin's kiss at parting, so I was encouraged.

Anne was quiet after he'd gone, but she seemed easier, as if some test had just been passed. She sat with lute in her lap, softly strumming, facing the gray rain.

A few weeks later, after Mass on the feast of Saint Michael, they sat beneath a little tree which was now shedding leaves. There was a carpet beneath their feet, and they drank wine and ate soft cheese and tart slices of late pears. We were in luck with another warm day, although autumn had deepened. I'd found treasure in the very bottom of a chest Duchess Isabel had belatedly sent. Without asking, I brought it forward.

"An excellent idea, Rose!" Richard's face brightened when he saw what I carried. Anne was surprised. When she recognized the small carved box, she shifted her gaze to me, suddenly anxious. She did not protest, however, so I beckoned to a servant and together we tidied their table. Then, between them, I unrolled a painted leather scroll of black and white checks and opened the carved wooden box which held the ivory and ebony chessmen.

"Do you still play to keep your horses, Lady Anne?" Richard flashed a smile.

A glow entered my lady's cheeks. I saw her eyes soften.

"You will just have to find out, my Lord of Gloucester." Anne was as cool as those sanctuary fish.

At their request, I took pawns, one of each, and, hands behind my back, traded them. Then, fists over the board, I invited them to choose their color, just as we had done long ago. A jeweled index finger tapped my freckled fist. I opened my hand, so he could have the piece.

His skin and hers, so alike! So fair, so fine, while mine, mine . . .

❧

Hugh stood by one of the gray arches, between the choir and the garden, a brown felt cap clutched in one broad hand. Anne leaned close to whisper, "Rose has a suitor."

I forced a smile in return and inwardly groaned.

"Go speak to him."

"I will with you to Compline."

"No. You will stay and speak to Master Fletcher."

"I am—am—afraid. Master Fletcher and I have quarreled."

"You are quite safe here. Besides, Rose, you are not afraid of anyone."

She left me, her rosary looped elegantly over one hand, veil floating behind her. Her sorrows, it was clear, were slipping into the past.

Mine, I thought with sudden insight, *have just begun.*

"Mistress Rosalba." Hugh bowed politely. His ruddy fair person looked well in blue and murray.

I folded my hands against my bosom, as my mother used to do before an unpleasant interview with Master Whitby. Remembering our last meeting in the garden at Crosby's Place, I couldn't imagine what brought him here. Had he come to shame me again? If so, it was just as well Anne had left the scene.

Well, if he was formal, I could be, too. I curtsied and said, "As you see, Master Fletcher."

"I have come to make amends for our last—conversation."

I lifted my chin and replied, "No need, sir. Truth is always best."

"Yes. Truth is best, but I was—uncharitable." He caught my arm. "But a man may be excused for some anger in such a case, I believe."

"A man may be excused for almost anything." I was tart as I dared. He was strong and had already demonstrated his temper.

"So you women will have it." He parried my thrust.

The courtyard here was full of dried leaves. In one slate-paved corner, a thin, lightly clad charity child slowly swept. We passed him by, me walking briskly, as if I had some place to go. Hugh kept pace at my elbow.

"Come, Mistress Rose. Let us forgive and forget."

"I am not angry," I said, turning on him. "Nor will I be, as long as you never dare to lay a hand on me."

"I was a fool. Beating is no good way to rule a woman."

"To rule a woman is no good way!" I snapped back, now tried beyond measure.

At this, he was at last provoked sufficiently to seize my arms at the elbows and hold me so that I had to face him. I rested my hands on his broad chest, feeling the uselessness of resistance. His sere, gray eyes flashed beneath shaggy brows.

"God's Blood! I never crossed swords with a creature stouter." He only studied me, although what was in his eyes was almost as bad as kissing. "Nor saw anything in skirts I liked better. Damn it, Rose! Say you forgive, for I have come on purpose to ask pardon. We shall begin anew. Do I not have some claim, at least, upon your friendship?"

He had saved me from death. He was close, warm and capable. Admiration flowed from him like heat from a banked fire. Desire equals flattery; herein lies its power. After the hot and thorough initiation I'd received, I was vulnerable.

"You are too familiar, sir." I glanced uneasily to where he gripped my arm.

"And I hope to be increasingly so. Now, come, sweet Rose, allow me the kiss of peace."

He bent to lightly brush his lips against my cheeks, one after the other. Astonished, I allowed it, not quite believing that he'd dared. As he did, his warm, hard belly pressed close; he smelled clean and fair.

"I give thanks for your forgiveness, Rose. But to speak frankly, I had hoped to be the man so honored."

I knew what he meant, of course, and that made me blush. Looking down, ashamed, I said, "Certes, it was a great folly, one which I do daily regret."

"We shall no more speak of it." Hugh spoke in a firm, almost fatherly tone. "Now that we are friends again, I shall keep you no longer from your prayers."

"Hush and follow!" Finger to my lips, smiling, just as I'd done with him long ago, I turned and began to walk. Richard, a smile of his own begun, obeyed. He signaled his servants to stay where they were.

It was cold now, the holy day of Saint Hugh. We'd gone to hear Mass, and now, within, my Lady played her lute, making music like the sweet caged bird she was. Her skill was not a thing she'd yet shared with the Duke of Gloucester, but I thought it high time.

She'd made excuses for not playing for him, prime being that a lady might know a few pretty songs, but it was not quite fitting to be as skilled as she'd become. These days my lady played the lute far better than many a fellow who earned his bread by the trade. I said I thought her music was quite extraordinary, but she'd only laughed and said it was "a wonder not to be much wondered at, as many hours as I've put to practice."

Richard had arrived today unannounced. Another piece of luck, I'd met him as he passed through the brittle, frost-edged garden.

"What is this, Rose?" He eyed me warily, as well he might, now alone with a woman whose veins still ran with the fire he'd started.

Wanting to tease him a little, I boldly caught his gloved hand and tugged him forward, into shadows and torchlight.

"Listen, My Lord!"

Within the cold leather glove there was a warm hand. He did as I asked, however, and at once his attention strayed from my impudence to the music. Anne's sweet voice was as clear and pure as a cut boy's. The lute accompaniment was both elaborate and beautiful.

Lifting the latch to the outer door, I bowed him into our fireless antechamber. My lady sat in an alcove beyond, hidden by a tapestry. Great bellied, it held heat within the smaller space.

    Shoot, false Love, I care not.
    Spend thy shafts and spare not.
    I fear not thy might
    And less thy spite.

    If thou canst, now shoot and harm me.
    So lightly I esteem thee.
    As a child I once deemed thee.
    Long thy bow did fear me.
    At last I do perceive
    Thy art is to deceive,
    And every simple lover
    All thy falsehood can discover.
    Then weep, Love, and cry sorry.
    For thou hast lost all thy glory.

I watched as he went to the curtain. One hand upon it, his pale face turned to me, questioning, framed against his dark hair. It would, of course, have been utterly improper for an unattended lady to have a musician in her bedchamber anywhere, not only within the sacred precincts of St. Martin's! I suppose I was wicked to do this to him, but, somehow, it had become an irresistible notion.

How could he imagine anything but a highly-trained lute player beside her? Now that the words were past, Anne began to finger a fair embellishment. The sound danced like a sparkling waterfall.

Pretending I hadn't a notion of anything amiss, I indicated, with an encouraging gesture, that he should open the curtain. Richard's lean jaw tightened as he reached, caught the fabric and then stepped inside.

Anne, deep in her music, was badly startled by his abrupt entrance, an effect I had not for an instant considered. She jumped up with a shriek. The lute struck the floor and sounded a noisy discord.

Fortunately for me, the perpetrator, there was carpet on the perennially cold stone flags, a recent gift of my Lord of Gloucester. The instrument, with its fat belly and long delicate neck, was not injured, though it did pop a cat-gut string.

"Saint Paul!"

Before my heart had time for another beat, Richard turned on me, Plantagenet temper up."My Lord—I—I— only—wanted you to hear her play!"

"Of whom do you speak?" He did not shout, but—far worse—spoke with icy precision.

It was time to go to my knees, which I promptly did.

"Your Grace—um—to hear my Lady—Lady Anne— who—who—plays—so magically!"

There was a little pause and I heard a swish. This was Anne in her furred, many layered winter dress, bending for the lute. Holy Mother Bless her, for this led to Richard's turning to assist. Just the sparks from his eyes could have ignited the floor under my feet.

"Your pardon, dear Lady Cousin." Richard presented the lute with its dangling string.

"Never mind, Your Grace! I—I shouldn't have been so silly."

"My Lady—I didn't mean to frighten you! I only wanted—his Grace the Duke—to hear—"

"Rose," Anne interrupted, waving me to silence, the pale tips of her fingers emerging from hand warmers. "Go fetch something hot for my Lord of Gloucester."

"Yes, my Lady." Off the floor in an instant, I scampered for the door.

"Rose!"

So close to escape! Already I had a hand upon the cold iron latch.

"Your Grace?" I curtsied low, not daring to meet his eyes.

"Call my servants."

"Yes, my Lord." I was halfway to shutting the door when Anne had another thought.

"Rose!"

Another curtsey and My Lady instructed, clear and

clipped, "Be certain you bring them directly. It would not seem well for me to be unattended." This last seemed a little strike at Richard, to let him know she'd witnessed his instant of suspicion. At last out the door, I trotted away, briskly, too, as you might imagine. Of course, I knew I was going to catch it, but emotion had not let me think clear.

Much mischief was set loose with this prank. In the moment Richard had swept back the curtain, I'd known he was wondering who he would find there. In the same moment, Anne, nerves still raw, had caught suspicion in his eyes.

I'd hurt Richard—yes! Made a bit of fool of him, too, but I'd also scared my understandably edgy mistress and hurt her feelings right along with his.

Why? I could see well enough all around the matter now, but what devil had prompted, had whispered there was no harm in my fooling? I slowed, needing time to get my wits about me. Besides, My Lord and Lady didn't really want me to hurry *too* fast. A few minutes, private, would right matters between them, of that I was certain.

When I came into my mistresses' chambers again, I arrived with the tail of the duke's attendants, hoping everyone would be occupied. Sure enough, they were encouraging the fire in the antechamber, setting out a table and chairs, arranging the refreshments the duke had brought in. There was wine and spice for mulling, baskets of nuts, apples and cheese. I slipped into the shadows, and remained unnoticed—for a few minutes.

As I'd hoped, Richard and Anne seemed well enough, even merry. Anne was explaining to John A'Parr why she had been shy of playing her lute in the duke's presence.

"I have been intending to surprise His Grace at Yuletide, but now Rosalba—"

"Has surprised me 'pon Saint Hugh's day, instead," said Richard. I noted how his dark eyes pried shadow to uncover me. I was in trouble with my Lord of Gloucester, and would stay that way.

Anne touched his glove, soothing him with the pale tips of her fingers. Her nails, of which we were taking great care, were lovely as ever.

"When we have refreshed ourselves, if you are willing, Cousin, I shall play again."

"I would be honored, Lady. What I just heard declares you have more than mastered the art."

There was a sizzle as a hot poker, heated in the fire, plunged into the mulling pot. A spicy, burnt smell filled the air. A bottle was already open and sat on the table between them. Richard took the glass offered by A'Parr and gazed at it, studying the red spark which shone within.

He took a sip, and then passed the glass to Anne. It was an honor, from a royal duke to an earl's daughter; it was communion shared by a knight with his lady. Firelight flickered upon the tapestries behind them, causing the woven vines to appear to curl and twine.

Anne lowered her lashes demurely, took a slow sip, and then said, "I began to study the lute after you went to court, Cousin. Anthony Reed instructed me. Do you remember him?"

"Yes, very well. Poor Reed couldn't see his feet upon the floor, but his music—his music! He ever delighted my heart."

Anne was as good as her word, and later played again, most exceptionally. Richard claimed astonishment once more and appeared genuinely moved by her artistry. He seemed to understand the effort which she'd put into the accomplishment.

When they exchanged their cousin's kiss that afternoon, I saw how they lingered close, hands resting upon each other's shoulders, how they gazed into each other's eyes.

He should not be so very angry with me, I thought, for I have brought him another step closer to his desire. But what of my own? My heart ached, loving them both so much, so hopelessly.

Chapter XVI

Milord?" I curtsied deep to my young duke. I had been
led to where he sat at a table bright with candles,
cluttered with empty wine bottles and the bony ruin
of an excellent dinner. Old friends were there, friends who had
also trained in arms at Middleham.

Here sat Francis, Lord Lovell, broad shouldered, ruddy
cheeked and brown skinned. The others were the Lords Dacre,
Greystoke and Fitzhugh. In the background stood Richard's
guards. A pair of heavy-headed mastiffs, big as ponies, sprawled
in the reeds, having taken up stations where scraps were most
likely to land. A Welsh harper with frizzy gray curls had been
supplying an appropriately martial ballad. His was the strong
tenor I had heard during my journey along the corridor.

I'd arrived in a knot of anxiety. For several weeks after the
lute incident, I had been waiting for the other shoe to drop.
Today, I could not imagine why I had been conveyed to
Crosby's Place in order to speak to him. I knew he enjoyed the
simplicity and peace of St. Martin le Grand, but here I was, far
off my ground, summoned to the great room of his townhouse.
No, I did not like the lie of this land one bit!

"Very prompt, Mistress Rose." He indicated I should rise
from my curtsy. "'Tis unfortunate you missed Master Griffyd's
song, for it was a brave story."

The harper bowed and the duke's friends added their
agreement. Richard's secretary, John Kendall, at the lowest end
of the table, stood to hand the harper a purse. The Welshman
bowed again, face shining in the reflected glow of Richard's
good will. It was clear the duke had pleased the harper at least
as much as the other way round.

"Come again to me, Master Griffyd, for tomorrow's
supper," Richard said. "Now, gentlemen and cousins, I thank
you for your company, but I must have a talk with Rose."

As the lords withdrew, there were friendly nods in my

direction, for they remembered me much as I remembered them. Acknowledgement was well salted with curiosity, for I was not so plain as I insisted upon imagining.

Secretary Kendall stayed put, so those who knew anything about anything understood this was business, not pleasure. That made me even more anxious than I'd been before.

Francis Lovell, who'd apparently drunk himself to right good cheer, strolled close and chucked me familiarly under the chin.

"Um glad to see tha' art safe, after great trow-ble, Roe-an Roose." His joking made me smile because his attempt at Yorkshire dialect was, as always, horrid.

"I am glad that you, too, are well, My Lord Lovell, and have likewise weathered the storm."

He studied me with merry black eyes. He and Richard— one so tall, the other so short—what a precious pair! Always together as boys, always talking about their horses, their hawks, side by side, day in and day out....

"I hear," Francis remarked in a stage whisper, "you get your way in everything."

"What? You jest, Milord."

"Oh, don't try to pull the wool over my eyes, Rose! I reminded the Duke of Gloucester that you were born under the Scorpion and will either have your way or have vengeance. So now I entreat you, play the docile maid. I heartily pray, bewilder and vex His Grace no further."

Another thing about this boyhood pair, it had always been Francis who loved to hear himself talk, the one who caught girls with lines woven of felicitous nonsense. Tall, lanky and gregarious, Francis had teased everyone, including his best friend. Richard, who said little and pondered much, was his exact opposite.

Bewilder? Vex? I gave Francis Lovell a look that said I had no idea what he was on about.

"It's good news." This added to my confusion. Then, after dropping a boyish buss upon my hand—as in the old days— Lord Lovell sauntered away. While this went on, My Lord the Duke was growing impatient and appeared to be within a hair of saying so.

At this juncture, I suddenly took it into my head that Richard had received permission from the king to marry Anne. Oh, to escape the confines St. Martin's and return to Middleham and our wide Yorkshire sky! Thrilled by the idea, I colored.

Richard noticed my blush. "Do you anticipate me, Rose?" A servant had appeared carrying a silver basin. He began to wash his hands in the scented water.

"I do not know, my Lord of Gloucester, but I do pray we shall soon make return to Middleham."

He dried his hands upon a towel presented by another servant and then motioned them both away. "Do you speak of my marriage to your lady?"

"I pray that is the matter, Milord."

"I pray that it were. However, it is of your marriage I wish to speak."

You could have knocked me over with a feather. My jaw sagged.

"My-my—marriage?"

"Yes. When the Countess of Warwick long ago took you to service, she promised your mother that in time she would provide you with a dower and a worthy husband. She is not able to complete her promise and this disturbs her. Among other things, she writes to me of this." A jeweled hand waved for confirmation to Kendall, who gravely nodded.

"This is of no consequence to me, My Lord. As long as I serve my dear lady, I am content."

"The Countess of Warwick, however, is not." Richard leaned back in his chair, trying on amusement. "Do you hear this, Kendall? Here stands a young woman who does not wish to be well married."

"Perhaps we should call the harper back?" Kendall obliged with a smile. "There's certainly a song in this, Your Grace."

"I know a stout fellow who wishes to marry with you, Mistress Rose, who petitions me for your hand."

Richard smiled. It was a lord's smile, reassurance and guidance aimed at me, his rudderless dependent.

"He is a man of appropriate substance, a soldier of confirmed bravery who had done me excellent service. Moreover, you owe him your life."

"Master Fletcher dares to speak of this to you, My Lord?" At last, I'd found my tongue.

Richard nodded. The smile stayed firmly in place, but I noticed that he'd begun to twist one of his rings.

"Daily he pleads his case." Kendall spoke for his master.

"But—but, Sir! I—I—have refused Master Hugh."

"Come, come, Rose," said Richard. "To marry is an act of prudence. Better to marry than to burn."

The sharp scorpion of whom Lovell had spoken wondered if my lord was talking about himself? Shadows stole in and out behind his banter.

Daily I felt the tug of desire for him. By this, I knew it was not simply my foolishness, my weakness. Richard felt it, too, and he'd decided that by marrying me off, he would end it. It made my heart ache, particularly since it was a very good plan.

Who knew better that he belonged to Anne and she belonged to him? Anything else would be mere lust, a sin on both sides. Our night of pleasure had been a double betrayal of a long held friendship.

Now, my good lord played his part, ostensibly looking after the welfare of a servant. The Countess of Warwick had promised and great lady that she was, in the face of all sorrows, a promise made was a promise which must be kept. Noblesse Oblige!

"Rose?" Richard raised one dark brow.

"Milord?" Whatever he'd been saying, I hadn't heard a single word.

"I should like to see at least one marriage during this blessed season. If it cannot be my own, yours must suffice."

"I cannot leave My Lady Anne, sir." I drew myself up as tall as possible in a last, futile attempt to save myself. "I wonder, Your Grace, that you can ask it."

"I have not asked you to leave Lady Anne." His rejoinder came equally sharp.

Candor seemed my last chance. "If I am to sleep with a husband—" I swallowed hard, "I shall not be able to care for the Lady at night as she requires."

"This presents no difficulty." Richard regarded me steadily. "There are Sisters of gentle breeding at St. Martin who will assume those duties and keep your lady well. And, you must not forget the ladies Grace and Margaret, from our days at Middleham."

Ah, yes, those pasty docile faces—those--interlopers!

"These ladies are with the Countess at Beaulieu, but Lady Anne certainly should be attended by those who have been trained in caring for her. Equally certain, Mistress Rose, is that you are too wise to waste your days simply dressing and undressing my dear cousin. You must get back to your garden, to your work."

I opened my mouth, but nothing came out, so I closed it again. That was when Richard delivered the *coup de grace*.

"Lady Anne and I have discussed it. She concurs."

Out-flanked, and deprived of them both at one stroke, I couldn't help myself. I sank to my knees and began to cry—and not with any kind of quiet dignity, either.

"Leave us, Kendall."

The secretary, sincerely discomfited, was up and gone in a flash. Heaven knows what he thought. No doubt that something was between us, which was, after all, the wretched truth.

Richard came around the table. A moment later, he had hold of my hand. I didn't dare look at him.

"Rose," he said, pressing my fingers gently between his. "What is this?"

"I have refused Master Fletcher, my Lord."

"Why? Fletcher is a good man. He promises to make you a worthy husband. He is brave, and forthright and he loves you. What more could you desire?"

His closeness was wrenching. What he said stabbed me to the heart—stabbed all women! Men know better than this and they demonstrate it whenever they marry for status and property, and then take a mistress to slake their passion. Why do they imagine us so unlike?

"Love, My Lord." At last I dared to meet his eyes, "Love."

He released my hand and gazed down with all the regal authority of which he was capable. When he fixed you with those bright falcon's eyes, you no longer saw him as spare and barely twenty.

"Love—" the Prince of York began, pausing as if to ponder a word in a foreign language, "will come. You have this man's respect, which is more."

"You love the Lady Anne, and she loves you." I don't really know how I dared to say it.

My speech was followed by a deathly pause. Then he said, "You, best of all, should know whereof and for how long."

I found my handkerchief and attempted delicacy while blowing my nose. Doubtless, I failed. The duke stepped back, rested his hand upon the corner of the table.

"For his good service, good character, and his preservation of your person, I have promised Hugh Fletcher your hand at Twelfth Night. So it shall be."

Unable to speak, choking on a mixture of rage and tears, I bowed my head.

"This is a good match. With it, the promise made by the Countess of Warwick to your mother is honored."

Perhaps there was more to this speech, but I, without leave, without the proper thank-you, leapt to my feet and took flight. Along the way, men at arms and servants stared after a weeping, freckled lady's maid on the run.

The driver who had come to fetch me, the one who would now drive me back, wore *Blanc Sanglier*. I had said only a few words to him on our way, but not a single word was passed between us during our return.

"Why, Rose! Whatever...?"

I arrived in a rage, slamming through the door. I was seldom angry with her, but this was different.

"You knew of this, Milady! And sent me off like a lamb to the slaughter!"

Anne regarded me, calm as a Madonna.

"You could have done me the courtesy to tell me of your decision, Milady. I am the one who will be yoked to that great brute for eternity, after all."

Anne lifted her chin regally. "You were, very recently, honest enough to point out the obvious to me in the matter of husbands. Now, I do the same for you." She was only a degree less chilly than Richard had been.

"This is different." Purposefully, I left off "Milady."

"Is it?" Anne refused the bait. "We, each one of us, owe these gentlemen our lives."

"I have no past with Hugh Fletcher.".

"Next year, you will," Anne replied, as if this made sense.

"No! No! By the Holy Well!" I stamped my foot in purest rage. "How can you talk to me—like—like—a man?"

We both knew what man. A long pause followed in which we measured each other. A log in the hearth broke in two, a fiery crash in the midst of our silence.

"Rosie." She patted the seat beside her. "Come here to me."

"No!" I stamped again, quite beside myself. "No! How can you do this to me? Send me to the knackers like an old horse? You know that I have loved you—always! How can you treat me so?"

"Rosie," Anne insisted. "Hush and sit with me." There was knowledge in her eyes which doused my fire. All of a sudden, I was afraid.

She had made friends with the cats about St. Martin's. Two striped grays, affectionate sisters, snuggled in a basket by her feet. Slowly, I approached and took a seat beside her on the high-backed bench. Anne faced me, back perfectly straight. Her blue eyes seemed to look right through me. I knew with absolute clarity what she was about to say.

"Rosie," she said when I had settled my gray skirt beside her. "I know."

"Milady?"

201

"About—about Dickon." She was not accusatory, neither angry nor jealous, just Yorkshire matter-of-fact. "He confessed to me, and he is very, very guilty—as he most certainly ought to be."

Senses reeling, I began to get down on my knees before her, but she held my hands and prevented it. This talk we would have side by side.

"Have we not been closer than I am to my sister? Now, dear Rose, tell me about this Fletcher, about why you are so against him. Talk to me about my Cousin Dickon, if you need to. Talk about—about—any of it." It was shocking to meet such authority in her familiar eyes. In spite of all she had so recently suffered, in spite of my four more years, at this moment, I felt a child.

"Oh, I did not mean to! I never wanted to hurt you! I love you! You must believe!" I hid a burning face in my hands. "Only—only—I—I love him, too."

"Yes, Rose. Yes. I know. I love you, too, as much, I think, as I love him, only—only—it cannot be. My mother said she saw it coming years ago. Remember when she sent you away to Mother Ash and brought Grace and Margaret to me?"

How could I forget that anguish, that first time away from my Anne?

"It is not fair to you, Rose, to pull you apart between us. It is best you be in your place, and I be in mine. There is no other way for people to live. In time, the king will certainly let Richard marry me, but you were twenty at All Hallows. Long ago you should have been rewarded for your faithful service and true affection. You should be well married and settled."

I began to weep. I was trapped, no way out. No way, it seemed, exactly as it had been for all the women in the world since....

"Master Fletcher is to be the Duke of Gloucester's man. You will live at Middleham Village near Mother Ash, who, I am informed, is not fit anymore. Soon, you shall succeed to her duties. Forever you shall have my heart and my gratitude."

I had never thought much about the future, but here it

was. What she said made perfect sense. There were barbs, yes, but taken in all it was a generous solution.

"And you and your lord shall ride among your castles, and I shall stay at Middleham and watch you come and go." This ended, as you might imagine, with a terrible sob. My dear lady—my sweet friend—put her arms around me and held me close while I cried my heart out.

"Do you forgive me?" Between us, this was the chief matter.

"No." Anne pushed my veil away so she could stroke my braid, "I don't think I do, but I can understand how it happened. At any rate, I've been horribly jealous."

"I was horribly jealous of the prince. He was so very handsome."

"So he was."

Was that a catch in her voice?

Anne and I hugged each other. Beneath her rounding bosom I could feel her heart beat, steadily, soundly. *My doing,* I thought. *I have made her strong, made her well.*

"Oh, Rose," she said. "I do forgive you. Was I not a wife? I know men do not play fair. They love as if it is a game they mean to win, while we—we—are different. We must believe in our love."

❀

There is a point at which we must simply save face. Nothing could be done. Nothing! I must simply do as I was told. The fact that I was to be forced into this marriage roused a fury which nothing could still. That Hugh was neither ugly nor repellant, that he seemed to want me very much, made it even more infuriating.

Anne and Richard in complicity! I was at everyone's disposal, to be put out of the way as soon as it suited. Darkly, I wondered if Hugh intended to abuse me after I was within his power.

Of course, Richard, both as good lord and as guilty man, would supply my dower. Another reason for Hugh, known as one to whom money stuck, would continue to pursue me. None of this may have been fair to think about, but even a cup of stinking strong valerian tea could not stem the tide of my black thoughts.

Grace Poleyn and Margaret Neville arrived a few days later, older as were all of us, giddy at their escape from the harsh conditions under which the Countess was kept at Beaulieu. Margaret was the same, cool and wary. Grace reminded me of a puppy with those big teary eyes, and the way she practically wet the floor in her joy.

"Merry meet!" She threw herself to the ground before My Lady. Anne raised her up, all welcoming smiles.

I was supposed to be mending, but my hands lay idle. A servant brought wine and cake, while Anne talked with Grace and Margaret as if they were her equals, on and on about her mother, about the war.

The ladies have arrived. Good dog Rose is sent to kennel...

They'd brought a letter from the Countess. After devouring it, Anne said, "And here, at the end, dear Rose, my Lady Mother greets you by name and congratulates you upon your marriage!"

The Countess had changed my life, all those years ago; she had been good to me. I certainly pitied her present hard circumstances. Richard had been negotiating with King Edward to obtain her release into his custody. In Middleham village they'd later quip that it was a fair Christian indeed who would desire his mother-in-law to live with him, even before he'd bedded the bride.

"So you will take used goods, sir?" I confronted Hugh while he stood at attention, guarding the black oak door of Crosby's Place. I will not detail the intelligence gathering, the scheming, or the effort it had taken me to get here. Francis Lovell had been right. The scorpion was roused, and I would have trekked through hell to lay a few stings upon my husband-to-be.

"A man may overlook a hump for a good dower." He grinned down at me, all red cheeked good humor. It was a clear, frosty December day, a thin scud of ice across the puddles, the ruts frozen in place. Hugh was hale and hearty, looking better than ever in shining helm and mail, a sword at his side and an axe in hand.

"You are sorely mistaken about that."

"A certain well-disposed Lord says I shall soon have it in hand, Mistress Rose, so I have decided to stay the course and make an honest woman of thee."

"So! It is for your own gain!"

"Not at all, Rosalba Whitby! You refused courting, which leaves a man with no other choice but to speak to her master. Besides, you went back on your promise."

"Promise?"

"Your promise by the river. How easily you set aside my true devotion!" He was now half way to joking, baring his teeth in an infuriating grin.

"Made under duress, you great, stupid ox!"

"Did you truly believe that after going to all the trouble of slitting a man's throat and saving your life, I was going to knock you on the head and throw you in the river if you refused?"

"I hardly know who or what to believe—then—or now."

"Well, here's a lesson for you. Put not your trust in princes." Hugh winked a frosty gray eye, older and wiser, from beneath the silver helm. "I assume you have had time to meditate upon your errors."

This was not going as I had planned. Now, he'd made me blush and this made me even angrier. How dare he rub my nose in that?

"Folly brings no reward."

"From this time forth, Mistress Rose, you must put your trust in me. I shall never fail you."

"A mighty promise, Master Fletcher, but I doubt time will prove you up to it."

"You don't know what's good for you, lass." He scowled,

injured at last. "You will learn that if this great ox wills his head under the yoke beside yours, so it shall be."

"You shall live to rue the day!" With what I hoped was the last word, I stormed away.

I hadn't got very far when I heard someone else shouting. Looking back, I had the small satisfaction of seeing Hugh's captain on the steps beside him, bawling, "Mouth shut and eyes sharp, you great northern bullock! You're not here to chat up serving girls."

·❧

Upon the twelfth day of Christmas, we were married at the porch steps of St. Martin's. Lady Anne stood in the open door as witness, while Grace and Margaret huddled behind her, half hidden in the dark doorway. Under her stern eye, I went through my part obediently.

As we kissed good-bye, however, there were tears. It had been arranged that Hugh and I would go north with some others in my Lord of Gloucester's service. We would not see each other again for a very long time. My new husband stood by patiently while my sweet Lady and I hugged good-bye.

At Crosby's Place a supper was provided in the kitchen, attended by servants of the duke's household. Richard had been right about a Twelfth Night marriage. It was just the thing to cheer everyone, a last feast before the gloomy, frigid winter. There was merry talk, a piper, laughter, and a good roast piglet. Everyone had a wonderful time. I was the exception, spending the evening holding my tongue while attempting to maintain my dignity. Hugh and I had been granted a bed in a cupboard within a locked storeroom. It was a luxury for folks in service to have this much privacy, even on a wedding night.

·❧

Don't think, I exhorted myself, clenching my jaw and resigning myself to what was about to happen. *He'll be quick and then snoring.*

"Think you are going to get away with that?"

I opened my eyes. There he was, braced over me on his forearms, all barrel belly and those muscular shoulders.

"I should check for knives. With you damned dales women, a man can't be too careful." This had to be a joke. He was as much of the dales as I.

"All who live by Scotland carry a weapon, as you well know, Master Fletcher."

"Therefore, again I ask: Have you set your weapon aside, Mistress?"

"Yes, but I wish I had not."

He chuckled, taking this in the spirit offered. "Come now," he said, rolling onto his side. "Talk to me."

I looked him up and down in the flickering light of our candle, which he would not—of course—blow out. There he was, the balding bear with bushy blonde eyebrows to whom I'd been eternally chained. We were under the covers, naked, and skin to skin. I was monstrously embarrassed. I had sworn, however, to wear bravery through this ordeal—*if nothing else.*

"Talk? About what?"

"About your heart."

"What do you care about my heart?" This conversation was proving to be as unnerving as anything I'd imagined.

"I had hoped, when the duke dropped you, your heart might turn." He assumed a lovelorn expression.

"It is not simply a case of one man or another."

"You *are* a woman, aren't you? With that vacancy within which yearns to be filled?"

Such—I guess—delicacy! Still, his joking angered me.

"You obviously know very little about women."

"I have had a few women in my time, lass, and I have made it my business to learn about you. For instance, I know you work hard, take yourself seriously and are clever as well as a nice armful. All that I like, for such a wife keeps a fellow on his toes."

"Stop trying to make an even bigger fool of me than you already have. What you mean is that a full purse makes up for my being used goods."

"To marry a woman with a full purse is plain horse sense. As to being used, that was simply a small slice of what appears to be an ample pie. Our generous lord doesn't seem at all inclined to another piece."

"Damn you to hell and the Duke of Gloucester along with you!" I swung at him, but Hugh intercepted. I was engulfed in big arms, crushed against his body, where an inch of fat covered layer upon layer of hardest muscle. There was no escape.

"Hush, Rosie. We've an audience."

From outside I heard smothered laughter.

"He's roused her," someone whispered.

"Nayh!" Hugh threw open the cupboard door and shouted, slurring as if he were blind drunk. "Never hinder me, woman! I'll end this riot." He'd leapt out of our bed, which responded with a great creak as his bulk lifted. Outside, there was shushing and hasty scuffling. Throwing down the bar of the storeroom with a great clatter, he banged the door open with a roar, massive arms raised over his head.

Even from the backside, it was something to see. There were shrieks, whoops, and a stampede down the stairs. A few minutes later I heard Secretary Kendall shouting, "Decorum! Wretched Churls! Is this how you reward our lord's generosity? Shall I set the guard upon you?"

Hugh closed the outer door and barred it. Grinning triumphantly, naked and still mostly erect, he returned to our bed and pulled the cupboard entry shut.

"That should be the end of that, Mistress Fletcher."

We actually shared a smile. When one of his big hands came about my neck and drew me close for a kiss, I did not resist. There were things about this man I had to own I liked.

"It's much the same with any fellow who's healthy and has his heart set on pleasing his woman," Hugh whispered as he drew me down.

"No!" I panicked at the sight of him looming over me.

"I won't crush you. He pushed up again on his big arms to demonstrate how he would keep from cracking my ribs.

"Easy, lassie; I know what I'm about."

He was surprisingly gentle. His natural sensuality proved exciting; his large body was fit and wholesome. After a time, he murmured, "Lets me into the city, she does, but hides the treasure."

"What?" Although I knew exactly what he meant.

"Come on, Rosie." He bent to graze my neck encouragingly with his lips. "Don't tell me that skinny little sprig o' the broom is a better man than this big, strong soldier?"

"I can't." I had begun to tremble. It was not supposed to be like this—not with him!

He responded by rolling onto his back. He never let go of me, though, and this brought us contrariwise, me on top. Huddling against his broad fuzzy chest, I prayed to the Blessed Mother that novelty would make him spend and then leave me in peace.

"I'll be the horse." His big hands swept warmly down the length of my back to fasten upon my hips. "Stay up, sweetheart, and I'll give you a ride."

My Dickon had been a hawk—ravenous, magical, all fire and air. Hugh was all earth, frankly offering me his marriage vow: 'With my body, I thee shall worship'. That night I learned every manner of man may prove a lover.

❦

It was different from my first experience, but, after all is said and done, much the same. Afterward, I went to sleep in his arms, not in tears, not humiliated, but released from my cares by this most humble, fleshy delight.

In the morning, however, I washed long, remembering the thorough manner in which Anne had performed the same task after her nights with the Prince. It was a strange and uneasy feeling, to recall what Hugh and I had taken and given, that wildness shared with our cousins, the beasts. I was relieved there would be some time before I would share a bed with my husband again.

❦

"I see you know how to bend the knee." We were withdrawing from the hall at Crosby's Place. Hugh had been humble in Secretary Kendall's presence.

Yesterday had been Saint Brigit's day, the first cross-quarter day, in which new contracts between servant and master were drawn. Richard had delegated our business, as I had expected, and we had stood in a line. Some were supplicants receiving largess, others looked for justice, while the remainder settled rents.

"And why should I not?" He jingled the purse as we marched arm in arm out into the thin winter sunshine.

"Are you not angry?" Personally, I had suffered, feeling as if everyone in the room knew exactly what I'd done to make the Duke of Gloucester so obliging.

"No," Hugh said. "This not only makes reparation, but is a sweet apology into the bargain. How often does a wronged man receive anything like justice from a lord?"

"You are not angry with me anymore?" I had been surprised to discover I actually liked Hugh well enough to care.

He did not answer right away. When we were well out of anyone's earshot, he halted.

"I will always be angry about what you gave away." Sunlight gleamed on his white brows. The eyes beneath were as chill and bleached as winter sky. "Now, don't look so put upon."

I suppose my face—and the inner groan—was all he needed to reckon my state of mind.

"Everyone is allowed a few mistakes. Now that we are married, however, don't ever make that mistake again."

"Or?" Never one to shun battle, I rose, fish to his fly.

"I will kill you, Rose." He spoke the words calmly. "From now on, you are mine."

With this speech, we were again a hundred miles apart. Looking up at him, I saw myself cast into the very pit he'd lifted me from but a few weeks ago. I felt small and bullied, terrified of him—and, of our future.

"You think threats will make me love you?"

"No threat. It is simply what will happen. Best you know it."

In the yard, he lifted me easily into a waiting cart. We would leave now, traveling with a contingent of the duke's men, sent north to help defend the Warwick inheritance. February blew around us, stinging and cold.

It would be a bitter trip, so far to the north. I settled my cloak around me and huddled down between the trunks, out of the wind. I felt little but fear. It was disturbingly like my long ago journey to Middleham.

Nothing was settled between the two dukes. The King equivocated. George and Richard played dogs; my Lady Anne was the bone. Temporarily, however, Richard had been put in charge of the maintenance and protection of the northern part of the Warwick spoil. Our journey would take us by way of Warwick Castle, Pontefract, Nottingham, and finally, to Middleham. At each post, a part of the company with whom we marched would remain.

Anne stayed in sanctuary. She was well-tended, wrapped again in a cocoon of privilege, with her own cooks and servants, presiding over a demi-household, all maintained, *sub rosa*, by the Duke of Gloucester.

Chapter XVII

I t was a long journey in the cold, bouncing over the frigid ruts, waiting out snowstorms that, fortunately, were more wind and wet than accumulation. At last, we arrived at Middleham.

I was kept busy righting the cottage we'd been awarded, one that had lain empty for many months. The things we'd bought in London were what we started housekeeping with—two cook pots, metal forks and tongs, blankets and linen, stools of differing heights and a bedstead. With these, and what remained in the house—an ancient monster of a cupboard with many shelves and countless mouse-droppings, a battered table and a high backed bench by the hearth—I set up housekeeping.

In spite of the minor disrepair of broken shutters, the cottage was sturdy. There were slates upon the floor and a well-built central stone chimney that a sweep cleared for us. The house had size, with a room before and behind the chimney and a loft above for storage and winter sleeping.

At first, we rattled within like two peas in a dry husk. There was plenty of joking that I must need breed quickly, and fill the place up. It was odd to find myself at chores that for years had been the province of mere house servants. I swept, carried ashes, and hauled both wood and water.

Hugh was also out of practice at domestic tasks, and I heard him cursing like a madman as he worked on the broken shutters, but he did the heaviest lifting and was always helpful. The bedstead and trunk were rope hauled into the dark, warm loft. Hugh lifted me up while I strung hanks of Sweet Annie, rosemary and lavender from the rafters to sweeten the air. Out of doors it snowed and wind howled. The towers of Middleham castle appeared and disappeared in flurries of slashing white. I was home again, but not in the way I had so long imagined. Sometimes it was bitter to stand in the shadow of the great keep and find myself a simple tenant living in the sparse northern village of a lord who was not presently at home.

"Do not grieve." Hugh caught me at it one day. He patted me on the back.

My first instinct was to pull away.

"Oh, Rosie!" He gathered me patiently against the heat of his big chest. "You should not. That is no life for the likes of you and me—running like a dog when they call. We can make something of our own now. I tell you, lass," he rubbed my shoulders and settled me warmly against his gut, "for years I imagined I had a good life, but what does a young fool know? This is contentment, to be well-settled, to know where I'll rest my head at night, and who will rest beside me."

He was happy, I could tell, hoping for no more wars, no more hardship, for a time of comfort and warmth. I tried—yes, I did—to be his good wife.

Mother Ash lived a street away. Of course, she was older than ever, a genuine crone now, all bent, her face twisted from a seizure. Still, she hobbled here and there, and her hands did not shake too badly. She was still the midwife of the village, although her practice was small. She simply did not have the strength to travel about these days.

"You have been missed," she said, taking up our conversation as if it had been in progress, irritated from the moment I entered. "I didn't teach you for all those years to have you go gallivanting off to France, playing lady's maid, you know! The Blessed Mother knows there are plenty of gently-bred ladies for that *fol-de-rol*. I've had to start all over again with a girl who is not so satisfactory. My time on this earth is not unlimited, Rosalba Whitby!"

Useless, I could see, to defend myself by speaking of Anne. Ash spoke with the imperiousness of the old and she was right. Our lives run through so quickly. We must make a mark while we can.

"Well, here I am again, Mother Ash, for the rest of my

earthy stay."

"Which you regret. Mmm..." She made a new considering sound I'd never heard before, deep in the back of her throat. "You have done well for a poor ignorant girl from the dales." Her brown eyes snapped with sly humor. "Let us hope you have not forgotten everything, and that you do not become interested only in breeding with that big bull husband of yours."

Fire reflected upon the rafters of her house, hung as always with bunches of simples, of scented lavender and rosemary and strings of dried fruit. A gray cat, as of old, slept under the fire bench, chin resting on a tidily tucked tail.

Stung, I defended myself. "I was given in marriage to Hugh Fletcher by the will of Lady Anne and Duke Richard of Gloucester. It is no love match."

"The best kind!" Ash leaned to cheerfully smack my hand with hers. The flesh was dry, like fine leather. A wry, toothless smile cracked her sunken cheeks. "Good! You will not turn housewife. Now, you can be the one to go out in the snow and catch all the new lambs."

The idea of suddenly practicing midwifery, when I hardly had done anything in that way at all, was truly alarming. It must have showed in my face for she said, "Come, come. It's not so hard. It's only that folks think it is. I'll teach you some good birthing charms and if the signs are bad, you can send for me. Surely you remember something o' what I taught?"

Her gaze was so severe that I did not dare say a word, except to humbly ask if we could begin to practice the charms right away.

Busy with my new home, busy with learning and new duties, I hardly had time to think for the first months, which was just as well. Hugh settled in quickly and gained the respect, if not the love, of his new cohorts in arms.

There was some jealousy at first, some sense that he had been promoted over others because of our marriage. It did not take too many Sundays, however, for the rest to see the kind of archer he was, or too many watches for them to learn that he knew his job. After a duty tour in which he and his company let blood a bandit gang who had been terrorizing the area, voices lifted in a cheerful greeting when he entered The Bear.

"They found an honest man and a good soldier for you, Roan Rose." This, delivered with an approving nod, was what I heard that spring, as the natural reticence of Yorkshire began to thaw. The comments jarred, of course, but no one knew what I truly felt—nor would they! That the remainder of the Earl of Warwick's household believed I had married well was a balm.

It was sad to learn how many of the older folk had died, many who had followed their Lord of Warwick into his bloody folly. Among them, gone into darkness, was my dear True Thomas. I wept sorely when I heard this long delayed news.

There was worse. I sent greetings to Aysgarth, to my mother, as soon as I was come into the country again, but she could not reply. She had died, and that, only a few months past, in the early winter. Bled to death from the womb, I learned, while walking to tend a sick child on the dales. She had lived forty-three years.

My youngest sister Lily was still in Aysgarth. She would be fourteen now, but, somehow, that was a tie broken. I would go see her in the spring, I thought. It was a decision I would later regret, but there seemed to be far more urgent matters. This was the true beginning of my practice of curing and midwifery. There were calls at midnight to travel through the snow with someone to tend a good wife's labor, or to try to help a child win free of fever or choking catarrh, or to hold an aged hand while life sighed away.

I had never shifted a child myself, so there were those who their doubts about me. It was rough going at first, facing down their suspicions with only my common sense and the word of Mother Ash or those ancient charms to spin their faith upon. White-faced men with broken limbs at least lay still, so I put on authority and used a strength that my teacher no longer had to set matters straight. Some, as in any winter, died: the old, infants, a woman three weeks from childbed. Years later, I could fall into bed and sleep dreamless after days and nights of watching and nursing the dying, but it was not during that anxious, always aching, first year.

"You have a son?" I was surprised, but should have seen it coming. As we approached April, Huge had grown almost diffident. He no longer lorded over me, the wise man, the old soldier primed for husbandry who'd scooped up a young woman with good dower. Bane of my life, but I've always had a quick sense about people—not that I ever pay the least bit of attention to that wise self which senses how things really are.

Fire glimmered over his strong features while he studied my reaction. He was square-headed, nothing like the long narrow head of Old Whitby. Had he shared that characteristic as well as his fairness, I would have bolted, leaving Hugh Fletcher, the noble Duke of Gloucester, and my dear Lady Anne as far behind as I possibly could.

"How old is the boy?" My heart sank. I could see us saddled with a rambunctious, neglected boy.

"Sixteen," said Hugh. He smiled as if this would cheer me up. "Thought I was going to bring you a jumping kid to rear, didn't you?"

"That is what second wives get to do—raise the first wife's children and listen to her husband sing the praises of a woman they have doubtless worked—or bred—to death."

"Ah," he replied, shaking his head, "so dour and wise and put upon, my Rosie." He lifted his mug and took a long swallow, probably in order to continue dealing with me.

"Well, why haven't you told me?"

"When? While I was saving your freckled skin and tenderly courting you, or while you were busy pouring bile and scorn all over my head?" He jutted his chin and his eyes held a dangerous light. "While you were pining over my Lord of Gloucester, who plucked the cherry and left the tree for another to tend?"

"That is not to the—"

"No, it's not. The business before us is that I have a son. After all these years I can make a home for him and I intend to do so. Is that so hard for you?"

"I never said—" and sputtered to a halt. It was, after all, neither his fault nor the boy's. "To care for your son is fatherly and just," I amended, schooling myself. Exactly as he'd said, I'd made everything hard for him, and all he'd wanted was to marry me—not only freckled, but unchaste, to boot....

"A better answer! We can use some help around here. We will not be able to do all we must upon the land allotted not to mention the service we owe the duke, without help."

"That is what cottagers are for."

"Or a man's sons, has he any. My boy Jackie is well-grown and strong. He'll be a big help."

There was a pause in which I, too, took a deep draught of the bitter brown. When I lowered the mug, there he sat, still staring.

"I shall make a drinker of thee yet, Lass."

"Indeed you shall," I replied, trying not to sound spiteful. "Have you any other secrets to share with your wife, Master Fletcher?"

"Not at present."

"Which means there are more?"

Hugh shrugged, his ruddy face a genial blank. I distrusted him most in that style.

"So tell me how you came by this son."

Hugh studied my face for a long moment before he began. "Jackie was born in Sandal Magna when I was sixteen. My father was a good man and beyond patient. When my Aldy got big by me, he let us wed and put us to work in his house. He had plenty and understood the way things are without a sermon every hour. Aldy was fourteen when she gave me Jackie. She had another at the breast when the Bitch of Anjou came." My husband's face turned to stone. Whatever the horror of that day had been, I knew it would never be told.

"My Jackie and I were about all of my family to live through it, only else my brother Rafe and his Margery who'd been lucky to visiting her folks when it happened. It broke my heart to leave Jackie, two-years-old and lost his mother, but there wasn't much else could be done. Rafe and Marge have raised Jackie all these years alongside their kids and have done what they could. Now that I am settled, I can do better by him—and them."

The tale was familiar. Soldiers from abroad returned home to reclaim their families, boys and girls who barely knew their own sires. Sometimes the trouble caused by these reunions ended only when the father marched off to more battles.

"Have you seen him very often?"

"Well, a time or two a year—sometimes not at all—as and when I could manage. When I was in Germany—well, it's no regular life I've led."

"A great lad of sixteen," I chose my words carefully. "Has he not fixed upon some trade?"

"He can shoot, like me," Hugh said proudly. "Jackie can split the eye of a running hare." Then, he added, "but it appears he'll never make a soldier."

"Why?"

"He hasn't the heart for it. He's farmed with Rafe and he's spent a year as a 'prentice to a smith, but he hasn't the patience. Has an eye, as I said, but can't be bothered." He shook his head and considered the remains of our supper. Suddenly, beside the bread and cheese, he slammed his knife into the table, which did not bode well.

"Will he be upset that his father has taken a wife? Will he work for us?"

"He knows how to work, that's for certain if Rafe and Marge raised him. That Marge! I can see her now, a stick in her hand and a young 'un bare-assed over her knee. As for you," he said, brightening, "the pup may be jealous of what the old dog has—but, as for my takin' a wife, well, it's none o' his business."

"It is natural to dislike change and the reason for it."

"Ah! You would know all about that, wouldn't you?" He reached out and before I could protest, had pulled me onto his knee. "Such an old, wise Lass! Now, don't start thy fretting! Not at bedtime, anyhow." A hand moved to my breast; his lips brushed my cheek.

I didn't want to argue, but I noted that, my husband, who

was no one's fool, had turned the conversation.

⚜

I was cooking, leaning red-faced from a stool into the fire, when Hugh came in. The door remained open, and behind came two more, a girl and a boy, a pair of baby-faced Saxons, fair as flax.

"Mistress Rose," Hugh spoke cheerfully. "Here is my boy, Jackie—and his wife, Bett."

As promised, there stood my new-made son, as well as the something more my husband had been unwilling to discuss. Wise for once, I didn't say a word.

They were both half grown pups, everything soft and awkward. The boy had a round face and held his cap in a raw, overlarge hand. The girl was doughy faced and big-bellied, weary circles round her eyes.

The son retells the father's story!

They gazed at me the way humbler folks did, slack-jawed. Hugh must have given them a great talking to about his high-and-mighty wife.

"I am glad you have come, and — and — I hope we shall learn to be family."

"Yes! We shall help each other get on." Hugh clapped the boy on the shoulder. At his touch, the round, scantily whiskered face grew sullen. I had a sharp premonition of how things were going to be.

Chapter XVIII

S ometimes the boar flew high above the castle ramparts, but I was not within. Now, I came and went, performed my tasks and went home. Here I'd see about supper and chastise Bett for what she had not done.

As I'd feared, Bett and Jackie were naught but a pair of children. The two of them would sit and sing prettily while he played a lute he'd brought with him from Sandal Magna, but work they avoided like the plague. Bett was in her last three months of pregnancy. She was frightened of giving birth and frightened to be so far away from her home.

Every day I'd ask her to do a task or two, but she would "forget." I would patiently remind her, and then she'd forget again. She boiled our oat porridge over and did it so often she came near to ruining my fine new three-legged pot. She would not weary herself scrubbing it clean, either. There was always an excuse.

Sometimes, I'd come home dead tired, and there she'd be, sitting on the stoop, feeding scraps to our red chickens and not doing another blessed thing. If she went into our garden as much as she said, it would have been the pride of the village, but instead there were as many weeds sprouting as vegetables.

And Jackie! Sucking ale and practicing his lute, joking and lolling about with any other do-naught he could find in the square or outside The Bear. Not much got done in our fields or for the lord, either. It got so bad that the bailiff knocked at our door to explain that if things went on as they had, we must give money in lieu of the boon-work we owed.

"It's a good thing I came home early today or there'd be no supper—at least, none we wouldn't puke."

Jackie and Bett put their heads down, two bad children, but kept shoveling what I'd prepared into their faces. Supper was bread baked a few days ago and fresh pea porridge thickened with last year's turnips. I'd set out boiled eggs and an end of cheese to fill in the holes. The last bean soup I'd cooked had soured, but lazy Bett had been perfectly willing to reheat it one last time.

Well, perhaps they did not want a fight, but I did. I told Hugh what the bailiff had said. This focused my husband's attention and a good old family row we had! The youngsters went sulking off together before we'd half got our shouting done.

"We'll have to pay a cottager to do his work, and if we do that—by Our Lady—there'll be nowt to put back! I can do much of my work--and hers--about the house, but I can't mow hay and thresh into the bargain."

"No! No! And why should you? By Christ!"

"I wish she'd drop that lamb. At least we'd have an end to that. She's sick! She's tired! Her back aches! I am up before the sun and to bed after it goes down, and I'm carrying."

"Eh?"

I glared at him, arms akimbo. No, I hadn't bothered to tell him. Why should I? A man, even one who was often gone on duty, ought to notice the lack of a certain woman's business, should he not?

"You heard me."

"When did that happen?" He tried to take my hand, but I was still angry and snatched it free.

"May Eve," I replied, and then felt softer, for Hugh's pale eyes silvered with pleasure. We'd watched the dancing and later gone for a walk that had ended in a nearby grove along with half the courting couples from the village. He'd been utterly intoxicated by our roll in the grass, although I'd been worried the whole time someone would see us. It touched me that he was tenderhearted enough to feel pleasure at my news.

"Ah," he said, chest visibly swelling, "get the lass back to her home, and see what happens!" His big arms warmly enclosed me. Outside, twilight draped the rolling green land. The last rays of sunlight haloed the high battlements of the castle.

Blessedly, neither Jackie nor Bett appeared to destroy our peace. Those hefty red chickens prowling in the yard did gather at our feet expectantly. A good thing about her constant cosseting was that one of them was soon going to make a very fine dinner!

The fires of evening trailed smoke across the roof tops. There was a murmur as our neighbors took ease in the long summer evening. Soon enough it would be haying and after, harvest home. Every hour of each long summer day would be spent in labor.

From two streets over, a rousing song floated up from outside The Bear.

"Probably Jackie." I sighed, resting against my husband's broad chest.

"Umm." Hugh agreed, arms close around me. "They aren't working out, are they?"

"No."

"Christ's bloody nails! Everything in my life is a damned battle." He heaved a sigh. "Rafe told me how it was, that he was at his wit's end with the boy. I had to know better."

"Which is why everything in your life is a battle, Master Fletcher."

"Well, damn it, I'm his father! I've a duty to try to set him straight."

"I hope you can, because I've got enough on my plate with Bett. She's in a dream all the time."

"You need help, my lass."

"Help costs."

"By Our Lady! I do regard a frugal wife."

"As you should, Master Fletcher."

"Ah, but here's a difference, Mistress Rose. Now comes my next child—God willing—and I have waited long to bring another honestly into this world. You shall have it easier from this day forth. I promise."

And, better than words, this paragon hauled water for the night and helped me clean the supper dishes. We went to bed and made love, as wantonly as we wished, with no one in the house from whom to hide our pleasure. This part of marriage had become a great delight to me, for Hugh was a hungry lover. Besides, the damage was already done.

Noses out of joint, they didn't come back—at least, not while we were there—but the next day while we were at work, they collected a bindle and went off haying field to field, where whatever landowner there was supplied food and drink. I couldn't imagine what Bett, unwieldy and unwilling, was pretending to do, but it was just as well they were gone.

For a time, they'd be earning their own keep. Harvest was fun if you were young and strong, rambling from one place to another, sleeping in tents and sheltering in barns when it stormed. There'd be ale and a good free supper. At least, they wouldn't be in my hair.

To my surprise, I discovered that Bett *had* done a few things, mostly those that could be done sitting down. She had spun wool and made a decent job of it. She had fed the hens and got the sheep to pasture and back. She had not milked much, but had let the lambkins suckle all they wished. If there was only a little cheese, this meant our first lambs were healthy and milk fat. Of course, neither she nor Jackie had mucked out often so we did lose one to the scours.

Livestock—both the two legged and the four—will soon fall ill if the shit isn't regularly taken away. Hugh was sufficiently humbled to take on this task himself and made a thorough job of it. In our Lord's field, though, as he did double time catch-up work, and cursed Jackie the entire time.

It struck me funny, though, the way our thick-legged hens missed Bett. They came poking their heads in the door, staring at me with their beady eyes, crooning songs of *braaawk-brawk-brawk*, which I took for questions about where their friend had gone. Still, it was a daily challenge to discover where each had hidden her eggs, for Bett had allowed them to nest just about anywhere.

At last we found a woman to do some cleaning and engaged her husband to muck out our shed as needed and to work the allotment. Hugh laid out some cash and I bartered simples and made a promise to attend the cottager's daughter-in-law, one whom would soon be lying-in.

.🐝

On a full moon night toward the middle of August, Bett gave birth in the fields, just like the silly little cow she was. Jackie sent for me, though there was a Granny in a nearby village who could have tended her. The ride in the moonlight with the young fellow they sent to get me was fun, though, once I woke up. We jounced along in a cart, over rutted roads, while I gazed up at the star-filled sky.

I swear, for the last mile, I could hear Bett screaming, which was rather alarming. I did not get too deep into the thought, for I'd stared at her lazy backside all spring, and it certainly appeared broad enough to me. No boy-hipped elegance like those Neville girls on this plump village hen!

"Why did you not sit with her, Grandmother?"

The aged crone drew herself up straight and glared from a cloudy, single eye.

"You! She will have *nowt* but you!" The words were spoken with justifiable irritation.

I took in the simple, resentful faces gathered round staring at me, the foolishly preferred stranger.

"You've delivered a year of days more little 'uns than I have, Granny Martin," I said, humbly. "I'd be glad of your counsel, if my daughter-in-law is in trouble."

A scream rose and fell from the shadowy grove beyond.

"She's in no more trouble than a cat. Yer welcome to 'er."

Some smooth address and Granny was more offended by Bett than me. I knew Ash didn't think much of Granny's work, but I put it down to a natural jealousy between practitioners close in age. Long years of experience would have brought this old woman much knowledge, so I didn't want her for an enemy. Before her neighbors, I'd offered to defer, hoping this would salve the insult.

The merrymakers had withdrawn from Bett's noise, while over our heads the night was black as a velvet robe. Shooting stars fell from the group that they say looks like a man carrying a lion's pelt. Some watchers had forsaken their campfires and were enjoying the thrill of fear such sights bring, and talking loudly about prophecies.

Shooting stars, Ash had taught me, fell from this acreage of the heaven every August. Only the kind of stars which can be seen during the day, Ash said, were dangerous to us, and the last day-star had shone a very, very long time ago, in the evil time when the Normans came.

Dawn would be here soon now, but all around plenty were still wakeful. It was the last of summer, the fat time, when even the poorest could enjoy life. Before you knew it, it would be winter. We'd all be cold and the less fortunate would feel the bitter pinch in their bellies. Such was the great wheel of the year upon which we all turned.

"Mistress Rose is come!" Jackie exclaimed, leaping up from his wife's side. "Bett would have none but you!"

They were both so young, greasy and now burned black from their long sojourn in the fields. Bett writhed on the ground, shrieking and flailing. In a fight with herself, I supposed. A skinny lass, a friend new made, sat beside her. She'd apparently given up trying to comfort and now just stared at Bett, jaw-dropped. She had, however, boiled water in a three-legged pot set on a small fire. I'd brought my basket with vinegar and clean wraps for the baby and rags for the bloody rest.

Men usually don't hang about, but Jackie had stuck by her, for which I gave him grudging credit. In the firelight hanging from a tree, I saw his lute.

Doing as little as possible in the fields, I'd wager, and singing for their supper! What a feckless pair!

"This is Mistress Fletcher, and this is our friend, Tansy Pickering."

"What's wrong w'er?" The girl, black as a gypsy, asked. "Is she dyin'? Granny said *nowt*."

"I'm going to have a look. Tansy, please hand me out of the basket what I call for."

The girl nodded. First, I got her to splash vinegar over my hands. Bett wouldn't lie still, though. She kept rolling, screaming and kicking her dusty skirts. Finally, out of patience, I smacked her face hard as I could and shouted, "This is the way of it, if you don't keep your knees together! Mind me, Bett! I can't help if you won't lie still."

It was cruel, and I never knew how cruel until I birthed my own and learned for myself how terrible is that labor pain. I'd seen Mother Ash deliver a box or three, however, with similar, calming results. It turned a young mother around, so she did not waste so much energy fighting what needed to get done.

At dawn, the baby came, a fat bald boy, dropped as smoothly as a cow calves. I didn't need to do much, just keep her in memory of how the cats did it, with shallow panting breaths. Jackie stayed through everything, as did Tansy, and I taught them both how to be useful before it was done. We waited in the grove until the next night, which did more to make us a family than all that had gone before. As it was harvest home, no cart could be spared for such an unimportant task until well after sundown.

Fortunately, it was a bright pleasant day beneath the trees for Bett, the new baby, and me. We lay on a bed of straw and took naps. There was no trouble at the teat. Bett began to leak the sticky first milk almost at once.

Folks brought us what was necessary—clean water, bread, a pot of wheat porridge, cheese and ale, and more rags, too, so we were well supplied. Once delivered, Bett seemed happy with her new task. She tended the baby with awkward devotion.

I sat under the trees and watched lines of half-naked sweating men scythe the dusty wheat, while scarlet-faced women and children raked the rows. Long ago, I'd had a task at gathering in, one I now saw other children performing. I had lugged shrub—a mixture of herbed, honeyed vinegar and water—in a jug about the field, offering refreshment. I'd sweated with the workers and breathed in the sweet choking dust. Today, I sat with Bett and the new baby and took in the scene. It was an unusual day of rest.

Hugh was well-pleased at our return and proud as punch of his grandson. The coming of the baby even stiffened Jackie's spine for a few months. He came home fit and brown and then went on to do his share of autumn clearing and plowing for the duke. His dedication lasted 'til the snow flew. Then, gradually, he fell back into feckless ways.

The baby was fine, strong, and blessedly regular in his habits. We took him to church, paid the pence, and his parents politely christened him "Hugh John." Soon enough he was "Little Jack" to us.

.❖

After the birth of the baby, Bett was different. Far from perfect, but at least trying, and it turned my opinion of her. "Little Jack" would eventually grow to be a fine man like his grandfather.

.❖

I was proud of myself and feeling strong, when a thing came to pass around All Souls, which nearly threw me, big belly and all, into the pit. Now that harvest was in, I'd gone down to Aysgarth to see how Lily was doing and discovered that misery was still a daily companion in that house.

Wicked old man! Evil came from him and spread through the rest of his family like the plague. Now, dirty, cantankerous, mind failing, he sat in the doorway on a stool, mumbling and cursing.

"Greetings, Father," said I, most humbly.

After peering up, he answered, making a feint at me with his stick, "Humph! Yer nowt o' mine, spotty bitch!"

So the visit began. He heaped insults on everyone who passed by, even his precious son, Clifford, his strong, blonde daughter-in-law and his fair grandchildren. Whitby's shouts and carping were the background against which our meal was taken.

My sister Lily was pale and thin. At first, I didn't recognize her among the cousins, for she was gangly and fair, very much like them. There was a huge, yellowing bruise on her left cheek, which she had "earned" for being slow in bringing the old monster his beer. She greeted me with a bob and cold eyes, but I took no offense. It was more than clear I should not have left her here without Mother's protection.

The meal we took in my old home swiftly soured my gut for Whitby found fault with everything and everyone. It was a hundred times worse now than it had been in my day. The children bolted their soup and rushed from the table, or served and gobbled standing in the kitchen.

After this anxious repast, Aldgyth asked me to look at one of their sheep, which, she said, was ailing. Out by the pen, a lantern between us, we sat on the rock wall. Here, I got an ear full, and the true reason she'd been so happy to see me.

"He pisses anywhere the urge takes him and forgets to put it away. He sits in the square all day and tells everyone Clifford is a fool and all his daughters are sluts. He declares your poor mother was a witch. Says she flew out the window every night and laid three devilish cuckoos in his nest."

"He has a madness which comes in old age. A choleric nature makes it particularly evil."

"Aye, and, B'Our Lady, he's healthy as a horse."

I nodded. The old man's knees and hips had gone bad, (those go quick on farmers) and he moved with difficulty, but his color was good. It was astonishing, as I thought of it, that he should still be so hearty, this man who was always putting himself into blood-boiling rages.

"Worse, the old bastard always has on a horse's pizzle. Tries to put my hand on it, he does. Catches my little Maud by the wrist and makes her touch it if I'm not watching—and she his blood! It's been hell ever since your mother died. She had draughts to quiet him."

I listened, nodding, but wondered where this was going. Soon enough, Aldgyth said, "Your mother taught you, did she not, Rose? Give me something and when you're gone, I'll put that wicked old man down like a dog."

A cold thrill ran through me. On top of the awful scene at supper, it brought me near to puking. Ash had warned the day would come when someone would ask me to use my knowledge to harm.

"What says my brother?"

Clifford had always been his father's self-righteous favorite, a mirror of his violence and strong appetites. Bad as things were, I didn't live here anymore. I had already decided to take Lily back to Middleham when I went home.

"Him!" Aldgyth was dismissive. "Men are little boys. They strut and roar, but they always want someone else to do the hard things for them."

Now, Aldgyth and Clifford had never been friends to me, nor, particularly to mother—at least, not in my time.

Was this a way to get rid of their burden and stick me with the blame?

I needed time to think, but Aldgyth, no fool, had my measure.

"Since your mother died, he has laid hands on Lily."

I gazed deep into those cold blue eyes and believed her. The noose of my neglect drew tight. *I hated that evil old man.* I always had.

"Let me think awhile," I said. "I will walk about tomorrow and see what I can find."

"We still have your mother's box." Aldgyth offered with a sidewise look.

Of course, now I was caught in her web. Had I not agreed, she would have kept mother's medicine chest and never mentioned it. In one way, though, it was now a kind of barter. Where property was concerned the Whitby's kept things straight. They might exert every muscle to cheat you beforehand, but once the deal was done, it was done, whatever the outcome.

※

"Take this vial. If you do exactly as I say, Clifford shall be master of all the next day. Just don't forget who *my* friends are." I added a threat she might believe. Hollow, of course, but worth making. I returned to Middleham that afternoon seated on a farmer's cart with mother's box beside me. I don't know if I would have done it at all had I known what would happen next.

It was a good three weeks after my visit when Clifford himself, face full of guilt and fear, appeared at my door. In private he told me that our father, with the constitution of an ox, had not quite died at once, but was lingering. Aldy was watching over him, he said, but they both thought I'd best return to Aysgarth to sit beside Whitby and pretend to care.

It is one thing to murder and walk away, another to watch the fruits of your work, as I did, for the three hellish days that remained after I arrived. Why I did not drop my baby in terror, I do not know.

Whitby had suffered mightily, swelling and unable to piss. Fortunately, the initial seizure had rendered him speechless. I told myself he deserved it, while sweating with fear that Aldgyth and Clifford would turn on me and get me hanged. They, however, were a couple made of stone, whose only complaint was about the length of time this "last illness" was taking. Each day seemed a year, but, finally, in the middle of the night, the old man gave a great hiss, very loud, and then died.

A wake followed and the next day was the burial, where the family, without tears, and in a hurry to return to the end-of-the-year labor, stuck him in the stony ground beside his wives. The whole time I waited for justice to swoop down and strangle me with a talon foot, like one of the duke's hawks. It did not happen, but my conscience was bad.

After I got home, I was as ill as I'd ever seen Anne, with coughing, headache, sore throat, and aching ears. In a fever, I'd stare into my mother's beautiful medicine chest and imagine giving myself, by accident, or in my sleep, the same dose I'd made for Whitby. I was afraid that if I died now, I would cause the death of my babe. This became a terrible matter. My baby was alive and I knew it, for she squirmed, kicked, and made her hunger known.

She must not come to harm, for nothing was her fault!

I had terrible dreams of Whitby accusing me, of dragged into fire—sometimes the stake here on earth, sometimes a flaming hell thronged with demons. Still, I dared not confess.

At the holy well, I prayed to Saint Alkelda.

It was Mother Ash to whom I finally confessed. I blathered on and on about the evil old man and about how he had treated his family. Then I spoke of how infirm he'd been and how mad, of the way Aldgyth had enticed me. I was so guilty....

All through my maundering, Ash ground a paste in her mortar, a honey-based wound dressing for one of the duke's soldiers. She nodded absently the whole time, almost as if she wasn't listening.

"This spring," she said, when I paused, wiping my eyes in a loathsome mixture of guilt and self-pity, "when the mushrooms come, I will show you a dark angel which will carry a strong man away without fail, in a heartbeat. Of course, you must find a way never be the one to give it, for a sudden death after a meal does start fingers pointing." She grinned, all gums inside those withered red apple cheeks. Shocked, I stopped crying.

"Goose! Do you think you are for hell's eternal fire over one wicked man? Do you see your fine strapping husband or our duke weeping and lamenting over those they've slain? A soldier kills at first to stay alive, but soon learns there's a kind of joy in his work. Did you understand nothing you saw while you were in the castle? Our masters—they do their murder cold. Sixteen heads, I heard, fell after Tewkesbury. I know these lords; they watch the axes fall and then trot off to dinner. Do they whimper and ask God's forgiveness? Fie on you, Rose! Put in some steel, or don't play the game!"

"I—I shall never do the like again! I have promised Our Blessed Lady."

"Why speak to her? Does she not, when her face is black, deal in death? Do you lack the stomach to use the mighty weapons I have put in your hands? Fie! Fie!" Her dark eyes were full of disapproval. "Know thyself, lass! What you truly regret is that the old man did not die at once."

"It would have been better, sure, if he'd gone quick."

"You should have asked me. You young ones! All alike! Imagine, after a year or two, that you know it all. But, the plain fact is, your memory is bad. More henbane, lass! What were you thinking? It takes twice what you gave to drop such a big man."

"If I had asked, I would have made you accomplice to my evil deed."

"So very evil was it? Whitby had his way for years, did 'e not? He'd bullied and beaten four wives and had his pleasures. Seems high time he took himself off, and left something to those unhappy souls he begot."

"But—but—who am I to pretend to be worthy to be his judge?"

"Do you think all who are born high, all who judge and send folks to the executioner, are without sin? That they are such pure, holy men they never make mistakes? Let me tell you the truth, as you don't seem to know it already. The rich hide their murders by use of a judge they've bought and with twelve good men and true whose balls are in their pocket."

I stood mum as a rabbit and felt a right fool.

"Now listen to me, Rose, if you cannot do the business with as much presence as my Lord Duke when he cuts the heads from his cousins' necks—whose only crime, when all is done, is to say *red* when he says *white*—you had best not do it. Guilt is the sure way to a real fire."

In her eyes, my wrong-doing consisted of having incorrectly prepared. Her notion of punishment was to have me recite remedies whenever she called out for them. When I got one wrong, I had to perform some wretched household task for her. Considering the old-woman disarray now spreading within her dwelling, it made me think pretty hard before I spoke.

I got over my guilt, much as Ash had said. Not so much as "boo" came from Aysgarth, except by way of Lily, who was here at every market day now, happy as a lark, selling eggs or cheese. I'd asked her to come home with me after the funeral, but she'd replied that she'd just as soon stay on.

"Thank you, Sister Rose, but now that Dad is gone, 'twill not be so bad." She made this little speech flat as a firecake while her gray Whitby eyes shifted away from mine.

At the time, I imagined she had a sweetheart in the village. Again, it was much easier just to let things with Lily go. With Bett, Jackie and little Jack, and my own baby soon to come, I thought I had my hands full. I was wrong once again, but we'll get to the how and why of that in time.

Lily seemed happy when I saw her. It did my heart good to see her merry and jesting among others of her own age, flirting with the boys. She grew rounder, and it suited her well.

Yuletide came again, and we servants were invited into the great hall to celebrate by the duke's steward. My first Christmas without Anne! How strange it was to play the Yule games in the great hall of Middleham and not to see the earl or his countess presiding from the high table.

It was, however, equally strange that so many of those who ruled here, from the steward and his wife, the chaplain and his clerks, to the chamberlain, and the commander of the knights of the *mesnie*--the military presence of our duke--were the same as they had been in the earl's time. In some manner, little had changed except the name of the master.

I was back where I should be, among my own people. I had married a fine upright Yorkshireman who treated me well, and, at the advanced age of 21, was big with my first child. Everyone teased, as they do all couples in this condition. Hugh's comrades-in-arms joked with that he was a grandfather before he'd managed to "honestly sire" a second child.

"Our Rosie bloomed as we knew she would for this lucky dog." Oliver Swan, who had lately become the village saddler, said. He gazed at me with regret. His had been the head that had received that famous deluge of wash water so long ago.

"She never would have had you." John Pullen jostled him. "You don't save your money. Our Rosie was waiting 'til she found a rich old man, who may," he added with a broad wink at Hugh, "soon kick his last."

"Oh! I'm in my dotage?" Hugh retorted, waving his tankard across the table, "I'll break thee over my knee any day, Pullen! An' do they come one at time, all o' your mates, as well."

How bright and gay Middleham was! Many were glad to

toast me and my husband, to heartily wish us "thumping luck and big sons." Some even came with small presents, saying that I had not been wed in the north and so had not received the *brideswain*.

Hugh was pleased by such shows of friendship. Times, he faulted me for being too much like those I'd served, and accused me of having forgotten my place, so it cheered him to see that there were many at Middleham who held me dear. It was lovely to be among old friends and hear the boys sing the carol:

Born of a maid, a virgin pure
Born without Sin, from guilt secure
So let us be merry, cast sorrows away
Our Savior Christ Jesus was born on this day

Chapter XIX

I confess to cursing my poor husband while I labored. Even though I had gained skill in delivery during the past year, it is another matter when you are the one who must perform the trick, must rend yourself to make safe passage. Birth is blood, sweat, flooding waters and dire pain, that ends in a baby—the eternal mystery, emerging, in the Christian father's malediction, "between shit and piss."

"You have a fine daughter, Rosalba." Mother Ash held up my baby, wet and gluey, the cord just tied off, then laid her on my belly while she finished below.

Hesitantly, I put a hand upon her, this naked wet worm. She squirmed and squalled. Mine—she was mine? The notion was excessively strange.

"What a pair of lungs!" Hugh's appeared at the top of the loft ladder. He must have started up at the first cry.

"Come, Master Fletcher, if you don't mind a mess," Ash said. "There's nothing here you haven't seen before."

Lying back, swamped in the peace that follows the storm, I'd tensed, imagining Hugh would not be pleased. Master Whitby had scorned his daughters. My husband, however, surprised me. He took up the cloth that was laid to ready, swaddled our child in it, just as nice as you please, his big hard hands gentle and deft. Prophetic, the way she quieted in his arms, and settled in to gaze at him.

We named her Alkelda, after the saint in whose church we now received sacrament and at whose well I sought comfort. We gave thanks to God for her, though, in my opinion, the God inside those four stone walls didn't have much to do with the lust, blood, seed, or pain that had gone into her creation. Alkelda was sturdy, fat and surprisingly fair, every inch of her plain Yorkshire.

Two years passed. Hugh and I worked, quarreled and made up, as couples do. I continued my work under Ash's tutelage and began to gain a reputation as the local healer and acceptance as her heir.

During the spring of 1475, Duke Richard and his Anne at last made return to Middleham Castle, finally a couple, the long ago promise fulfilled. I thought it was the end of the interrupted fairytale—from now on it would be 'happily ever after'. At the time, we who had been of Warwick's household imagined so, and the idea gladdened our hearts.

Middleham Village greeted the lord and lady, blazing with banners. Men in armor, men in brigantine and mail, carrying swords and bows, jostled in the bailey. Castle and town spilled over with folk of every quality. Servants made the best shift they could, sleeping in haylofts.

The duke's visit, however, was all business. Richard, hardly glancing to right or left, rode into the yard seated upon a tall bay warhorse, reins in one gloved hand. This castle where he had once served as a sickly princeling was now his spoil.

They dismounted and went directly into the hall. Here waited an impatient, hard-eyed crowd of northerners. They had brought their quarrels before him. Numerous parties had arrived from all around the district in the last few days, accompanied by trains of servants.

The gentry came to seek justice, or, perhaps, to persuade my Lord of Gloucester to enforce their view. Those with deep pockets arrived for politics, to ingratiate themselves with this new power. Marriage to Lady Anne had brought the northern portion of the Neville-Beauchamp inheritance, and now Richard must administer it and cultivate the old family affinities.

There were the usual feuds and commotions between rival lords and their men-at-arms to discuss, as well as trespasses and arguments over property. Quarrels over the marriages of heiresses and rights of wardships would also be brought before him, for wealthy widows and orphans were ever pawns, played for advantage.

On the duke's side, there was much to be considered: justice and the law, of course, but also the delicate business of balancing the wants of his friends against the rights of his foes. I now understood far more about the great game my Lord of Gloucester played, understood far better the stakes. Not only by report, but with my own eyes had I seen the heads of once powerful men set upon city gates, food for ravens.

Nothing was certain. Nothing was forever. We bowed low before Richard of Gloucester, but he had been born as naked as the least of his subjects. In an eye blink, fortune's wheel could spin, and he might be cast down, as low as he now rode high.

Anne had time for her lesser subjects and began with a walk about her old home. The castle had her first, naturally. I was in the herb garden, directing the spring digging and clearing when at last I saw her, coming along the path.

I had not imagined her out-of-doors so soon. It had been two years since we'd kissed each other's cheeks at the door of St. Martin. Today, in a dirty old dress, I was spading around the feathery green of the perennials. There were cottagers to help me, but Mother Ash cautioned they could not always be trusted among the rarer herbs.

Yesterday I had gone to watch while she and the duke arrived along with the rest, all in our Sunday best, lining the road and the inner wall of the bailey, to greet them. Stubbornness, I suppose, sent me to stand at the back.

Today Alkelda was with me, sitting in the grass playing with a pile of pebbles and a cracked wooden cup. She was tethered to an apple tree and pleasant spells of quiet were followed by ear-splitting shrieks of temper when she abruptly remembered the end of the cord I'd tied to the leading strings at the back of her dress.

My workmates punctuated their digging with visits and chat that distracted her, and older children came and went. It was not so difficult to run back and forth, but it was annoying. I kept having to rethink what I was doing, but at home, Bet and Little Jack had runny noses. I'd wanted to keep Alkelda away from their wretched sniffling and coughing, out in the healthful sunshine.

There was a great commotion at the bottom of garden, and there she was, among cries from the children.

"Our Lady is come! Our Lady Anne!"

Gazing across the spring green at this cheerful mob, all those humble folk in dusty clothes running to greet her, I felt the old thrill of delight.

"Our Lady!

In that blue she favored, the kirtle covered by a matching blue *hoppelande* with white fur trim, she approached. Her head was covered by a simple veil and coif. It was old-fashioned, but just right for us. I watched, wanting to go curtsy with the others, to put myself in her sight, but somehow I could not.

I put my head down and started to dig again. This task needed doing, but I'd been so distracted today by Alkelda—and now she was wailing again because everyone had left her.

With a groan, I stuck the spade into the dark, damp earth and went across to her. At once, grubby little paws lifted.

"Miserable brat! What now?" I bent to pick her up, for she cried louder and louder as I'd approached. "Here." I settled her on my hip. "What's the matter? Eh? What's the matter, my mouse-meat?"

My daughter dropped her fluffy head and pressed her face against my bosom. She was tired, peckish and wanting the comfort of a breast. I sat down on a rock that served for our seat in this place and opened my dress. She knew what to do, so I could quickly slip my cloak around to cover us. Peeping into the gloom, facing out of the wind, I could see my freckled, bare breast, Alkelda attached. She paused to roll up her eyes and smirk, so I knew it was for attention she cried rather than for hunger.

"Got your way as usual, brat."

Although this was said with a jounce that drew another smile from her, it amazed me how little patience I possessed.

I'm certain I must have been just as selfish and cunning as a child, but, as I remembered things, my mother had always been most forbearing. Hugh said I was too quick to smack her fat little hands when she did wrong, but I retorted that she was always a perfect angel when he was around. Of course, he didn't help matters, doting on her as he did.

Alkelda could do no wrong! It was a love story between them, right from the start.

"Is this you, my Rose?"

There stood Anne, even lovelier than I remembered. She was winter pale, with just a copper crescent of hair visible above her high forehead. Lady Grace, looking uncomfortable as she always did out of doors, stood behind her. There was also a half-grown beautifully dressed child, doubtless one of the duke's wards. Three sweet-faced boy pages grappled with Anne's spreading train, attempting to keep it from the damp ground.

"I am most sorry, Lady Anne," I said, "that you should have to walk here, but this one," I added, indicating Alkelda's fat legs, "thought she was hungry."

"I wished to stroll beneath these blooming apple trees, Rose, so never you mind."

An old woman among the crowd, one who remembered us in the old days, spoke up. "Rosie has got a new mistress, Milady."

This drew laughter. Despite the uproar in my heart, there was a glowing sense of the past, of all of us being where we were supposed to be at last—at Middleham, together.

Hearing the fuss, Alkelda, sat up, leaving me uncovered. The red, stretched nipple, so suddenly abandoned, was embarrassing. I covered myself quickly.

"Oh! What a pretty little girl!" Anne said the same as every other well-wisher. "What an angel!"

"Thank-you, Milady." I got to my feet, with Alkelda hugged close. It would have been improper to go on sitting while my mistress stood.

My daughter was adorable that year, with a goodly amount of white blonde hair and her round rosy cheeks. She clung to my hip, staring, jaw dropped, at this new admirer who'd apparently come on purpose to meet her. A marvelous lady was this, radiant, and as beautifully and cleanly dressed as the Madonna!

Anne smiled. I'd forgotten how lovely she was, how perfect, her eyes, her brows, her tender mouth, her glorious hair...

"Oh, Rose!" She gazed at my child with longing. "What is her name?"

"Alkelda, Milady."

"A fitting choice."

"Thank you, Milady."

"Will you say hello?" Anne spoke to her, leaning close.

First, as was her way, Alkelda played coy, closing her eyes and shrinking against me. Then she turned and said in her piping little voice, "Hello, mi'lady."

Everyone chuckled and said "how clever Rose's baby is to talk so well to our duchess." Against my bosom, Alkelda swelled and preened.

"How old?"

"Near 17 moons, your ladyship."

"So big!" Anne studied her.

"I am very glad that you have come home to us again, Milady."

"And I am very glad to be here, Rose. It has been far, far too long I've been away." Her eyes turned toward the castle, and then, with an expression of delight, took in the rolling green which lay beyond.

"It does us all good to see you so well, My Lady, and to have you here with us at last." I offered a little speech which would include the other happy faces which had gathered round.

"I cannot say how much I have longed to be here, and to see all of you." Anne opened her arms to the adoring crowd. Everyone beamed and blushed, shuffled their feet and looked mightily pleased.

"A kiss, Rose!" Anne said, so I came close and touched my lips to her fair cheek. She smelled wonderful, of lavender and angelica, of her own fair flesh. The scent of her swept me straight into a vat of pain. I had put aside how much I'd missed her, but seeing her now, being so close, brought all my loss and longing back.

"Come to me tomorrow, after Mass. We will talk."

I bobbed a curtsy with Alkelda, that warm, damp, living millstone, firmly in place. Milady walked away beneath the blossom-drifting trees, her pages and ladies like petals around the heart of a flower. Spring, a brief pink, gold and white, dotted the ground beneath the trees.

Alkelda, for once, stayed quiet, gripping the front of my dress and watching Anne depart. Her fat lower lip quivered, and I could hear her breathing hard, as if she'd had a vision.

Meanwhile, around us, whispering went on.

"And what do you suppose Milady wants with Rose?"

"To talk about babies, of course."

"What else can young wives talk about, eh?"

Chapter XX

You are to come at once, Mistress Rosalba." The page stood in the door, lit by a harsh spring moon. "The duchess needs you."

My Alkelda shifted in her sleep, but quickly found her thumb. Our three colored cat, alarmed, leapt from the foot and dove under the bed as I climbed out. "Shut the door, Master Geoff!" I groaned. The chill of that cold night rushed straight inside.

Hugh bolstered our girl with a pillow so our daughter would not roll out, then thrust his legs out of the other side and sat, his sparse blonde hair standing up around the bald spot like a young duck's. The whole house sighed. At 3 o'clock, sleep is either absent or deep. Tonight snores were the rule, both in the loft and down here by the fire.

The woolen shift I wore to bed was crumpled and a little milky, for I had nursed there before sleeping, but the anxiety in Geoffrey's voice was plain. I had better simply throw a dress over my undergarment and go.

I pulled the first thing off the peg and began to slip it on. Hugh came behind and gave a hand, holding out a sleeve. A-bed in his tunic and baggy hose, but willing to help, even when I knew he was as tired as I. Tying the belt over my own belly, I hoped faithful use of mother's measures would keep me from soon again being in a fix. It was, of course, different for Anne. Noblewomen were expected to breed regularly.

My hose, hung by the hearth after a good rinse, were plucked from the line, still damp. I sat, tugged them on and then stepped into my shoes. At the door, Hugh handed me first my basket of supplies which I kept ever handy by the door, next my shawl, and then gave me a peck on the cheek.

"May the Holy Mother lend her grace."

"Indeed! Narrow as Milady's hips are, we shall need her aid."

We went, Master Geoff and I, to the castle. There were fires here and there along the curtain wall, marking the posts of guards. In the west tower, lights burned brightly.

I was—thank the Blessed Mother—not alone. Mother Ash had been summoned. Earlier we'd agreed that Anne was probably much like her sister. The long process of bringing forth through such a narrow gate would be a painful and dangerous process for mother and child alike.

.❀.

The birth was as we'd feared, long and difficult. The baby presented head first, no difficulty there, but it took the poor duchess a wretchedly long time to get the job done. Grace and Margaret were present as well as Ash and I and two senior housemaids. I felt a bit like a fifth wheel, but Anne was glad to see me. She greeted me with a wan smile.

"Rosalba! I am so glad you have come."

Grace gave me a worried look, but stepped aside so I could hold the pretty hands which reached for mine. The duchess wanted me right by her side, so I held her hand and soothed her brow. Occasionally, Ash and I consulted, although I had nothing to add to her understanding. I would rise from my place, leave Grace holding her Mistresses' hand, and go down to have a look with Ash. Together we exchanged hot cloths soaked in preparations of said to ease birth. The little crown with its bloody, brown fuzz, presented again and again, like a fierce eruption attempting to burst through her reddened skin, but she could not pass it. The color of what baby flesh we could see stayed high, but Ash and I both knew a long travail would do the child's brains no good, not to mention the fact that the precious infant might strangle in the cord.

Herbal infusions and wine, a sip here and there we gave, to help our Lady endure what was for all of us a very long day. We prayed over Anne, and secretly I thanked the Virgin that my own travail had passed so easily. Ash and I went out at different times, and there, by the head of the stairs, stood Duke Richard, solemn in his red robe of office, a great chain of gold about his neck, paler than usual, eyes burning with anxiety. A *Book of Hours* was tucked beneath his arm, so I knew he'd kept to his usual schedule, taking time from business to recite prayers from *The Little Office of the Blessed Virgin Mary*.

I could see him attempt to remove himself, knowing that this was woman's work, as declared by Nature and God Almighty. He was patient, for our suffering is ordained. At the same time, knowledge of Anne's danger, of his part in her agony, of his helplessness, gnawed at him.

Three of the clock came again and passed. I fretted, worrying about whether Alkelda was being a good girl, if there was milk enough to spare among my neighbors. I hoped that she would not tumble into the fire. It was odd to think that since I had come to live here, I had never been away from my own hearth for more than half a day. How dear my humble home had become!

About evensong the Duke of Gloucester's heir came forth, a boy of proper size with a strongly molded head. He was as tired as his poor mother and the cry he gave was little more than a thin bleat, but his color was not bad.

"You have a fine son, Milady, a fine son!" Voices came from every side, encouraging and congratulating. Anne slumped on the pillows, tears pouring down her cheeks. She had entered that perfect moment of body joy, the peace and silence which follows the storm of birth.

No sooner had Mother Ash and I begun to congratulate ourselves, I assisting at the basin as she cleaned the child, then Anne and Lady Margaret, as one, gave a hideous shriek. Mother Ash shoved the son and heir at me and ran. I, in turn, laid the child in the arms of the wet nurse, who stood behind me, eagerly waiting for her most noble charge.

I grabbed wads of wool from our store. Anne had delivered the afterbirth and begun to bleed like a fountain. I had heard my mother tell of this, but had never seen it. Sometimes a woman, long in labor, may deliver all and then find a swift and bloody death by expelling her own uterus.

Mother Ash's ancient hand was in now, deep, still the bright blood came, pooling between her legs. Anne shrieked with what remained of her voice.

"Hold her, Margaret! Hold her! She must swallow this."

Margaret was attempting to do as she was told, but her terror had overpowered her. She was sobbing near as loud as her mistress. I rushed to the head of the bed. Margaret was easily moved aside, while I caught Anne's thin, seizing form in my arms.

"There, there, dear Lady!" I used all my strength to hold her close, so her hands could not reach the vial and spill the precious liquid. "Drink it! Drink it! Now!"

She almost retched, but the stuff stayed down. Her eyes rolled wildly in her head, back and forth from me to the flood of gore between her legs. Then, abruptly, she went slack. Blonde lashes closed.

"Blessed Mother, save her!" I pressed her limp body close, as I had done during those terrible fevers of her childhood, the times when she had lost consciousness. Then, from deep inside me came the chant, over and again:

Three ladies came from Northern land,
Each with a knife in her hand,
Stand blood, stand!
Bloody wound, in Holy Mary's name,
Close!

"Snow!" Mother Ash called. "Clean snow! Clean, mind you! Dig it from a drift! Hurry!"

A housemaid went running. Margaret huddled on the floor at my feet, rocking and weeping. I lay beside my duchess, holding her close. Anne was breathing, but so lightly I could barely feel it. Whatever Ash had given, it had near killed her. I prayed her measure was good. Otherwise, I would have dealt my dear lady death with my own hand.

"Does she breathe?" Mother Ash's old body shook with effort, her hand still deep within.

"She does. Praise Our Blessed Lady."

My teacher nodded. Slowly, she began to withdraw, inching her hand free. More blood came, but nothing like the fountain of earlier.

"Keeping saying it."

I spoke the charm again. The room smelled like a slaughterhouse. Nausea rolled over me, as I remembered the rolling, claustrophobic cabin, the channel waves, Isabel's terrible screams....

Still, in this room, life went on, as it will. In the corner, close to the fire, the nurse rocked, holding the precious first born son of the Duke of Gloucester safe against her warm bare breast.

The door opened. I looked up, as did Ash, expecting the snow. That was here, but hard on the heels of the maid, came the duke himself.

"You have a fine son, Milord," said Mother Ash. "Straight as an arrow." Sleeves up, red to the elbows, she indicated where the young goodwife sat, crooning softly to the noble child. Richard gave a cursory glance at the warm picture by the hearth, but his gaze returned at once to the blood on the old woman's hands, to the bed where I lay, holding his wife.

"The duchess lives, My Lord." It must, I thought, take a mountain of self-confidence to speak in such a manner to an anxious prince. I wouldn't have wanted to be the target of that fierce gaze.

"But things are not well. Your Lady Wife bled heavily just after delivery."

Mother Ash then went on with her business, packing the snow from the basin onto Anne's shuddering belly and groin. Richard bent over me, dark hair falling over his shoulders.

"How is my dear consort, Rose?"

"I do not know, My Lord. She is in the arms of the poppy." Suddenly, I wanted to weep exactly as her ladies were now doing.

"Poppy stills pain," said Mother Ash, "and it will slow the blood. The duchess is now in God's hands."

The duke's hand passed over me, to tenderly touch Anne's brow, to graze her white cheek, where copper strands were stuck with sweat. So close to me he was, closer than he had been in years, those mobile lips, lean cheeks, and those beautiful hazel eyes with their woman's lashes. I could smell his fear.

There is no good explanation for where the mind goes, memories flitting like dry leaves. Holding Anne against my bosom in that bed filled with her blood, I remembered the night when Richard had forgotten his high estate and had taken me, Roan Rose, in his arms.

"You will stay with her until she is better, Mistress Rose." Those were his words, but his eyes saw nothing but Anne.

"Yes, My Lord." I bowed my head so he could not catch a glimpse of the feeling flooding through me.

He crossed the room to better examine his son. The nurse opened her robe. The baby was exhausted, like his mother. He was asleep, tiny face pressed against her breast. This woman had been chosen carefully and Anne had enlisted my help in the search. She was a clean and virtuous wife who had raised three fine children already. Of course, she was a last minute part of the business, for the candidates must all be recently delivered and their milk in full flow.

Mother Ash had advised Anne to nurse the baby herself whenever she could, believing this was beneficial to the womb. Anne surprised both of us by agreeing. It seemed her mother, a most sensible woman on every score, had been a staunch believer in this notion.

"An elixer is sucked in with the true mother's milk, something which cannot be obtained from surrogates." Anne had explained her mother's teaching. It was unfortunate the Countess of Warwick was still in sanctuary. I knew that she would have been a great comfort to My Lady.

I stayed on at the duke's request, inside the great walls of Middleham. It was peculiar to be in the castle and once again part of a noble household. I was far better pleased, I quickly realized, to be the mistress of my own humble abode.

The constant fear of overstepping bounds, the jockeying for favor, was beyond wearying. Over and over, I bit my tongue and deferred to those whose opinions I did not respect.

Besides, I feared the loss of routine which would result from my prolonged absence. Jackie and Bett—Irresponsible and Scatterbrain—would let everything fall apart. I thanked God that Hugh was given duty at the Castle, for he would keep things in order.

In the afternoons, when Anne was sleeping, Bett did bring Alkelda into the kitchen to visit. I hugged her, and then obliged with the breast. She didn't truly need it for food, just for comfort. Of course, she loved being in the castle kitchen, where everyone admired her. It was generally agreed that she was an adorable, clever little girl.

Those weeks inside the castle, I discovered I missed my bossy girl with her demands for suckling and attention. I even missed her endless prattle! I worried that she would come to grief without her mother. After all, she was just learning the ways of the world, the busy street beyond our door, the bubbling pot on the fire.

How strange it was to realize--at last--that my home was no longer this great castle! Middleham was the same stone warren in which I'd lived as a child, but now too much had changed.

Chapter XXI

Their son, another royal Edward, named for his Uncle the king, lived and grew. In five months, Anne and Richard, Duke and Duchess of Gloucester, were gone, ridden out of my life again. Their colorful train, as great as a hundred, stretched behind them. There were the loaded wagons, strings of horses, knights, squires, ladies, laundresses, cooks, maids, servers, secretaries, clerks, the falconers and the birds, the hunting dogs and their keepers—everyone in the world but me—and it no longer rankled.

Time passed, and the duchess gave birth to no more children, nor did she kindle. When she was at Middleham I was often called upon to make potions and pray with her. I knew only too well for what she prayed. Richard kept no other women, nor was he ever known to upbraid his wife for her barrenness. Whenever they were together, it was well-known they shared a bed. When she was at Middleham, and if I'd been summoned to her, I saw Anne glow after a night with her Dickon. Even he, usually so somber and care-worn, would seem in better cheer after a respite in her arms. The affection they shared, so obvious, was commented upon by all. It was as if they were country cousins who'd married for love.

Myself, I had the other problem women have, setting myself to rights, which I did once, even though I was ill for almost a week after. My husband, who knew no more of this than other men, comforted me. Finally, as was bound to happen, one stuck, and there I was, swelling up and tired again.

Alkelda was a strong and willful three and a half by the time our Will was born. They were pretty babies, two of a kind, fair and fat, with dark gray eyes that would never change. One way or another, my mother had written Whitby out of most transactions. (My sister Marigold had Mother's freckles and auburn hair.) Only Lily completely took after her father. My two children by Hugh, on the other hand, were fair and square, Saxon to the core. Looking at my babies, I wondered if I lacked the same force of will my mother had possessed. Over time, however, all my children raised some freckles, a dusting of golden flecks across their noses.

Hugh was not around in those days any more than Richard. The duke was constantly on the move and his soldiers, archers and men at arms went with him. There were skirmishes on the border, rebellions and private warfare of lords upon one another, as has always been the way in our turbulent north country.

Sometimes, when the ducal couple were at Middleham, I would happen upon Lady Anne in the garden, for she liked to go there in the evenings before Compline. She always had Edward and his nurse with her. It was said by some she fussed and worried too much, but what else could she do? This delicate child was all God had given. He must be kept in health to take the reins of the wild northern steed his father was now working so hard to tame.

Edward of Middleham was a pretty child, a nice mixture of both parents, with a sweet thin face, chestnut hair and blue eyes. He was bright and quick to talk, but so tiny at a year that his words seemed nothing short of a miracle. Anne doted, as did Richard.

Little Ned had terrible fits of coughing, very much like Anne. Poor little boy! He, like his mother, learned to swallow a medicinal sludge, heavy with black honey and herbs. For him, his illness was worst at haying time and in the first warm days of spring. He slept on a fine wool mattress covered with linen, for he sneezed and choked if put to sleep on featherbeds or upon Our Lady's Bedstraw. When the family was in residence at Middleham, I was often in close attendance, and Mother Ash's recipes traveled with Edward's nurse as they went castle to castle.

These I had finally recited for Anne to take down, so that she would have them always and in a "good script." My writing had never become fair. That is an art which takes time to perfect.

Their family made a pretty picture, sitting in the garden while Edward played with a puppy or quietly maneuvered toy horses and soldiers upon carpet the servants had laid down. Anne, gentlewomen at her side, would ply the needle. Richard's robes and coats of arms were always most beautifully embroidered, glowing with color and fine detail.

He stayed a little apart, at a table daily carried to wherever he chose to work. Kendall, his clerks, squires and pages came and went, bearing the petitions and letters which arrived in a steady stream, and, for which a duke must always have attention.

"I am very sorry for it, My Lord Edward, but it is time for your medicine."

"Oh, Mistress Rose, must I?"

"Indeed, you must." The duke would answer before I could. "It will make you strong, just as Mistress Rose's medicines did your mother."

"Come Mistress Rose." The child extended a fair hand to me. "I must do my duty."

How alike they were, this father and son! I brought a tray and a mug of something which would help the medicine go down, a decoction of something pleasant like hot milk and chamomile, spiced with ginger and sweetened with honey.

If Edward was ill, I was would be called. Duchess Anne and the duke might be there too, if he were not dealing justice somewhere, making war upon those Scots, or treading some careful dance around the Percies, those old northern rivals. Once little Ned was so bad, we tented him over so he could breathe a steaming broth of herbs.

I'd never seen a royal child so watched over by his parents. Even the Countess of Warwick, who I'd call a good mother, had only spent an hour or so with her girls each day.

Like all the noblewomen of that proud family, Anne's mother had traveled with her husband, peace and war alike.

Lammas was a day for bringing bread and cakes for the Queen of Heaven. We village women also took time to decorate St. Alkelda's Well. The pavement around sputtered with lights. Offerings of bread and fruit were carried in small baskets. Everyone brought something, and everyone, if they chose, could take something away. The priest took some of this offering, too, but he did not forbid us the ancient devotion by the water, which has happened in other places.

One summer when they were staying at Middleham, Anne brought Richard to the well. Whether she'd meant to pass here or not, it was on the way to our village church, which they had been about to honor with their presence. With the strange attraction which remained among us, we'd all arrived at the well at the same time.

I'd arrived first and was in the act of arranging my gifts upon the step, when the duke and duchess appeared. On my knees, after lighting a candle with a twist of straw, I turned, and there they were. They'd seen me too. I knew they sometimes missed me, but they missed the girl of long ago.

Today, kneeling here, I was just another peasant woman, broadening as I ate less meat and bore children, my freckled skin burnt by the sun. I stayed where I was and watched others pause and bow. The priest was with them, as well as the family chaplain and two clerks. The priest's eyes lit upon me with irritation.

"She makes more of an offering at the well than in the church, does Mistress Fletcher."

"Rose?" Duke Richard chose to pay attention to him.

"I do not deny it, my gracious Lord."

"Is not the Mother of Our Lord as important as your saint?"

I'd hoped for a gleam of something like humor in Richard's eye, but it wasn't there.

"My eldest child, as you know, noble ones, is called Alkelda." I was as humble as I knew how to be and indicated my daughter's solemn little face. "I have a special devotion to our saint."

The priest nodded wearily. He had heard this tale one hundred times from one hundred different women. Churchmen have listened to this excuse since the beginning of the rule of the fathers. Lady Anne laid a white restraining hand upon her husband's arm.

"Mistress Rose has a deep devotion to Our Lady, this I know."

Richard was mildly surprised. Anne was not the sort of noblewoman who was in the habit of correcting her husband-- at least, not in public.

"Today she tends our Holy Well. These offerings, My Lord, are for the poor, for the old and infirm." She used the alarmed male silence which followed to strike home the nail. "As you certainly must remember, here it is of old the custom."

There was a pause in which Richard studied us, the women, children and grannies of town bowed down at his feet. He cleared his throat.

"My Lady reminds me that charity is ever a blessed custom. It shall not shorten, even by a tithe."

The priest bowed, his pale face curdled milk. The rest of us bowed again as Lady Anne went past on her husband's arm. She was, like Our Lady Herself, a blessed intercessor!

Anne offered the nosegay she'd carried and a fine hank of bright blue silken thread, which we village women would later share out among us. When the lord and lady moved on, the crowd parted. As in the Earl of Warwick's day, we knew there'd be a pig brought from the castle for our feast.

"Rose, you must attend tomorrow at the stables where the warhorses are kept. I wish you to be present when I surprise my Lord Richard."

I had curtsied, hands full of the lavender and sage I'd been gathering. Impulsively I offered her a sprig of lavender. Anne stroked the grey-green needles to raise the oil and then lifted the stalk to her nose.

"It's 'specially lovely when fresh cut."

"Indeed it is, My Lady."

"You must attend when I give My Lord husband a special present. Whatever else you are to do, you have my leave to be absent."

I couldn't imagine what she was up to, but she was clearly excited. I couldn't imagine why I would be summoned to attend what was noble family business. When I arrived, however, dressed and scrubbed as well as I was able, I found not only other old servants and prominent villagers there, but gentry from the castle. There were even solemn burghers from York wearing long black robes and golden chains.

"Now, My Lady, you must say." Richard appeared puzzled and more than a little embarrassed. "What is this gift?"

"I have searched for years, and at last I have found perfection." Anne's cheeks were pink as apple blossom, her braid of copper peeked, country fashion, from beneath her veil. She raised her voice and cried:

"Masters! Bring out White Surrey!"

Into the bailey came pair of young grooms all dressed in blue and murray, leading a beautiful war horse. He was white, except for silver-grey dapples on his withers and high round rump. His muzzle was steel. His eyes were black.

The horse lifted his head, flared velvet nostrils, tossed his head and stamped. For Richard, it was love at first sight. We, the onlookers, were delighted. We loved Anne and we loved her all the more for how much she loved her husband.

"I've searched everywhere, and, here, my Lord! Have I not found?"

"Saint Anthony…"

The grooms led the magnificent horse in a circle, so we could all admire him. An uncut stallion with a short back, the *destrier* was not as massive as some of his kind. There was a look on his face I had never seen on any horse before, something like the keen edge of our north wind. Blood other than that of the ordinary thundering French warhorse flowed there.

Richard stepped forward. The horse pricked his ears, seeing whatever it is they see from the sides of their heads.

White Surrey appeared more interested than alarmed. Although he kept his ears forward, he didn't startle.

Anne kept pace with her husband. A maid followed her carrying a basket of apples. A fair green globe passed into My Lady's hand and from there into the hand of her husband. It was a ritual of service, and their jewels flashed in the sunlight. With a prick of sadness, I remembered when such sweet tasks had been mine.

The duke took the bridle in hand. He and the horse studied each other. They were two noblemen, both small and fine drawn, but proud warriors nonetheless.

"White Surrey is trained by a great Irish horse master. He carried his rider to the palm at his first tourney and he is judged both valiant and wise."

Delight haloed our duke. Anne followed her husband, waiting to see Richard astride his present. There he would be—her perfect, gentle knight, exactly as she had so long ago dreamed. The horse was saddled, this also at her summons. A murmur ran around, the men noting that the horse seemed calm for a stallion. Anne was having difficulty maintaining composure. Without us about, I had a feeling she'd have started a girlish dance of joy.

"Is this not the noblest steed that ever was, Mistress Rose? Is he not?"

"A most noble creature Milady." I made a deep courtesy and others followed my lead. The warhorse was truly beautiful, another magical being who would live in castles crowned with their love.

Richard, in the saddle now, began putting the horse through his paces. First, they walked, next performed a neat reverse. After, they trotted a figure eight which rose to a cantor. The horse's white legs changed lead smooth as silk.

The duke, flushed and smiling, had just pulled up when a train of men and horses paraded through the fore gate, all decked with summer flowers. Some were falconers with their hooded charges set upon their wrists.

In secret the household had been readied for a merry ride! Anne's mare was led up, all in the best tack, a black mare with three white feet. The day was ideal.

"My Lady, you know gentlemen of York attend me on grave business." Richard shook his head. It seemed that despite everything, he was going to decline her invitation.

"They will wait, sir, for I have asked them."

Richard swung down from White Surrey, whose bridle was instantly caught by a groom.

"I beg your pardon, Milady. Their business is pressing."

"Not so pressing it cannot wait until the morrow, My Lord Duke." A black-robed, great-bellied alderman moved forward and bobbed a stiff elder's bow. "How could our business be of more importance to you, My Lord Duke, than your Lady wife's pleasure?"

Richard sent Anne a look, and I knew as if he had spoken that he would privately insist she never do such a thing again. Still, the gathering remained all smiles, including the merchants of York, whose business had been put off. To see Anne of Warwick happy, to allow her husband a carefree day upon the dales, appeared, just now, to please these great men well enough.

"Gentlemen, care for my wife's happiness shows great kindness, yet I cannot allow you to be inconvenienced. Time and tide do not wait, not for the merchants of York, nor for their duke."

"Ah, my dear Lord!" The alderman spoke again. "Again allow me the impertinence of age, to say that when youth and happiness come, a man best seize his joy. Sire, you do attend our needs in all seasons and have been our good lord. Go forth and rejoice in God's blessings." His white hair blew in the breeze, for, aged and wealthy as he was, he had uncovered his head to address his lord.

Richard stood speechless. He shouldered his burden, but I think he never expected thanks. Being a good lord he saw as his duty before God, and he truly was a better lord than many others. It may be pleasing to hear that on that golden day, the Duke of Gloucester, his wife and his noble household took a holiday, riding and hunting their hawks upon the green hills of our wild land.

ChapteR XXII

That next winter George Duke of Clarence finally got his comeuppance, although it was almost mud season here before we heard this sensational piece of London news. He had been imprisoned for mysterious "acts of treason" and then executed--in secret--at the Tower.

What had finally brought about his downfall was a long story. His wife, Lady Isabel, had managed, over the years, to bear two live children, a girl and a boy. The girl was said to be pretty and healthy, but birth trauma had left the boy, as folks said, "not right in the head." Isabel's final childbirth had killed her and her baby too.

George, in one of his mad fits, had accused Ankarette of using black magic to murder Isabel. Acting the part of the king—and as judge, jury and executioner—he'd tortured Lady Isabel's most devoted woman servant and then hanged her.

The unlawful death of a commoner was a small thing, certainly, but by this time, the king was more than ready to use anything against George for a host of other acts that smelled to him like treason. As soon as the duke was imprisoned in the tower, the queen and her family pushed hard for his execution. They had reasons, chief being revenge. George, if you remember, had 'headed Elizabeth Woodville's father and one of her brothers during the Warwick rebellion.

Hugh said he was not surprised to learn of the Duke of Clarence's mean end. As for me, I confess that while I went to church and said prayers for Ankarette and Lady Isabel, I did not say one word on the duke's behalf to Our Lady.

Chapter XXIII

I, the oldest of my mother's daughters, was said to be: "Quiet and grave, but still waters run deep. Always about with her mother, so much alike you might take them for sisters!"

My second sister, Marigold, had married young and gone away to another village. We sometimes met on market days and had a chat. Her husband's dad had a little farm where the family labored to produce flax and wool. I gathered she worked hard and bred regularly. Her husband was a bit feckless, but a gentle sort, rather too easy-going for his own good.

We talked over our big bellies every market day that summer. She it was who told me there was talk about Lily—even in her distant village. It was said she was wild, a "free woman." Once, when her name came up, I saw men nearby put on their gargoyle faces, which gave me a notion the rumors were true.

I didn't worry about it too much, though, as I was at the end of another pregnancy. This one, who would be named "Rosemary" after my mother, came over the course of a few hours. Bett brought me the things I asked for and sat with me, though I cut the cord and the rest for myself. The boys, who always slept like stones, woke up at cock crow the next morning and then made us both laugh by their surprise at finding their Mam still abed with a new little sister.

When Lily appeared at my doorstep one chill autumn day, a stick in hand and bundle on her back, I can't say I was entirely surprised.

"Good day to you, Sister Rose."

"Good day, Lily."

She stood, hesitating on the threshold, so I bade her come in. There was an air of finality about the way she laid down her bundle. Then, she put her hands into the small of her back and stretched, displaying a full belly.

"Ah, so you've got caught!"

Mother to the world, was I?

"Didn't do it by myself." Lily gave me an irreverent, careless grin.

In spite of my respectability and my station in the village, I opened my arms. I didn't know what I'd tell Hugh, or anyone else, for that matter, but she was my sister, the baby I'd cared for before I'd come to Middleham. I should have gone to her, as soon as I'd heard that Mama had died, but, thinking only of my own business, I had not.

I brought her hot cider. She shivered and warmed her hands upon the cup while I sat down again on my stool and stirred our supper stew, which bubbled over a small fire.

"Aldygyth says I am to stay with you."

"She does, does she?"

"Yes, for Clifford says he will not keep a whore in his house."

"And where is the man who is responsible for this?"

"In France, with Dickon."

"Dickon, indeed! You had better learn some manners here at Middleham."

"It is his own soldiers who call him that, Nick, Roger, and Jamie, too, very often. Not to the duke's face, of course." She smiled, enjoying the impudence.

"So, little sister, was it Nick, Roger or Ned?" I asked, testing thickness of our supper by letting a gluey stream fall from my wooden spoon.

There was a pause, in which Lily looked, at last, ashamed. Finally she said, "I—ah—don't—exactly—know."

If Hugh had been home, the house might have landed about our ears, but he, too, was "with Dickon in France", and so in our sullied Lily came. Bett had the sense not to play haughty, and lo, there we were, an entire household of women. Bett and Lily soon locked together like lodestones, and it was good for both of them because her Jackie had taken to disappearing for months at a time with the traveling players.

As might be expected, I got grief from the castle and the church about Lily as I knew I would, but they didn't dare do more than complain to Lady Anne. I could not imagine Milady agreeing to drive my sister away, so I ignored them. Anne did eventually rule upon our scandal, in a message sent from Pontefract. She said that as long as my sister behaved modestly and went to hear Mass and made her confession, she could remain. Further, she said "Mistress Rose should be commended for her Christian charity."

"Do you think any of them will marry you?"

"I would like to marry Jamie, but he has a wife," Lily said. "As for the others—well..."

"What?"

"Nick is a bit too fond of drink."

"I see. Lily, dear," I asked, studying her belly, "did you get this baby Maying?"

"How did you know?"

I sighed, attempting patience. "We figured a due date near the Lady Mass, didn't we?"

"Oh—right."

Her men were Scot free, this we learned upon the duke's return. A'Parr offered to find us a decent man willing to take her, but I asked him not to. A forced marriage was nothing but misery.

Lily rather surprised me by saying she was no longer attached to any of them. In fact, to my astonishment, I soon learned she was on the verge of getting a name right here in Middleham, in spite of the promise she'd made to behave herself and in spite of her big belly.

I was afraid she'd lead Bett astray and I was angry with her, too, but she knew very well I wouldn't toss her out. She was my sister and I would stick by her. I did not approve of Lily's way of life, but she got by on her wit and beauty for many years and died comfortably in a nice warm bed in York. Such, in her case—and, in many another I could recount—were the wages of sins of the flesh.

A fine babe we named Robert O'Grove was born to her

just two days before the Lady Mass. Hugh, who had a terrible soft spot for the little ones—he who had been so high and mighty about Lily when he'd first come home—dissolved like a lump of sugar.

The birth—maybe the pain—changed her for a time. Lily grew quiet, almost inward. She asked me to teach her the ways I knew to prevent conception and how to set herself right when the flow was absent, all of which I did, while cautioning her of the dangers involved in the latter course.

Lily didn't go out looking for excitement anymore. She did her work about the house and also took effective, if not particularly affectionate, care of Robert and the other children. Aldygyth had, it seemed, trained her well. We now had a regular pig's pile of children, two of them Hugh's grandchildren, Jackie and his newest brother, Oliver. With Robert, Alkelda, our son William and little Rosemary, that made six. At night the loft and the downstairs were full of sleepers. It was a good thing Hugh and I earned sufficient to keep us. Our necessary always had some skinny backside or other capping the hole.

For two years, Lily pleased Hugh and me well, but it turned out it was only her way of gathering strength. One day, at Saint Michael's Mass, she went to market and did not return. We heard she had ridden away with a servant of the Percies, into the north. Robert O'Grove wept for his Mama-Mama-Mama in vain.

Hugh damned Lily to hell and I joined him, but what were we to do? Bobby was a beautiful little boy and kin, just as Bett's babies were. He grew up calling Hugh "Dad" along with the others.

⚜

Midsummer came. I bent in a field with my basket beside me, a pair of shears ready. Old Mary and I and a few other village women were ready to begin our harvest of Our Lady's Bedstraw. First, we'd cut it and spread it in the sun, and then take it to finish drying in the rafters. The plants sprawled and splayed. They were four angled, like mint, small yellow flowers borne on woody stems. The smell was sweet and clean. When it dried, it would be added to newly re-stuffed mattresses or pillows. Much of it would go to the castle, to be mingled with the rushes that covered the floors of upper chambers.

The best tops we'd clip to be used in making an acidic extract. A miracle, how at a time of plentiful milk, this useful plant ripened, providing a curdling agent for making cheese. Plant and animal united in providing for us, human kind! The tops also provided a yellow dye used in all sorts of ways: to color butter, cheese, wool and silk yarn. Some ladies even used it to color their hair. After this harvest, we'd leave our patch of bedstraw alone until autumn, when it would be time to divide roots. Like the roots of madder, those of bedstraw yielded a fine red dye.

So much to do, and so little time between dawn and dusk, even in the long days of summer! My children were with Hugh in the field, for it was that time, too. Children can't do much to ruin hay, and some good work can be got out of them there. In the herb garden, however, we didn't need little ones running riot, bruising the plants and scattering seed. Conversely, in the hay field, old timers weren't as useful as youth and energy.

Hugh sometimes complained, saying he did more child-rearing than I. The fact was he had more patience. From me, they got chores and lessons. I praised if they'd done well, but if they did not, a lecture or a spanking was coming. At night, after home and castle, I'd fall into bed exhausted, and hear him sitting up in the loft, telling the little ones his stories.

Our lord and lady came on horseback, across the hayfield in the early morning, through the first heat and dust of the day. I was there, with other mothers, in the shade of a lone beech of great age shading one side of the hill. A spring welled there, so it was a good, green place to lie.

We with young children were carrying shrub to the thirsty

workers, cooking and tending any who fell ill or suffered injury. Of course, an added task was watching children, as everyone in the village went to this work.

Rosemary was shy and suspicious, and unhappy to be with anyone other than me. Large and fair, she was a pretty posset, but just now, out in the hot field, she was stuck against my bosom like a heavy, wet rag.

Our lord and lady approached slowly through the stubble in the first heat of the day. Their companions came to get water from our spring, while we gathered the children out of the way. Falconers rode in carrying hawks, as well as Anne's ladies, and a host of beaters and excited, barking hounds. All our work must wait until they moved on.

The duke had not been much in residence during the last year and we'd got out of the habit of having him among us. As soon as he and Anne rode in, the other women began to poke me.

"Go greet them, Rose."

"Yes. You know what to do."

I tried to hand Rosemary away to a Granny she ordinarily liked, but today she would have none of it. So, to prevent her screaming, I ended up serving my lord and lady with one free hand while another woman drew the shrub. All the time, I was keenly aware of Rosemary's body, of our dusty, dirty clothes and my milk-stained bosom.

My little girl finally turned her head to cast a dubious blue gaze upon these two brightly dressed strangers. Lady Anne dismounted. She wanted to hold my daughter, but this Rosemary would have none of. She wailed and buried her face against my bosom.

"She does not understand the honor," Richard said. He smiled but stayed right where he was, on his white horse.

"She's plain ornery, Your Grace." I jiggled Rosemary crossly, flushed with heat and annoyance. "I am sorry I cannot make her behave, Milady."

"No one needs manners when they are so young and fair." Anne reached to graze the tips of her long fingers across the yellow curls gracing my daughter's head. There was so much longing in her, it made me sad.

"She's very attached to her mother." Lady Grace, poor thing, from her seat on a mare still tried to be gracious to me, even though I'd been little but sulky and rude to her over the years.

"In every way." Richard indicated the fierce grip Rosemary maintained.

I was in no mood for jesting. I'd been up before dawn for two weeks in these fields, with three-year-old William and a hot, needy babe of eight months. Her clinging did not uniformly stir my maternal instincts. Instead I often felt quite opposite. I had moments that summer when I thought if someone of good repute and upright habits offered me a nicely filled purse for her, I would have made the exchange without a second thought. Rosemary was the neediest of my babies. Even with the other two, who were energetic enough, I'd managed to find time for myself. This child was a creature who was not only helpless, but who must always have her way.

Latin mumbled in our ears as the priest ducked and bobbed before the altar. Around us dogs scratched while babies fussed and babbled. It was Sunday Mass and the whole village was supposed to be in attendance. There was a haze of incense and sweat, although most folks did try to clean up. Men dozed, leaning upon their wives. Women nursed here and there and occasionally rose to take a child or one of the gray hairs out to answer the call of nature.

Hugh was one of the sleepers, but he'd wake up for good and all once we escaped the gloomy confines of the Church. He'd happily return home for his bow and then to the village green with the other men, bright with good cheer and ready to win a wager or two on the flight of his arrows.

I remember a wonderful summer feast day, blazing blue and hot. Every man at the butts had removed his shirt and stood bare-chested, looking brave as could be. There were bellies on the older fellows and scars too. Beatings, brandings, old wounds, all etched into man-flesh, now burnished by summer in the fields to brown and red.

The green of that year! There had been good rains and so much sun! Most of it was even well-timed, so the hay didn't spoil. Beans flourished and did not mildew. We and our animals were well fed straight through the winter. It was a fine fat time.

Our Alkelda was fair, all pink and white. She was haughty sometimes, especially when she and Hugh were in something together, but she quickly learned all I taught and took pride in a job well done. She was not, however, much interested in following in my footsteps.

Her father had had the notion to teach her letters and how to add and subtract. She picked it up fast, far more quickly than the boys, which Hugh said he'd expected. Now and then he talked of apprenticing her to a shopkeeper in York where she could "make a good marriage." At the time, it had all seemed far away, even unlikely.

There was nothing more fun than the midsummer's fair, always capped by an archery contest with prizes from the castle. Competitors from villages near and far came to compete, from as far west as Aysgarth and as far east as Thornton Steward. The square by the church bustled with bright things for sale, from eggs, cheese, meat and vegetables, to pots and utensils, as well as bright ribbons, silks, medals and charms. Players came, too, along with fellows who could juggle almost anything. A stilt walker roamed in a patched, trailing jacket and a long-nosed mask, delighting and frightening the children. Rosemary's jaw had dropped at first sight of him. She'd stood still as a stock, her fist wound tight in my dress, her eyes round.

The best part of having children is observing their wonder. I remembered my sister Lily screaming when she first saw the stilt men, and how the other children had been cruel enough to tease her about it for a long time after. The players, later, would give us the tale of John the Baptist because this June day was his feast. It was always a favorite because of the bloody severed head carried in by the wicked princess at the end.

Bett had been sad again when Jackie proved not be among these rag-tag rascals. The summer after Oliver was born, he'd disappeared for good. We had word of her husband occasionally. He moved from troupe to troupe, not even, it seemed, able to stay long with a group of players. I thought he probably did not want to come to Middleham anymore and skipped any commission that did. Poor Bett still wept for him. Hugh grieved for his lost child as men do, by getting angry and declaring: "That boy is no son of mine!"

"Where are the horses?" Rosemary asked. She was remembering the hobby horses of Saint George's Day in April. These were always my favorites, too, with their long flowing manes and tails and the men dancing about inside.

"Not 'til Saint George's Day comes around again. They belong to the brave saint who will slay the dragon."

"Oh." She was saddened, I could see. "Will that be a long time?"

"Not until this summer is over and next winter is done. Then, we will have Saint George's Day again."

"Oh." Rosemary speedily lost interest. It was far off for a little one to imagine—and now up the street came a young woman with a tray of sweet buns.

"Look, Mam!"

Where I'd never been indulged as a child, we didn't stint our babies. Hugh had made certain this morning that there were cut pence all shined and ready to put to use for all our pretty ones.

Feeling rich, I smiled at the seller and brought her to a halt. Rosemary already had a wand decorated with ribbons and topped with a shriveled, carved-and-painted apple head which was supposed to be John-Baptist's. Most children had them. Some were waved solemnly like wands of office, while others, ribbons streaming, were used for poking, hitting, and throwing. A few heads had been knocked off in this rough play. Now, beady eyes peering, they lay abandoned in the grass.

Like magic, Alkelda, Jackie and William appeared at my side as soon as the sweet bun seller stopped. They pushed ahead to get theirs while I lifted Rosemary onto my hip so she could pick from the tray. Her rosy cheeks glowed; her breath went in and out steadily. Clear blue eyes considered her choices. Rosemary weighed plenty already. Packed solid like all of them, my Yorkshire lamb!

Munching sweet bread, we headed with the crowd toward the archers taking their stance. Brown legs and bare feet lined the green, the competitors all in a row, shooting at targets set at the very bottom of the green. There were many contestants to start, but, soon they would be whittled down to just a few. Hugh would be in that group, though whether he would carry the palm away on this occasion was much wagered upon.

A famous champion from Nappa, Watkyn Wright, had arrived today to try his luck. A purse was offered by the duke and this fine prize had drawn archers from far and wide. Our lord was in residence today and the white boar was flying at the castle—as we locals said, "The pig is up the pole." Tomorrow, the gentry would ride in to see jousting. It would be an entire day spent watching our betters compete—that is, for those of us who were at leisure, which meant young folks, dressed for Sunday and flirting. I was one of those who had too much to do. Hugh plain hated tourneys.

"I've seen enough knights charging in my line of work. A tourney is a show, nothing like a battle. The real thing ain't so pretty."

In the end, that Watkyn fellow beat my husband by a finger paring's breadth. We of Middleham were disappointed and Hugh was more than a little upset. He'd already been planning to put the coins in that purse to use. Still, he'd won second place, which was one silver coin and a piglet. When we looked over the available litter, I asked for a sturdy sow with an eye to enterprise.

"I thought you would never keep pigs." Hugh leaned on his great bow beside me. "I thought you said they were dirty."

"They are and I did, but I have thought again, Husband."

"Changed your mind, have you?"

"Yes, I have, Master Fletcher."

"Humph! So, it's a good idea now that you're the one that's thought of it?"

"No," I replied, teasing him back. "Raising pigs was always a good idea, even when I didn't think so."

He played this to his friends gathered round, rolling his eyes. *Women!* Obligingly, everyone laughed. Then the men went off to celebrate with a few pints, leaving me, the children and the piglet behind. I shrugged as I watched him go. Joke he must, but I had my pig, now that I more perfectly understood the business.

I'd chosen a fine sow from a litter of nine, a fortunate number. She was hearty and fat, of the black and white spotted kind from our duke's Gloucestershire properties. When I'd held out an apple, this fair lady had been the first among them to come.

Chapter XXIV

There was sun and rain. Seed went into the ground. Where were the years going so fast? Compared to the long stretch of childhood, the last decade had flown. Days passed and spring began in earnest, along with the next sowing. Piglets scampered in the pen with my dear sow Belle. Young Jack broke a finger in a fight. I set it and did a fair job of setting the nose of the boy he'd hit. I did it for free, too, because I thought Jackie had been in the wrong.

Our William was growing into a fine sweet lad, my favorite, I confess. He had just been in his first archery competition among the youngest boys, and he'd placed well. He was proud as punch when the men slapped him on the back and called him a "chip off the old block." William liked to walk the hills looking for plants with me and he was a dab hand with our animals, too. I imagined he'd rather be a farmer than a soldier.

Somehow it had come round to April—again. Rosemary had been ill but we'd pulled her back from the brink, and so our family had once more survived another winter. We were looking forward to summer, when shocking news came from the south.

Duke Richard's brother, our virile, golden King Edward, had died! Only forty-one, yet this bright warrior had spent every drop of his strength and health in a long wallow of gluttony. His son, another Edward, was but thirteen, so our duke had been summoned south, to assume new duties as the boy king's protector.

"I am happy that the Lady Anne has not called for you. You ought to be here with our children. It is sufficient that I must follow the duke down to London."

That was the way Hugh wanted it, but fate was soon to arrange otherwise. Not long after, more strange news came from the south, stories of plots by the queen's kin to waylay and murder the Duke of Gloucester. Next news came that the Duke of Gloucester and his cousin of Buckingham had taken Lord Anthony Scales and others of the queen's family captive and seized the young king on his way to London. Rumor flew like leaves in a storm.

Lady Anne was anxious—even more so than usual—about her son. She summoned me at least five times during one week to consult, though there was no more wrong with the boy than there had ever been.

We were not surprised when a summons came for Anne to join her husband at Westminster. I did not expect to be called, expected, in fact, to have nothing to do with this, although I knew my Lady had not been sleeping well. She rarely worried about Richard, not when he was at war or otherwise, but she was afraid for him now and made no bones about it.

"My Lord detests the south—as do I! There is nothing but scheming and wickedness in London. And, see, Rose, it is plain the queen and her family have plotted to harm my husband, and only because his brother named him lord protector."

It was clear something was up, something beyond what we ordinary folk would ever understand. Still, it never crossed my mind—*simpleton that my husband says I am*—that our duke would do what he next did.

I hated even the thought of London, of the dirt, smoke and noise, of the stink of that filthy river, but when my mistress summoned me to come with her, I could not decline. It would mean leaving our children, but these days I trusted Bett. She'd come a long way from the dazed girl she'd once been. She had a fair hand with our mob, even with Jackie and Robert, both of whom were unsteady boys at an unsteady age. Robert O'Grove was a handsome devil, a bit heartless though, and needing a great many whippings before he understood right from wrong. Hugh declared, he clearly took after his parents. Oliver and our Will sometimes rubbed on each other and fought, but they were pretty well matched, and were, down at the heart of it, more brothers than cousins.

I decided to take Rosemary with me. She'd been ill over

the winter, so ill, in fact, I'd found myself glad—for a change—that although she was over three, I still had milk to give her, for she'd been unable to swallow anything else.

It was, however, with no happiness that I left Middleham and rode south in the train of my lady. As we traveled in the household wagons, preparing to take up residence at Crosby's Place, we heard more news. King Edward's widow, Elizabeth Woodeville, had fled to sanctuary, taking her younger son and all her daughters along with her. Her brother, Edward Woodville, had stolen more than half the royal treasury and put to sea with it. He said he would return with a foreign army at his back.

London Town was afloat in rumor. Their distrust and fear of us Northerners was as deep as our distrust and fear of them. Soon after I arrived, the Lords Vaughn, Grey and Earl Rivers, who had been arrested at Northampton, were beheaded at Pontefract Castle in the north, thus dispatching an aged chamberlain who had long served as tutor to the Prince of Wales, as well as one of the queen's sons from her first marriage and her brother, too, the learned, elegant Anthony, Earl Rivers. These gentlemen had raised an escort of a 2,000 men to accompany the prince to London, and had brought along carts filled with extra weapons and arms, as if planning for war. The queen had been rushing to have the boy crowned before Richard could arrive from the north. These were the facts as I heard them. Whether this added up to treason or not, is for lords to decide, not for me. If my Lord of Gloucester saw danger to himself and his family, he took the only course open to him. That the queen and her family had actively pushed for the execution of his brother, George of Clarence, was a fact not far from anyone's mind.

The next great one to die was Richard's old comrade at arms, Lord Hastings. He was accused of plotting with the Woodville Queen, Bishop Morton, and the Lord Stanley and his Beaufort wife against the protector. We heard that Richard made the allegation during a council meeting. Lord Hasting's execution occurred minutes later, performed on the Tower lawn. This mighty lord, boon companion to the late Edward IV, lost his big blonde head upon some lumber, just a step beyond the room where the assembled lords had been in council. Lord Stanley and Bishop Morton were arrested by armed guards and committed to the Tower.

I did not understand any of this maneuvering then and I still can't say I do. That there were plots and counter plots surrounding the accession of a minor to the throne was the ordinary course of things. That our Duke Richard should be the man sending so many men so hastily to the block was not.

Anne said not a word about any of it. On the other hand, if Richard had not looked entirely the part of "Old Dick" before, when I saw him again in London, I thought he'd aged ten years.

"Why Hastings?" I dared to question John A'Parr, as he and I huddled over a supper in a shadowy corner of a kitchen. "He was a friend to my Lord of Gloucester. Wasn't he the one to send news of the plots laid against him by the queen and her family?"

"It had to be." Parr shot a glance over his shoulder to make certain no one was listening. "Hastings would not give way on crowning the prince. He wanted the Woodvilles put down and was happy to have the duke to do it. I think his plan was to sit back for a few years and wait for our lord's fall. Hastings, indeed, might have gone high in the boy's favor, especially now that his Woodville uncles are gone. Did Hastings not mightily please King Edward?"

This made as much sense as anything else I'd heard. There would be no way for Richard to find favor in his nephew's eyes, even if he hadn't already beheaded the boy's half-brother and a beloved uncle.

"It had to be done quickly." A'Parr continued. "I don't think His Grace could have held his course had he waited. After all, he and Will Hastings shared escapes and battles together, back in the old days."

We talked in whispers, heads close, although we were

ostensibly alone. It was a time of whispers, of knots of men assembled in shadows, knots which speedily dissolved, each man going his separate way as soon as words were passed. Plots flew through the air as witches are said to. It was, all told, the darkest, most fearful time early summer time I'd ever lived through.

I'd never seen Richard in this mood. A shadow seemed to follow him. For the first time, I saw fear in the faces of the men who bowed before him. Of course, it was the south—the south of treacheries and lies, where we feared them, and they, in their turn, feared us.

The court mourned in black and it suited the grim mood. The shadows of the great palace, the flickering, smoking sconces, the pallor of those indoor faces! How watchfully they turned toward the Duke of Gloucester, who was now indisputably the young King's protector.

June deepened. Young Prince Richard was still in sanctuary with his sisters and the Queen Dowager. Plans for the coronation of the boy, who would be Edward V, went on apace. The whole thing seemed a fever dream, but so it ever was in London. It was my humble estimation that what had just happened was the chickens coming home to roost. The very idea that those popinjay uncles should take England for themselves! Especially when their opponent, the lord they thought to oust, was Richard of Gloucester, our new "Hammer of the Scots." He'd dispersed Scales' two thousand with hardly a drawn sword, or as the late Hastings had remarked, "without so much as a cut finger." We'd all lived through the turn and turn-about before, and the soldiers knew which leader to follow. Still, it was a time of great danger. Heads had fallen and more would be parted from their shoulders before it was over. The business had most surprised those who knew Richard best.

At last, the youngest prince was given over by his mother, Dowager Queen Elizabeth, released from sanctuary and sent to be with his elder brother at the Tower. The place was like all castles, a town in itself with a garrison and their families, the cooks, laundresses, and haulers of night-soil and all the rest who kept it running. We had moved there ourselves, the Lady Anne, her husband, and all their retinue.

Here I saw the princes playing on the green, shooting their bows and playing some French game that required paddles with strings and little balls. They were handsome fellows, even from a distance. The crown prince, Edward, was tall for his age but thin and pale. He was fair—radiant, like his mother— but appeared to be of a solemn temperament. No doubt, he mourned for his lost father and uncles and feared the stranger uncle who now ruled him. His little brother, Richard, was nine and had not yet begun to grow. An adorable red head with chubby, high-colored cheeks and a ready laugh, he put everyone much in mind of the late king.

Duke Richard passed by us, the ladies and servants of his wife, in a fine sweep of black robes. Rubies and sapphires gleamed upon his gloves. I could not see his face, for, like the others, I had dropped a profound curtsy.

Nobles, the highest and proudest among them the dark, handsome Duke of Buckingham, waited upon him. As ranking dukes and royal kin, Buckingham and Richard made the customary greeting of "Cousin," and then departed side by side. The others bowed and followed, falling into step behind. The door to the private room from which the Lord Protector had emerged remained open.

Through it, I saw Anne. She had followed her husband almost to the door. Her pale face was framed by a veil, which floated about her shoulders. Just one look at her face told me there was trouble. Grace, seeing Anne's distress, too, started toward her, but Anne made an imperious wave. She beckoned to me, so long her closest familiar.

"Rosalba! You alone! Come here!" So, past the jealous eyes of her well-born ladies, I entered. As she directed, I closed the door behind me. Not standing on ceremony, she simply took my hand and drew me toward the window embrasure, away from any listening ear.

We sat in indirect light, for this window faced north, the shadow side. All the time, she kept a tight hold on my hands. I could feel a tremor in hers, a chill in her slender fingers. London never did either of us any good. As short a time as she had been in residence, she already looked unwell.

"Blessed Mother Protect!" I dared to speak first, gazing into her eyes. "What has happened, dear Milady?"

She tried to speak, but instead began to cough. I seized the bottle from my apron pocket and offered it. There was a time in which she gasped and swallowed hard, attempting to master the throat-closing spasm.

"Rosalba—a sermon will be preached Paul's Cross today declaring King Edward's sons to be bastards."

If the heavens had opened and spat fire down, I could not have been more surprised. I shuddered, put my arm around her and waited for the rest.

"My husband will take the crown."

We fell into each other's arms, both of us trembling, both of us weeping. I can't say which one of us was more shaken, amazed—or afraid. It was long before either of us could speak. Anne finally began, the words hurrying, coming pell-mell.

"Long ago, in the presence of Bishop of Stillington, King Edward plighted troth to Lady Eleanor Butler. He had his way with her and then did not acknowledge his promise. Shamed and brokenhearted, Lady Eleanor retired to a nunnery and died a few years later. Bishop Stillington it is who brings this tale."

"Did—did not--the—Duke of Clarence tell—something like—?"

"Indeed he did. It now appears he died for knowing it to be true."

"Blessed Mary Mother!"

We released each other and searched for our handkerchiefs. There was a clash of arms somewhere below, breaking the hush. The protector had passed, on his way to destiny.

"Richard says there is no other choice." Terror and tears flooded my Lady's eyes. "I—I begged him to hide it, to put it away, but—but—he says it is immaterial. He says I must remember what happened before, of the terrible wars that always come to lands where children rule. He says it has already started and that there is no turning aside, that English blood will be shed. He says that whether the boys are bastards or no, it will come, soon enough, to the loss of his head. The worst part is I believe he's right. He is in great danger, and the power of the crown is less with a boy king. Our cousins will begin to tear each other—and England—apart."

Who would know better than Anne, who had watched her father's earthly career?

"A party will form around the young prince, who is angry with my husband for the things he has already done. As happened under Henry VI, favorites will rob the treasury and the people, and set faction upon faction. The commons will be trampled over by battles and our wool trade will be ruined. It will only be a matter of time before the Woodvilles and their friends have off My Lord's head."

I could feel the fear, coming straight through her fingers.

"Oh, I wish for nothing but Middleham, to have my husband safe and to hold my precious boy in my arms! I want none of this! None! Neither does My Lord, but he says he must, although he is damned to hell whichever road he takes."

"Hush, dear Lady." I drew her close, for her voice had risen in the desperation of those last words. I knew, deep in my heart, she was right. The nobles would jockey for favor with the young King. Unlike Henry V's widow, Edward's beautiful queen would not disappear to a castle on the Welsh marches and content herself with a handsome young lover. A leopard cannot change her spots, nor could Elizabeth Woodville. Her need for power was too strong.

If Duke Richard had let Grey, Rivers and the others live, it would have been a fatal mistake. Killing them was a mistake, too, for young Edward—oh, that cold thin face spoke his mind all too clearly. Richard had found his nephew hostile, and the death of his closest councilors would not improve things. The boy would be contemptuous, too, as his mother and his Uncle Rivers would have doubtless taught.

To play the role of protector was to begin a game Richard

could never win, a game which started with every card in his opponents' hands. The end would come at the Prince's majority and the triumph of the Queen Mother. The Duke of Gloucester would work like a slave for the ungrateful brat for a few years and then end his earthly career on the block.

Not Richard.

"Your husband the Duke is at a terrible fork."

"True. And all ways lead to hell. I fear Westminster, these time-servers, these—dissemblers! I hate it here. Again I meet that hideous creature, Bishop Morton, once Queen Marguerite's deepest councilor, and that braying Lord Stanley and his wife, Lady Margaret Beaufort, with her Lancastrian blood. She has that Tudor son of hers lurking in Brittany, waiting his chance. I look into their eyes and none dares to meet mine, except for the Beaufort woman—and her eyes! Mother of God! A serpent looks kindlier. Oh, Rose! What will become of us?"

I did not know, could not speak. An abyss yawned before us, and we both saw it clear. All I could do was hold her close and share her terror. It was like being caught in rapids. Each rock, each boiling whirlpool must be negotiated, one at a time, without a moment's thought for anything else. Not for where we'd been, or for where we'd end.

It all happened as she said. The Princes in the Tower were declared bastards by the Reverend Shay, who preached upon the text, "bastard slips shall not take root." The citizens of London, so fond of their late King Edward, did not cheer when Richard was called upon to take the crown. Instead, they simply melted away. The comely sons of Edward IV had become, to all intents and purposes, the Duke of Gloucester's prisoners.

The nobility was not so nice in its judgment. A few agreed with Richard's claim and his reasons, although many did not. They were, however, quite ready to accept him—for the time being. His strong move across the board had taken them all by surprise. Even those who hated him kept silent, content to wait for a better time in which to advance their cause.

The coronation of Richard III and his Queen came and went like a fever dream. It was the first double coronation since that of Richard II and Anne of Bohemia, and had been prepared in two weeks, all that splendor. Anne and Richard were consecrated, blessed and the spirit of kingship entered into them.

I was nowhere around when this happened. Just another servant, I waited her return at that stinking pile, Westminster. I was ill. Filthy city! The place was a stewing pot of contagion and one had fastened upon me. I coughed and ached, and, as if this was not sufficient, also spent a great deal of time in the *garderobe*. I must have contributed the contents of my exploding gut to every privy in the palace. Thank heaven others of my humble sort helped with Rosemary.

I had seen only a glimpse of their solemn procession toward the abbey, and later another from a servant's distance, the great feast, the panoply, the splendor, beyond anything I'd ever believed possible. Still, beneath the surface, beneath all the kneeling and swearing of fealty, my vision blurred. Perhaps it was the illness, but in the years that followed I remembered the sense of illusion the day had, as genuine as the anxious, sickly sweat running down my back.

Things were unstuck, great things, matters beyond me. Like a shimmer of heat above a summer hayfield, it would end in thunder. As the time for their royal progress around England approached, I did not get better. Anne kept me at a distance. A queen could take no chances on catching something as ugly as what I had.

As for my healer's art, it was a case of "physician, heal thyself." I wasn't making much headway, though I stuck to Ash's remedies. What need had a queen for such a creature? I was lonely, ill and at loose ends. I sat among the seamstresses and mended. There, not surprisingly, I was judged a slow worker.

The Court had moved to Windsor Castle when I caught Grace Poleyn hurrying along a corridor. With a low curtsy, I begged for her attention.

"Yes? What is it, Rose?"

She's in heaven now, with a queen to serve. She and those other well-born ladies of the north, Alice Skelton, Anne Tempest and Elizabeth Babthorpe ever accompanied Milady. They were the ones privy to her confidences, the ones who tended all her wants and needs.

"I wish to beg leave to return to Middleham, Lady Grace. The Queen has no need of me and my child and I are ill."

"It has already been arranged." Grace shared this news with ill-disguised satisfaction. "You will go north from here in two days with Master Wheeler and some baggage the Queen is sending back to Middleham. The village, no doubt, has need of you."

And the queen does not...

Out loud, I said, "Please convey my grateful thanks to Her Majesty, Lady Grace."

The disease, whatever it was, had at last shrunk to a cough and a runny nose, so, as tears pricked my eyes, I began to sneeze. As I searched awkwardly for the handkerchief in my bosom, Grace stepped backward, tugging her skirts away as if I was a wet dog who'd begun to shake.

"I shall convey your gratitude to the queen." Magisterially turning, she abandoned me, a pool of skirt and sorrow, blowing my nose down upon the clammy stone floor.

Together with three other servants and a small contingent of armed men, (happily, among them, Hugh) Rosemary and I went home. It seemed, after all these long years, that I was finally erased from my lady's ledger.

At the time, there was nothing but except relief. In Middleham, I was important and useful. At the court, it had been far otherwise.

Hugh and the soldiers sent from London had one thing in common; none of them were young. Most had followed Richard since Barnet and had gone many times across the border after the Scots. It was hard to believe that a king actually had taken the time to think about his foot-soldiers, but it seemed he had. All of them, to a man, rejoiced to leave the city and retire to the north.

We all brought home some London news, but the stories Hugh could tell were best. I had not known it for we'd rarely seen each other, but while I was at Westminster and Windsor with the Queen, he had served many weeks at the Tower. As a master bowman, he had been called to the archery lessons of the princes.

"Prince Edward, now, he doesn't want to listen. Thinks he knows it all. Tall he is, but not too strong yet. I reckon a few years will put meat on those long Norman bones. He's nearsighted, though, and there's too much scholar's chatter in his head. He'll never make an archer, nor yet a soldier, I deem, no matter how hard he tries."

The others, scarred veterans like him, listened and nodded.

"The little fellow is a fine lad. Just as merry and sweet as anyone could be who has lost his Royal Daddy, his favorite uncles, and then had Lady Luck turn whore on him. A man's heart in a boy's body there! He's true royalty, like his great father."

"What do you suppose will happen to them?"

"Nothing, an' the king knows what's good for him. But Lord Richard will not hurt them," Hugh replied. "Why should he? They cannot harm him now. Nor, no more, can their witch of a mother."

Plunging back into the country was good medicine. I soon regained my accustomed good health as did Rosemary. There was no time to brood upon the past. I was home, another pair of hands to the haying, and, therefore, universally blessed. Upon these dales I would remain, minding my own business, my hearth and children—or so I thought.

It was not long before Hugh ate a mess of a kind he had never looked to sup upon again. By mid-September he was down in the southwest on active duty, fighting with the King against a rebellion started by the King's "good cousin" the

Duke of Buckingham. My husband was released from attendance upon His Grace as soon as that action was ended, toward St. Martin's day. He came home in the cold, bearing tales of war and bone-chilling rumors none of us cared to hear, these being about the late king's children.

.❧

When Hugh came through our door there was much rejoicing. Bett was glad to see him, as was I. No one among us who had been down in London could have predicted that King Richard's "dear cousin" Buckingham would be the first among the wolves to try treason.

"I swear I never thought I'd fight again in England, not in my life after the whipping we just gave the Scots, and there I was again, down in bloody Wales, the rain coming down like cow's piss!"

He told of the fighting, of the wild Welsh soldiers and their strange language, and how their horses, arms and all their mettle had washed away in the biggest floods he'd ever seen. With children and neighbors crammed inside our door, he shared a whole new set of war stories. Not only of sodden skirmishes, but my husband could also say, "The King did this," and "The King said that."

We villagers were still growing accustomed to the change, that our duke, in whose life and in whose comings and goings we had long been familiars, should now be the greatest in the land. At last, the dreaded subject arose. Someone asked about "The young lords in the Tower." My husband shook his head slowly and pursed his lips with displeasure.

"They have not been seen since September. My friend, Dick Blanchard, says there's the foulest stink he's ever known about the Tower middens."

Everyone's eyes grew large. An icy chill knifed through me.

"King Edward's children have been—put—to silence?"

"I have heard it said here and there, although I've never been one to believe that our Lord Duke had the stomach for it.

Nevertheless, I have heard men say, 'what else can a king do'? A king's troubles are not ordinary, after all."

"He could have sent them away, to Brussels, to Duchess Margaret," said I. This was a possibility I had overheard Anne speaking of with her lady, Mistress Babthorpe. "And that the Tower middens stink is hardly news. What castle with a host in residence, does not? After all, the whole city--the palace at Westminster included--smells far worse than my pig's pen."

The women laughed and looked relieved, but the men shared a look, as if they were wiser.

"Brussels is not likely," my husband said. "Margaret is not that fond of King Richard, this, too, I have heard, and foreign alliances change, that's the only thing certain about 'em. The Duchess of Burgundy has no children of her own. Perhaps, with her brother King Edward's children in hand, she might send them with an army into England."

"She is the king's own sister!"

"Would be nothing new for Plantagenet blood to hunt its own." These words came from the oldest, most grizzled veteran, one who sat close to our fire.

"His Grace would never do that, for if those boys are bastards, what need has an annointed king to slaughter them?" Everyone fell silent, acknowledging my close acquaintance with the man under discussion.

My husband gave me a measuring look before he spoke. "Ah, Rosie, our Dickon is king now and a king does as a king must, if he wants to keep on bein' a king. He headed his cousin Buckingham without a blink, and who would have seen that coming, after the way they were arm in arm all last June?"

Another of Hugh's mates spoke up. "Even if those boys were not born bastard, I don't want children ruling from London. The country will drown in blood without a man on the throne who is strong enough to keep his damned greedy cousins down."

"Aye!" sounded from every corner of our fire-lit room. Every stool and bench in the house—and some dragged from nearby houses—was full of folks who had wanted to hear the returning soldier's news.

"So it was in Henry VI's time. First his uncles stealing us blind and murderin' each other, and after them, that French bitch and her friends."

"Aye. The North shall never forget that bloody French whore. Elizabeth Woodville, she would be the same, mark my words."

On every side, heads bobbed in affirmation, although they knew nothing of the lady. It was sufficient for most of them that she was a haughty southerner.

"The older boy was a dog who would bite, like his mother. The younger one, though, little Lord Richard, he was a stout, merry fellow." Hugh sighed at the memory. "If our king has done for that sweet lad, 'tis a rare pity."

A soldier at the back of the room, a man who sometimes served at Sheriff Hutton, where Richard's own son was frequently housed, next offered an opinion.

"There are other places besides Burgundy to send the royal bastards. A king keeps many castles and he and his lordly friends have a host of children settled among them. What's two more boys in such a mob?"

All eyes turned toward this well-respected speaker. *Did he know something the rest of the world didn't?* Could the princes have been sent secretly to live with their cousin, Edward of Middleham, now in residence at Sheriff Hutton? The castle was already host to the children of Richard's friends, put to their knightly training in the clean safety of a country fortress.

"Well, what have we to do with them so high-and-mighty?" A late-coming graybeard who'd lived long and seen much, rapped his walking stick impatiently on the floor, bringing the room to attention. "They must be fightin' each other an' killin' each other. Noblemen, ha! No finer than rooks brawlin' over a gut pile. Best the likes of us can do is keep out of their way."

The crown of England likened to offal! This is often the way such deep matters are seen by those who have not walked in the castle, but I understood. Our blood, our labor, our sons and daughters were given for the distant glory of others. Escaped from the plagues of Westminster and the disregard of my mistress, I could almost believe the graybeard right. And even with all I and others had said, it was hard to put those handsome boys out of my mind.

A year passed while King Richard moved restlessly about his kingdom, hoping to keep order, to keep watch upon his lords and what plots they were hatching. We in the north minded our business. In the spring of 1484, in April, a terrible blow fell upon us and upon King Richard's hopes. His son Edward of Middleham, the new little Prince of Wales, died at Sheriff Hutton.

We heard he had died after several days of agony from a burst gut. Dear Blessed Mother! The date was April 9th, the same day his uncle King Edward IV had died! We all noted the date and shuddered. Was it divine retribution? Had Richard indeed slain his nephews and then been punished with the loss of his own much-loved child?

I wept for the child's suffering and for the queen my old friend, imagining what she endured, and remembering how Ash and I had done what little we could during her long and terrible labor. I wondered if Anne still consulted doctors and midwives, ever hoping, ever praying, to fill her scarred womb?

Summer came. In the village we planted. We sweat in our fields and gardens and then reaped harvest. I tended folks at the castle and supplied the village and the soldiers with my herbs, infusions and tinctures, as Ash, now gone to her rest, had done before me:

Horsetail is to stop bleeding. Feverfew is for headache. Knotgrass for diarrhea and hemorrhages, juniper berries ground for a spice. Marjoram is for an upset stomach and for sore throat gargles. The sweet clover, Melilot, was for animal forage and to nourish the bees. Mustard, violets and nasturtium were for our summer salad. Nettles planted around the hives kept off frogs...

My children complained when I served them stewed dishes of wild greens and nettles several nights in a row as a tonic, but they were so hungry that some of the mess went down their gullets despite all that noisy complaining. The following week I was busy dosing the tanner's crew of arse-scratching little ones for worms and the day after was spent making blue dye from chickory and brewing oat straw tea for women's aches and pains.

⚜

Toward Christmas of 1484, I was astonished to receive a summons from Queen Anne to Westminster. Hugh was furious.

"She has twelve physikers, all speaking Latin! What need has she of—of—my wife?"

Whenever he took that stance, I wanted to sling a pot at his head. 'My wife' indeed!

"She is our queen, Hugh."

"Sent you away like a dog, did she not? Or, have you so soon forgotten?"

"She did not send me away like a dog. I asked leave and was given it."

"Came home all sad, you did. My Lady Anne does not care for me anymore! She is queen now with great ladies at her side. What does she need with poor little me? And here you were in my arms, weepy as April! Aye, and this was the shoulder upon which you cried, Rose, so don't pretend otherwise."

"You don't understand what it's like, Hugh. Don't start."

"No, I suppose I don't, but you are no longer a poppet to warm her ladyship's bed, Rose. You are a woman with three fine children of her own, three more who are our kinfolk to tend, and a hard-working husband. You should rejoice to stay here with us."

"Anne is the queen. She summons me. I don't have a choice."

"You may ask her pardon and refuse. It is winter and a bad time to travel. Say your children are ill."

"It is always a bad time to travel and the children are not ill."

"Winter is hard on children. Rosemary is sniffling again, or hadn't you noticed?"

"Winter is always hard and Rosemary always sniffles, summer, spring and winter too. Alkelda knows how to take care of her perfectly."

Hugh stared at me with his pale eyes, his body immoveable as a bull's.

"Rumor is the queen has the lung contagion."

"Are you afraid I will catch it?"

"I am afraid you will bring it home to kill my children."

"Oh, your children, are they?"

"They had better be!" He made an angry feint, hand upraised.

I shrugged as if what he thought was of no importance, which always infuriated him.

"They are mine, indisputably, Master Fletcher. Therefore, as their mother, I am bound to love them, which even a man as thick as you must recognize."

"Bitch," he said, enunciating. Dragging out a chair, he sat down at the table heavily. "So you will go running off to London again? Anne Neville's good little dog, who takes a kick and then is right willing to come waggling back?"

"Anne Neville is the Queen of England, sir. The likes of us do not refuse her."

There was a long pause in which he studied me grimly, his big hands toying with an empty tankard still upon the table.

"I have heard it said that women might be—one and all— lawyers," he said after a time. "I used not to understand, but I do now."

"I must go and make ready if I am to leave." I sensed his anger and suddenly wanted very much to quit the room. As I turned, that self-same pewter tankard flew past my ear and smashed into the wall, where it fell to the slates with a great clatter. I knew his aim. He could have hit me easily, but had chosen not to go quite that far.

"Hugh. Please! Don't be angry with me." I was still trying, in the face of provocation, to speak softly.

"Why not be angry? You do whatever you like, don't you?"

"You would not refuse an order to attend His Grace in London, would you?"

"You are not a soldier. You are not even in service anymore."

"Why can't you understand?"

"I understand well enough!" He slammed his fist into the table. "I understand that it is them afore me and afore mine and afore your own blood! Always and forever! Well, go your way, Good Dog Rose! Go on! Go tonight!"

Chapter XXV

W*here are the princes?"*

The question hung in the air all around us, the question no one dared to ask. Rain, mud, the dead leaves piled—the sighing of long dreary twilights that wrapped that grand and filthy palace like the new coal fogs shrouding the winter city.

Anne was pale, coughing, nervous and irritable. I encouraged her to take a nap after the long mid-day ordeal of the royal dinner. As we were preparing for one of these retreats from the public—I, in the act of handing her a glass of wine—she suddenly said:

"The King My Husband says he has sent them to the care of a monastic order in Burgundy." We were quite alone. Her words, apparently an extension of an ongoing dialogue in her head, took me by surprise. "They will be for the church, where learning and good breeding will be to their advantage. It is a secret, Rosalba, one that may not be spoken to anyone."

"You tell me?" I was so amazed that I left off the honorific; so amazed, I was sharp.

"Yes. You must be the hole in the ground," Anne replied, trying to pretend she was at ease. "I cannot bear what you— you—might be—imagining."

"Only what the rest of England imagines, Milady."

In a flash, she'd slapped the wine out of my hand. The golden cup splashed me on its way to the rushes.

"How dare you?" Two red spots appeared on her white cheeks, glowing like coals. "You dare to speak so about My Lord, with whom you were privileged to share your childhood? How dare you speak so to your queen?"

There was nothing for it but to drop to my knees and seize her skirts. It was no time to be sent away. Whether she knew it or not, as soon as I'd arrived it was plain that she was dangerously ill. She needed me now more than she ever had.

"Forgive me, Milady! You surprised me. Please! I beg you!"

A tug of war began, Anne trying to pull her skirts away, hissing like a furious cat. She slapped me, too, repeatedly. I desperately hung on.

"Wicked spotted creature! Remember who you are! I can have your evil, lying tongue cut from your head!"

She could, this I knew. A thrill of fear stabbed me. King, queen—was such power sufficient to transform my gentle childhood companions into monsters? I counted the heads— Lord Hastings, Lord Scales, the Marquis of Dorset, Sir Richard Gray, Sir Thomas Vaughn, Sir Richard Haute, Buckingham, as well as the terrible public drawing and quartering torture of one imprudent Master Conyngham for treasonable speech...

Dear Holy Blessed Mother! Those beautiful red-gold boys—the younger only a few months older than Anne's own sweet lost Edward! Was it true, what Anne said, or was the rumor true, the rumor Hugh recounted—of a stench, which had, last autumn, saturated the inner rooms of the White Tower?

"Would Dame Woodville come out of sanctuary with her daughters if things were otherwise? Would she have brought her children to court? Devil take you, wicked ingrate!"

I held on while she swore and hammered me with her fists. Who knows how long it would have gone on, but the king suddenly came through the door, an unexpected event at this time of day.

I heard him snap his fingers at his escort and the door slammed, leaving us alone. In the next instant, he had his wife by the wrists and was dragging her away from me. At once, the queen began to sob hysterically.

"Even she—even she—thinks—" Anne began, gasping like a fish out of water. Then, she began to cough, that hollow, retching cough.

"Get out!" The King's eyes blazed. In tears and terror, I staggered to my feet and fled the room.

I feared I would be put to silence; I prayed to be sent home. Neither came to pass. That very evening, Anne called for me again, commanding me to prepare a sleeping draught as I had of old.

᠅

"My darling son is dead! And—more—the king must put me aside! Oh, Blessed Mother! I cannot bear it! I cannot!"

"My Lady, the king your husband would never—never —"

"He will do what a king must. My Lord always has done his duty—and now he is king, nothing is more important than an heir. My husband is not the man he used to be. He is king, and that is another life."

"My dear lady—"

"And I am queen and that too has requirements. In this case, my duty is to accept divorce or die. I prefer death. Yes, death is best. Ill and barren as I am, I am useless."

"My Lady! No! You must not say these things! You must not!"

"Long ago, Rose, Mistress Ash cautioned me there might never be any more children. Though I did not want to believe her, she has proven right."

Nothing more could be said. Ash had given me her opinion after the birth of Edward. Too bitter a dose for a young woman to swallow, she had said. Then she had taught me all the charms and potions she knew for childlessness, and we had applied them. After Mistress Ash died, I had gone on with the prayers and charms whether I was with my mistress or not.

"It is not good for her to believe she will have no more children," Ash had counseled. "So there must always be hope. However—in her case..." She had sighed, and ended there.

Those charms and potions—not one—had worked. So Anne had gone to other healers, to doctors, one after the other. As Ash had foretold, none had been able to make a child stick much past quickening.

And now the illness, the trouble with her lungs, kept coming back. Another evil, I feared, which I could neither fathom nor cure. Anne came to me for comfort now, for nursing, but her doctoring was in the charge of others. She took my draughts in the morning, though, paste of lemons, feverfew potions, ginger and hot cider. They did, she said, clear her throat and warm her chest, hold back the chill that camped there.

At least the yearly royal progress was done and she had settled for the winter, but I had begun to believe my queen would never see another spring. Many had this disease here in London, this wasting disease, the sore throats which never quite went away, the fevers which rose every afternoon, and at last the coughing, till the bright lung spit blood and the patient wearied and died.

My beautiful wan queen presided at Christmas—her duty— to be on display—to be seen in her glory. She was kind and generous to King Edward's daughters, sending gifts and inviting them to dance at parties. She even presented Lady Bessy, the oldest, with a magnificent dress made exactly like her own. At the Christmas revels, the two of them walked side by side, my fading, copper-haired mistress and the red-gold bastard beauty. It was the talk at the court, the Queen's generosity and kindness twisted by their evil tongues into something sinister.

I watched from the shadows as the Beaufort woman with her priests and her cat's cold smile, daily visited the Queen Dowager, now styled "Lady Gray," in private. I saw the ushers come and go bearing messages between them, heard the whispers that stopped and the false pleasantries as I passed.

January came. I watched as my dear Lady, Anne, the Kingmaker's daughter, willed to die. There is no other way to describe what happened in that bitter, black, smog-filled London winter. At Christmas tide, I think, my Lady looked into Lady Bessy's blue eyes and had seen reflected the strong beauty of her own youth, not so many years gone. Perhaps she began to imagine a sinful way to heal the breach within the House of York, a marriage which would require a Papal dispensation...

Not only King Richard knew duty, but so did my darling lady. Oh, how she loved him and served him! Milady pined for her little boy, fretted for her lord, and, but twenty-nine years of age, let go of her life. I wished her body could have gone home to Middleham, or, better, have been brought to Sheriff Hutton, to be laid by the grave of her dear only child.

My sweet mistress died in March, when the world was busy gazing at the spectacle of an eclipse. No one in the palace paid much attention to the end of a barren queen, only her sorrowing ladies--and the King. I was holding her hand when she let go of her last long sigh. I helped to lay out her long, thin body. I combed her beautiful copper hair across her shoulders, thinking this would be the last service I performed for great Warwick's daughter, closer to me, even since she had become a queen, than my sisters.

During the final days, she had asked me to take on a few tasks after her death and with those wishes I have faithfully complied. For as long as I could make the journey, I traveled to Middleham and laid the gift beside Saint Alkelda's well, praying as I did for Lady Anne's sweet soul. Better mistress a poor woman never had.

My queen was buried in Westminster Abbey. Although it was a grand place, it was lonely, so far from the Nevilles and the other great northern families whose blood had run in her veins. With all my heart, I wished she had been carried back north, for I was never able to visit my dear lady's resting place again in my life. Anne Neville—last Queen of the White Rose! It was just as well she did not live to see the end of the House of York, which was to come a scant five months hence.

"What do you think the King has done with his dear brother's children?"

It was past midnight, not a week since Anne had gone into the crypt. I had been summoned from my bed. Not knowing why, I'd compounded a sleeping potion and carried it hence, for I could not think of any other reason why His

Majesty would have wanted me at this hour.

As he spoke, the king stared at me out of those sleepless hollows which had become his eyes. A black gloved hand, all blazing with jewels, caught and crushed my wrist, forced me onto my knees. Exhausted and half lost in sleep, I was swiftly terrified, a sparrow caught in a falcon's fist. The cup I'd carried splashed into the reeds.

"Speak, woman!"

"My Lord King—men say—men say—say…"

"Whatever men say is true." Richard spoke from a face of stone, a face exhausted, anguished. "But, hear us, Rose, for we've question which you must answer. We've long been pondering on it and imagining what light your Yorkshire wit can provide. The King could ask learned councilors, of course, but…"

"Sire?"

"Do you know what Truth—which God alone knows—has to do with what men say?"

"Good My Lord, please!" I thought my wrist would break. All I wanted was to flee from him as I would from the devil. "No, My Lord! And if I did—I should never…"

At this nonsense, he cast me down into the reeds. I rubbed my poor wrist, the bones aching as if a thousand demons had tested their jaws upon it. At that instant I believed, as some among the court already did, that since Anne's death he had gone mad.

"Do you wish to leave us?" He gazed scornfully at me, now huddled on the floor at his feet. "My dearly beloved consort, the Queen, is gone to her eternal rest. Your humble service is at an end, Rose."

I sobbed, remembering my adored Anne upon her bed, a dales flower, withering in the poisoned air of the south. Before she had died, she had asked me for another boon, besides bringing the ancient tithe to Alkelda in her stead. At the very last, she had asked that I care for her husband, "as if he were your very own. You must, for the sake of our old love, until he marries Lady Elizabeth, or," and here her lovely eyes had blazed with grief, "one of the royal ladies of Portugal, with whose ambassadors I know he even now speaks."

I'd blushed at the image that had come to mind. Even in such terrible times I could still think this thought, even when, on every side it was whispered that King Richard was a cold, mad killer.

Anne had pressed my fingers with hers so long and white and said, "You will do what is right, dear Rose, what is needful. You always do. And whatever you do will be right, this I know." My Lady had smiled a sweet smile that spoke of long ago. "After all, Rosie, a hawk will quickly take a loose hen." She'd tried to laugh at the ribald jest and I had blushed, but it had ended in coughing, the bright, living blood mingled with her spittle.

On this awful midnight, remembering Anne, I wept fresh tears at his feet.

"I cannot leave you, Your Majesty."

"Cannot?" A dark brow arched. "If the king so much as imagines you gone ..." Mockery flowed across his face, "you will quickly find yourself ..." the gloved hand waved, the ruby flashing against the darkness, "Gone! This, after all, has happened to people far, far more important than you, Rose."

"I—I beg your pardon, Good My Lord, but I promised my dearest lady, your queen, I would not leave your side. Until—until..." My throat closed with fear. I'd never, ever seen him in such a state. I was as frightened of him as any other person in the household that night—maybe more—because, to me, the change was so profound. Richard was now truly a foal of the Nightmare.

"Until?"

I swallowed hard, and looked up at him, praying not to see the king, only my Yorkshire Dickon. When I could not speak, there was silence. He simply stared back with those burning eyes, full, as always these days, with bitterness and rage.

Ah, Mary Bright! Where was my Dear Lord Dickon? Lost, buried in the same stinking midden as his nephews, leaving us at the mercy of this crowned, terrifying stranger?

"Until you take a new queen, Your Highness."

"Do they say this will be very soon? For, the king tells

you, every soul in this domain knows more of his doings than he does."

"Diverse notions…" Dredged from somewhere, fear summoned courtier's language."…are—are--abroad, Your Grace."

He looked down at me, and I had a flash of his brother George, about to make a vicious joke at someone's expense. Instead, he looked past me, into the darkness. After a time, with some effort, he returned his gaze to me.

"So! You wish to stay with the king, Rose?"

"I—I promised my dear Lady—Queen Anne—upon her death bed, my noble lord…for the sake of the love which I have so long…"

"If you do not wish to keep that promise, the king releases you. You shall return to Middleham at once."

"I most humbly beg your pardon, Your Grace, but you--you cannot release me. I made this promise to my sweet lady, Queen Anne, before That One Who Sees All.

"That One Who Sees All…" He studied me gravely. "Is there such a being, Rose? Have you seen him? Have you heard him speak?"

"No, you'll pardon me for my ignorance, My Lord."

"The King speaks to God, to his Blessed Mother, to his most blessed saints and angels, and to all the company of heaven, many times every day, Mistress Rose. The King has given him, and his blessed saints and angels, faithful homage, hour-by-hour, every day of his life, as you well know. The king has done good works and charity of every sort; he has administered justice for rich and poor alike, though this brings him no thanks. The king has given alms, has endowed chantries, performed good Christian works too many to catalogue. Yet God gives the king no sign. We wish to know if God speaks to such a humble creature as you, Rose?"

He paused, and in his eyes I saw an inquisitor with a query for which there was no right answer. Whatever I said, it would simply provide another excuse to tighten the ropes.

"Please do not ask me, Your Majesty. I am as your Grace says—common—and—simple."

Richard flashed a triumphant smile. "So! God does not speak to you, either."

"My understanding is not equal to—"

"Shame, Rose!" He cut me off. "You talk like one of these southerners and think you can make a fool of your king. Remember, the king knows you of old. We order you to speak plain."

By the Black Virgin! I trembled at his feet, beside leather boots ornamented with jewels. Richard was a falcon, bright eyes, beak gaping, poised to tear flesh.

"Here is another hard question for a common woman." He scoffed when I made no answer. "How is it you still fear God?"

"Your Grace!" Remembering my own mortal sins, I shuddered.

"The king no longer fears God. God does not speak so the king can hear. God most assuredly does not listen to these endless prayers his subjects offer. His justice is blind, his mercy is the hangman's—a sharp knife busy in the gut—until his obedient servant can vainly cry out no more."

The torches flared, and, Mother Mary, I looked up, expecting to meet Divine Wrath and vanish in an explosion of heavenly fire along with the most noble blasphemer.

"Be of good cheer, Rose. Nothing will happen." He leaned toward me, as if making a confidence. "Nothing at all! Those words, spoken by the meanest slave—or by a king—bring no divine punishment." His thin lips twisted. "And what service did my dear consort ask you to perform to keep the king in cheer until he marries again, Rosalba? Come, now! Look up! Dare to speak plain as was once your wont."

I lifted my head as commanded, but could not reply. Richard, his expression merciless as any of his bloody-handed royal ancestors, stared down. His face was alabaster, his long nose, his burning eyes, twinned the devil's. To say I was terrified is to fall far, far short of the mark.

"Chess, Your Majesty." I surprised myself, I think, as much as I surprised him.

"A poor conceit! To defeat a woman—a simple, common

woman—whose little charms and foolish little potions have lately proven so worthless? This will neither take much effort, nor make for much amusement for the king."

At first, I could not think how to answer. From his point of view, all he said was true. Nevertheless, his scorn, especially the part about my failure to save our beloved Anne, sparked a towering rage. The fresh tears now spilling down my cheeks arose from temper. I had lowered my head so he would not see, but he bent, and a flashing, cold hand jerked up my chin. It was hard to look at him, but I knew I must now, or risk a blow of royal displeasure.

"You are angry now. Good! Good! That will make for some sport."

Richard released me and took a step back. Lifting his sparkling hands, he clapped and called into the shadows.

"Bring the chess board."

I had imagined we were alone, but, of course, you never are in a palace, not for an instant. Out of the darkness beyond the flaring torches a servant soon materialized, carrying a board and an elaborately carved wooden box.

From that hour, I entered My Lord's Kingdom of Night. The impassive face of those northern guards, the only ones he trusted, watched us, graven statues on either side of the arched door.

I touched his shoulder for the first time in years and felt mail beneath his robe. Dear Blessed Mother! He even slept in it! Later, after fatalism set in and he had gone out of London-- that seat of his undoing—only then did he relinquish the practice.

I knelt beside him, for he had again called me, then required me to remain after I'd handed him the sleeping draught I'd brewed. It was difficult to judge his dose. The king was not a big man, but the demons which kept him wakeful were strong. At the same time, he did not desire the sleep of the poppy. It lasted too long and left him slow-witted.

Chronic sleeplessness is a most difficult ailment to manage; all healers agree. What works for a time will soon cease to have effect. In large doses of opium, death lurks. All in all, treatment is a conundrum.

"Will it help?" The king appeared doubtful.

"I do not know, Sire." I bowed my head, mentally telling the ingredients, the amounts, all over again, while he drained the cup. It ought to work, of course, but he was different—now, more so than ever.

I received the cup again, offered by his jeweled hands. They sparkled in the clear light of a fine bee's wax taper. He was studying me.

"Medicine is no certain thing, is it Rose?"

"No more than any other, begging your pardon, Your Grace."

"Only God knows the answer, certainly none of us."

"Perhaps, Sire, not even God knows."

"*Not even God!* Excellent! We shall make a canon—or a heretic—of you yet, Roan Rose."

"Our Lady forefend!" I spoke with feeling, the fire leaping in my mind.

The king watched my face and softly laughed. He knew he'd frightened me.

"By your leave, My Dread Lord." I curtsied, more than ready to escape, but he caught my hand.

"You do not have leave to go." His eyes, deep in their hollows, met mine. He'd made the decision quickly, as was always his way. "Walk with me." My hand in his, he led me across the chamber with those regal hangings, and pushed through the curtains. My heart flew into my throat and stuck, for here stood his bed, all gilded and hung with the arms of England.

"Are you entirely at the king's service, Mistress Rose?" The candles were guttering, hissing fingers of wax, pooled at the clawed feet of the candelabrum.

I swallowed hard, raised my eyes. Behind him, the leopards shone rampant. A promise had been made to his queen, my dearest lady, and she knew, as well as I, there are other ways beside draughts to put men to sleep. Desire, which had flickered between us for so many years, shot a lewd tongue.

"I am at your service, Your Majesty."

Gently, he drew me close. There was no mail beneath his shirt this night. It was something of a surprise, this lack of suspicion, but at this moment, the Court was at Windsor and not in the dark city.

There had been a time when I'd dreamed of his kisses, imagined I longed for them, when I'd summoned the memory of his lean body, but we'd reached a point where Time had warped everything. The man of my dreams had taken a King's oath, become destiny's creature.

And, what else? Usurper, certainly. Perhaps even the coldest of killers, murderer of those lost, red-blonde lambs. I did not know if he had slain them, but the thought was in the back of every mind, on the tip of every tongue. If the Duke of Buckingham, as his loyal northern guards forthrightly believed, had had them killed during Richard's first summer progress in order to further his own aims—well, that too was a sin at Richard's door. He had taken a mighty oath to protect his brother's sons.

So many vows broken! Now, at this turn of events, I too would break a long ago promise made to my husband. His lips touched mine, gently, but with his usual decision. There was the unfamiliar sensation of a man small and slight, not a whit taller than myself, but astonishingly strong.

He smelled the same, felt the same, although he was now harder, muscles denser, than our legendary long ago. Memories flew to old roosts, memories which are not words.

The first kiss was detached, as if he wondered whether his heart still pumped, wondered whether he was still a man, one who could be roused by a round woman and the proximity of a bed. His mouth tasted of the draught, of honey, burnt wine, and, last, the lingering medicinal.

"Rose." We drew breath together, the same deep breath we'd drawn so long ago. "Rose is still Rose."

Men and children are much the same in their needs. They seek the breast first, remedy for all their ills. When he came at last to kiss my lips, his mouth was limned with the milk which ever lingers. Ah, here is another flavor of that bitter herb called love!

After, the King slept, and I lay with him. Before dawn, however, the spell of the draught wore out and he roused himself. Just as long ago, I dressed and left the chamber, escorted straight to my own, by one Master Hundell, a guard who'd watched in the antechamber.

As had happened long ago, I was ashamed to my soul, all the while knowing that I would do it again, whenever the King asked. I was afraid the whole way to look the guard in the face, afraid of what I'd see there. Thank whatever angel is in particular charge of me, the man behaved as though I just another routine morning detail.

I suppose this is why he—Master Hundell—was where he was. Richard knew the hearts of his men, though he did not know the hearts of his lords. But, wait. I run ahead. Bad news will keep.

"He made a mistake when he headed his old friend Lord Hastings, aye, the king did."

"Better, he should have headed Lord Stanley or that serpent wife of his."

"Ha! Or both of 'em! 'Deed he should, and now he rues it."

"The king rues may things, I think."

"Aye, but that's what it is to be king. He wanted it. He must stand the course."

"If Edward's queen ruled, I wonder how long my Lord of Hastings would have lasted at her court?"

"Not much longer, perhaps. Old Will was ever riding for a fall."

We hoisted a pint together. Hundell was a bull who reminded me of Hugh, another stern northerner and now my partner in crime.

"You have a good husband, Rose." Hundell sighed and considered me.

"I do, Master Hundell."

"You have done him wrong."

"I have. I shall not escape reckoning—not in this world, nor in the next."

"Well, well. Take no offence. 'Tis nowt, Mistress. Do the likes of us say no to a king?" Hundell shrugged broad shoulders. "His Grace can plaster over the mar, I have no doubt. He is a just lord and as open with his purse as was my Lord of Hastings."

"I pray my husband never learns of my—service--to the king."

"Well, I shall not be the one to tell him, Mistress Rose. Have no fear on my account. There are secrets which must be kept when you are dealin' with a king." Hundell warmed to his subject. "I am of the chosen company who fight beside His Grace. I guard him through the night. You rock him to sleep. A company will not survive battle if the commander does not sleep. What you do is not just—just—whorin', it is—for—England."

His broad, pitted face blazed red, as if to speak so long, on so common a matter, embarrassed him. Hundell was, after all, not the kind of man who ordinarily made excuses. I turned hot with shame.

"I—have tried every draught, every charm and potion I know to make him sleep."

"Your husband's wrong is the king's right, lass." Hundell gruffly conveyed his absolution. After a pause in which he again hid his discomfort in the tankard, he added, "'Tis the best thing for putting a man to sleep on this green earth."

There might have been a wink, but he refrained, gaining stature in my eyes. A good man and just, was Master Hundell. He swallowed several pints quickly, then he was on his feet, and after excusing himself, away to find some sleep of his own.

I was relieved he viewed my truancy with plain soldier's logic. Hugh would likely have been of the same mind, too, had the woman involved not been *his* wife.

I lay in the king's bed, waiting for him to give in, to end his wandering and return. Armed men stood outside, the loyal ones who followed Richard like dogs. Not a word would slip. I could hear them shifting and coughing. The past winter had been hard on all of us. I was sleeping when he came at last, waking only as he lifted the covers. With a deep sigh, he lay back.

"My Lord," I whispered, praying he wouldn't reach for the dagger that always, here in London, lay beneath his pillow. "'Tis Rose."

There was a moment in the darkness where it was, I believe, touch and go with his understanding. Finally, Richard laid a hand on my face. His long fingers were like ice.

"Rose?"

"So you may sleep." I was embarrassed to the core.

In the darkness behind those heavy curtains, I slipped my arms around him, drew the King of England close. He was cold, shivering in my arms, for he'd been long wandering those dark halls. I knew servants watched, ever trailing him. Some cared for their master. Others, in the pay of his enemies, reveled in spying upon a man who did not appear to have the stomach for his own terrible deeds.

I wondered who had followed him tonight, and if my presence in the royal bed would remain secret. I prayed it could, for he needed comfort, and I—I would have had him, my haunted and hunted Lord—any way at all.

That night, he simply lay in my arms and I warmed him. We were quiet, like the children we had been long ago. He was drained, exhausted. It was like holding a boy upon my bosom, thin as he'd grown, but he did, at last, sleep.

A'Parr did nothing to change the order of the guards as they came on and off duty. Only on the nights when those who were faithful—to the bone—did I come with that night-time posset and then remain, slipping into the royal bed.

Richard never asked. The devising was A'Parr's—and, mine. We did what was needed and when and as we could. Richard could not be king without a single safe place. It could not be asked of any man. And he was a man, after all. The next time we lay together, he played the part.

It was a long time, there in the quivering light of a single candle, with hands and lips, long warming embraces, my arms around him, hoping to drive the cold grief out, to hold it, for as long as I could, at bay. A kiss, a caress which lingered, an answering shiver when he put his hand upon my breast; thus he was led to the balm of earthly pleasure.

I opened body and soul, but he—he could not. I caressed his arms, his sides. I sighed and wriggled, playing my part, kissed his shoulders and his hard chest.

"Your Grace, what would please?"

He raised himself a little, and we looked at each other.

"Such a courtier, my Rose!"

I put back his dark hair, now falling over his shoulders. It had been forever—a lifetime for both of us—since our first and last embrace.

"So long ago, when you were a maid," he said, his words somehow following my thoughts. "I should not have done what I did. It was a sin then; it is a sin now."

"I was a maid. As for then—and, as for now—well, I am a simple woman, Sire. I follow my heart."

I touched that old-young face. All the time I had been moving, just slightly, as if I could not master my longing for him. He bent for a kiss.

"There are still strawberries in your mouth, Rose."

That was when I understood how to help.

"Dear Dickon." I said the old name, ever so softly, locking arms around his slender waist and hugging him tight. "Dickon." This soon proved the charm.

Our hearts were full of pain, but they still beat strong. We were yet on this earth, in the flesh—Richard and Rose—and we were together. I, common as a stone pried from the earth of my native dale, was possessed, transfigured. I flew with my Lord, the sun's royal falcon.

⚜

"And what is this?"

It was another night. He'd lifted my pendant. He smiled, as he asked, the same question he'd asked before in another time and place.

"I always wear it, Milord."

It lay, soft against my freckles, that ivory white rose.

"*Lenticulae.*" Idly he traced patterns upon my flesh.

"What?"

"Freckles." He broke into one of those rare, beautiful smiles. "It would take me a very long time to kiss them all."

"Indeed it would, my Lord."

"Shall I attempt it?"

His lightness was charming, though hard to believe. Richard was not made for gallantry, and, yet, when he played the part, it was easy to see another self which might have been, one more provocative, more playful, more like his wanton brothers. Perhaps House Plantagenet was, as they say, begotten upon Melusine, the Devil's daughter. Even serious, care-worn Richard knew how to make love.

If, afterward, he slept in my arms, it was all for the good. My sweet Lady Anne would not be angry with me if this was the only way he could rest. She would understand.

She had told him to do what he must, wed Bessy, or to marry one of those Portuguese princesses who carried the blood of John of Gaunt, founder of House Lancaster, whatever it took to hold his crown. That final, many-faceted sin—let the boys die and marry their sister, his niece—he could not bring himself to commit. In fact, he had just issued a statement that emphatically denied any such intention and ordered severe punishments for those who passed this "rumor."

Silently, I wondered that Richard would shrink from anything now. If he did, it must be because Bessy was truly a bastard. This claim was, after all, the foundation of his

Kingship. Perhaps he did it out of tenderness for her, but I thought both ideas false. The lady would have been happier with the man who had let her brothers slip into the hands of wily, cruel Buckingham than with Henry Tudor, that avaricious, soulless bane.

.⚜.

We lay together in an upper room at Nottingham, the river winding below us, beneath sheer rock and the castle walls.

"I have lain with more women in the last few months than ever since I was a bachelor."

"There are some rewards for being king."

"Rewards? I was counting them as sins. There is a great deal to be said for your view."

I wasn't entirely surprised by the confession, though, I'm not sure why. Woman's intuition, I suppose.

"The Lady Bessy?" *Why not ask?*

"She is angry with me, as is her mother, but nothing there can ever be mended."

"Imagine!" I dared to tease. "You make love to her and then renounce her and send her away to Sheriff Hutton."

"She wanted me. Was most insistent, in fact, so I refuse to take all the blame. As for making her queen—the time for that would never be right. The North, after all, is all I have, and the North came from Anne."

"But, my Lord, I have heard it said that Henry Tudor makes plans to marry her."

"She is a bastard, yes, but this seems not to matter a whit to many people, especially to Tudor and his friends. Her blood daily increases in value. She is lusty, beautiful, and seems, if her mother is any indication, like to breed."

"You are far more wicked than I or anyone ever imagined, Richard Plantagenet." I stroked his lean cheek.

"More of a self-righteous forked fool at the beginning. Now, perhaps, you are right. 'Wicked' suits the king's purposes far better than 'good'. Remember how I repented after lying with you?"

"Yes. Why did you? It made me feel so bad."

"It made us both feel bad. What a fool! I wanted you and I wanted Anne, too. I could not understand how this could be, so the desire, and acting upon it, had to become a sin. Now that I no longer speak to God, I am not so certain about these rules anymore. I wanted to bed you and I did. I wanted to be your first, Roan Rose."

"I loved you very much, my Lord."

"You still love me." His lips began a traverse of my throat.

I sighed, and settled against him. He lifted a long strand of my hair and studied it.

"Nothing," he finally said, "can be settled until Tudor comes. If I kill him, there will be more to my story. I warn you, Rose, I shall commit a great many more mortal sins. To start, I shall cut off almost everyone's head. Next, I shall wed a Portuguese princess–if one of them approves the portrait I've sent. Perhaps I shall marry Bessy to one of their Portuguese cousins—the ambassador suggests Duke Manuel of Beja would make a suitable match. However, if Tudor kills me, Elizabeth shall marry him, and, God Help her, be his queen. Lady Gray, I have no doubt, will dance with joy on the occasion and comfort her child by saying that to open her legs for one man is much the same as to open them for another. If that is how it happens, it will be a sorry end for the House of York."

He seemed distant now, as if not talking about himself. I hated his withdrawal, as much as I hated the thought of him dead.

"Tears?" He stroked my cheek. "Not for any of that, I hope?"

"For you, My Lord. Your subjects most heartily pray such evil never comes to pass."

"Many of my subjects pray most heartily that it does! God will throw the dice when he pleases and I shall stand the hazard of the cast."

There followed a long pause in which I hid my face against him. The cold possibility of what he said entered like a knife. That he, as well as Anne, might die!

"Do you think this is correct?"

"My Lord?"

"That one man is much the same as another. Mistress Shore believes this."

"Leave her be, Your Grace. Especially when you are lying with a married woman.

"Who is the king to call the kettle black?"

"Yes, Sire."

"Impertinent as usual." He lured me on again. "But you haven't answered my question."

"If you weren't my king, I'd kick you out of bed. After all, *is* one woman much the same as another?"

"Yes—and—no."

"Why do you men pretend to believe we women are so utterly different from you?"

"Well, in my case, appetite has always been most particular. Some men—and, some women, too, I trow, will eat anything."

"The Lady Bessy was in love with you, Your Grace."

"Do you think so?"

"Yes." I had watched the young beauty before she'd been sent north, sadly following the king with her blue eyes, ever on the brink of tears.

"She is in love with a dream. That is the only answer I can find."

"If the Lady Bessy loves you, she will never love Henry Tudor."

"God—or the Devil—I make no favorites—Help me save Lady Elizabeth from lying with that base foreign scoundrel."

"If you have taken the lady's maidenhead, Your Grace, she will be yours forever, whatever comes to pass."

"Ah, Rose!" He stroked my face and smiled. "What fancy is this?"

"If Lady Elizabeth gave you the flower—then—then ..."

"Is that why you are here?"

He began to move, making the suggestion with his body. Between us, there was so much to say—and so little. Our only candle guttered, choked and flared again.

I could speak of the charge our beloved Anne had given. I

could declare that what I'd just said was true, that his taking of my maidenhead had changed my life for good and all, in ways neither of us could have imagined, but now my king had lost his compass, had fallen upon me, a hawk from out of bright sky. He'd taken nourishment for body and soul, just as he did tonight. He needed no more burdens. That was not what I was here to do.

"I, like your royal niece, endure a dream of you, my Lord."

His response was to part my legs with his. As he did so, he whispered, "Let us make it come true, then, Rose."

I was in love now, hungry between times, impatient with waiting. Everything was stolen, forbidden, and, therefore, impossibly sweet. The nights we lay together were given to pleasure, in all the ways experience makes possible. When I first arose from his bed, the hot trickle between my legs kept me well in mind of the sins I had committed during the night.

A knock sounded at our tower door.

I barely noted it, coming as it did from somewhere beyond my dream, a violent dream of spilled cups upon a royal table, cups which were knocked over by the diners as fast as I attempted to right them.

I had reached the point of frustration. The gentlemen and ladies seated about the table were never angry, although a flood of wine ran over an expensive damask cloth, a red flood of ruin. In fact, they seemed to take a cold kind of delight in overturning, and then simply asked me to pour again. I could not understand, and knew that somehow I must keep the cups upright, keep the red wine within, but they would not let me. With their own jeweled hands they tipped those cups over as soon as I filled them. Then, shockingly, I saw what flowed out was not wine, but blood, congealing in gelatinous strings, dangling from the edge of the rare white damask ....

The knocking became an escape to which I ran...

I had fallen deep into sleep after a night with Richard in a tower chamber at Nottingham. My exhaustion was not so much caused by attending my lord during his restless nights, but a new worry over what seemed yet another disaster. It had been overlong since the moon had called me to pay her debt.

As if there wasn't enough anguish in our bitter pleasure! I had become certain that Richard had bred me. I was sleepy beyond all measure, just as I always was in the first months. I hadn't told him. Living, as we did that summer, on the edge of the abyss, the last Plantagenet summer England would see, a peasant's full belly would be the final cruel joke at his expense.

"Rose." He stroked my cheek, my hair, and then ran his hand tenderly along the bare length of my torso. It had been warm that night and I was naked, lying with my leg over a pillow, belly down, in the softness of that royal bed. It was the last time in my life I'd sleep in such luxury.

"Rose, wake up."

"Yes, My Lord." Forcibly rousing myself, I pushed the pillow aside and sat. Even with that nasty dream, sleep was so welcome! Legs over the side of the bed, and there I sat, knuckling my eyes and attempting to hide a yawn. He put his arms around me, kissed my forehead.

He threw on a robe to open the door, but he did not girdle it, only held it closed while he spoke with A'Parr. Richard was bare beneath, muscle and sinew embracing his crooked spine, but not a spare inch anywhere. When he returned, hands at my waist, he lifted me down, easily as Hugh might have done.

By Our Lady! For such a little man, he was strong!

I put my arms around him and kissed. My Lord kissed back, not quite ready to put comfort behind him, as if he were as loath as I. Flesh to flesh, feet on cold stone, the first light seeping in through that one high window, he passed tender hands over me.

"Ah, my Roan Rose."

Without another word, I knew our time together was

done. Gazing into his eyes, I could almost see him disappearing, into another world, one that would take him away forever.

"Ah, My Lord! What has happened?"

"Tudor has marched, unfettered by a single one of my faithful vassals, deep into Wales. A'Parr has brought confirmation. We shall soon know who among my lords has been biding his time till he betrays me."

I did not know what to say, but locked my arms around that slim waist and held on as if I would never let go.

"You must go now." He spoke against my hair.

"Go?"

"Yes. You leave at midday."

"My Lord?"

"Yes. For you, it's back to Middleham."

"Please, no!" Swiftly, tears rose and spilled.

"At midday, my Rose."

If he had become cold and commanding, I couldn't have borne it, but he held me close, and he was gentle, in the moment of putting me away forever. From God knows what yet unquenched fount of sweetness in his nature, he stroked my cheek and then couched his explanation in purest Yorkshire.

"Ah've nowt time na for lasses," said the King.

Chapter XXVI

O h, yes, I obeyed him and I went, but not far. It turned out to be easy enough to do. The five old soldiers with whom he'd sent me had no wish to be away from their lord's battle either.

We started, but ended by turning back, past Nottingham. The king and his company had gone down to Bestwood to hunt and wait for the coming of the enemy. We walked to Leicester, waited a time, and then marched in ever greater haste, as we heard the news that Richard had gone, without any of the help promised by the Lords Percy and Stanley, down to meet Tudor and his miscreants near Market Bosworth.

We lay up in the hay fields by night, where the locals told us we were only a few hours stride from the fires of armies. About the time of lauds, the old soldiers and I, all of us the king's friends, began to move.

In the gray which proceeds dawn we came upon the king's pickets at the rear guard. Here, my soldier friends went in and I stayed among a little group of women of the army waiting in an orchard. In the camp, the lords were arming. There were gay banners and the flash of metal on the hill above.

From that distance I heard canons begin to boom and heard the distant thud of gun stones. Into the summer dawn rose a black smoke, as if hell had opened a gate. There came next the battle roar. At last, in the valley behind the hill, I began to hear the terrible cries of the wounded.

Some of the women simply stayed under the trees. Myself and a few others, pale and full of fear at what we knew in our hearts—we went forward—to help, to look for our men. In dread we skirted the hill which had been the king's camp.

A mob of ravens had already gathered, a murderous racket in the trees. Hearing them, the hair on my neck prickled.

There were three ravens sat on a tree . . .

The grim old song! Crossing myself, I began to walk. If the crows gathered so eagerly, there were none left to do me harm...

Down, down in yonder green field
There lies a knight, slain 'neath his shield...

The dead lay everywhere. I stepped among them and then over them. Of the first lords I saw was one who lay belly down, arms extended, hands still gripping his battered, emblazoned shield. A trail of gore marked his progress through the crushed grass. He had been crawling, stubbornly refusing to release his arms. The shield was dented and battered, the corners actually hammered out of shape. One heraldic quartering had been obliterated, but the other was still identifiable. It was my Lord Duke of Norfolk, ever true to the house of York.

As I approached, the ravens flew up with a chorus of caws and a funereal clatter of black wings. They did not go far, just rose, circled, and then landed again in the nearest tree, confident of their feast. It took my breath way to round the hill and come upon this rare work of men—broken strong bodies and dead horses, the fallen, trampled standards, the greasy sheen of blood upon long August grass. A haze hung in the air and the wind was rank with dust, black powder from the hellish guns, and that slaughterhouse stink. I crouched to see if any still breathed, but stiffening death was all I saw. On every side lay Richard's men, men I knew, tabards emblazoned with the boar, now soaked with their own entrails.

Now for good and for all, sorrow's knife entered my heart. What did I see high across the plain, but a red dragon banner blowing in the wind! The banners of the Lords Stanley, of Talbot, of Percy and the Blazing Star of the Earl of Oxford I recognized, too.

Dead and dying horses, legs broken, guts spilled, lay on every side. I entered the heart of the slaughter, picking my way through the bodies, stepping over oozing remains.

Soldiers were in the king's camp farther back on the hill, a great pack of them, baying like a pack of murderous hounds.

There were screams as the wounded were knifed. If I had been in my right mind, I would have run, but I did not. Blood hammered in my brain, and one word—

Dickon!

The field poured gently down to a creek bed and to a plain with a few thorn trees and small patches of briar. Another crowd of soldiers boiled at the bottom. By stooping and moving slowly, I avoided notice, but it was here, on the slope, I found White Surrey. His foreleg had broken, and he'd been shot through with longbow arrows, leaving pools of dark, grainy blood. There were dead men all around me, and I could name each and every one.

On every side they lay, without heads, without arms, men whose gut spilled in fly-covered piles. Not only Richard's soldiers, not only Wilfred and Niles and other guards who had stood, silent sentinels on so many secret nights. Here too I saw among dead Secretary Kendall, my dear old friend, A'Parr, the stalwart Hundell, even the King's ushers, pages and servers, all of them lying among his bodyguard. Even clerks and humble body servants had followed the king into battle. I knelt beside the beautiful, still warm body of the white horse, laid my head down upon his froth-covered neck, and sobbed.

Dickon!

On every side lay blood and ruin. I could not bear the soft pleading of the dying horses. Their dark liquid eyes, filled with astonishment at what had happened to them, followed me. Drawing my blade, I crawled across the filthy ground, putting first one and then another from his misery, plunging the knife deep in the neck vein. Hot blood gushed over me, but it didn't matter, except their suffering end.

Shading my eyes against the sun, I peered toward the dragon banner. I could hear sounds and see a busy crowd which raised my hackles with fear—sounds which brought to mind a rape—soldiers laughing and screaming, a crowd of them clustered at some wicked business down in the hollow by those twisted thorn trees. I knew they were at the Devil's work.

Then a knight—Sir Thomas Burgh, it was—moved. His face was turned to one side, the helm and chest plate gone.

Matted brown hair spilled upon the torn earth. They had done a poor job of killing and spoiling him. His black lashes rested against a shattered, bare cheekbone.

To my horror, helpless as an infant, he groaned, rolled over, seized a fistful of grass and tried to pull himself forward. I crawled to take him in my arms. A moment later, uncorking the bottle I carried, I let water trickle into his mouth. As I gave him drink, his eyes focused.

"Thanks, Rose," he whispered through split lips. I held his battered head in my lap and stroked his cheek.

"Our king—slain." Sir Thomas coughed. Blood trickled from his nose, from his mouth.

I held him close. After a minute or so, his entire frame shuddered fiercely and he died.

There I sat, upon the battle ground, cradling a dead man. My back was again against White Surrey and I brushed away the flies which kept gathering. This was how it was when a group of soldiers wearing Stanley's Griffon Claw badge noticed me. They made a braying, threatening approach.

"And what is this? One of these traitors' leman?"

I knew what they intended, yet I did not move. I would be raped by all upon the bloodied earth of the King's household, spat upon, mocked, and killed.

"S'Blood! What are you at, you stupid bitch?"

Fortunate, I suppose you'd call it, on this day of utter ruin. It was Hugh, with the battle rage still on him. His face was blood-spattered; his steel gray eyes were bright.

"You know this spotty whore?"

"I do." Clearly, he did not want to claim me as "wife." He raised his sword.

The others did not wait to see what he would do, just moved off. There were plenty of other throats to be cut and women to rape.

As Hugh dragged me to my feet, Sir Thomas rolled from my lap like a log. Around us other soldiers had turned their attention to the bodies and to knifing those who still breathed.

Good profit, spoiling dead gentlemen!

"What do you think you're at?" Hugh dragged me after

him. "Christ's blood!"

"They've killed the king."

"Damn right! I saw 'em split his head."

I tried to tear myself out of his grasp, gorge rising, for I'd just noticed his jacket. There, staring me in the face, was Stanley's griffon claw badge!

"For once in your life," he shouted, slapping me hard back and forth across the face, "do what I say!"

"Got yourself a choice piece of the baggage?" A passing ruffian cheerfully suggested.

"Ay!" Hugh pushed me and then delivered a hearty kick. I staggered, fell, and began to retch bile upon the bloody grass.

"Get up, bitch! Get up!" He was right behind me, hammering me with his fists. "Damn you! Heartless whoring bitch!"

※

Beside my husband, I marched among disorganized, rag-tag companies. There were Welshmen shouting war songs and a hoard of filthy, murderous French who looked as if they'd just been loosed from irons. Trumpets blared; soldiers sang lewd songs.

It was impossible, impossible! This quaking nobody, to have slain the warrior, Richard! Even with traitors on every side—impossible! And my husband! To have changed sides, to have fought beside a cowardly, French-speaking foreigner who'd cowered behind his soldiers through the whole battle! I couldn't believe that, either.

In a trance, I staggered in the van of the conquerors, made up of English traitors, a hoard of brutal French mercenaries, and woolly Welsh barbarians, all marching behind that flying, snapping dragon. Birds flew. The sun shone. The land was green and hot. It was a beautiful August day, in the very heart of England. I seemed to float, several feet above my beaten body, watching my own progress down the sunken, dusty lane with something approaching disinterest.

At the bridge of the town, we drew to one side to allow

prisoners and booty from the tents pass. Suddenly excited, Hugh grabbed me by the back of the neck and propelled me forward.

"Here! Here! Look at this, slut! Look!"

A horse was coming in the midst of it all, carrying one of the heralds. His scalp rained blood, his white boar tabard was covered with dirt and gore. The poor wounded man was quite unashamedly weeping at what he was being forced to do.

The king's body was tied, belly down, stripped entirely naked, a halter about the neck, as if he were a felon. I could not believe they had so dishonored Richard Plantagenet, his ancient blood royal, God's anointed. He had been stabbed countless times, hacked and slashed. There was hardly an inch that did not gape. The contents of his bowels, where some contemptuous pikeman had thrust, ran down his legs. Flies crawled and swarmed about the horse which lashed his tail in disgust. From the clotted mass of brain wobbling, it seemed they'd got him down and then smashed his head. His fingers, looted of their rings, dangled, dripping.

What had been his head banged every other step against the gray bridge. I wanted to rush forward, to throw my apron over him. God help me, I even wanted to kiss those awful gaping mouths oozing royal purple, but Hugh had a ferocious grip on my hair. He could not prevent me from sinking to the ground, which I did, knees and hands in the choking dust. Horse's feet and men's boots paraded past while my tears fell into the August dust.

"Get up!" He kicked and then yanked my hair savagely. "Get up!"

I obeyed, stumbling forward. He let go of my hair, but only to deliver another kick. I took a few steps, just enough to embrace the stone bridge. It was wonderfully cool, that gray stone, even on such a warm, bright summer day. I pressed my face against it and sobbed, thinking, as I hadn't in years, of the stony plain above Aysgarth.

How good to go there now, to huddle in one of those cracks in the earth, to gaze up at the sky! To listen to silence and wind, to see a bright falcon glide on a ray of sunlight, to hear again his sweet, piercing scream ....

"Come with me now, or, by God, you can stay here." Soldiers and villagers were pouring over the bridge, a tide sweeping everything along. I didn't look at my husband, just clung to the bridge, fingers wound in the ivy, clinging as if for dear life.

"The Devil take you, then!"

I didn't look until I was certain he had gone, taking his hatred with him. I was dizzy and bruised, but free.

People went on passing, now mostly villagers and the occasional knight with a small company trotting behind them on foot. My knees trembled, and at last I allowed myself to slide down the stone wall against the bridge. Something sticky smeared my cheek. I reached up to investigate, touching my face and then examining my fingers. Raising eyes to the stones above, I saw shreds of dark hair and clots from Richard's pitiful, battered head.

Carefully I reached into my sleeve and extracted a handkerchief. Using this, I wiped the mess away. Huddled against the bridge, I sat and regarded what I'd gathered, blood, and a strand of hair, still attached to a bit of scalp.

Why remember more? I found a humble cottage by the edge of the town and asked the old woman there if I could lie down in her stable shed. She saw me, the state of my clothes, and, her eyes knowing and sad, let me. In the dark coolness, smelling of her dairy cow, she brought me a blanket, water, cider and a piece of bread. I drank, but could not eat.

"I will go away soon, Mistress. I will give thanks for your charity to the Blessed Mother."

"You must sleep now," she said. "I will make a tisane."

"I cannot sleep, but I will rest." Slowly, every muscle throbbing, I lay down in the straw. The smell of new mown rye rose to meet me.

"Everyone sleeps," the old woman said. "One way or another."

Yes, one way or another. Even though every memory made we want to shriek, another notion came, hard and fast upon the heels of my grief. My King, poor haunted creature, slept at last. Therefore, so could I.

❖

"You are become Stanley's man?" In the morning light I stood staring at my husband.

"You had best be glad of it," Hugh said shortly. "If I had stayed with Richard there would be no one to save your sorry ass—again."

"You betrayed our Lord. After—after—"

"Yes. After!" His "after" carried a very different meaning from mine.

So, he knew! This morning, I didn't care.

"The king is dead. Long live the king!" I waved my hands in the air, giving the words all the sarcastic emphasis I could.

"Yes," Hugh said, evenly. "And if you're as clever a woman as I've always thought, you will act as if you believe exactly that."

Chapter XXVII

At home, blessedly, Rosemary dashed to leap into my arms. Her tow head was still beautifully golden.

"Mama-Mama-Mama!"

I buried my face in her sweet neck and kissed her, felt her little soft hands, smelled her child's body. Tears filled my eyes. Hugh had shouted abuse most of the way back. It was a balm to see someone was glad to see me!

It had been a long way home, many barns and stables and a long dusty road. Even without my husband's curses and blows, I knew I had done wrong. I must keep my mouth shut and endure whatever Hugh dished out, exactly as mother had done. I must do my work, love my children—and serve my husband, if I could not again love him. Above all, I must protect the secret I carried.

Alkelda appeared in the doorway, a bucket of water yoked on her skinny shoulders. She stared at me and then at Hugh. My eldest showed no pleasure.

"Your mother is home at last," Hugh said. "So you will soon to York."

Kneeling on the floor, holding Rosemary close, I was shocked by his preemptory tone.

"What?"

"She is to go into the house of Wilfred Fuller of York and serve her term there. She is of age."

"You have not said anything to me of this."

"You were not here. I have made arrangements for the children as I have seen fit. Alkelda is near twelve. She will have a better chance of making a good marriage in York, in Fuller's house. He is a shopkeeper whose wife needs help."

Little wonder Alkelda had greeted me like a portent of doom!

Boiling, I faced him, Rosemary straddling my hip. "And did you get a good price for your daughter, Master Fletcher?"

"Yes," he replied, cool as you please. "So, it is to her benefit and to ours. Spare your breath. The business is long settled."

I marched away, out the door I'd just entered, Rosemary clinging anxiously to my side. Alkelda had shed her yoke, so on my way I seized her hand.

"Walk with me."

As we went down the lane, my elder daughter abruptly said, "Why did you come back?"

"Where was I supposed to go?"

She shot me a black look and tossed her head, with all the hauteur of which twelve is capable. "Papa said you had taken another man."

I wanted to slap her, but I did not, just kept pulling her along. The words were her father's. Nevertheless, when the queen lay dying, I had put the needs of Richard Plantagenet above those of my own family.

"I am sorry if this is what he thinks of me, and teaches you to say." After a pause, I asked, "How long before you are bound?"

There was a moment in which she only glowered, but finally she spoke.

"The next cross quarter day, Saint Michael's. Father says they will meet us at the market. The contract has already been signed and witnessed."

"Do you want to go?"

"No." The look with which she favored me held nothing but scorn. The pain of my abandonment, my betrayal, she'd already walled inside. "But," Alkelda went on in a voice so resigned my heart came near to breaking, "Papa is right. He says there is nothing here for us. Now King Richard is dead, he's right. He says he will soon go north to service with Lord Percy at Alnwick. We are to leave Middleham anyway."

If she'd struck me in the chest with a dagger, it couldn't have been worse. I couldn't walk anymore, just stopped, there in the lane with summer all around, in the warmth of the stone walled, sunken road. I had just lost the last ten years.

Having delivered the knock down blow, Alkelda stared at

me steadily, watching my emotion with all the satisfied vengeance of which the young are capable. It was beyond dispiriting to see so much hatred upon my daughter's face.

Pulling her hand loose, she turned silently away and retraced her steps. In the distance, I could see Hugh standing by the door, his big arms akimbo. Blinking back tears, I hugged Rosemary and headed toward the limestone paths.

Perhaps an hour later, about supper, I returned, walking through the streets of Middleham. Those who knew me nodded, but dared no more.

Change as the wind blows! Whitby cried, loud and clear as if he stood before me in the street.

I set Rosemary down. She hurried inside, anxious to see her father, her siblings, happy to see food on the table. I'd as soon never eat again. It had crossed my mind not to return, to lie gazing at the gray Yorkshire sky until I died, but, I had a final duty to perform for my dead, dishonored lord. I must do my best to bring the fluttering life within my body to the light of day.

Supper went in near silence. Bett shed a few glad tears at the sight of me, but it was clear that things were not as cheerful in this house as when I'd left. Her boy, Jackie, I learned, had already gone to serve in the house of a local carpenter, another of Hugh's arrangements. Oliver, Robert and William barely dared a word. If they spoke to me, they watched Hugh's face. Fear of angering him was palpable.

"I am just as glad you are back." Hugh finally spoke as I cleared. "I need your help. You can take the children to Aysgarth. The potter's cottage there is empty. I have shaken hands with your brother Clifford on it for next year."

I began to wash up. Life, all too clearly, had gone on without me.

"And before you ask one of your stupid questions, you had better get used to the idea that the only thing which gives you importance these days is that you are the wife of Hugh Fletcher. I have again pulled your fat from the fire, apparently my calling in this life."

I went on washing. He wished an argument, but I was

well and truly vanquished. All I wanted was to take Rosemary in my arms and lie down in darkness.

"Did you hear me?" He leaned close and shouted.

"I did. I suppose it is better we should leave Middleham."

"You suppose!" He snorted contempt. "Do you think you can remember how to do an honest day's work?"

"Yes."

"Good, for I'm leaving tomorrow to begin my service with Percy. Otherwise, Bett and Alkelda would have to do all the work of moving and neither of them have the wit to do it right."

"Bett manages well." I began to dry dishes. Bett had taken shape as a housekeeper. It had only taken her twice as long to figure it out as any other women I've ever known.

"Well," Hugh said, unbending slightly, "you will do better."

I hung the towel over the back of the chair. "And when will I see you again?"

"What do you care?"

I started to walk past him. I planned to draw some water, wash and find a bed.

"Where are you going?"

"To draw water," I said. Over our heads, I could hear anxious whispering in the loft. Bett had taken the children upstairs.

"Draw water and then sit." Hugh sternly pointed at a chair. "We have a few more things to talk over, you and I."

I drew my water and returned, feeling close to the walking dead. At last, I thought, I will brew a chamomile tisane, so I dropped in another bit of wood and fixed the kettle. Hugh stopped behind me with yet another tankard of ale in hand. I prayed he was not drunk. He didn't seem to be, and he waited for me to finish my tasks while sucking on the thick brown stuff.

As soon as I sat down, however, the harangue began anew.

"You don't care, do you?"

"I care."

"Then, why don't you speak?"

"I'm tired, Hugh. You are tired. Do we have to fight now?"

"Yes, we do. I'm as tired as you are! Didn't I just save your sorry spotted ass?"

"Please don't shout at me anymore. I can't bear it."

"You will have to!" The words came in a roar.

I covered my eyes and began to weep. I didn't want to, but exhausted and covered in bruises as I was, I couldn't stop it.

"Your grand days are over, Rose. Either you stay in my house and make the best of it, or you can get out and get on with your whoring. I don't care."

"I am no whore, damn your lying tongue!"

"Oh! You didn't open your legs for him?"

I stared into his eyes, tears racing down my cheeks. "I was Handmaid to our Liege Lord," I said. The ancient words crossed my tongue, bringing an otherworldly satisfaction.

He sprang up and slapped me. I saw it coming, but he was still too fast. Though I ducked, there was a stinging, jaw-rattling blow. I saw stars.

"Whore! Whore!" He had me by the arms, pulling me close against him. "Say it!" he roared. "Name yourself!"

His hands were bands of iron; he was swollen with a mighty rage, spitting poison, an honest man betrayed.

"Stop! You'll break my arms!"

"Say you're a whore! Confess!"

"To you? The Devil!"

This got me thrown down in front of the fire, but it gave me a moment free to reach the knife. It was out in a flash.

"I'll break your goddamn arm," he shouted, raging louder at the sight of steel. "I taught you everything you know!"

"Go on then, dear husband! And cut my throat, too, while you're at it! Big, brave man! You're a damned traitor!" I kept my ground. Let him come to me. In his rage, I'd find an opening.

The rest is a blur, for he hurled himself upon me. I drove the knife in low, just as he'd taught. He deflected the blow at the end of my thrust. Still, his weight was descending, and the

blade did find flesh, glancing off his hip bone, slicing a bloody
track into his buttock. He hit me, across the jaw, and I saw
stars again, leading into a dark, roaring tunnel.

When I came spiraling back, he was on top of me, rooting
as hard as he could.

"You're mine! Mine!" He hissed through clenched teeth,
his breath hot on my cheek, his seventeen stone pressing me
into the slate flags of the hearth.

He rolled off, onto his back, put his hands over his face,
and lay there, panting. Done in anger, it had taken a long time.
Blood drenched the side of his tunic. Though in agony, I
crawled away.

Pulling myself up by using a chair, I'd staggered to the
water I'd just brought in. It was hard to know where to splash
it first—on my face or upon what his violence had macerated.
He paid no attention to me at all, although he did get up, bare-
assed and bleeding. Once situated in the other chair, he began,
with some difficulty around his beer belly, to examine what I'd
done to him.

"Bring me bandage!"

I fetched, like the dog I now apparently was. I would not
come close to him, though, and tossed it into his lap. Then,
before he could do anything else, I started up the ladder. I was
amazed when he took after me again, grabbing me around the
waist.

"Where the hell do you think you are going?"

"Away from you!" I cried, hanging onto the ladder.

He yanked, and the ladder fell, making a great crash.
"No!" he shouted. "You're going to be my wife! You're going
to patch me up, and then you are going to lie beside me."

"It's your own damned fault. You cut me, you evil
whoring bitch."

Morning had come. My jaw was swollen. In this beating, I'd lost a tooth and both eyes were blacked. I'd peered into a basin of water out of doors at sunrise, assessing the damage.

Bett was sorry, but she was scared too. She wouldn't have dared even sympathy if Hugh hadn't been on his way out. The children, of course, were terrified. They went pale at the sight of their father, packing up his arrows and bow, donning his sword and chest plate, all laid out atop the table. They gave him the widest possible berth, hurrying away to chores in the stable.

Will, bless him, had swelled with rage when he saw what his father had done.

"I pray, William, that you never treat any woman of yours so. Nevertheless, do not quarrel with your father. His temper is up and I would not have you used in the same manner."

My darling Will, not ten, was gone that very day, away with his father, and into service with that cowardly, thrice-damned caitiff, Percy, who'd shirked the field at Bosworth. It was, I heard from Hugh's own proud lips, a "foresighted arrangement" he'd made with the Percies, "before the battle." When the time came, I blessed my beloved son, pressed swollen, split lips to his forehead and prayed hard to see him again.

Alkelda hardened her heart. She only said, "I am sorry it has come to such a pass, Mother, but you stayed away because you had another man. You left me and Bett to care for everything. You have broken my father's heart and driven him to this madness."

"Alkelda, I most heartily pray you find a husband of the same noble perfection as your father."

As you might imagine, I could not abide the sight of her from that instant. How could I have raised such a daughter? How could she look at me, straight into my two blackened eyes, my smile ruined, and still take that brute's side?

Alkelda did her work and helped us ready for the move, but I packed her off to York as soon as I could find a trustworthy person traveling that way. I did not wait for Saint Michael's. By the time she went, seated sullenly atop a wagon load of grain, Alkelda was just as glad to be gone from Middleham—and her sinful, shameful mother—as I was to be rid of her.

No one in town had much to say, and it suited me. It was known I had been beaten for "just cause," and so there was precious little sympathy for a woman who had not lately lived much among them.As for Hugh, I thanked the Blessed Mother he was gone.

When I had time, I went into the fields, off and on for days after, searching for herbs of the season. At last, I found all that was needed to make a potion so deadly it would take down an ox. With great care I prepared, and then poured it into a brown glass bottle I'd tucked in the back of the medicine chest. Around the neck, as warning, I knotted black thread and a fragile bird's bone.

This was for Hugh, if he came back. To pray that I did not have to use it and end up hanged, I sat with my three-legged pot quite late during the next dark of the moon. I had carefully sewed a poppet, stuffing it with his hair from a brush and snips of cloth from a ragged sweat-stained shirt he'd left behind.

I wished him impotence. I wished the wound I'd given would fester. I wished the last of his hair from his head. I took my knife and slowly sawed away the legs at the knees, one at a time. I dug pins first into the eyes and then into the heart. Lastly, I spoke a charm I'd made:

Black Lady freeze his soul
Black Lady eat him whole
May he burrow like a mole
May the Devil be his dole
Cold his flesh and damned his soul,
Down in Hell's nether hole.

The work, the charm, and the greasy flaming of the poppet as it burned, made me feel a great deal better.

I bled after he'd forced himself upon me. I swore that if I dropped the King's child, it would soon be the end of Hugh Fletcher. I swore before the black night sky to follow him and kill him if that happened. I prayed the bleeding was injury to the passage, not to the womb.

My prayers for the safety of the child were answered. Staining ended, but the ache of his abuse lasted longer, subsiding only after a span of a month. After my husband left, I did receive visits from others who had served Richard and Anne, folks who were still about the village. In one house where I was led, an old groom had made an altar at his hearth. There we lit candles and prayed for the souls of our lost royal family, for Queen Anne and little Ned, for the betrayed and murdered king, our Good Lord.

A humble soldier who had fought at Bosworth passed through in secret one night. He was healing from his wounds, and on the run. The usurper had set his men to pursuing everyone loyal to Richard, even down to ordinary soldiers like this, to steal what they little had, and take their lives.

Henry Tudor claimed these men were "traitors" for fighting for their anointed king against an invader! From this poor soldier, I learned exactly how our Northern King had died, heard the story at last.

Richard had fought as he had so long ago in the melee, fought and fought, fought when his men were gone, fought on foot, after White Surrey had been slain. He'd fought, even pierced with an arrow. At last, all alone—and, even then it had taken a gang of them—for someone to get behind and ax him.

I could see it—the pack of savage curs, the boar at bay...

"They say it was yet more proof he was a devil. Even with his head broken, his body would not stop moving."

I'll see you in hell . . .

We wept and gave each other comfort and aid as best as we could. It was beyond strange to look up at the castle and wonder who next would live there.

Our family moved on Saint Michael's as planned, the white she cow and the ox pulling a hired wagon, our best hens penned in withy cages. What we took was piled inside or hung from the sides. Robert, Bett, Oliver and I walked, driving a pair of sows. Neighbors came to say good-bye as well as those who had served my lord and his lady in our happy days. I shed a few more tears, and then turned my back on Middleham.

.❧

Autumn was spent cleaning and getting ready for winter. Bett and I lectured the children of the dangers of the river and the falls, things new to them. Robert O'Grove had fights with the local boys—all the ordinary stuff of moving.

It was peculiar to be in Aysgarth again, to be passing Whitby kin in the street. They made polite greetings. I was one of their own whom fortune had raised up and then cast down. No one asked about my injuries, or, significantly, about the whereabouts of my husband.

They knew I had "seen Bosworth." Perhaps they assumed my black and blue was a result of insults dealt by soldiers. It often happened that a woman so befouled would never know her husband's touch again. As for Richard's death, there was a hard core of sorrow. The reeve and others of the local Moot, I learned, were already missing their "Good Duke" and his even-handed justice.

.❧

I came to terms with a shepherd who now served Aysgarth. He watched all sheep in common upon the high pastures and then had a share of our profit from their wool, cheese, and meat. He was not a Thornton.

It seemed most of that family had perished after a contagion-filled autumn followed by a bad winter. They were gone, every one, the brothers Mark and Matthew and my poor friend Jane. A boy and girl of hers survived, but that was all of the family that had once dwelt in the croft.

I'd known this man long ago. He'd been a cottager who'd sometimes go soldiering and then return at the end of each spasm of violence. He'd been strong and fierce, and well able to make his living at war, but he kept coming back and resuming his labor for hire.

His name was Alban Bart and he was an old man near fifty now, though astonishingly hale. He lived in the Thornton's ancient stone croft with a herding dog. I remembered Alban as good with animals, so this livelihood came naturally. He and my mother had once healed a poor sheep that had been mauled by a dog, and he'd always been a great favorite with us children. Everyone said the Thornton orphans couldn't have found a better caretaker.

One day I set out, staff in hand, Rosemary trotting beside, onto the dale to look for him. I drove my own small flock before me. It had been awhile since I'd handled sheep, but it is a skill that is never lost.

You stare at them. They stare back at you. If you do it right, the matter is settled!

More sheep than I owned and you needed a good dog, but that was another expense and more livestock to care for. It seemed better to pay a tithe and have a skilled and honest shepherd care for them.

It had pleased Hugh to stable an ox and a cow instead of sheep. It was a richer way to live, and, of course, a cow makes money, as did the ox. Now, without Hugh, I had decided it would be better, on this thin ground, to keep sheep for cheese and wool and to sell the cow and the ox. They would be expensive to winter over.

The children had cried. They knew the cow and the gentle ox, had grown with up with them. Still, it needed to be done. The facts were, we would be living poor.

I walked the Dale as I hadn't for many a long year, rediscovering paths I had known before. The sun was warm, the fields stubble, with animals wandering here and there, finishing up the harvest.

Wind blew. A hawk sped past. When he circled over my head, sun-gilded and swift as the wind, I began to cry. Rosemary, pretending she didn't see, began a tuneless song. She didn't like how her Mam had come home, so sad and strange, but it was hard to see a hawk without remembering

Richard. Mother of Sorrows! I imagined my Dickon—broken, in agony—but still fighting those villains with his last breath.

I paused, touched my belly, for within there was a flutter. Joy sprang up in my heart, overcoming the grief. I was not ashamed of what I carried, for had I not got this child "in liberty"?

The old croft was set on a gentle incline overlooking an undulating wave of green. To Jane's girl, Joan, I'd brought a gift, a little medal of the Virgin upon a silken necklace.

She looked at me as if I'd dropped from heaven when I presented it. I explained that her mother had been my dearest friend many long years ago. With tears in her faded blue eyes, she thanked me and then offered a tisane of mint.

We put my sheep in a holding pen of stones. I suggested that Rosemary stay with Joan for a little. She was far younger than Joan, but lonely for her Middleham friends and shy of the children in this new place. Leaving the girls together to get on with whatever would develop, I went out to see if could find Alban.

Not much later, I did. He was by the hilltop spring, watering his flock. His dog barked, but was so well-trained he did not rise or run at me.

"'Day!" Alban Bart was almost exactly as I remembered him, except perhaps thinner. His hair was now steel gray.

"I am Missus Fletcher that was Rosalba Whitby."

"I know who you be."

He looked me gravely up and down. Master Bart was freckled over a pale milky skin, as much a "roan" as me. Something in his straight carriage reminded me of True Thomas, gone for so many years now.

Dear True Thomas! Long dead alongside his lord, the Kingmaker, at Barnet...

"I have come to talk about my sheep."

"Ten o' them, aye?"

"And three lambs."

"But three?"

"Yes, five this year were born bucks and sold young."

"'Afore our Good King Richard fell."

I nodded.

"Then 'twill be time to put them all to a ram."

"Yes. They come into season soon."

We talked about price. I didn't dicker; it wasn't polite. I'd already discussed this part with one of my new neighbors. Still, when Alban named it, I was pleasantly surprised to hear it would cost a trifle less than I had been led to expect.

"I must look them over and see if they be in good stride. Can't muck bad ones in with the good."

I agreed, telling him they were already penned at his croft. After, we shook hands. When I began to take my leave, he interrupted me.

"Not so fast, Missus Rose." There was a twinkle in his dark eye, "Have you been in high places so long you do not remember me?"

"I do remember you, sir. You and my mother healed a fair ewe together. The owner was right grateful."

"No else?"

"That you were a soldier and that you often went away to fight. That you always had good dogs, and that you would ride us children on your back, and that you made merry at May Day and Lammas. That you sold us roasted chestnuts at the All Saints fair."

Recollection made us both happy. I was pleased that he was pleased to talk. I hadn't expected it from a crusty old dales' man. We stood quietly for a time, gazing over rock and green, across the backs of his black-faced sheep.

"And what has hurt thee, Mistress Rose?"

"Men do what they like with their wives." I shrugged, but nevertheless I was sorely ashamed of what had happened to my smile.

"Your husband has done this?"

"He never has hit me before, though this time he had some cause." I offered the customary speech of the beaten. "He will never hit me again, though, of that I am certain." I had not intended to end on that note, but it came as it would. No one, not even a man, would mistake my meaning.

In my medicine chest lay a certain bottle . . .

Alban Bart neither smiled nor frowned. He just went on studying me with his bright brown eyes.

"Spoken like your mother's daughter."

Clouds were moving in from the north. Wind gusted, hissing in the grass and tearing autumn leaves from the tree that sheltered the spring on the hill. Like a bolt of unexpected lightning, I knew...

"You fathered me." After all these years, it was as if an angel had stepped out of the clouds, all bathed in white light.

Alban nodded. "So your mother said." He allowed himself a slight smile. "'Tis truly all we men have to go by."

"Well, sir, I am glad to know you at last," I said, feeling tears well. "For my mother always said she did love my father."

"She did me the honor." Alban said. "Take heart, woman. Thee ever wish it, I'll come stand at your side."

From the other side of the hill, Jane's boy Matt came up with a pair of erring sheep trotting ahead. I was pleased to meet him and admire the carrot-colored shock of hair he'd gotten from his mother. He even had her two gated front teeth.

I left Alban and Jamie Thornton moving their herd to the next hill. When I returned to the croft, the girls were chattering happily, sharing the task of baking scones. Little Rosemary patted them into shape while Joan built up a sheep-dung fire to heat their wall oven.

Although there was much to do back in Aysgarth, I stayed on, letting the girls continue making friends. I checked the croft larder to see what herbs they might need before winter. That was one item I'd brought plenty of from Middleham. When we returned to the village in the twilight, Bett was justly irritated at my dereliction. I wished I could have told her truly why we'd stayed so long.

.❧.

It was a time of putting one foot in front of the other and staying alive, trying to keep the grief for all I'd known and loved bleed my heart to death. The hardships of returning to ordinary life, of establishing the family at Aysgarth, kept me hard at work. Robert O'Grove was a great lad now, feeling his oats. True to his breeding, he was a tough one to keep in line.

So much had to be done before winter came! I feared the coming of the bitter season.

❧

Parsley, sage, rosemary and thyme...I was planting again, those bedraggled little plants I'd dug before leaving Middleham. The garden behind the Potter's House was neglected and tangled, but ashes would ruin the ground, so instead of burning, I'd had to cut and clear all by hand. I needed to plant now, as soon as possible. There was not much left of warmth or sun, but if I watered well and covered the sets with leaves and old straw, I could hope they would show me green again in the spring.

Bett and I worked together at cleaning and cooking, but I soon learned I could not count on her for much longer. Bett had a man, and the day would come when she would go to him, live with him and keep his house, back in Middleham, and be damned to what people said. Her sweetheart was a leather worker who'd been left with a pair of young daughters after his wife had run off.

❧

Here in the lonely grove I knelt and removed an earring. Drawing the knife through the pocket hole, I began to dig. After a quick check to be certain I was not observed, I poked the earring, silver hoop and dangling beads of German crystal, deep into the dirt. Mother Ash had said that they liked shiny things very much.

Last, I took the hilt of the knife and tamped hard. I hoped they would not be cross that it was not two earrings—the other was missing.

"Oh, you spirits who dwell under the earth, you miners of riches, who know where treasures are hidden," I said, doing my best to speak to them politely. I couldn't recollect the exact charm I was supposed to use and hoped that this would suffice.

"Accept my humble gift, Earth Spirits, and bring me some money!"

Pease porridge hot, Pease porridge cold. Pease porridge in the pot nine days old...

Here it was again, the grimy three-legged pot and the peas, oats or cracked wheat, with whey and a drop of honey to dress it up. A thin slice of sheep's milk cheese and maybe a boiled egg, washed down with a swig of bitter ale, was, these days, a feast. As winter came on, I hungered for meat.

Ah, I'd been born at Master Whitby's house--and, lo, and behold--here I was again! Living under thatch which dripped in a hard rain, cold feet treading a floor of broken flags and packed earth, the border of my rough dress ragged and stained, the barnyard smell from the old shed behind filling my nostrils.

When I was feeling very sorry for myself, I'd make myself recall what I'd seen at Bosworth—all those brave comrades, lying blue and bled. At least, I told myself, I'd avoided that.

At butchering time, I went to Naseby Manor to assist, though it had been years since I'd been near such work. The blood and guts and sorry bawling of the poor frightened cattle made me weep and puke, but I kept at it. In the icy dark, I struggled home with my reward, offal, in a dripping basket.

Though ready to faint with weariness, I roused Bet and got her to help in slicing the best of our trophy, half a heart and a veiny chunk of liver. That same night, Bett and I and the children sat and gorged, mopping up the juice from a drippings pan. The taste of beef in my mouth made the day I'd spent suffering easier. Overhead, we hung another prize, an ox tail, which, tomorrow, we'd reduce to a fatty, marrow laden soup. It would improve the endless porridge.

I'd lived long among the gentry, but how quickly, now

that fortune's wheel had turned, did I come to resent those in the castle. Hares, scampering across the windy heath, drew my attention. I knew they belonged to someone—the Usurper in London, the Manor of Naseby, our Bishop, someone, anyone, certainly not to a meat-starved peasant.

Still, I coveted them. I dreamed about ways to snare them, to cook and eat them without getting caught. The half-royal child growing within craved meat. He must be fed!

.❧

The poor creature was half strangled, and looked up with pitiful, bulging eyes, too exhausted for any more terror. With one blow I almost took off his head. Then, I sat down and shed tears. It had been years since I'd killed a hare.

As Hugh said, I'd grown soft. The killing was almost unbearable to me, the light going from the poor creature's eyes. The hare and I were one, trapped, strangled, nothing more to do here than pray for a quick death.

"Hey, lass!"

I almost jumped out of my skin. It was, luckily for me, none other than Alban Bart. If it had been the gamekeeper from Nappa Hall, I might not this day have all my fingers.

"Blessed Mother! You scared me!"

"This is not a good spot to be poachin', lassie." Alban glanced over his shoulder. "Nor a good place to repent, neither." He picked up my kill by the back feet. "We'll up to the rocks."

When we were better hidden, he cleaned my kill, a young blue hare buck. I watched his freckled hands neatly draw out the guts and then pull the skin from the body like wet hose from a leg.

My father's hands! I watched his nimble work.

"Safest to eat it here."

I felt ashamed. The risk I'd just taken had not been for my family, but for me alone.

"Let us share." I was thankful he had helped me, but suddenly uncertain how my ill-gotten supper would sit in a queasy stomach.

Alban studied me with his level gaze. "You're breeding." It was not spoken as a question, just a stated fact.

"Ay."

"Indeed, yes, such a hunger your own mother had for meat when she carried. Stay, then." He lifted his head and scented the wind, much as his dog might. "We'll be safe enough here."

We made a fire in that sheltered place, cooked and ate the hare, sharing out with the dog, in perfect silence. All the best parts were handed, without comment, to me.

"Don't it risk it again." He collected the hide and stuffed it into his bag. "Cunningham, the gamekeeper, has a bad temper. He don't wait for the law to settle, neither, but would have had your fingers right here. You send to me, an' you get a taste for blood again, lass. Old Alban shall see you get what you need."

⚜

We endured a rough winter of cold, sickness and thin rations. Then came the first of April—the Fool's Day—and spring again. My mind returned to last year, to the death of my queen, and farther, to the spring before and the death of dear little Ned, the day when our once bright world turned black. It seemed naught but a dream.

Only a year ago I had been a lady with clean, soft hands who dwelt in a palace, who was ever warm and who ate well. This year I was a soldier's abandoned wife, reduced to living in a world of thatch and daub, scrubbing, broken-nailed, scrambling to keep body and soul together. It had been an angry spring so far, wet and raw, the snow late to melt. Now, here was a warm day, the first really so!

In the Asygarth, knots of young people were ignoring their work and loitering in the afternoon sun, playing sweet games of flirtation. Even their parents were seduced by the weather, and the whole village seemed to be finding ways to take the day off. Where was the harm? It was too wet to plow.

The unremitting labor of planting would come soon enough.

Winter had been bad indeed, but here no one's belly was flat empty! Beer and pickles, a little cheese and a little bread, a little dried fish, all mixed in messes of pease and barley, sufficed for our rejoicing. It might have been worse, considering that once again the country had suffered a change in government. We were far from the center of things, off the beaten track of Kings and armies. For the people of my village—for me and mine—it was just as well.

I went—a fool on this Fool's Day—out to search for a ewe, one which I had not taken to Alban. I'd traded for her in Middleham when Bett and I'd traveled there during a break in the snow, to The Lady's Mass Market. Bett and Oliver had stayed behind there with Bob Brown, her new man, and I had come back this pretty runt ewe.

She dropped her lamb soon after. Perhaps because I was missing Bett and Ollie, I'd kept the new sheep in the shed with my geese and chickens, and made a pet of her. She was a docile thing and never wandered far, even if she slipped her collar. Today, though, one of my elderly neighbors, poor, tottering Master Tennant, had stuck his head inside to report he'd seen her across the water, wandering up the hill with her lamb.

It was a careless thing to do, as close to delivery as I was. I was afraid my sheep would fall into a hole in the limestone—or, more likely, the lamb would fall—and she, foolish and faithful, would stay alone on the dale. As always at the term of carrying a child, I wept easily. Simply imagining the ewe's anxiety and devotion and brought tears into my eyes.

Rosemary and Bobby had gone off with some new friends and were nowhere to be seen. I should have asked Master Tennant if he knew a grandchild who could go after my ewe, but I had little faith that there would be much diligence in a search done by any of the children, all busy whooping and frisking in the spring sunshine or pitching rocks into the icy river. Besides, the warm day called to me, just as it had to everyone else.

I thanked the old fellow for his news, then quickly put a crust of bread and a bottle which contained the last few swallows of weak bitter in a basket—in case either the sheep or I needed encouragement—before setting out.

The going was slow up to the stony heights. At the bottom, it was very muddy. I went carefully, picking my way around slippery stones and holes full of water and muck. At the top, I took a rest.

The valley below was greening—amazing what a day or two of nice weather can do —but the high ground where I was headed remained a patchwork of tan and sedge. The broken clouds were gray, like beggar's rags fluttering against blue. In the distance, on a shocking emerald knoll nourished by a spring, I could see Alban leaning on his staff, watching his sheep.

He didn't acknowledge my wave, but that was fine. I wanted to be alone. The warmth, the lack of wind, pleased me. Birds sang and whirled in a patchy April northern sky. I was inspired to lift my arms and let the sleeves fall back to reveal winter pale skin. The sorrow which had plagued me, those low, dark clouds of grief, the dark shroud in which I'd so long mourned, lifted.

I was alive, and tolerably well for a pregnant woman near her time. Things were not easy, but we were getting by.

Oddly exhilarated, I followed the narrow sheep path leading to the stone table of the ridge. It loomed above me, the rocky jumble today resembling a gray, beached ship. An ark, I thought, sitting on high ground after the great flood. Rather like me, it was a survivor of a watershed time. It was a common thing for straying sheep to get in trouble up on the rocks. Surely, this was where my missing ewe had gone.

It came on fast, which was not the first thing different about this pregnancy, although it was hard to credit a change of sires as actually mattering in woman's business. I should have paid more attention, especially when I'd suddenly felt so lively, so strong, so absurdly hopeful. Perhaps, however, things were meant to go exactly as they did.

I'd worked my way across the dome of stone, occasionally getting down on all fours to peer into holes, no doubt looking as absurd as a great, round beetle. At last I reached a flat space where I could sit and listen. I was in no condition to keep scrambling.

Borne on the wind, just as I'd hoped, I heard the lamb, a thin little baa, followed by the deeper *blat* of his mother. Then I started the slow task of moving a little and then listening again, trying to locate them among the rocks by sound. I managed to find them, too, although, now that I remember it, the whole episode smacks of madness.

By this time I knew the way of birthing as well as anyone, yet I could not see how it was with me. The strength, the energy, the rush of high spirits, all should been sufficient warning. I'm not even certain how I imagined a woman so pregnant would be able to carry a lamb back to the village, but somehow I did get down to where she'd fallen, at the bottom of a crevice. I even managed to push her back up beside her mother.

They didn't move off at once. The baby was hungry and immediately began to feed. My pet patiently stood for those butts, nuzzling her newly restored lambkin. She gazed down gratefully with her dark eyes.

As I reached to get a purchase on the rocks and begin my own climb out of that hole, my water broke with a splash. With it came pain, an agonizing contraction such as I had never felt in any other delivery.

So sharp, so deep! Breathe and breathe, straight through the crushing iron hand!

I screamed. The pain was all, so keen and cruel. In a respite, I tried to climb once more, but now it was as if I was shackled to the ground. I couldn't seem to make my legs obey. Usually, I went from cramps to contractions to birthing, all in an orderly train. Rosemary's had been such an easy labor, and I'd never expected anything so different from my body.

Did the seed of a lover come forth in another way from the seed planted by a husband? Those Devil-born Plantagenets!

Deep in the throes of another white wave, I imagined a

vicious creature, one bred in adultery, gnawing its way out of my sinful womb.

The ewe stood above, puzzled, but she had her lamb, so she was content to wait. The foolish fond thing lay down, the lamb beside her. Over my head, clouds thickened and the wind picked up.

There was not an instant free from the pain. Contractions came so fast, so hard! I knew what it meant. The dead king's child would be born here—and soon. I had better hope that I would be well enough after to climb out, or we would be in deep trouble.

A dagger thrust again and again into my belly. I feared to faint. I feared I must bleed out as Anne had, but, finally, I felt my burden shift and move.

The child was coming. Like the father--sudden!

Holding onto the rocks, I braced myself, forehead and knees against cold stone. Rain fell. Water trickled, then poured. A little pool gathered. I could feel each drop as it splashed my bare legs, icy cold. Lightning flashed and thunder boomed, but I was hidden in the rock. Within each world-shaking stroke, I could not hear myself scream. Above me, the ewe's tail appeared as she sheltered her lamb.

I caught the hot wet thing, drew the bawling chrysalis of a man onto my belly and fell back into a sitting position. Gasping for breath, I wrapped the baby in my apron. The afterbirth, in a rush of its own, delivered.

There was a renewed surge of the earlier joy. Perhaps, all could yet be well. It tempted fate to imagine anything else. I made do with what I had. My blade and some yarn in the pocket finished the work. Then, I simply sat, shivering in that sodden dress, my new son wrapped in the apron, watching water trickle down the rocks.

The storm was gone as swiftly as it had come. An echoing boom in my ears signaled its passing. I wet my dry lips from a constant trickle down the side of the fissure, enough for a long drink of sweet rainwater.

It seemed best to rest a moment, to put the child to my breast. Soon, soon, I told myself, I would be able to climb. At least, I hoped so.

That was how Alban found me, down in the rocks, drenched and shivering, suckling my boy child. He'd seen me, great bellied, go into the stony maze. He'd seen the storm come and go, but had not seen me come out again. Wondering, he'd left his dogs in charge and had walked to investigate, for which my son and I must be eternally grateful.

His grizzled head poked over the rim and his eyes sparkled as he cried, "Ho, woman! Hast thou but swapped places with thy sheep?"

Not too much later, the sheep and her lamb—and I and mine—came back to Asygarth, piled into his little cart.

It was baby time again, the torn part healing, the yellow shit, the eternal washing and hanging to dry, the feeding, the bleeding, the lack of sleep. Outside, the weather grew warmer. Alban lent me Jane's help and took Robert O'Grove out of the house for some months after. In the end we left it that way, which was better for both children. Jane was happier with in town, and Robert had reached the stage of needing the strong hand of an older man.

I had my baby christened long before I was churched. Alban Bart and Master Tennant sponsored him to the church. Master Tennant reported that the priest had lifted an eyebrow, but in silent acknowledgment of the fat hen with which he'd been presented, he wrote down the child as instructed: "Richard Fletcher, born on the day of Saint Richard of Wyche to Hugh Fletcher the Archer and his wife, Rosalba."

Dickon was small and had, from the first, a shock of dark hair. In a backwards blessing, he was strongly freckled, "roan," like me. When my neighbors came to study him, he seemed no stranger to the Village of Aysgarth.

Chapter XXVIII

Alkelda, the cleverest of my children, did well in the York shop. I think she was often sad at first, but the city life seemed to suit her. William ran away from his father around July of that year and came back to us when Dickon was four months old. He stayed with us, ever still my blessing, until, at fifteen, he found work on property owned by the Cistercians at Jervaulx. He came to visit when he could, and told me he was learning about the hives the monks kept. The bees and their mysterious, industrious ways fascinated him.

Will was inward, a quiet presence, although he and I could sit and visit the day away—all about nothing. Will would never have money put by like his dad, but I was pleased his heart was in the land.

My daughter Rosemary was as unlike my mother as I could imagine, ever shy and entirely ordinary. Despite this carriage, she had a quick wit and absorbed all I taught her. She liked to dream, yes—she and Will were a pair in that way—and I found I loved her more and more as she grew. Almost every day, I wished I'd been more patient with her when she'd been an anxious baby.

Up in Middleham, Bet and her Master Brown stayed together. Oliver was a charming joker who grew more handsome every day. Sadly, Bett told me when we met one market day, that he was unreliable. She saw his father in him, but tried to keep his feet on the honest path and hoped for the best. Her older boy, Jack, was steadier, shaping well under the guidance of the carpenter who held his indenture.

Robert O'Grove went for a soldier the year my Dickon turned two. Alban and I agreed it to be the best course, for he was like to get himself hanged if he stayed here, all the mischief he got up to. He traveled north, to Alnwick. Bobby left the pretty girls in Aysgarth grieving—and their parents praising God that he'd gone. Months later, word came from Hugh that they had met at Alnwick. The next year he wrote again, to say that Bobby had moved on with some young bloods bound for Germany, all of them intending to join a Company of St. George and fight on the continent. We never heard of our Bobby again.

·❧·

Ash Wednesday of 1493 arrived. It was now eight years into the usurper's reign, an April afternoon when the wind blew sharp from the east. I had my head against the back of a sheep which had just walked up the stand for milking. I suppose that is why I did not hear him come in. The cats were making a clamor, demanding their share as they always did. They knew that even in lean times I'd indulge them.

The top milk went into a jug for us. The dregs, with whatever might have dropped into it, I splashed into a bowl for my cats. After some head slapping and hissing, they sorted it out, the two queens and half grown kits which caught the mice and rats in our barn. I talked to them as I always did as "my lasses." They were just like me, solitary, their menfolk gone a'wanderin' and fightin'.

"Ladies! Ladies! None o' that! There's plenty for all." I stopped milking and turned to lift them around so that each busy tongue got a share.

"So--it's come to this, has it, Rose?"

There stood my husband, Hugh Fletcher, leaning against the shed door, watching me.

"Down to waiting on pussy cats, are ye?"

They scattered at the sound of his voice. Only a young orange Tom, devil-may-care, kept on lapping. I shot to my feet, heart pounding. There was a pitchfork nearby and I'd use it if I had to.

"What do you want, Hugh Fletcher?" My husband had occasionally sent money during the first two years, but the custom had soon died. For years I'd been managing without him and I was proud of it.

As he entered, I moved, toward the pitchfork. That was

when I saw what had been hidden by shadows. Hugh only stood by the grace of crutches. Below his knees, there were no legs.

"I'm out of work. I came to see if I could make myself useful around here."

"Your lord will not employ a skilled Fletcher who has given his all in service?"

"I've had a belly full of lords, Rose."

For a long moment we stared at each other. I remembered George of Clarence, another of whom he'd had a "belly full." My husband's face was yellow and gaunt, his cheeks hollow. The loose folds of his once great belly lay like an empty sack.

I heard Dickon enter. He'd just finished tossing hay to the white cow on the other side of the shed wall and must have heard our voices. I knew the red freckles across his long, pale face wouldn't hide his paternity from my husband.

"Who be this then?"

"Dickon Fletcher, sir." My son eyed the crippled stranger uncertainly.

"Dickon, eh?" Hugh did not look at me, only at my son. "And how came you by the name o' Richard, young fella?"

"I was taken to the font on St. Richard's day." Dickon's voice stayed steady. He was small and thin—yes—but never afraid to speak.

To my relief, Hugh simply nodded. "Well, young fella, I am Hugh Fletcher, which, as it seems, makes me your mother's husband—and—your Dad. I've had some bad luck, as you can see and am come home at last."

The rage between us had burnt out. By claiming Dickon, Hugh had disarmed me, thrown himself upon my mercy, being first to sue for peace. Needless to say, my boy's hazel eyes flooded with astonishment.

"It is as Master Fletcher says," I said to my son's wonder. "Come now. Let's go in to the fire. Master Fletcher has journeyed far in bad weather and is anxious to see Rosemary again."

Bowing to the fate those restless dale winds had blown in my door, I took my son's small hand and gave it a comforting squeeze. A boy needs a father in whatever guise he comes, even a crippled, broken-down soldier.

We sat before the fire. Hugh—what remained of him—slurped the pease and turnip soup I'd made earlier. After an intial look of hesitation and fear, Rosemary hugged him. Hugh shed tears too, breaking at the sight of her. In better light, he appeared even sorrier than he had in the barn. After the children had gone into the loft, we had a time by ourselves. I brought him the last of the porridge, which he set upon at once.

"A poor time of year to travel, husband."

"Yes, but I had to, after rallying. I've been sick a long time."

"What happened?"

"Around St. Martin's day, a young lord rode his horse over me when I was out beating for a hunt. Broke my legs, rib or two and near finished me. Said it was my fault. I coughed blood for weeks. The legs had to go, or I'd now be serving my time in the ranks of hell." This last, spoken with his old humor, came near to my heart.

"No merry Christmas."

"None indeed."

"I am sorry." True, I was. My strong soldier had suffered the worst of fates, to live beyond his usefulness.

Hugh leaned down and set the bowl on the hearth stones. "I've come to ask forgiveness, Rose. I should have left your chastisement to the Almighty and remembered charity."

"Or remembered love."

"*You* might have remembered love. We were joined before God and for my part I did love you. Bad reason though it may be, love was the root of my anger."

Inwardly, I shrugged. It was man's oldest excuse.

"We're eight years past that piece of bad road, aren't we, lass?"

I managed a nod. Still, even after so much time, memory of that night made my gut churn.

"I have left the service of all lords, Rose, except Him Above. I had hoped to die in harness, but it was not to be."

We were silent for a time, watching the fire. I knew he would speak more, and that silence was what would make it unfold. I could not trust my own tongue; that I knew.

He nodded at the pitiful stumps, "In spite of what is lacking, I can make myself useful."

I nodded again, but said no more. There were two children whose need for Hugh was far more immediate than mine. Rosemary had hardly left her father's side since he'd come in the door. She, and Dickon, too, had silently served this apparition, bringing first a stool for a seat and then water for washing and a cloth to dry, giving, as I'd taught, attentive, silent hospitality to a stranger. I'd noted the way my son's eyes continually dwelt upon Hugh. Dog-like attention had sprung from that single most important of words. "Dad" already used, set the seal upon my decision.

"Go on as you have begun. Be the boy's father."

"He wants one, don't he?" Rheumy eyes studied me.

"All boys do."

I could tell that this was no decision made spur of the moment. My husband had decided to enter like this long before he'd come swinging on his arms into village. That made me glad, for it showed the man I had once been proud to be married to.

"Here," I said. "Let me draw more ale. We shall drink on it."

"Good ale, Rosie." Hugh said, after a long draught. "The best I've had in many a year. You brewed it?"

"It only takes a little care in doing. I wonder that folks hereabouts made it so poorly."

"You are the alewife?"

"I am," I said proudly. "Mother Ash taught me many things."

Hugh smiled. The sight still warmed, even though he was a jack-o-lantern.

"You always were a clever one."

We shared in silence my strong, rich ale and the heat of the fire. Outside, a noisy rain mixed with sleet began to drum on the sides of the house.

"St. Hugh of Grenoble's feast is but two days before the feast of St. Richard of Chichester." He'd spoken at last.

I might have said something—anything—but I only nodded.

"You never learned to lie, did you, Rosie?"

"Oh, I have learned. Since our Yorkshire King was slain, I have learned to lie and to steal, too, for that is how a peasant lives. Still, Fletcher, you are still my husband, to whom I at least owe honesty."

Wearily, he shook his head, but in his eyes I could see the man who'd once loved me, valuing straight talk. Raising his tankard briefly in my direction, he drained it to the dregs.

By his own choice, he slept that night on straw by the hearth, like any poor traveler to whom we'd offer hospitality. It wasn't until the next day, stripped, sitting in a chair, washing himself from a basin we'd arranged on the table, when the sight of his angry, mottled stumps reminded me of the spell I'd cast at Middleham all those years ago.

The knife, the firelight glinting upon it, as I'd sawed off the poppet's legs . . .

Such a chill washed over me! I might have been standing out of doors in January. Hard to believe it had worked, and that it had taken so long. Now, when my fury was almost burnt to ashes, I should see the outcome.

There was fear then, fear such as I had not felt since I'd made the draught for Aldygyth to give. I would to hell, certain! Then, I remembered what Ash had said as she lay dying.

"Don't weep for me, Rose. We flow into a dark lake, are washed in deep waters. Then we sink down, down to the old roots of the world. We forget who we were and we shall be born into this world again. There is no hell, nor no heaven neither, just the great wheel on which we all turn."

That memory comforted.

Then, I remembered the rest of the spell— how I'd dug out the eyes of the poppet—and shuddered. I sent a quick silent prayer that this would never come to pass.

Poor Hugh! There wasn't much life left in the body that returned. He never asked for anything more than kindness from me and a roof over his head. I fed him and he helped about the place as he could, for he had bad weeks at a time. For my part, I nursed him, even, with Rosemary's devoted help, cosseted him, for which he was grateful.

He taught Dickon about fletching and told him a thousand soldier's stories, which they both enjoyed. The clever long fingers of my lad were quick to learn, and Hugh, and surprised by this, thoroughly praised him. None of his own children had been interested in their father's birth trade.

Hugh Fletcher lived only for a year. One day, stubbornly off on his crutches on some errand of his own, he dropped dead. Alban found him on the winding road that passed his croft. Hugh was lying on his back, cold as a stone. The crows he chased away had already pecked out his eyes.

Chapter XXX

great lady and her retinue stopped by the church. The parade of horses and men at arms, of knights and banners, put me in mind of my childhood. Like my mother, however, I had better things to do than gawk and I kept to them.

We were out in the backyard, feeding our fine spots sow and her piglets, newly moved into their own pen, when I heard the geese hiss and bang their wings. To my amazement, armed men had come running down the lane. Behind trotted a priest and close beside him, seated upon a beautifully tricked out mare sat a tiny wizened woman, wearing the habit of a rich abbess. When I recognized her heraldry, my heart almost stopped.

"Blessed Mary Mother save us!"

Dickon and Rosemary had gone into the pen to feed the piglets scraps. It was all I could do not to scream.

"Rose Fletcher?"

Sick to my stomach, I waved to the children. "Stay where you are!" The more distance I could put between the boys and those men . . . I curtsied, low in the dust.

"Come here." The priest gestured with a black-gloved hand.

Rising, I obeyed, passing the rowed up men at arms, toward the woman on the mare. She had always seemed old, and so she hadn't changed much. The richness of her somber clothing was suitable for a widowed queen. I didn't dare look behind me, only prayed that the boys were, for once, doing what they had been told.

"Is that you, Rose Fletcher?" The old woman asked. There she was, the wicked usurper's wicked mother, in her tiny cruel person, like nothing so much as the shriveled husk of a locust.

I dropped another dusty curtsy to collect myself. "To

what do I owe the high honor of Your Ladyship's presence?"

"Get up and come here." She was so eager to behold my ruin, she kicked the mare forward.

I kept my eyes down, stared at the small booted foot in the stirrup, but she spoke again, "Look at me, Rose. Where are your manners?"

I obeyed and hoped my eyes did not flash what I was thinking.

Viper in the bosom of York! You, evil flicking tongue of poisoned rumor! You who carried my sweet queen's coronation train with your hands, even then, plotting to murder her husband . . .

A thin smile cracked thin lips, a corpse face. I wondered if the usurper was as hideous as this dried she-monster, with her ferret's eyes and sharp nose.

"Times have changed, have they not, Mistress Fletcher?" She seemed to relish the sight of me in a grease and dirt-splattered apron.

"Even and ever for the better, My Lady." I played the part of a blank peasant.

I am better here than at court, watching those traitors preen, watching that wretched simulacrum pass for a king, watching him sneak like a felon into the bed of a golden Plantagenet princess whose boot he is not good enough to lick!

Margaret's eyes narrowed. Perhaps she heard my thoughts.

"It is said you have a son."

"I have two sons, most noble lady." My hand slipped inside in my skirt to grasp the handle of the ever-present knife.

"I mean a son born to you during the rule of King Henry VII, you stupid creature." The face within the linen of her headdress was sharp as a hatchet.

I was ready to die, to take that *evil-bitch-of-one-whelp* with me, when a scuffle began at my back, along with cries I recognized only too well—those of Rosemary and Dickon. As I turned, I saw several of her foot guards in our pig pen, chasing our piglets.

Rosemary, tall and fair now, had ducked through the fence and hidden behind Master Tennant. Dickon, now a fine upstanding eleven, stood and protested. The men laughed, and one of them caught him by the scruff. My heart froze, as did my hand.

"This one, Your Highness?" The soldier called out. My wiry Yorkshire lad kicked, struggled, and called the soldier "Rogue and thief!"

"Yes, that one. Bring him here."

It was all I could do not to fall on the ground, to beg and plead for mercy—but this would have been to fall into her trap.

I played at confusion. "That is my Dickon. What do you want, Most Noble Lady Margaret?"

"To look at him." She said it with a foxy sideways slew of her colorless eyes.

"Dickon!" I said. "Come straight to me."

Dickon, though wondering, once set upon his feet, obeyed. He was so brave, my dark angel, his hazel eyes fearless. When he came to my side, he bowed his head, hands at his side, as he had been taught. I gripped my knife and judged the distance between me and Lady Margaret Beaufort.

In his struggle with the soldier, Dickon had been pushed into the muck of the sty. He arrived at my side malodorously splattered.

"Richard? Whereof comes this lordly name?"

"Tell this great and most noble lady, my son. Speak loud, so all can hear."

Dickon swallowed hard. "I was taken to the font upon Saint Richard of Wyche's day, My Lady." He recited this oft-told tale with innocent pride. Still, the fear he was catching from me sent him deep into our thick northern dialect.

He had lifted his head to be heard, gazing up as he spoke. I could tell he sensed the menace that floated, just perceptibly, around. I tried not to shudder, imagining her talons gripping the throat of my child and offered prayers to the universe.

Holy Mary, Mother of God, preserve my beloved son!

Saint Alkelda of the holy well, protect us!

Black Mary of Barcelona, turn the knife of my enemy into her own heart!

Blobs of mud added to Dickon's copious, red-brown

freckles. In evening light, they looked like moles, the ugly velvet kind that stand up. It was, of course, only sty mud, but Lady Margaret no longer saw well.

She leaned to stare at him, and he, poor child, suddenly affrighted by the yawning abyss that had opened, paled. I encircled his meager shoulders with my free hand.

I shall kill you if you touch my son. I shall die as did my King, blade red....

All at once, Margaret made a creaking, hissing noise. It was a mirthless laugh.

"This is what you have brought me so far to see?" She rounded on the priest. "A dirty, birthmarked peasant tending his mother's filthy pigs?"

Without another word, she kicked the mare forward, knocking us aside. The priest, discomfited, followed her. The guards scrambled to fall in, though the men in the pen made certain of two piglets.

They hurried away fast as they had come, straight out of the village. I did not yet dare to embrace Dickon and cover him with kisses. Not yet—one of them might have looked back—even the Great Bitch herself!

Rosemary, peeping out from behind Master Tennant, watched them go. Other neighbors began to creep out into the street. I said, as off-handedly as I could, "Come, children. Let us take care of what they have left us."

We moved to secure our fence. The remaining piglets, having seen murder done, were much afraid. They ran from us, hunching together in a corner and trembling. One of Tennant's grown sons silently moved to help, shaking his head.

Rosemary kept exclaiming, quite amazed,. "They killed two of our pigs! They stole them!"

"Wouldn't have happened in the Duke of Gloucester's time." Young Tennant spoke under his breath. I nodded and blinked back a few tears. I was grateful for the unintentional perfection of his condolence.

It wasn't until the next day that anger at the Beaufort woman's insults, capped by her men's wanton theft, struck me. Relief, however, was the main thing.

We had survived an inquisition by the Mother of Treachery!

There is a rush of joy in survival, after which our poor world has the look of heaven. The moon, for the next few evenings, arose in silver robes. Twilight birds sang *Gloria* finer than I'd heard in any chapel. I rejoiced, knowing the boar had hidden the last child of his body.

That night, though aching tired, I left Rosemary in our shared bed by the fire and went to the loft to watch my Dickon asleep. Once there had been a pile of snuffling, dreaming tow-heads, but now there was but one little boy left—His—my dark treasure.

Chapter XXXI

Alkelda's young face had grown so hard. She had Hugh's look, with those broad Saxon cheekbones, but there was no longer any girlish bloom. She was twenty-two now, ten years a city dweller, who labored in a shop from dawn to dusk. She'd grown plump and pale, like a partridge raised in a cage.

"I have come to ask your blessing, Mother." She held her head high, and studied me as I sat, spinning before my hearth.

"You will do whatever it is with or without my blessing, but say on."

"I am to marry Robert Fuller, head clerk in the counting house Master Wilfred goes to. Robert is a widower of thirty-two with twelve year old son just apprenticed away. Five clerks are in his charge, and he earns sufficient to keep a house on the Silversmith's street."

I had expected some such. Horse sense was her banner.

"I have a letter from my Master Wilfred, written to you."

I conned the letter slowly. Reading was not something I often did anymore. At last, because I did not want her to see how hard it was for me, I said, "I'm certain your father would have been well-pleased, as Master Wilfred says this is good match. If you are marrying this Robert Fuller of your own free will, I freely give my blessing."

"Don't *you* approve?" Her strong jaw jutted.

Ah, my Alkelda! Always looking for a fight! She was my strong-willed daughter through and through, although she'd die rather than admit it.

"Liking is for you, daughter, not for me."

"You have an opinion." She raised her voice. "Speak plain, Mother."

"An' you wish it."

"I do."

"Then I say this is a good marriage. However, I must also

say that the heart often regrets decisions made by the head alone."

She must have been waiting for this for immediately she shot back, "In this family we have a tradition of making prudent marriages, do we not, Mother?"

She was quite correct. My mother and Master Whitby, myself and Hugh, we had done what we must, what made sense, in order to live and raise children.

We gazed into each other's eyes. I tried to send my love to her. She was so hard, still young, so certain of herself and her ability to stay whatever course she set. Taking her hands between mine—hers soft and stained with ink— I declared, "I bestow a mother's blessing upon my very dear daughter Alkelda. I commend her to the care of The Blessed Queen of Heaven, to the guidance of her holy name saint and all the angels. May they always watch over you, and send you wisdom for each and every decision you make."

Alkelda lowered her capped head and closed her eyes to receive my words. When she opened them, I saw tears. Casting my arms around her, I drew her to my bosom. When she let me, I felt as if a hole in my heart closed. It is a bitter thing to be estranged from a child!

It wouldn't last, for we lived far apart, but the closeness she had briefly permitted was sufficient for my happiness.

"Thank you for your blessing, Mother." She put on her stern face again, as if she'd gone further in reconciliation than she'd ever intended.

"Your coming here has been my blessing. If ever you need aught from your mother, you have but to ask."

Chapter XXXII

t was not easy to lower myself between the stones. Every joint hurt and the thing in my belly pained me. Heavy it was, but not like a living child, for it was one of those dead things which somehow know how to grow. What I carried this time was killing me.

It was no mystery. I'd seen tumors. Worse, my mother before me had died of something like. There was no sense in clinging to life, clattering about like a crab dropped alive into a hot pot. Best to go down quietly while I still had a few shreds of dignity left and get it over.

The sky overhead was clear, the wind very cold. Tonight, after the sun went down, it would freeze. Between the cold and the vial I'd brought with me, I'd be dead by morning.

I had wanted to be strong, but I wept as I crouched down inside the cold stones, down in the crack below the twisted tree. No matter how terrible the pain, how stern the resolve, it is a cruel decision to leave this life, to leave the green leaves, the sun, the silver rain, the flowers and sweet scent of a mown meadow.

Still, there was no more joy to be had. I could only watch the lambs playing, no longer jump like one, no longer shout for joy or throw a ball with my grandchildren. All that lay before me was to be abed, to have pain as the tumor feasted upon my flesh, to watch the eyes of my dear ones turn bitter and resentful as they were forced to tend a shit-covered old woman.

Above me was the twisted oak. Today it reminded me of Ambien Hill and the sorry, broken trees. Here was my place to die, beneath this smaller, but much older oak, reclining in the stony arms of mother earth.

Deliver my soul into this stone womb and thence into the roots of this ancient tree! Perhaps I'd be born again, as Mistress Ash had said. God the Father might rage at the notion, might punish my act, but The Blessed Mother would understand, just as the women who trained me and loved me always had. Our Lady of the Blue Robe would calm the Old Man. She would know that this sin was to benefit my family, just as so much else in my life had been. I do not claim all my acts selfless, certainly, for there was, after all, my Dickon, but a great deal had been well done besides.

The taste of the Belladonna and henbane was bitter, cold, sickly. It would kill the pain, a flaming sword daily in my belly. I'd have a sip now, the rest later. When I was drowsy, I could better keep it down. The rock felt good against my cheek, just as it always had. I was at home now, already buried upon the dale.

Above I heard a cry, a hawk coursing. There he was! I'd known he'd come—cloud rider, his glinting talons, floating between my eyes and the long rays of a rare, cold April sun.

He spiraled—here and gone, here and gone—a savage angel mastering the arching sky. What a gift it was to see him, my true love come for me at the end.

Dickon Fletcher came balancing through the rocks. He could hear the others who had come out with him shouting, but to him their noise was useless, offensive. With such bawling they couldn't hear, couldn't even see. He remembered his mother explaining exactly that, asking him to be silent while they searched for a strayed sheep.

He was certain he knew where she was, so he followed the path they'd taken so many times, across the barren rock, jumping over the cracks, and balancing along the ledges to get around the narrow deep breaks when it was too wide to jump. It was difficult going, even for him, and he didn't know how she, so ill and weak as Rosemary had said, had managed to get here.

Something kept him going, in spite of the gusty, frigid wind, in spite of his reason still nattering away, saying Mother was in too much pain--not to mention, too sensible--to force her dying body across this fissured terrain.

At last he reached the tree, the most stunted, twisted, wind-tortured, water-and-earth-deprived living thing he had ever seen. He looked down into the crevice, and there she was, just as he'd known.

Yes, here, this place she took me to when I was small, when I was sad, when she wanted to tell me secrets....

The wind gusted, slashing through cloak, stockings, tunic, everything. He shuddered, feeling about as warm as if he'd walked out naked.

How could she have ever come so far?

As he prepared to climb down, he heard a hawk. He lifted his dark head, but he could not see the bird, for he was dazzled by the sun in that clear, cold sky, now blazing like a smith's fire as it set.

Dickon returned to looking down, let his eyes adjust to the gloom. She was wrapped in a worn brown cloak, pale beneath her freckles. With joy in her eyes, she said, "Dear my Lord! Have you come at last?"

She was intent, yet he knew she didn't recognize him. She spoke to someone else, someone from her past, from the bright years before he was born, when she had served the mighty Duke of the North and his duchess, those most high princes who had once dwelt at the now empty Middleham. His mother had even lived—incredibly—in the great palace in London, a servant to that Anne Neville who had become— briefly—tragically—Queen of England.

Dear My Lord...

Dickon shivered and it traveled all the way to bone. All his life he'd known he was different. He remembered the way that old crippled soldier, the man said to be his father, had sometimes studied him.

Dickon's Master, Geoffrey, Physician of York, prized him, his attention to detail, his dexterity, his quick intelligence, his hard work. Now twenty-two, he had been brought into the family. The hand of the Master's elder daughter, sweet Alys, would soon be his. He'd walked a long way to tell his mother of his good fortune, but it was too late to tell her anything now. She could no longer hear him. He could see in her eyes that she had entered the past.

The heart stops and the soul is left in once-upon-a-time...

Dickon squeezed down beside her. There wasn't much room for two grown people, but he managed, pulling his knees under his chin, as he'd done as a child, sitting and listening to her fabulous stories, some told in this very place.

"Mother!" He touched her cold, freckled cheek. It was bitter to think he would never speak with her again. "Mother, it's Dickon."

"Dear Dickon," she said. "Where is our dearest Anne?"

Dickon noted the dilation of her pupils. He did not try to speak again. He understood what she had done. It was hard to learn so much all at once and Dickon Fletcher shed tears, holding her against his shoulder. Rose was barely breathing. Her extremities were ice, the warmth already devoured by the surrounding rock.

What she had done was wrong, against God's command, but if she had chosen it, there must be a deeper right. As for the rest, as for whose son he was...

Am I a king's bastard, son of an evil usurper, a man whose hands were stained with the blood of his two young nephews? Or am I the bastard son of "Good Duke Richard," a lord of whom the wise old men of York still spoke with reverence? This was a Lord, the old men said, who had taken trouble to see justice done, even to the humblest of his subjects.

If my mother loved King Richard ...

He felt her body jerk. She had leapt to her death, as to a lover's arms.

With her silence, with the harsh peasant's life she'd chosen, she'd kept her secret. She'd kept him, child of the last Plantagenet King, alive. Dickon knew only too well what King Henry had done with the rest of that royal kin, both the high-born and the low.

"She asked me to deliver it to you and to you only,

Dickon." Father Martin, the first priest he ever remembered his mother liking, had handed him a flattened, stiff leather wallet. Now, the sun well-risen and some distance from Aysgarth, he'd stopped by a pool. The land was quiet, bare, no one else on the path to worry about. It was, after all, a little early in the year to be a traveler.

Birds sang in the nearby thicket, telling the world that spring, the miracle, was come again. His heavy heart rose at the thought, for he and Alys were to marry as soon as Lent and the Holy Feast of Easter were past. It had been arranged to take place at once, before the unlucky month of May began.

Sitting on a rock close by the backwash from the river, he reached inside his tunic and removed the wallet. He was not certain why it had been so easy not to open it sooner, but now that he was alone, away from the village, away from his grieving sister Rosemary and her too-inquisitive husband, the desire to see the contents was strong.

The wallet had been folded for a long time. Through the exterior, he saw the outline of a pair of rings and something long, perhaps a chain. Slowly, he brought them to light, possessions so precious his mother had not kept them at home. He laid each article in his lap.

A gold sovereign came first, stamped with the head of Edward IV.

"Thank you, Mother!" By weight alone, this was a great deal of money!

Then, sure enough, two rings appeared. One was a woman's ring, very old, from the look of it. Dickon wondered if it would be too small for Alys. The other ring was heavy, old tarnished silver, 'graved with a boar, the dead King's emblem, *Blanc Sanglier*.

Once again, he wondered at the intimacy in her last words. There had been no titles, only a sweetly spoken diminutive. The very idea! Rose Fletcher was a woman who had spent the last years of her life milking sheep, tending the sick, growing herbs and brewing ale.

Last of all, he drew forth a chain with a beautifully carved charm, a white rose made of ivory. This would make a splendid wedding gift for his York bride!

At the very bottom, lay a handkerchief, crackling with ancient blood and folded small. When he broke it open, there was a hank of human hair. The bit of scalp to which it was attached had dried, the blood fell into his lap as a fine ochre powder.

For an instant, Dickon considered simply dropping this dreadful relic into the rushing river, but, in the end, he simply tucked it back again into the farthest corner of the wallet.

This last should have gone into the ground with Mother, but the best I can do now is to take it back to the oak tree someday.

Slipping the wallet inside his tunic, he rose, retrieved his staff and tightened his belt. It was a long tramp back to the City, but the black heaviness he'd felt began to lift as soon as he broke sweat. Swinging his oaken staff, Dickon Fletcher marched down the road leading to his future, a slender, upright form haloed in the present splendor of a rising sun.

The End

About the Author

"Not all who wander are lost." Juliet Waldron earned a B. A. in English, but has worked at jobs ranging from artist's model to brokerage. Thirty years ago, after the kids left home, she dropped out of 9-5 and began to write, hoping to create a genuine time travel experience for herself—and her readers. She loves her kitty-cats and grandkids, taking long, lonely hikes, reading non-fiction and filling her yard with messy native plants. For adventure, she rides behind her husband of 50 years on his "bucket list" black Hyabusa.

Other Books by Juliet Waldron

Austrian, 18th Century:

Mozart's Wife and *My Mozart,* a duet
Nightingale

Red Magic
~The Magic series continues soon with~
Black Magic

American Revolution:

Genesee
Angel's Flight

And, coming soon to Books We Love:

Hand-me-Down Bride

Note from the Publisher

Thank you for purchasing and reading this Books We Love Book. We hope you have enjoyed your reading experience. Books We Love and the author would very much appreciate you returning to the online retailer where you purchased this book and leaving a review for the author.

Best Regards and Happy Reading,

Jamie and Jude

Books We Love
and
Books We Love Spice
http://bookswelove.net

Top quality books loved by readers,
Romance, Mystery, Fantasy, Suspense
Vampires, Werewolves, Cops, Lovers.
Young Adult, Historical, Paranormal

For a spicier read visit
http://spicewelove.com

Notes

Printed in Great Britain
by Amazon